Eternal Night

A Novel by *Jessica Barone*

Book One of the Dream Series

AmErica House
Baltimore

First printing

ISBN: 1-58851-050-6
PUBLISHED BY AMERICA HOUSE BOOK PUBLISHERS
www.publishamerica.com
Baltimore

Printed in the United States of America

In loving memory of David Eisnor. . . .

"Love is eternal
Like the circle of a ring
Whole unto itself
Its beauty never ending
But going on forever."

—1977 Hallmark Cards, Inc.

An Eternal thank-you to the following:

My Mama, and her words "Stand tall, and keep your head held high."
My Mother, as always.
Michael, for all the suggestions.
And to my Father and Subby for the trips to Vermont.

PART ONE

The Beginning (August, Nineteen-Eighty-Six)

1

Step for a moment into the past. Relinquish all holds on your fabricated reality.

What was life like before this time?

Remember, Remember.

Ten years ago, fifteen, twenty. How long ago were the 1980's? How long ago was that time?

From where your life began you will remember it differently. Were you a doctor then? Did you wear flashy clothes, big hair, and cosmetics? Did you listen to bands like Depeche Mode, Billy Idol, INXS, or David Bowie? What were the movies we saw then? *Star Wars, The Lost Boys, Legend.* These were the days of twisted innocence, aluminum dreams and stained-glass hopes.

Children ruled it all.

A child of the eighties played in this wonderland, lost somewhere between the decade of hippies from which it was born and the decade of darkness that had become an immediate future.

A child of the eighties was not prepared for her past nor her future, but languished in an iridescence of colored lights and corrupted purity.

Her name was Julia Anderson.

Born and raised in the state of Connecticut, U.S.A, her life would be completely and irreversibly changed in the year 1986. Something dark and frightening would come for her, something out of the past itself, to lead her into an immense future.

It all began in Connecticut, where she lived in a relatively stable family with one sister, a mother, a father, and the father's mistress.

Julia loved her father as most daughters do, but for reasons that he could not change about himself, although the mother wanted him to, he left them all to a fate worse than death, it seemed. What was this fate? Divorce - loss of a parent for two young girls, bankruptcy, and the lay off of the mother in a time of financial repression.

There was nothing left to do but move.

Julia, at the age of sixteen, became instantly removed from life, as she knew it, subjected to a new world that held absolutely no interest to her at all; the shadowy, backward world of upstate Vermont.

11

In Vermont, rent was cheap. In Vermont, there were jobs. In Vermont, a world of her mother's far past, they were all to find happiness again, this new little family of women.

Julia was not happy. Father gone, home gone, bitter toward her mother, whole life overturned, here in this new land, all she had was her writing. She wrote and wrote, stories about pain and losses too giant to possibly be her own, stories about the forbidden and completely opposite world from that which she had been brought up in, the world of the vampire.

And miraculously, she sold one book immediately. It wasn't a big sale, but gave her a means of transportation. A small 1980 Yamaha motorcycle. And now, working on her second book, that could quite possibly lead to greater things for all the Andersons, she had come to something that all writers must deal with, no matter how old or young they are: writer's block.

Julia sat on the edge of her bed, pencil in hand, staring at the words on the page before her. The words never changed, not at all, for the past two weeks. They simply sat there, staring as stubbornly at her as she stared at them. She stared until her eyes watered and tears ran, unnoticed, down her soft, childish cheeks.

She listened to the sounds around her. Crickets and motorcycles outside, the television playing *Dukes of Hazard* downstairs, her mother talking and laughing loudly on the phone.

What good is any of this? She thought so loudly, it seemed that her words rang aloud in her own ears, as if she had spoken them. She couldn't find the ending to this story. There simply was no ending. Maybe there were just some things in the world that never did end, simply went on and on. A vampire is evil, she reasoned. Therefore, the heroine should kill him, shouldn't she? But maybe he wasn't really evil at all. Maybe he was just misunderstood. God, that sounds so corny...

"Julia, you're talking to yourself again!"

The shouted words from her mother downstairs broke her reverie. Frustrated and aggravated beyond belief, she flung the notebook into the closet and the pencil to the floor.

Standing with a sigh, she journeyed into the bathroom that separated her room from her younger sister's. Once in there, she placed her palms down on the cool tile of the sink, and stared at her reflection in the mirror. On the inside looking out, or the outside looking in, it was still the same girl she saw every day. The same blond, shoulder length hair, curly with the falseness of a perm. The same blue/green eyes staring back, searching the same tanned face from August sun, and scowling at the same rash of adolescent pimples.

12

Who am I? Julia thought this to herself for what seemed like the millionth time. "What am I doing here?" she whispered as she rubbed her face, turning this way and that, looking at her reflection in the mirror.

She pulled her tee-shirt tight against her skin, looking at her breasts and wishing yet again that she were a full-grown woman, instead of being stuck in this form, in this limbo between childhood and that magical age of eighteen when womanhood in all its wonderful forms would be revealed.

Julia never really had a boyfriend, nothing serious, not even really passionate. She felt so awkward at times like these, wondering what she was doing wrong, and why all her friends could dress like Madonna and get any boy, or man for that matter, that they wanted. If Julia dressed like that, she knew she would just end up looking silly. She simply had to be herself, or she would feel like she was betraying the only person she had left, herself.

"Guys have always thought I'm weird," she said, staring at her confidant in the mirror again, the one who could not help her. "Julia, get a grip," she muttered to herself as she left the bathroom. "Think of what Christi would say. And you know what she would say, don't you? You need to get out more."

Christi had been her best friend as far back as Julia could remember. There was nothing that could keep them apart. Not silly arguments, not popularity, nothing. Nothing, that was, but Vermont.

Julia sighed, went to her closet, and pulled out the dress that Christi had given to her as a going away gift, back in June. It was a light blue summer dress, made of soft, crinkly cotton material, which almost tickled her bare legs as she pulled it on over her underwear, after she had discarded her tee shirt and shorts.

The dress was special because Christi had worn it; even though Julia had washed it several times, it still smelled like pink powder, and there was no other way to describe it. It reminded Julia of very good times, times when Christi had invited her to sleep over, staying up all night watching music videos and drinking forbidden beers.

It reminded her of home.

Julia pulled on white ankle boots over her small, delicate feet, and tied a white scarf around the waist of the dress for a belt. She used a smaller, but matching scarf to hold back her hair.

After tucking a wallet and keys into the pockets of her black leather jacket, she made her way down the stairs quietly, only to be halted by her mother.

"Where are you going?" Jeanne Anderson demanded not too gently, cupping the talking end of the phone with her hand. Julia almost laughed

13

aloud with the sight of this ridiculous gesture, knowing it would achieve nothing. The person at the other end of the phone would simply receive a muffled version of a mother antagonizing a daughter.

"I'm going to the park." Julia said, adjusting her bra strap with a carefully planned element of sarcasm.

"Getaway Park?" Jeanne asked, raising one eyebrow.

"Yes Mom," Julia said.

"It's eleven o'clock, Julia. You are only sixteen."

"Mom, will you please stop reminding me?" she sighed, shouldering her way past her mother to the door. "It's still summer after all, and before you can say it, no, I won't be doing this once school starts. I'll be home by one, and I'll catch up with you tomorrow at the mall."

Before Jeanne could utter another word, Julia was out the door and gone to the small garage, preparing to ride a motorcycle with her dress on. Frowning because she had to do it so carefully, she thought of the mistake she had just made, committing herself to visiting her mother at work. Jeanne worked in the mall, in a department store, as a sales person.

Not quite happy, but looking forward to the adventure of the evening, she roared the little bike to life, and was off. Winding down the mountain trail, Julia found that it had suddenly become quite difficult to think about her problems at all. Riding at night was such an exhilarating experience. It seemed as if the wind had a form, shape, and life all its own, stroking her hair, caressing her body as it blew all around her and through her. She began to wonder why she had ever been unhappy, and before her mind could quite rationalize, she arrived at Getaway Park.

After paying a parking fee, and entering the main gate, she began to feel a bit queasy with excitement. Pulling the little Yamaha next to four big Harley Davidsons, the air seemed to crackle with anticipation. What was going on here? She wondered. Almost turning around to go home, Julia smiled, inwardly scoffing at herself for being so silly. It's only because I've been in solitude for two weeks. Only that, she thought, but a small voice whispered, that of her conscience perhaps, are you so sure?

Passing the night away at Getaway Park was a relatively easy task for Julia to accomplish. The park basically expressed itself and everything in it by the name it had been given, a Getaway. A break from all the hardships and trials of everyday life. It seemed that everywhere you looked there was another distraction from the worries you had left at the entrance gate; another ride, another game, another item of delicious food that a young girl could not pass up. It was a neverland of toys and playthings, however, it harbored within it things that were neither pleasurable nor diverted.

14

Getaway Park, like any other amusement park one could encounter in a lifetime, was an unknown mask for things that occurred far beneath the vision of a teenager's naked and exposed eye.

Julia was being stalked.

Almost from the instant she had stepped within her playground, their hunting ground, he had watched her. Had desired her, and all that was her youth, her innocence, and her grandeur. And for all Julia knew, they were simply a group of boys following her, as boys often do to young girls, especially when they are alone.

In no mood to be frightened, Julia was openly aware of them, the four of them, and the one who watched her almost constantly. However, she kept to her business, thinking simply, let him watch, I don't care. Surrounded by people, and even park security guards, she didn't for one moment think that he could hurt her. Only that he might be curious about her, although there was something entirely different in his eyes when she turned to check if he was there. Something that made Julia a bit fidgety.

By the end of the evening, their presence behind her had eventually worn her nerves thin. One more ride, she thought, and then I will confront him, the one who watches. Curious that they never ride.

As Julia got on the carousel, she noticed that the respectable gap between her and the man was rapidly closing. Finally frightened, she all but ran to the platform, just out of reach of this dark haired, dark-eyed pursuer. Breathing a deep sigh of relief, she climbed up onto the horse closest to her, believing she'd be safe while the ride was in motion.

As the carousel took her in a wide circle, she heard two male voices arguing. As it brought her to the point of her entry, she saw that the dark-haired one was arguing quite hotly with an older, more prominent looking young man. Quite quickly, she registered the fact that she had not taken in the physical appearance of these other men at all, except for the fact that the watcher had long, dark brown hair and dark brown eyes that seemed too sad to be those of a stalker, and now, came the appearance of the one he argued with.

This man appeared to be a little taller than the watcher, maybe just over six feet. Dressed in black from head to toe, his hair splashed an interruption of orange color down to his shoulder blades. His eyes were light blue, icy and cold, dangerous as the argument heated up. From the way the light hit his cheeks as Julia went by, she could see a slight dusting of orange hair upon his face, and for all his slenderness, he looked far more threatening than the dark-haired one. Julia knew he hadn't been watching her. If he had, she probably would have run to the nearest security guard and begged assistance.

On the next turn of the carousel, Julia decided to watch the watcher. His hair was indeed long, falling almost to his waist. Some shorter pieces of hair fell across his face, possibly a weak attempt at bangs, sometime in the past. A light mustache grew along his upper lip, and a silver earring glittered in the flashing lights of the carousel, dangling unnoticed from his left ear. He wore a black leather biker jacket and nothing at all beneath it, with the exception of a silver chain with turquoise stones hanging off of it, resting gently against the flesh of his skin. Tight black jeans encased his legs, running down into black leather biker boots. Around his right boot, tied on by an ancient-looking strip of rawhide, was a dyed red feather.

All of this collecting in her mind as the ride once more drew her away from them, Julia found herself admitting to the fact that yes, he was a handsome man. And then, she chastised herself for it. What kind of nut case was he for chasing her around all night? And what kind of nut case was she for enjoying it?

As the ride drew her closer once more, the shouting got louder. They're fighting about me, she surmised. That was the only logical explanation.

A very loud explosion of a voice shouting "No!" interrupted Julia's thoughts. She jumped at the sound of it, not surprised at all when the people around her began talking about security and how fast they should move away from the ride when it came to a halt. Never mind them, something inside Julia warned. What will you do?

Julia's horse swung around now to face the little group of men, and in an instant, her heart stopped. The watcher was gone. There, next to the platform, stood the orange haired leader, fixing his blue ice upon her, the other two watching, helpless it seemed, behind him. *But the watcher was gone!*

Terrified, Julia jumped down from her perch on the horse, shaking the jacket into place. Sure he was here on the ride with her, she spun around to look behind her, wide-eyed, but he was not there. Where was he?

Heart pounding in her throat and in her ears, Julia made her way through the moving horses, collapsing on a stationary chair, pulling her legs up to her chest beneath the dress, trying to be as inconspicuous as possible, and wondering how the hell she was going to get out of the park alive. The people on the horses looked at her strangely, but Julia didn't care. What am I going to do now? Shaking, she almost yelled out to the operator to stop the ride, but then, something extraordinary happened.

A hand, warm and soft, and light to the touch as a summer day, came from behind. It came out of nowhere it seemed, and pressed itself very firmly upon her cheek.

In an instant, her fear melted. It was gone. Her body relaxed, legs sliding to the floor with a thud, she briefly wondered how she had remained upright. And then she heard the voice, echoing in the air, in the mind, all around her, as warm and as comforting as that gentle touch.

Easy, easy. Be calm. I will not harm you.

Julia's sight seemed ready to vanish. The people staring at her had become liquid, phantoms swimming in another world, another life that was no longer her own.

And then, her head turned, and he was there beside her, holding onto her, her fingers interlaced with his, and she could not pull away, could not move except to shiver, to uncontrollably shiver with the knowledge that she was no longer in control.

He planted little kisses all over her hair, whispering strange things like, "You've come back to me, you're here again, and you won't leave me now, will you, no, never."

Julia shook harder, her brain struggling with the intoxication of his voice, his touch. Let me go! She wanted to shout but she could not, and in the very instant when she felt that she would drown, falling forever into those dark eyes, and had accepted this, the booming voice once again shouted.

"Jonathan!"

Julia blinked back tears, instantly reanimated. Her body, her mind, everything was in her grasp once again. She looked up, surprised yet again to see that she was no longer on the carousel, but practically laying upon a park bench, one conveniently removed from the prying eyes of the park's other patrons.

Sitting up, Julia realized that she was not alone. There, around her, stood the four boys that had been following her all night.

Abruptly, the watcher spoke. "Are you alright? You passed out back there." he said, gesturing to the ride in the distance.

"You made me pass out." Julia said, her voice shaky, not totally convinced of her own words.

"Don't be ridiculous." the orange haired one said, scowling.

Julia sat back further into the chair, pulling the jacket tighter around her chest. "What do you want?" she asked them, the watcher in particular.

He smiled gently; yet, something remained behind that smile. Julia knew something was wrong with him, with all of them. Their silence was impossible to over look. They simply didn't behave correctly.

"I've wanted to speak with you all night." he said, reaching a hand down to pull her up. "I'm called Jonathan."

His voice, so deep, it called to her more than the words did. It cascaded down Julia's body, making her skin itself tingle. Despite her better judgement, Julia reached out and grasped his hand, much to the annoyance of the orange haired man. He practically growled his aggravation, turned, and stalked away. Julia watched him leave.

"That was Jason." Jonathan said.

Julia looked up at him, he being so much bigger, overall, than her. He couldn't be more than nineteen, she thought, and yet, there was something about him that really intimidated her. He seemed so much older.

Jonathan smiled again, more hunger in his mouth this time, and Julia pulled her hand out from his quickly. "What is your name?" he all but breathed.

"Julia," she whispered, a little too quickly.

"Julia," he repeated, his voice dark and rich like too much chocolate. After a pause, he turned to the two others still standing with him; the ones Julia had been aware of, and yet, had not really looked at. "This is Devin, and Andrew."

Devin was a little shorter than Jonathan was. He had waist length layered blond hair, and deep green eyes. The white jeans he wore were somewhat dirty, stained here and there, green and brown. Black cowboy boots encased his feet, and a black tee shirt, which was a bit too long on him, covered his upper body. He held in his arms a black leather jacket, decorated crudely with silver dog chains.

Andrew looked younger than the others did. In fact, he looked more like the boys she had gone to school with, her age. Andrew's jet-black hair was long in back, hanging down in a single pony tail, but spiked up and short on top, as was the punk-rock fashion of the time. His eyes were soft and grey, not a bit threatening. He wore a pair of tight black jeans, black boots, red tee shirt, and a beige suede jacket. An earring dangled from his left ear as well, and instantly, Julia remembered that Jason and Devin possessed similar earrings.

Jonathan looked at her expectantly.

Julia supposed she should say something, but not a word came from her mouth. What should she say? Hi, nice to meet you and your friends, and by the way, why did you hypnotize me back there on the carousel?

As she thought of what to do next, Julia noticed that Andrew and Devin begin to wander off in the direction that the one called Jason had gone.

"Where are they going?" she asked boldly, pointing at their retreating backs.

"Nowhere." Jonathan said softly. "Tell me, beautiful Julia, where are you going?"

Julia, startled, looked up at him. "Home." she said softly, inching away from him. She didn't like being so close to him. It bothered her.

"Can I come?" he smiled, so innocently, so smoothly. So...perfectly. Too perfectly.

"No." Julia said, walking around him.

He caught her arm as she tried to pass. Shocked, she opened her mouth to speak, but he silenced her immediately with a swift, but oh so gentle kiss on the lips.

Fire seemed to awaken inside Julia, born from a place she never knew existed. Torn between agony and ecstasy, she grasped the hand that held her, struggling not with any outside force, but with her own judgement.

Finally, he pulled away. Their hands slipped back together, seeming to know by their own where they wanted to be.

"Tell me where you live?" Jonathan asked.

Surprising herself, Julia told him, and as she did, it seemed to surprise him as well.

"I live right near there," he said softly, looking puzzled.

"Do you live with them?" she asked. Jonathan only nodded.

"I have to go," Julia said once more, pulling away. This time, Jonathan let her go. She began to walk away from him, confused for all that had happened. She stopped as Jonathan called her name.

"I'll pick you up tomorrow night, at eight!"

"What?" Julia called, wondering if she had heard him right.

Jonathan ran to her, covering a lot of ground in a few steps. "Tomorrow night, I'll pick you up at eight, at your house." Jonathan paused to toss his hair back over his shoulder. "That is, if it's alright with you."

"Yeah, sure." Julia said softly and then a bit louder, "why not?" She smiled at Jonathan, and he smiled with her, the first person to want to be in her company in a long, long time. "Would you come in? Meet my mom if she wanted to?"

Jonathan's grin seemed to grow. "Am I invited then?"

Julia giggled, pleased with the outcome of their meeting. Even if he was a bit peculiar, Jonathan was quite cute. "Yes, you're invited."

"Thank you." Jonathan replied, reaching down, grasping her hand, and kissing it lightly. "But perhaps you should know, Julia, as long as I'm invited, I will come back to you. You can't get rid of me now."

Julia wasn't so sure she liked the sound of that last sentence. He sounded strange again. Like the sound of his voice on the carousel which she was trying so hard to forget about. She pulled away from him, confused beyond belief at her feelings and her own choices.

"Good night, Julia." he said softly, bowed, and walked away, perhaps trying to make it easy for her to leave.

Light headed, Julia left the park, trying very hard all the way home not to fall asleep while riding the motorcycle. When she arrived home, Julia could barely stand up.

Ignoring her mother's perusal up the stairway with a lecture about being late, Julia all but crashed into bed that night. Still fully clothed in a dress of memories and dreams, she began to think to her future, and the new dream she had finally become a player in.

2

As the young girl slumbered in her bed, no insight had she as to the game that was truly afoot. Julia rested now, but further up, on the same hillside that she rested on, sat the mystery of mysteries; the home, or lair, of the one called Jonathan.

In the dark, the great house that served him and the others as home slumbered not so quietly, being old and well past the time of condemnation.

Closing in upon this home, a sound rings out through the night and the living forest, the echo of a grandfather clock ringing out the time. Three chimes vibrated through the mansion, but those inside it paid no heed. Time had no meaning to them anymore, and the clock was no new object, simply a relic, symbolic of so much more than simply the clock itself.

Jonathan stood apart from the others this night, wishing for things that had no words, being simply longings. His mind on the land below the hillside, and the young girl, Julia, he gazed out a window like a lovesick Romeo. Not surprisingly, Jonathan received no consolations or words of advice. He knew a lecture was in order from Jason, and that it was sure to come in the near future, and did not look forward to it. Sheer respect was the only thing that held him here now, when he longed so much to be free from them all, and the ways he had kept for a century.

Jonathan turned away from the window to look at the others. Andrew and Devin sitting upon the couch, munching on leftover pizza that they did not need to eat, talking in short open-ended sentences. Jason sitting regally in that big wicker chair that Devin had once found somewhere, smoking a cigarette. It was a habit that he had recently acquired, Jonathan knew not from where. Jonathan was not surprised as Jason turned and looked at him.

"Jonathan, I want to talk to you." he said, and then looked at the others sitting on the couch. "Alone."

Devin looked up at Jason, exasperated, and stood. Andrew stood with him.

"Outside again," he said to Andrew, his mouth full of food.

"Another fight." Andrew stated, giving a look of sympathy to Jonathan as he passed.

Jonathan stood stationary long after they had gone. He neither wished nor wanted to talk to Jason. He knew what he was going to say, after all, and had no explanations or replies to give. He simply wanted to be left alone. However, knowing beyond a doubt that solitude was a false hope, Jonathan left his place by the window, dragged a wooden chair over to Jason, and sat slumped, defiantly folding his arms over his chest.

Jason's eyes flickered to Jonathan, but he did not say a word, and the recognition lasted briefly. Jason's eyes drifted across the room, lingering on things that he only could see, thoughts thicker than air, thicker even then the smoke rising from his lungs and out of his mouth. Jason's thoughts were completely masked from Jonathan, just as they always had been, draped just as black as the overcoat he wore. It seemed like forever until he spoke.

"Jonathan, this girl you dragged us all after tonight, what is her name?"

Jonathan tried not to look at Jason, but it was damned near impossible. Jonathan knew what he was thinking, somehow, just knew. "Her name is Julia, it's not…"

Jason cut him off with a wave of his hand. "We don't need to speak of that, Jonathan. I was curious, that's all."

Jonathan raised an eyebrow. He wasn't so sure.

"Are you in love with Julia now?" Jason said, slightly smiling.

Jonathan frowned. "You're too cynical." he muttered, looking down at the ground.

"Yes, perhaps." Jason said, his voice icing over, the smile lost. "Jonathan, I don't see how you expect to love her, or to spend any time with her at all. You resisted your nature just barely tonight, I remind you, but who knows what you would have done if I had not been there. And I will not always be there. What will you do tomorrow night, and other nights? She is a temptation to you, because of who she is, and more importantly, whom she represents. You won't be able to resist your first impulses."

Jonathan lowered his head, covered his face in his hands, and sighed.

"Jonathan," Jason continued, as he extinguished the cigarette in an old coffee can, "I tried to explain all this earlier tonight. I'm only trying to protect you from yourself. You know that you'll never forgive yourself if you kill her. I should have done more to keep you two apart. You should not have met her. It is impossible for you to love her, a mortal."

"It is not impossible, Jason." He looked up at Jason slowly, anger and hate clearly etched upon his face. "It is only impossible to you because you cannot love anyone or anything." Jonathan rose out of the chair, fists clenched at his sides. "And if you truly want to know, yes, I feel something growing in my heart for this girl, as you call her, and it has nothing to do with my memories, or my lifestyle, or any other reason. It is because of who she is, yes, but everything about her. Her very soul is sunlight to me. A wish that only I seem to hold onto here, in this place."

"Jonathan, stop it." Jason said, all but growling the words out. Only then did Jonathan realize how angry he had become, and what it was exactly he was saying.

"I don't care what you feel for her, or what you think of me. Jonathan, sit down."

His eyes on Jonathan as he reclaimed his seat were very cold and deadly. Jonathan knew he had pushed Jason a bit too far, but because he had not yet been dismissed, he decided to take the issue a bit further.

"You are right when you say that I cannot love a human as I wish to. I do not trust myself with her, it's true, and you know it. But then you also must know that there is a way around it. If she was like us, I could not hurt her. Make her like us. Use the wine that you used to turn Andrew. She would not be harmed that way." Jonathan looked up at Jason, his eyes pleading, searching.

Jason sighed, looked away. "She could indeed be harmed, Jonathan. I don't know what the side effects would be on her. It's always different on each individual. But you should know this already. There is also the fact that she could go mad." He looked at Jonathan out of the corner of his eyes. "She might never accept you. Are you sure this is what you want? Consider all the consequences carefully."

Jason looked at the young man before him, sitting in silence, sadness and hope rising in the darkness of his eyes. Jonathan's answer came without saying.

"Yes, I can see you have already made up your mind on this matter. Alright, I'll do it for your sake. Andrew, Devin!" he called as he rose to his feet. "Should I give the news, or would you like to?" he asked Jonathan.

"I am forever in your debt, Jason." Jonathan said, standing as well.

"Yes, I know." Jason replied, grinning devilishly, extending his arm around Jonathan's shoulders. "And who knows? Perhaps this little adventure will prove to be amusing yet."

3

The following evening, Julia Anderson prepared herself for a date that she had no idea why she had accepted to go on. Except, of course, for the fact that in her eyes, this guy Jonathan was extraordinarily cute, and had taken an interest in her when no one else had.

Seven-thirty found Julia rushing around her room trying to decide on an outfit that she could feel comfortable in. Suddenly, her wardrobe seemed far too small, and the clothing that was in it far too revealing. Her little sister, Gayle, was no great help in that department. Being ten years old, she thought any item of clothing was fine for a date, if in fact, you chose to go on one.

"Boys are only good for one thing." Gayle said, rummaging through a stack of tee shirts that Julia had dumped onto the floor.

Julia walked into the bathroom, hugging a tight-fitting short-sleeved sweatshirt to her chest. "Oh?" she called back to her sister. "And what's that?"

"I don't know, but when I find out, I'll be sure to tell you." Her green eyes narrowed, and her freckled nose crinkled up, as Julia walked back into the room, tossing the sweatshirt onto the floor at Gayle's feet.

"I can't find anything to wear!" Julia's shoulders slouched with the helplessness of her situation. "And what are you making faces at, Gayle?"

Gayle grinned, and then began to laugh. "I just wish you'd put some clothes on, Julia. You look funny walking around in your underwear."

Julia smiled, tension gone for a moment. "Oh, I do, do I?" In a second, she had crouched down beside her sister, and began to tickle her, with no relief. "Now you're the one who looks funny!" she cried.

Gayle laughed and laughed, hiccuping breath until she shrieked, "Okay, okay, stop it, I give up! You look fine!"

Julia ceased to tickle her sister, rolling over onto her back, staring up at the ceiling.

"I do wish you'd get dressed though, Julia."

Julia looked at her sister helplessly. "Me too." She sighed aloud, feeling the pile of clothes rustle underneath her skin. "Gayle? Could you just pick me out something to wear?"

'Yeah, I guess," her sister replied, getting to her feet.

Julia sneezed as her sister's long auburn hair tickled her nose. "When are you getting a haircut?" she said, watching as Gayle moved to the half-emptied closet, searching through Julia's clothing.

"What's Jonathan look like?" Gayle asked, ignoring Julia's question.

"Why?" Julia said, standing now as well. She smiled, looking down at Gayle. The little girl was frowning again.

"How can I help you dress if I don't know anything about this guy, Julia?" Gayle said, facing her sister with her little hands planted on her hips.

Julia shrugged. She didn't see the logic in Gayle's question, but decided to answer anyway. "Jonathan's about six feet tall, with long dark hair and eyes, he wears biker clothes, and jeans that hug his legs…he's so hot."

Gayle rolled her eyes. "He sounds like a hippie." she said, turning her attention back to the closet.

Julia pouted. "He is *not* a hippie, Gayle. He's…" Julia trailed off as the digital clock in the corner of the bedroom caught her eye. Panic rushed through her in a hot, red wave. "He's coming in ten minutes!"

Julia darted into the bathroom, glaring at herself in the mirror. "My hair! And I don't have any make-up on, Gayle where are you? I need an outfit, now!"

"Yes, Master!" Gayle shouted in her best Boris Karloff impersonation, appearing swiftly in the doorway, holding out a pair of leather pants and an off-the shoulder white blouse.

Julia stopped dead. "What do you propose to dress me as, anyway?" she demanded, snatching the clothes from her sister and tugging them on.

"A biker." Gayle said, as if it made all the sense in the world. "So, what did you and mom talk about today anyway?" Gayle asked, watching as Julia ran a very wet brush through her curls.

"At the store?" Julia winced as she tugged through a snarl.

"Yes,"

"Nothing much. She was just yelling at me again for the usual stuff. You know, not being around enough, not having a job, not talking to her, coming home late…would you grab me a barrette?"

Gayle sighed. Trying to get information from her older sister was like pulling teeth. She reached down onto the floor, picking up a forgotten silver barrette. "Mom said to grab you a barrette?" She handed it to Julia.

"Yeah," Julia growled, slipping it into the side of her hair, pulling the now wet curls off her face.

"Why don't you ever tell Mom anything, Julia, or how about me? Sometimes I think you don't like us anymore." Gayle leaned against the doorway, watching as Julia applied red lipstick and dark blue eyeshadow.

"Don't be silly Gayle, of course I like you. You're my only sister."

"And mom?" Gayle asked, raising her eyebrows.

Julia tactfully decided to ignore the question.

"Are you still mad at her because of the divorce?"

"I don't want to talk about Dad, okay? Can't you think of something else?" Julia asked sadly, tracing her lower eyelids in eyeliner.

Gayle fidgeted. "I had a nightmare last night." She lowered her head, trying not to sound like a baby. She didn't want to let Julia down. Above all else, Gayle wanted her sister to remember that she was growing up.

Julia, however, did remember. She was painfully aware of all the changes that had been occurring in her life, and in her sister's life. Placing the makeup back into the tray, which had been set upon the sink, Julia turned and asked her sister, "What was the nightmare about?"

Gayle however, did not look up. "It was a man, with yellow hair. He watched me sleeping. He scared me, and I tried to scream, but when I finally could, he was gone."

Puzzled, Julia hugged her sister. "I don't remember you screaming."

"Well, I did." Gayle pulled away. "And, I think he heard it, too."

"Why?" Julia asked, genuinely curious.

And then, the doorbell rang.

"I'll get it!" Gayle shrieked out, bounding out of the bathroom, into Julia's room, and down the stairs.

Heart fluttering like a caged moth, Julia went to her bed, stuffing her wallet and keys into the pockets of her leather pants. Then, pulling on the leather jacket, she too went down the stairway. There, in the entryway at the bottom of the stairs, a curious sight met Julia.

Gayle stood at the door, staring at Jonathan, who stood beyond it, staring back. Gayle seemed paralyzed, her back laced with tension beneath the green tee shirt she wore. Jonathan, however, looked at her as if...

No, it was too strange, Julia thought, going to the door and giving Gayle a little nudge out of the way.

"He's like the man from my dream." Gayle whispered, tugging at the cuff of Julia's jacket.

"That was just a dream, Gayle." She retorted, pushing her out of the way a little harder the time, and opening the screen door.

"Hello." she said, looking up at Jonathan, his eyes finally resting on her instead of her sister.

"Hi." he said quietly, seeming to hold something back. Something that he didn't want Julia's sister to know.

"Would you like to come in?" she asked him after a moment.

"Your mother is not home." he stated solidly. It was not a question.

"No, she isn't, but..."

"Shall we go then?" he asked, flashing her a smile, and holding out his hand to her.

"Alright." Julia said, taking his hand within hers. She shivered subconsciously. Jonathan's hand was cold. "By the way," she said on the way out the door, "this is my sister Gayle, and Gayle, this is Jonathan."

They exchanged quick greetings. Julia thought perhaps too quick. An element of mistrust hung heavily in the air. Julia shook it off as she stepped off the front porch. "Tell mom that I'm at the park with some friends!" she yelled back. "Don't let anyone in! I'll let myself in tonight!"

"Behave!" Gayle yelled back at Julia, as she slammed the front door shut.

"Your sister loves you." Jonathan observed, smiling down at Julia as they walked the short distance down the driveway to where his Harley was parked.

"Yes, I know." Julia gazed ahead of her at the big, black bike. Silently she wondered at the exchange between Jonathan and Gayle. Why wouldn't her sister like Jonathan?

All Julia's worries were forgotten as she slid up behind him upon his bike. Wrapping her arms around him as they pulled away from the house, she buried her face in his hair, pressing her forehead against his back. He smelled of leather and woods, exotic. She decided right away that she liked it. No, she more than liked it, she loved it. It was in that instant she knew she was falling in love with this mysterious man from Vermont. She knew she would follow him anywhere.

4

Roaring through the cool and dark August evening, with a mortal girl riding on the back of his motorcycle, Jonathan's happiness was greatly reduced by an infinite sadness, which border-lined pain.

It was true that he'd do anything for Julia, give her any diversion or pleasure she desired, but from this he received no satisfaction. He knew what had to happen this night, and for some inexplicable reason, did not look forward to it.

When Julia had asked where they were going, he told her to choose, not wanting to go back to his mansion so soon, not wanting to trick her so completely. Julia trusted him, of this he was certain. Why, because Jonathan pretended so well. He pretended to be normal, like her, to actually be out on a date, to be human, to be a nineteen year old boy. Outside he was at peace; inside, his heart was breaking.

He made pleasant conversation at the restaurant they went to, but as hungry as he was for other things, Jonathan could not force himself to eat a bite. The movie was uninteresting to Jonathan, so involved as he was with the little things that Julia unknowingly did.

She sighed at romance, clutched Jonathan's hand when she was scared, tossed her hair in frustration when she was annoyed, showering his hypersensitive senses with a myriad of little sounds, and assaulting his nose with fragrances of flowers and spices.

He could hear her heart beat faster, every time his cool fingers stroked her skin, from anticipation or revulsion, he couldn't tell. Jonathan could have found out anything he wanted to about Julia, by peering into her mind, but he didn't want to, yet.

After the movie, they sat side by side in the parking lot, Julia talking non-stop, it seemed, but Jonathan didn't mind. She was nervous, she was attracted to him, she couldn't help herself, and he knew it. He didn't want to tell her anything yet about his life, anyway, didn't want to betray the horrible surprise that awaited her.

Jonathan watched her eyes sparkle as she talked of her books, vampire novels, he noted with a smile, saw her sadness as she talked of home, of her father, of her friend who lived in Connecticut. It was obvious to him that Julia had no one to talk to really, and so he let her go on, and on, for an hour or so, not once stopping her. The humanity of it all was so rare to him; he couldn't let it go. He began to feel the things she spoke of, and he knew he could understand her. Her loneliness matched his.

"So, where to next?" he asked her after she had paused for quite a while.

"Why are you being so nice to me?" she asked, smiling warmly at him. It wasn't an accusation at all, just a question that needed no answer. Standing, looking fondly at her as she held her hand out to him, his heart sank as she said, "Let's go to your place."

Back on the Harley, Julia snuggled ever closer to Jonathan, as they rode up the side of the mountain, past her darkened home, up the dirt path that extended through the woods. He could feel her warm, soft hands gently stroking the flesh of his stomach, her thighs cradling his hips and buttocks, her head resting against his back. She was so content, so at peace, while Jonathan was in turmoil.

He had never felt more the monster, than this night. Cursing himself for not feeding before he left, knowing that there had been no time, he was angry at Jason for keeping him busy. He was angry that Jason was right. Jonathan struggled with his true nature, just as he had been all evening. However now, he was losing the internal battle.

As time had progressed, so had the hunger, knotting in his stomach like a disease, trying to take over his mind, his will. Half of Jonathan wanted to pull the bike to a screeching stop, rip Julia's pretty, soft throat open, and drink from that tender skin, her sweet, sweet blood. Julia's blood, her innocent blood.

Ah, how good it would taste, burning on his tongue, and she would struggle and moan in his arms, as he defied his new found love, and took her, in final triumph.

Stop this! He told himself, and tried to concentrate on the road ahead. He tried to focus his anger at Jason; it was Jason's fault after all, not giving Jonathan a chance to feed tonight. Jason and his damned lessons. Jonathan scowled. Jason had done this on purpose, to give Jonathan a battle of wills to see which side would win out, Jonathan's nature or Jonathan's pretense.

Jonathan had finally uncovered the love he had buried away so long ago. Now, this damnable hunger was trying to beat it. He was so hungry. Just a bit longer, and the knotting pain in his veins and stomach would take over, and then he would...he would...he would do nothing, nothing to hurt Julia. She didn't need to be hurt in this, didn't need to be frightened, or used in order to fill Jonathan's hunger. His jaw ached, reflecting the gnawing deep in the pit of his stomach. *No! Do nothing!* His body uncontrollably shuddered.

"Are you alright?" Julia asked, shouting over the rush of the wind.

Jonathan ignored the question, glad that she did not repeat it. Julia snuggled even closer to him, holding him tighter. So innocent, Jonathan thought, you have no idea what you are holding onto. He felt her fingers spread on his aching stomach, causing the thirst to return sharply. No, he thought, wait for Jason to bring out the wine. Jonathan decided that when the wine was given, he'd drink before he gave it over to Julia. Jonathan didn't know exactly what was in this mysterious elixir, but he remembered previously feeling Jason's presence inside it. He was sure that it would make him feel better, at least for a while.

"Do you really want this?" Jason's words echoed on and on in Jonathan's mind.

"Yes, I do." Jonathan whispered, too soft for Julia to hear above the roaring of the motorcycle and the howling of the wind. "I really do."

As they drove into the old, overgrown dirt driveway of the mansion, Jonathan began to wonder if he was doing the right thing, after all. But then, as he cut the motor and watched Julia slip down and stand beside him, looking up at him with wide, trusting eyes, he could feel his love grow, and along with it, the hunger. He knew what he had to do, and that it was for the best. If she felt even remotely similar to how he felt, he knew there was to be no going back to their separate lives. Julia must be his.

Silently, he slid off the bike, paused for a moment, than reached out and swiftly, brought her to him. Arms pinned at her side, she appeared slightly startled, her face flushed, the smile gone.

"Julia, Julia," he breathed her name, like a plea, the wind whisking his words away. "Your life is going to be different from now on, but I think you'll like it here, with me." He raised one hand to her face, fingers toying with her curls. "I'm falling in love with you."

"What?" she whispered, struggling feebly to get away, not able to. "What do you mean, I'll like it here? Why are you looking at me that way?" Her words became so soft, Julia wasn't even sure that she had spoken them. Then, suddenly, she didn't care. She felt like she was drowning again, his eyes...they were so luminous in all their darkness, and she fell into their endless depths, deeper and deeper, and she couldn't get out into reality again. She didn't care. So immersed within him. Julia didn't even know that her own eyes had closed. However, Julia was not frightened. It was so peaceful, floating here, with Jonathan at her side. All sounds seemed so far away, and time? It hadn't even been invented yet.

As Julia fell forward, hypnotized, against him, Jonathan sighed, picked her up, and walked the short distance to the mansion where Jason waited at the door, his face blank, emotionless.

All but ignoring him, Jonathan brought Julia into the sitting room, setting Julia down upon one of the couches strewn with blankets of all lengths and colors. She did not stir.

There, in the circle of couches, chairs and cushioned seat that surrounded the coffee table and fireplace, sat Andrew and Devin, each of whom studied the girl, their faces, and emotions, unreadable.

As Jason came into the circle, sitting down upon a cushioned chair, Jonathan sat on the couch beside Julia, taking one of her hands in his. Only then did he release her from the bonds his mind had forged.

Julia came around slowly, groggily. Disoriented, weak and dizzy, she blinked back the darkness from her eyes, only to see Jonathan sitting over her. Funny though, she thought, he didn't look concerned.

"Julia, are you all right?" he asked.

"Yes, I think so. What happened?"

"You passed out."

"Again?" she questioned, rubbing her eyes with one hand. "This always seems to happen when I'm around you." she murmured. A small laugh came from someone in the room. Who it was, however, Julia was not sure.

"I'm going to have Andrew get you something to drink, alright?" Jonathan asked slowly, evenly. Why? Julia, at the moment, was too drained to care.

"Yeah, sure." she mumbled, wanting above all else, to go back to sleep, back to that place of peace. Even now, she closed her eyes, not really listening as Jason asked Andrew to get the wine, Jonathan asking about crystal glasses, and Jason saying that it will go down either way.

Andrew produced the glass and the bottle of wine from somewhere in the room, poured it into the glass, gave it over to Devin, who gave it to Jason, who handed it to Jonathan. Hesitantly, looking all the while at Jason, Jonathan sipped the wine. A slow, approving smile spread over Jason's face. Jonathan, feeling the hunger dissipate as the wine entered his stomach, smiled sheepishly back.

Jason gestured to give the crystal glass to Julia.

Julia lay very still upon the couch, holding her head in her left hand, Jonathan's hand clasped in her right. She could barely tell what was going on; she felt so strange. But now, she could hear Jonathan's voice very clearly, every word ringing into her thoughts, into her sleepy mind.

"Julia, I want you to drink this. It will...make you feel better."

Slowly, as if rising from the depths of a pool of tar, Julia forced herself to sit up on the couch. Her legs, as they hit the ground, felt made of lead.

Reaching for the glass, and holding it in her hand, seemed to be the hardest thing physically that she had ever done. However, her sight, murky as it was, seemed to focus clearly on this glass, filled with the darkest wine she had ever seen. "Are you sure?" she mumbled.

"Yes, go ahead. It's very old wine, but it's good. I drank some. Try it, Julia, it might help. Trust me." His voice convinced her more than anything else did. It was so soothing, so helpful, and she didn't want to insult him. She was, after all, his guest here.

Julia tipped her head back, and drank the whole glassful in a few large swallows. It tasted fantastic, sour and bitter and sweet all at the same time, rolling over her tongue like liquid candy, warming her stomach and numbing her throat.

Suddenly, the grogginess was gone, and a new feeling came over her body, something that she had never felt before. Unknowingly dropping the glass to the ground, she raised her hands to her face, not even really feeling it. Her body shook slightly from head to toe, an army of goose bumps raising up on her skin. The heat from her stomach spread rapidly, losing itself outwards from every pore in her body.

As soon as the pleasure had gone, came a moment of wretched sickness, nausea forcing her to want to throw up, and then came the darkness of oblivion; perfect sleep. The last thing she thought before the darkness took over was, I think I'm drunk.

Jonathan sat a moment, watching Julia as she slept, somehow knowing that she would be all right, that he need not sit vigil over her sleeping body.

"We should go out now." Jason said quietly, reaching to Jonathan's shoulder and pulling with a firm hand. "You need to feed, as do we all. Join us outside."

Jonathan nodded. He listened as Jason and Devin left the house. He felt Andrew approach his side, filled with the quiet kind of support he had always seemed to give.

"She's strong." Andrew said, observing something that Jonathan had already guessed.

Jonathan leaned over Julia, placing a lingering kiss on her lips. And then he left with Andrew, locking the doors shut to keep the sleeping girl safe.

It was one in the morning by the grandfather clock when they finally returned to the mansion.

It was then that Jonathan discovered that Julia had not yet awakened, but was tossing in her sleep, burning up with fever. Slightly panicked,

Jonathan snatched his hand away from her forehead, and turned to Jason, who was lighting up another one of his cigarettes.

"She has a fever, Jason, what can I do?" Jonathan said, approaching him slowly, asking for help with nothing more than the tone of his voice.

Jason took a long drag off the cigarette, blowing it out slowly. He seemed to be weighing all the possibilities in his mind. "Bring her home." he said finally.

"Home?" Jonathan questioned, looking doubtfully at Julia, and again at Jason.

"Well, there is nothing more we can do for her here. You know that. Besides, in a few hours it will be dawn, and she can't stay with us now."

"Why?" Jonathan demanded.

Jason scowled, stalking across the room, ignoring Julia, ignoring Jonathan, glaring into the flames of the fireplace. "Bring her home." he repeated, his tone aggravated, threatening.

Jonathan knew that the discussion was over. Bending down to pick Julia up, her leather jacket slipped, unnoticed, off her body and onto the floor. Before he could notice it was missing, Jonathan was out the door and into the night, willing himself to go upward, into the sky. Landing at Julia's home, he walked up onto the front porch, and placed her gently on the swing there, noting that from the cool of the night, her fever had seemed to recede slightly.

Now noticing that he had forgotten her jacket, he shrugged off his own, and placed it over to cover her. He then knelt down beside her, watching as her forehead tensed with some inner turmoil.

"Julia, can you hear my voice? I'm going now. Someone will find you here soon, I'm sure, but you'll be all right, I think. I will return for you at nightfall." He knelt there for a moment more, drinking in her young, innocent beauty. With his fingertips, he traced her forehead, her nose, and her lips. Leaning over her, his hair falling across his bare shoulders like a dark curtain, he kissed her, surprised as her mouth moved along with his.

"Jonathan?" her voice was scratchy as she called his name.

"Ssh. Rest now, Julia. You're home." He said softly, tossing his hair back over his shoulders. He didn't want to go, didn't want to leave her here, but he had to. Once again, he told himself, it was all for the best.

Jonathan backed off the porch, the cool wind blowing against him, but he didn't really feel it, for his thoughts were absorbed with Julia. With one last longing gaze at her, and at the house, he ran down the driveway, and flew into the night.

5

Gayle awoke the next morning to the persistent ringing of the telephone, located in Julia's room. After the fifth ring, it became obvious to Gayle that no one was about to answer it; it could be Mom calling from work. She rose from her bed with a moan, walked through the connecting bathroom that led to Julia's room, and answered the phone with a sleepy, "Hello?"

The voice at the other end was a girl's. "Hi, can I talk to Gayle?"

Gayle, however, didn't really hear the question. She was wondering where Julia was, why her bed hadn't been slept in, and why anyone would be calling at nine-thirty in the morning, especially during the summer.

"Can I talk to Gayle?" the voice repeated.

"Yeah, this is her. Who's this?" she asked, wondering for a panicky moment if the phone call was about her sister.

"My name is Ellen Pursivic. My Mom works with yours at the mall. She said you were new in town, and that you haven't really gotten to know anyone here."

"She's right." Gayle said with a yawn. "I've only been here two months, and not many kids are around to make friends with."

"Yeah, tell me about it." said Ellen with a smile in her voice. "This town is kind of a drag. That's why me and my sister Eyleen were wondering if you'd like to come over for a while."

"I don't know. My sister's not around, and I don't have a ride. Where do you live?"

"Not very far away, just a couple of streets below yours. We have a swimming pool." Ellen said, her voice full of hope.

"Do you have any ice cream?" Gayle said, yawning again. "I'd sure love some strawberry ice cream about now."

Ellen laughed. "No, but we could all go out for some if you came over."

Gayle rubbed her eyes, trying to wake up. The offer of ice cream was too good to pass up. "Okay, I'll call my Mom and tell her. Where do you live again?"

"Arrow Street. Five houses down on the right. A white Colonial."

"Alright. I'll see you soon. Say hi to Eyleen for me."

"Will do, bye."

The phone clicked off in Gayle's ear. "Bye," she said quietly to the dial tone, and hung up. That was kind of weird, she thought, shrugged, and went back into her room, exchanging her nightgown for a pair of jean-shorts and a yellow tee shirt.

After she called her Mom to ask if it was okay to leave the house, she asked where Julia was. Jeanne told her, aggravation quite thick in her voice, that Julia was lying out on the front porch, and would not be woken up. Gayle thanked her mother, and hung up.

Going out the front door, Gayle found Julia just as her Mom had said she would be, on the swing, still asleep, covering her face with that guy Jonathan's jacket. At least, I think it's his, she thought to herself. But why did Julia have his jacket and not her own? And why was she asleep on the porch, dressed in the same clothes she had left the house in the night before? Why hadn't she come in to bed last night?

Gayle walked over to Julia and shook her, none too gently. "Julia, get up!" she yelled, and when she received no answer, shook Julia a little harder, and yelled a little louder, "Get up, lazy, it's ten in the morning already!"

Julia stirred within the blackness of sleep, groaned, and lowered the jacket, squinting as the sunlight fell across her face. Surprisingly to Julia, it seemed brighter and hotter than usual. It hurt her eyes and her face. Throwing her right arm across her face, she sat up and yawned, gazing up guiltily at her bewildered sister.

"What's the matter with you?" Julia asked, "Why are you yelling?"

"Julia, why are you sleeping on the porch?" Gayle demanded, crossing her arms over her chest.

Julia glanced around her, looking down at the jacket on her lap, trying to no avail to remember the previous night. "I don't know," she said quietly.

"Do you have a hangover or something?"

Julia looked at Gayle. "You shouldn't even know what a hangover is, sis."

Gayle continued to interrogate Julia. "Where did you guys go last night, anyway? Where were you? When did you get home? Do you know how worried I was when I saw your bed empty?"

Julia groaned again, slowly getting to her feet. For some reason, she was exhausted this morning. "Please, Gayle, spare me the twenty questions. You sound just like Mom. I was with Jonathan last night, and where we went is none of your business. I did have wine last night, and I did pass out, but no, I don't have a hangover. I'm just tired. So you can get that look off your face and go to wherever it was that you were going."

Julia turned to the door, and then, curiosity got the better of her. "Where are you going, anyway?"

"Ellen and Eyleen's house."

"Who are they?"

"Just these girls," Gayle said, bounding off the porch.

"And I'm the one who doesn't talk." Julia muttered, yanking open the screen door with Jonathan's jacket clutched in her hand.

"Julia!" Gayle yelled from the end of the driveway.

"What!" she yelled back from the doorway, turning once more, to see Gayle sitting upon her three-speed bicycle.

"Mom's pissed at you for leaving last night! She says she's going out with the Mother's Group tonight, and that you have to stay home!"

"Sorry, I'm not staying home. And don't say pissed!"

"She said you'll be grounded if you don't. And your attitude stinks!" Gayle then peddled away, leaving Julia alone to slam the door shut on no one.

"Stay home, stay home, can't I have a life?" Julia growled under her breath, climbing the stairs to her room, wincing at the onslaught of light pouring in from her window. Dumping Jonathan's jacket onto the bed, she pulled the curtains shut, and when that wasn't enough to blot out the light, she pulled a blanket from her bed, wrapping it securely around the window frame.

She then closed and locked her door and the door to the bathroom, and knocked the phone off the hook. Sighing as she looked over the mess on the floor, littered with clothing and other miscellaneous objects, she stripped off her clothes to her underwear, and flopped down on the bed next to Jonathan's jacket.

Breathing in the scent of Jonathan that still clung to his jacket, she was soon overcome with tiredness, and fell into a deep, dreamless sleep.

During the travel on bike to a local convenience store to pick up ice cream, Gayle enjoyed the company of the two twelve-year old girls, Ellen and Eyleen. Being twins, and young, they still enjoyed looking similar. Their height, four foot ten, was equally matched, both had similar haircuts; very short, with the only difference being the braided tail that Eyleen wore down the back of her neck. They both were clothed in blue jean-shorts, army green tee shirts, and black sneakers. Their personalities differed slightly, Ellen being outspoken and vivacious, Eyleen quiet and shy. They seemed to Gayle nice enough, and fun to be with, that was, until, she went with them back to their home, and into their room.

Once inside that place, Gayle stood in the center of what seemed to be organized chaos, with a totally shocked and surprised look upon her face.

Old grenades hung strapped to the walls, as did crossbows and arrows, spears, swords, and several other evil-looking things. Dart guns were positioned over the door and the window. Helmets, combat outfits knives and canteens were among the items thrown into a large, open trunk. The bunk bed was strewn with camouflage netting. The trophy shelf was lined with commando comic books and, certificates in Vampire Hunting.

This is too weird, Gayle thought to herself.

"Well, what do you think?" Ellen said a bit gruffly.

Gayle watched Eyleen flop down onto the lower bunk, obviously distressed. "Ellen, she's gonna think we're strange." She looked up at Gayle with pleading in her brown eyes. "We lose all our friends this way."

"Knock it off." Ellen told her sister, turning to face Gayle again. Smiling, she whispered into her ear, cupping her hand over her face as if it were a great secret; "It's just something we play at."

"What is?" Gayle asked, becoming just slightly more interested than shocked.

"Vampire Hunters." Ellen rocked back on her heels, crossing her arms, grinning smugly. Eyleen groaned.

Gayle's eyes lit up. "Cool!" she exclaimed.

"Not so cool." Eyleen said quietly.

Ellen ignored her, showing Gayle all the different weapons that they had acquired from the Army Surplus down at the mall.

"How did you get them to sell you this stuff?" Gayle asked, turning a real sword over in her tiny hands. It was so heavy; she could hardly lift it up.

"Five finger discount. No, really our cousin works there." Ellen shrugged. "Wanna join the crew?" she asked Gayle, taking the sword from her and placing it back on a wall hanger.

"Ellen, I don't know. What if she tells her Mom about all this stuff?" Eyleen said, gesturing around the room.

"She won't," Ellen said, before Gayle could utter a word, "will you Gayle?"

"I won't tell," Gayle said, "but I don't know if I want to join up with you guys. I mean, it sounds kind of fun, but I just don't know." There was something going on here that Gayle couldn't place, something weird about Ellen that she could see Eyleen already knew about. "I just don't know," she repeated.

Ellen smiled a false warm smile that Gayle did not really like. "You can read some stuff if you like. Here, sit down." she said, placing Gayle on the bed next to Eyleen. "Read these." She dumped some books onto Gayle's lap.

Gayle looked down at the books, only to discover several Vampire Hunter comic books, and a Christian Bible. Looking over at Ellen, who was still smiling, to Eyleen who was frowning, Gayle opened up the first of the comic books, and prepared herself for the most unusual day of her life.

6

Sunset in Vermont, Julia awakened at last from a lethargy that had persisted the entire day.

Rubbing her face, she walked to the window, ripped down the blanket, drew up the curtain, and opened the window, lifting the screen. Not caring that the neighbors might see her in her underwear, which was already more than a day old, she placed her palms on the windowsill and leaned out a bit, closing her eyes and drinking in the fresh, cool air of twilight.

After a moment, she went over to the center of her room, changed her underwear, and pulled from the pile of clothes on the floor a pair of blue jeans and a plain, black tee shirt.

Gazing down at the pile of clothes, re-adjusting the barrette in her hair, Julia listened to the voices downstairs. Mom was home, and with her were a group of mothers.

Remembering all that her sister had told her in the afternoon, Julia made a face, and messily dumped all the clothes onto the floor of the closet, where her unfinished book still lay. Sliding the closet door shut with an audible bang, she unlocked the bedroom door, remembered the phone off the hook and replaced it, and opened her door, venturing down the stairs to see exactly what was going on.

Julia looked around, squinting, as she traveled loudly down the stairway. Why were all the lights on down here, she thought, rather annoyed at the fact, that, and the loudness of the four women and her mother chatting loudly in the family room. "These lights are too damn bright," she muttered, walking into the family room, and turning off the lights as she went.

Halfway there, through the dining room and almost to the entrance of the room, which was her goal, her mother glanced up from conversation and called her name.

"Julia, I'll be right there!" Jeanne called, and Julia groaned. Talking alone with her mother always meant a lecture.

Julia waited, leaning on the table, wondering what she was going to do about her date with Jonathan. It was the first thing she asked when her mother came to her.

"Call him and cancel." Jeanne said.

"I don't know his number." Julia replied, lightly scratching at her arm.

"Some guy, Julia, he won't even tell you his number? What's his last name, where are his parents?"

"Come on Mom," Julia moaned, knowing that her mother would not like the answers to these questions, "do I really have to stay here tonight?"

"Yes," Jeanne said, frowning. "I didn't like how you took off last night. I don't want it happening again."

Julia glared at her mother for a moment, dangerous thoughts creeping, unbidden, into her mind. Surprised at herself for even thinking these things, she decided to give up the fight. "Fine Mom, whatever." Julia sighed, rolling her eyes.

Jeanne began to say something, but then, the ladies came over to them, filing out of the house one by one. "I'll be right there." she said to the last of them, who nodded, and then took her leave as well.

"Are you riding with them?" Julia asked, feeling as if she had to say something.

"Don't take my Jeep, Julia." Jeanne replied, reaching to pick up her pocketbook, which was lying on the table.

Julia subconsciously flinched. "Mom, what the hell do you think I am!" she shouted, "Take your car, really!" Julia turned to go, pausing at the stairway, and looking over at her sister, who stood in the kitchen.

"Julia, I don't want to hear of you drinking again." Jeanne said, pulling open the screen door.

Julia glared at Gayle, who turned back to the counter, looking guilty. Julia faced her mother. "I just can't do anything right, can I, Mom. Now I'm not only a thief, but a drunk, too. What's next?"

Jeanne paused, anger and sadness fighting for control of her facial features. "Just stay home tonight, okay?" she asked, but before Julia could answer, she was out the door and gone.

Julia stood for a moment in the darkened dining room, and then turned to the kitchen, glaring at her little sister's back. "Thanks, Gayle," she said, flopping down on a chair next to the small, not-so-formal table, as the one inside the dining room. She was not surprised at the fact that her sister had ignored her comment.

Julia decided to take a calmer approach to conversation, seeing as she'd have to stay home the entire night, anyway. "What did you do today?" she asked.

Gayle lifted the plate of food she had been eating, and brought it over to the table, feeling as if it were now safe to sit, and eat, next to her sister.

"You know those two girls I told you I was going to hang out with?" Gayle asked, chewing rather noisily on a French fry.

Julia thought for a moment. Everything about last night, and the morning after, seemed relatively hard for her to recall. Finally, she simply gave up, and said, "A little."

"Well, I went over their house today. I wish I hadn't, Julia. They are like the Twins from Mars, or something, I swear. Well, Eyleen wasn't so bad, but that Ellen, she's just weird."

Julia had no idea what her sister was talking about. Confused beyond belief, she simply said, "How is she weird?"

Gayle took a big bite out of her burger, swallowed it, and drank a gulp of soda, seeming to ponder the question. "Well, they play Vampire Hunters sometimes, and Eyleen said she does it just for her sister. But Ellen, she really believes that stuff! She thinks she could kill vampires for a living, if she ever was lucky enough to find one. Why would that be lucky? I don't get it. And they want me to play too!"

Gayle took another bite of her burger, and proceeded to talk with her mouth full. "I mean, they had me read all this stuff; comic books and bibles, and you should see the stuff they've got! Swords and grenades..."

At this point, Julia stopped listening to her sister. Her mind drifted to Jonathan, knowing that he was coming over sometime tonight, and wondering how she knew this. She wondered what she was going to do. How could she get out of babysitting?

"Isn't that awful?" Gayle said, finishing off her soda, and slamming it down on the table, so loud, Julia jumped and covered her ears.

"Do you mind?" Julia hissed, bolting out of her chair and stalking out of the room.

Gayle sat at the table a moment, staring at her empty plate, and wondering what she had done that was so wrong. She heard her sister enter the family room, briefly flip through the television channels, curse, and turn it off again.

Gayle, after a moment, stood up, and placed her dish into the sink, listening as Julia went up to her room. Feeling bad that she was the reason why Julia was so angry and depressed, Gayle eventually went up to her sister's room.

Gayle found Julia sitting on her bed in the darkness, playing a Billy Idol tape rather softly.

"Can I turn on the light?" Gayle asked, watching as Julia turned to face her. There was an angry light in her sister's eyes, something she saw not very often.

"Yes," Julia said finally, her hand out to touch Jonathan's jacket. Pain shot into her eyes as light flooded the room.

"What's the matter, Julia?" Gayle said, concern heavy in her voice.

"I just have a headache," Julia lied, turning to look at Jonathan's jacket, and noticing, for the first time, some sort of dark stain along the collar. "Nothing's wrong," she whispered. The truth was, everything seemed wrong, but Julia could not place exactly what it was. She felt funny; hyper, jumpy, and very agitated.

"I'm sorry Mom made you stay home because of me, Julia. I didn't want you to be in trouble." Gayle poked around at the items on Julia's bureau, eventually picked up a needle and thread from a tiny pink pincushion.

"Well, it's too late now, isn't it." Julia replied, bitterly.

Gayle walked to Julia, standing with her head down, trying over and over again to thread the little needle. "I don't want you to be mad at me," she said.

Julia suddenly felt the anger flare up, hot and hard in her body and soul. Gayle would always get what she wanted, Julia decided. She will get everything I can't have . . . freedom, love, a mother to care for her.

"Go away!" Julia growled, giving her sister a shove that sent her backward into the bureau.

"Ow!" Gayle exclaimed, dropping the needle and thread to the floor, holding her right hand in her left.

Instantly, the smell of blood flooded the room, causing Julia to snap her head up in attention. Her eyes were drawn to the sight of her sister's blood; bright red, as it leaked out of her palm, and dripped to the floor.

"Gayle," she said softly, standing, approaching her sister's hand. "What did you do?"

"You did it!" Gayle shouted, tears in her eyes, but Julia did not see them.

Julia stood motionless, an inexpressible hunger forming in her stomach. The smell of blood was all around her, so thick, so red, she could almost taste it on her tongue. And then, came the pain. Hunger shot up into her ribs, tearing at her guts like a serrated blade.

Julia fell to the floor at her sister's feet, hands over her stomach. The pain knifed its way through her body, traveling, it seemed, through each of her muscles, each of her veins. A roaring filled her ears, her sight momentarily gone, her heart burned and beat so fast, she thought it might explode.

And above all this, she could hear her sister screaming her name, her sister's hands on her face, the blood smell expanding as Gayle smeared it onto Julia.

44

Julia's sight slowly focused on the bleeding hand above her, on each drop that squeezed forth. Her brain and stomach cried out to her for blood. Her throat was dry, so very dry.

Julia stood slowly, one hand grasping her sister's palm, the other clutching at her stomach in agony. She could not feel her sister struggle, could not hear her pleas. There was only the wrenching pain in her gut, the roaring in her ears, and the blood.

Gayle stared up at her sister, crying, shouting, "Stop it Julia, Julia! You're scaring me, leave me alone!" She pulled and pulled, but now Julia's face, lined with sweat and pain, was lowering to the bleeding pinprick on her palm. Gayle finally stopped screaming, thinking quickly, and she said calmly and loudly, "What would Dad say?"

Dad. Sadness erupted in Julia, flooding into her mind with all the effect of water being poured onto a fire. The pain dissipated from her, cooling, leaving her feeling sick, drained, sore, and entirely confused. Coming back to herself, she saw Gayle looking up at her, the bleeding hand clasped within her own. Immediately, she released Gayle, stepping back a few paces.

Gayle, choking back sobs, stood, rubbing her wrist. "Why did you do that?"

Julia, tears of her own welling up, as she realized just what had almost happened, said softly, "I don't know." She looked at her hands, rubbed her aching stomach. "What happened to me?" she whispered.

Wiping her tears away, Gayle backed away from Julia, into the bathroom to run her hand under the water. After a moment, she heard footsteps behind her, and then, a gasp of such horror, Gayle was afraid to look up.

In the mirror Gayle saw herself, and Julia behind her, only Julia wasn't really there. Her reflection was more like a shadow, outlined in shades, and transparent enough that she could see the bathtub behind her.

Julia covered her mouth to keep from screaming. "I'm not there?" she whispered, staring at herself as Gayle turned to face her. The horror in Gayle's eyes matched her own.

"You lost your reflection? But that would mean..." Gayle stated quietly, and then, "Julia, your tears are pink."

Julia swiped at her face then, turning her hand to the light. Yes, Gayle was right. Her tears were a strange sort of pinkish-red. Julia's mind suddenly flooded over with every story she had written on the subject, that of vampires, and before she had the chance to say a word, Gayle screamed it out for her, her tiny hands clutching at her neck.

"You, you're a *vampire!*"

"Gayle," Julia protested, her voice shaky, weak, "don't be silly, I am not."

Wide-eyed with terror, Gayle could do nothing but stand there and nod.

"That's ridiculous, Gayle, come on, think, I'm your sister." Julia held out her hands to Gayle, wanting her to know, and to believe that it was not true.

"Don't you *touch me!*" Gayle screamed out, backing away, into her own room, by use of the bathroom door, and then slamming it shut on Julia's stunned face.

Julia stood there for a moment, listened as her sister locked the door, and then, the door within which led to the hallway. She wanted to say something, but what? "Gayle, I am *not* a vampire…it's just…"

Julia trailed off, staring at the reflection in the mirror once again. "What the hell is going on here?" she whispered, and began to sob, helplessly. Entering her room, she switched off the light, and flopped down onto the bed, cradling Jonathan's jacket in her arms.

About an hour later, she heard the motorcycle pull up the drive.

Julia knew without having to look that it was Jonathan. She could feel it as surely as if she had gone to the window and looked.

Blinking back dried tears, and exhaustion from too much crying, she rose from the bed, locked the door to her room, and the bathroom, and shut the shades. Locking herself in her room would not make the problem go away, she knew, and it might not even make Jonathan go away. But, being terrified, and damn near hysterical, there was nothing else at the moment that she could do.

When the doorbell rang, she choked back a scream, and sat down next to the bathroom door, pressing her body back into it. She didn't want to see him now, didn't want him to know what she was thinking, even though it might all be true. Time to think, that's what she needed. And when the doorbell rang again, she shut her eyes, and hugged herself tightly.

On the second ring, Gayle decided that Julia wasn't going to answer the door. Gathering her courage, she went to her vanity, upon which was strewn many small items of jewelry. Digging through a drawer, she found what she was looking for. A cross, small and silver, she had received it ages ago, from a forgotten family member. All Gayle remembered about the cross was that it had been blessed, and according to Ellen and Eyleen, a blessed cross would protect you from a vampire and from Julia.

By the time the doorbell rang for the third time, Gayle had her chain on, and was going down the stairs. She wondered briefly why whoever it was at the door hadn't given up and gone away. Maybe somehow, the person at the door had known that they were home. Shaking her head, muttering, "That's silly," Gayle opened the front door.

Jonathan stood beyond the screen door, wearing a black shirt in place of his jacket. He opened his mouth to say something, but shut it just as quickly. His eyes were fixed directly on Gayle's chain, on the silver cross. His face paled, his hand suddenly clutching at his chest, as if he were having a heart attack. He stumbled off the porch, and backwards into the driveway.

Gayle didn't understand at first, but then, an idea hit her. Maybe he was a vampire too! Her heart began to pound, and she almost closed the door, but she heard Jonathan say, "Wait, Gayle, I need to talk to you. Come out to the porch. Come on, I won't hurt you, it's all right."

Gayle saw his eyes by the light on the porch, and despite the distance between them, they were very clear to her. A calm settled over her, as she realized, yes, he wouldn't hurt her. She would be safe, with him. Gayle opened the screen door, and walked out onto the porch.

"Put that chain away, Gayle, I'm not a religious man."

She believed him. The thought that he might be lying about it didn't even cross her mind. Gayle had to believe him when she looked into those eyes. They were really nice eyes, after all. If she were a few years older, she might even find him attractive. Gayle put the cross beneath her shirt.

Jonathan stepped forward into the light, standing below on the driveway near the porch steps. Softly, as if not to alarm her, he said, in explanation of his earlier reaction, "I have asthma attacks once in a while. You know how it is."

Gayle did know. One of her friends in Connecticut had asthma.

"Look, I came here to see Julia. Is she ready?"

Gayle stared at him for a moment, and then said, "For what?"

"For our date."

"No," Gayle replied, thinking quickly. "She can't tonight. She's sick with something. She had some kind of attack in her room. She went to bed."

"Oh," Jonathan said, almost, almost smiling? That just didn't settle right with Gayle. Neither did the fact that he turned and left without saying another word, climbing onto his motorcycle and tearing off into the night.

Gayle went into the house, locked the door, and went up the stairs. Julia waited at the top.

"That was him, wasn't it?" she asked.

"It was Jonathan." Gayle confirmed.

Julia sighed, went into her room again. "What did he want?" she asked, when she noticed Gayle following her.

"He wanted you."

Julia sighed; that was the understatement of the year. "Gayle, listen to me, okay? I know you're scared, but I am too. I've never hurt you, right? I'm not going to hurt you now; you have to believe that. Don't you trust me?"

Gayle stared at Julia, remembering the look on her face when she had held her wrist so tightly, comparing it to the scared, lost look that presented itself now. "I trust you, sis. You won't," she paused, the words sticking in her throat, "you won't kill me, will you?"

"Never!" Julia exclaimed, her heart breaking.

Gayle walked to her sister, studying her closely. Then, she forced a smile, and hugged Julia around the waist.

"It will be all right, Gayle, I'll figure this out. I'll just go right to the source, confront the problem, and reverse it."

"What if it doesn't work?"

"It has to," Julia said quietly.

Gayle pulled back, silently thinking for a moment. "Julia, Ellen told me that a person can become a vampire by drinking vampire blood. Did you ever do that?"

"I thought of that, but no, I don't think so." Julia's mind strained to remember the previous evening. It hurt her head far too much to try and think of it. She remembered the red wine, but the peculiar taste of it couldn't have been blood, could it? She remembered that Jason had something to do with the wine; however indirectly, it had come from him. Julia frowned. She hadn't thought Jason was altogether normal to begin with.

Just then, Julia and Gayle heard a few cars pull up.

"That must be Mom." Julia stated. "Gayle, I'm going to find out what's wrong with me, but I need you to keep this a secret. Tell Mom that I got sick, passed out, anything. I just need to think about all this for a while, and I don't want to talk to *her*."

"But Julia…"

"No. Don't tell anyone, please, promise me."

Gayle nodded slowly, standing and leaving the room, closing the door with a bang behind her.

Julia locked the door, and lay back down on her bed. She eventually fell into a broken sleep, tossing and turning the night through. Her dreams were all nightmares, bloody and full of agony, her body breaking out into a cold sweat. Sometime, during the day as she slept, she tossed Jonathan's jacket, unknowingly, to the floor.

7

Gayle awoke the next morning rather early. She had not really slept at all; nightmares had haunted every dream of her own.

Joining Jeanne downstairs for an early breakfast, Gayle learned that her mother had the day off from work today, and wanted to go on a long picnic, at one of Vermont's many lakes.

"Would you and Julia like to come?"

Gayle looked up at her mother, slowly, from the bowl she was washing. "Julia's sick Mom, remember?"

"Well, maybe if she's feeling better, she could come along." Jeanne offered, taking the bowl from Gayle, and wiping it off with a cloth. "Why don't you go up and ask her?"

"She won't come." Gayle said, "She'll be mad that I'm waking her up this early." The sun had just barely risen. However, Gayle left the dishes to her mother, and traveled up the stairs to Julia's bedroom door.

Gayle paused for a moment outside the door, listening for any sign of life within. Hearing none, she knocked. There was no answer. Even when Gayle called out to her sister quite loudly, there was no answer. Finally, Gayle just yelled down to her Mom that Julia would not be woken, and asked if they could just leave her a note.

"I guess so, Gayle," Jeanne said quietly from the first floor.

Gayle felt bad for her Mom. She really did want Julia to be happy with her. What mom didn't want for their daughters to be happy, after all?

Entering her own room, Gayle wrote out a short note to Julia, dictating where she and Jeanne were going, how long they would be gone, and added a bit about Julia's particular problem.

"I'm going to help." Gayle read aloud, after the letter had been completed. "Don't worry about anything. Ellen and Eyleen will have a cure for you, I know they will. And yeah, I know that in your books the only cure is to kill the vampire that gave you the blood, but we don't know who that is, do we? Julia, what if it's Jonathan? He's a little weird, you know. I won't say anything yet, but you've got to find out. Well, I'm going now, goodbye, Gayle."

Note finished, Gayle went into the connecting bathroom, and slid it under the crack in the bottom of Julia's door, hoping that she'd find it and read it, whenever she woke up.

That done, Gayle returned to the kitchen, and dialed Ellen and Eyleen's phone number. Hoping to reach Eyleen, Gayle's heart sank a bit as Ellen answered the phone.

"I can't talk long," Gayle said, nervously wrapping the cord around her fingers, watching around the corner of the room for her mother.

"What's up?" Ellen said.

"I was just wondering…" Gayle trailed off as her mother passed by.

"Well?" Ellen's voice agitated on the other end of the phone.

"Do you know of a cure for half-vampires?" Gayle said, sounding really silly to her own ears. She felt relieved when Ellen did not laugh or ask questions.

"I've been working on that for a while now," she said, chewing on something. "You know, to cure a half-vampire is to kill the vampire that gave it the blood in the first place."

"I know, but…"

"Hold on a second Gayle, do you want an answer or not?" Ellen said, a bit impatiently.

"Sorry."

"To become a vampire you have to drink vampire blood, right? Well then, if you're not a full vampire yet, why can't you drink something else to reverse the effect?"

"What is it Ellen, what can change you back?" Gayle said, hope and curiosity reflecting heavily in her voice

"We don't know yet, but we'll keep you posted." Ellen said. There was a pause, and then, her voice somehow shifted. "What's going on Gayle? Why are you suddenly interested? Yesterday you were doubtful, but now you're really digging for a cure. Is there a problem at home?"

"What's going on, Ellen?" This came from a softer voice beyond the phone, one Gayle knew to be Eyleen's.

"Ssh." Ellen said, and then turned her attention back to Gayle. "Well, are you going to tell me or not?"

Gayle nervously chewed on her hair. What to do, what to do? "I don't have a problem, I'm just curious."

"Yeah, right." Ellen said. "Anyway, I think I'm going to hang up now. If you ever decide to be straight with us, call."

One click and the conversation was over. Gayle stared at the receiver in her hand for a moment, not really knowing what to do. At least, there was a possibility of a cure, and to get one, she'd need to tell Ellen everything. But Gayle seriously had doubts about this whole thing. As scared as she was, she didn't really believe what was going on, not really. She'd just have to talk to Julia before making any decisions, she decided, and hung up the phone.

Later, as Gayle and Jeanne Anderson readied to leave the house, having packed up the jeep and locked up the house, Gayle sat in the front passenger seat, staring back at the house as her mother revved the ignition.

"Julia will be fine," Jeanne said, thinking Gayle was worried about her older sister's health.

"I hope so." Gayle replied sadly.

As they pulled away from the driveway, Gayle couldn't help but think to herself; it's funny how the trees seem to close in around the house.

8

Julia Anderson opened her eyes and sat up. In the place between dreams and reality, she had heard something, or someone, calling her name.

Looking around her darkened room, Julia could not find a trace of what it was that had called to her. She listened, but there was no voice. Finally, she simply let it go, and looked down at Jonathan's jacket resting down on the floor beside her.

Instantly, all the thoughts and worries of what had taken place the night before came flooding back to her. All the terror, all the doubts. Jonathan, had he done this to her? And what if she really was becoming a vampire? How could she ever face it, the horror and darkness that came along with it?

Julia sighed, swinging her legs off the bed, and getting to her feet. She knew that she'd have to face all the possibilities and consequences sooner or later, but at this very moment, she'd much rather it be later.

Julia thought for a moment about showering, but decided against it. She wasn't feeling very well this evening, and was rather depressed. The thought of standing in a shower made her feel queasy. Making the decision final, she changed her clothes, pulling on new underwear, a white tank top, and tight blue jeans. Walking to the bathroom to fix her hair, she discovered the note poking out from underneath the door.

Relieved that her mother and sister were out for the time being, but not so happy that Gayle was involving two outsiders in her problem, Julia crinkled up the note, and tossed it over her shoulder into the room behind her.

Once inside the bathroom, Julia picked up a brush that rested on the top of the sink, and glanced up into the mirror, out of habit, in order to fix her hair. Seeing her shadowy figure reflected back at her, Julia was instantly and completely sobered. She ran the brush through her curls a few times, tucked her hair behind her ears, and threw down the brush, stalking back into the dark recesses of her bedroom. Once there, her heart caught in her chest, causing her to become almost paralyzed.

Her name was being called again. It was a voice like no other, for nothing she had ever heard matched the quality of it. It did not come from an outside source, Julia realized with growing panic. It was inside her mind, inside her head.

Julia.

Again it called to her. It resonated through the core of her being; sending winter chills down the back of her spine. And she knew, beyond a doubt, as it lured her, that she could not refuse it.

Julia, come to the window. Open it, open it wide.

Julia began to move to the window, before she even registered that she was doing it. It seemed that her body was set apart from her mind. Julia was no longer in control, and all she could do was to sit back and watch. Her hands, shaking, drew open the shade, the big, glass window, the screen. Her face felt the gust of cool air, her eyes, which stared out at the horizon and the mountains, which populated it, watered because they could not blink.

Julia stood there like a statue after this task was done, realizing that she could not move until the voice told her to. She was frightened, out of control, yet her face, that of an impassive mask, could not show it.

Julia, bring us in now, one for each of us. Say it now.

Is this really happening? Are these really my arms? Such were Julia's thoughts, as her arms outstretched to the roadside. Is this really my voice? Her words came from her mouth, "Come in, come in, come in."

As soon as she said this, the spell was broken. Julia was left with an image in her mind, an imprint of sorts. Orange hair, blue eyes. Clasping her hand over her mouth, she realized just whom it was that she had seen, and what she had done.

Backing away from the window, tears of pain and panic trickling, unbidden down her cheeks, Julia watched helplessly as a strong wind began to blow through the room, causing objects to fall over, some items smashing to pieces against the hardwood floor. Julia felt the bedroom door hard and unyielding against her back as she came in contact with it, and she reached out for the lock.

It was then that he appeared in the room before her, the one who had spoken into her mind, the one who had given her the wine. Jason, it was Jason, standing there in her room, when there was no way to get up here, from the ground to the second floor. Hysteria took over at the sight of him, simply standing, as he was, in the center of the room, and Julia screamed, collapsing to the ground on her knees, watching through fingers clenched to her eyes, as Jonathan, Devin and Andrew, were suddenly there in the room as well.

As Julia's scream died out, they remained silent, watching her, gauging her every move. Beyond her choked sobs, there was no other sound to be heard in the house. The mysterious wind had gone. It was as if she was the only thing alive here, and she began to laugh with the irony of it all.

Jonathan, at seeing her reduced to this state, began to walk to her, knowing she needed comfort. But to Julia, he was just another threat.

"Stay away from me!" she shouted, rising to her feet, backing into the corner between the bedroom door, and the closet. She smiled as Jonathan stopped dead in his tracks. "What are you?" she asked calmly, and when she received no reply, shouted again, "What are you!"

Jonathan opened his mouth slightly, perhaps to talk, but before he could answer her, Jason spoke. "You must know by now. My blood must have taken effect, by now."

Julia's eyes shifted from Jonathan to Jason. "Your blood? What blood?" she questioned, knowing how crazy all of this sounded. "The wine, right? It was in that damn wine, oh, what have you done to me?" she sobbed out.

Looking back at Jonathan, watching his expression, she said, "How could you do this to me? I trusted you; I wanted to be with you! I loved you!"

"Julia," Jonathan whispered, moving toward her, trying to pull her small, shaking body close to him, and he felt her anger as she violently shook him off.

"How *could* you?" she insisted, eyes wide, helpless. "I know what it is to be a vampire, Jonathan. I wrote the book! Last night," she shook her head, wiping the tears on her wrist, "I almost killed my sister. My own sister! I was so out of control, I didn't know what I was doing. I don't know what I'm going to do now. My whole life is gone," she glared at him, feeling her anger build. "Gone! What the hell is going to happen to me now?" Suddenly, the helplessness took over, rage draining out of her body in a river of tears. She let Jonathan hold her, sobbing against him, somehow still wanting him near. She needed him still.

Jonathan held her as she sobbed, looking over at the others for support of his own. Receiving none, he knew he had to resolve this problem, quickly. "Julia," he said, softly stroking her hair, "Julia, look at me."

She sniffled, raised her head to meet his. "I'll take care of you now. I want to be with you, too. As a vampire, I could not do that without harming you, a human. If you are a vampire, I cannot hurt you."

"You're hurting me now." she whimpered.

"Julia, I have loved you from the first moment I saw you. I wanted more than anything to be able to love you. I looked into your heart and saw that you felt the same about me, and so I asked Jason to make you like us. Our lives could never have been the same again, if we were apart. I had to do this, don't you understand?" he asked, raising her chin with his hand.

Julia looked into his eyes, seeing the love there, the endless possibilities, and the hope that he had in her, alone. "I...I guess so." she whispered, her tears trailing off to a halt. "But I can't be this. How could I ever kill people?"

"You'll get used to it." Devin said, so rationally, so casually, as if he were discussing the time of day.

Julia stared at him; shock, fear and disgust made her want to run all over again.

"But I'm only sixteen," she protested.

"I was sixteen," said Andrew, rather softly.

"Come with us." Jonathan whispered in her ear. "You'll never have to be lonely, or frightened of anything again. I'll care for you, I'll love you."

"But my mother, my sister. How can I leave them?" she asked, turning to look into his dark eyes.

Jonathan stroked her face gently. How could he tell her that she'd have to leave them eventually? When the hunger got bad enough, they'd be in great danger of her and her new found appetite.

"Enough of this." Jason said, breaking the tension and silence of the room. "She can come or stay, but we're leaving." With this, he left the room the same way he had come, by the window. Devin followed him first, then by Andrew.

Julia gazed up at Jonathan, who had never left her side, never broken physical contact. The air seemed to grow thick, as she stood there, with him, painfully aware that the others were gone, and she was now alone with him. Unaware that she had done so, she now found herself holding onto him, afraid to let go, afraid to be alone.

"I have to go." he said softly, caressing the back of her neck with his hand. "Do you have my jacket?"

"It's near the bed." As much as Julia hated to admit it, he had been right. At this moment, she could not picture being without him. She wanted to be with him, to be a part of him, always. And it scared her to death.

Moved by emotions deep inside her, Julia leaned forward and kissed him softly, feeling waves of pleasure wash over her, as his cool lips touched her mouth.

"Will you come with me?" he asked, pulling back.

"I don't know," Julia said, "I...can't."

Jonathan walked to the bed, picked up the jacket and pulled it on over the black shirt. "Your jacket is waiting on my bike," he said, smiling warmly. "You can ride with me."

Julia wrung her hands indecisively. She wanted to go, but also, needed to return. "Can I come just for tonight? Can I do that?"

Jonathan's smile grew wider. "Get your keys." he said.

Julia grabbed them from where they lay on the bureau, and went to Jonathan, where he stood, by the window. She held his hand, and looked out, down at the ground. It really seemed like a long way down.

"Trust me." Jonathan said. Before Julia could take in another breath, Jonathan had pulled her with him out the window, and they were now descending. But, much to her amazement, they were not falling! It felt as if the wind had suddenly grasped them in a giant, invisible hand. It rushed over Julia, through her hair and clothes, making her skin tingle, and her insides feel light. Together, they landed next to the Harleys, and the others, a good twenty or so feet away from the house.

Julia pulled on the jacket as Jonathan climbed up onto the bike, starting it up. Looking at the house, Julia was amazed that she hadn't fallen, and wondered briefly if she could actually get up there the way she had come down.

"Come on, Julia." Jonathan's voice interrupted her thoughts. She looked to see him gazing at her, waiting for her, inviting her with more than words.

She climbed onto the bike behind him, holding onto him, and wishing she never had to let go. As they all pulled out into the road, Julia could not help but be amazed that she was with them, these men who were not really men at all, and she wondered if her life would ever be normal again.

ETERNAL NIGHT

9

Julia walked through Getaway Park, along with what she now knew as "The Vampires", clinging tightly to Jonathan's hand. Although she didn't quite believe that they were really vampires, she knew beyond any doubt, that she had stumbled upon real trouble. She could feel it emanating from them, from Jason in particular. It was in the way they looked at all the people who surrounded them.

To Julia, crowds were something to be avoided, at all costs. In crowds, people were many. Emotions raged higher than a fever sometimes, causing even the strongest willed man to stoop to things he normally wouldn't. Things like riots, harassment, and not to mention horrible, claustrophobic, pressing of bodies. These things were unbearable to Julia, and now, to her dismay, it seemed as if everywhere they went inside the park, a crowd circulated around them.

Girls approached Jonathan and the others carelessly, recklessly, coming on to them with such audacity, at first Julia had thought they might be drunk. But then, with fast approaching fear, she wondered how all of these young girls could be drunk at the same time.

And that was when she realized that yes, if they were indeed vampires, they would be able to manipulate the emotions and sexual feelings of others, in order to suit their needs. And what needs would that be? Julia shuddered to think of it. However, the energy that flowed between them and the girls was too powerful to deny. Julia could see the deliberate hunger in their eyes, and with a sinking heart, she began to believe that they were vampires. Either that, she reasoned, or some really good hypnotists.

I'm caught, Julia thought, watching Jonathan and Andrew smile at a couple of girls as they passed by. Her hand tightened on Jonathan's, but he didn't seem to feel it. She shook her head slightly, looked down at her feet. He caught me as easily as one of them, and I fell for it, and now it's too late.

Julia began to withdraw then, deep into her own personal despair. She didn't want to see anymore. No more hungry, sexual looks they gave over to the girls, no more willing advances. She was deeply frightened by them and trying hard not to show it, failing miserable.

Wishing she could talk to Jonathan privately, and knowing she couldn't, Julia thought hard, as if she were talking to him and her thoughts said, *I want to go home.*

Immediately, Jonathan stopped walking. Julia stood beside him, only after a moment realizing that the others had walked on without them.

"Why do you want to go home, Julia?" Jonathan asked.

Stunned, Julia looked up at him. "How did you know what I was thinking?" she demanded.

Jonathan raised a hand, and touched her forehead. "If you want for me to know something, and you push hard enough with your mind, I just might hear your thoughts."

Julia grinned, embarrassed, as a couple of boys passed them by, overheard what Jonathan had said to her, and laughed.

"But that's impossible." Julia protested, after they seemed out of earshot.

Jonathan stared at her for a moment, and before she knew what to expect, his voice came down, into her mind. *It is possible, Julia.*

Julia's eyes widened. This vampire thing was getting all too real for her. She had heard him speak, and yet, his mouth had not moved. It reminded her of what had occurred earlier, back in her room.

"So, tell me, why do you want to leave? I thought you wished to come with me for this one night." Jonathan took her hand, kissed each of her fingers.

"Because, Jonathan, you're doing it to me, too."

"What?"

"You know what. What you do to those girls." Julia waved her free hand around them.

Jonathan smiled. "No, I'm not. I didn't force you to come with me, Julia."

Julia frowned. He was right, of course, but she had been so sure. And now, she found another problem at hand to worry about. "How do I keep you out..." she trailed off, began to walk forward once more. She felt so silly asking him these things, as if she were in some sort of cheesy horror film.

"You keep me out of your mind by simply willing it. Don't think of me, or even that I might get in. It's not a battle of wills. Just think of something dark, opaque, like fog, or walls. If you concentrate, without fear, you can accomplish anything."

Julia smiled, knowing the hidden meaning behind this. She knew that if she did not fear Jonathan, her future, and the myriad of things she did not understand, the love she had for Jonathan, and his for her, would grow, to heights only reached in fairy tales.

By Midnight, it was obvious that some unspoken tension in Jonathan, and the others, had risen to a breaking point. They had finished with flirtations, becoming far more serious. Deadly, Julia thought. Observing their mannerisms was becoming increasingly like watching a tiger pace in a cage. Julia felt constantly on guard, her instincts reverting once more to a primitive time, when her long-ago ancestors had learned to fight or flee.

Soon, all conversation ended. Crowds began to avoid their company. And just when Julia thought she would not be able to take anymore, they left the park, wordlessly, and she did not know where they were going.

Relief flooded through her, as they pulled into the driveway of the old mansion, however, none but Jonathan actually cut the motor.

As Julia slid off the motorcycle, she overheard Jason say, "Catch up to us." As she turned to watch them, they pulled out of the driveway, and into the darkness. At this exact moment, the moon dove behind the clouds, leaving Julia and Jonathan bathed in silver shadows. She could not see his face.

"What's going on?" she said, hating the sound of her voice. It was so small, so scared.

"Nothing."

Julia backed away from him as he came forward. Something inside her knew, simply knew that he was not just a man standing there. Her legs tensed, aching to run away.

"I know something's going on, Jonathan. I'm not stupid. I can feel it, more than if I could see you." Julia took another step back.

"Don't be afraid of me, Julia." Jonathan's voice changed again. No longer frightening, it soothed her. He once again seemed more like a man. "Take my hand, we'll go inside."

Julia looked at him for a moment, trying to read his face, but with the light blotted out by the clouds, she couldn't. In the end, she swallowed down her fear, stepped forward, and took his hand. It was cold.

"Where did they go?" she asked, as they walked together to the front doors of the mansion.

Jonathan was silent for a moment, thinking over an answer. "To an appointment."

"What appointment?" Julia asked.

No answer.

"Are you going too?"

"Yes."

"So where are you going, and why can't I come?"

Jonathan groaned low in his throat, unlocking one of the big doors, and ushering Julia inside. Lighting three candles, stationed on the coffee table, he turned as he heard Julia dump her jacket onto the floor in frustration.

"I want the truth." she said, hands on her hips.

"Well, the truth is that I can't tell you, not yet. But I will say it's something you are not ready for. Jason said you aren't strong enough to handle it yet, and I don't want you to get hurt. I will take you in a few days, all right?"

"Fine," Julia sighed, but she wasn't content. "But I still want to know what's going on with you guys. Why were you acting that way? Why…"

Jonathan stepped close to her, taking her into his arms, kissing her to cut off the flow of words. He kissed her hard, a little rougher than what she was used to, the hunger inside him pushing him to do so. Once again, he felt grateful to Jason for giving Julia that wine. Jonathan didn't want to think about what would have happened now, if Julia had been human.

Finally pulling away from her, he gazed at her, watching her lips part for more kisses, the hunger in her eyes a small parody of his. "I have to go," he said with a frown, abruptly turning, and slamming the door behind him as he left.

Julia smiled as she listened to the Harley pull away. She had seen the longing in his eyes. Her peace of mind, however, did not last long. Standing in the dead silence of the mansion, long ago forgotten by anything human, and now inhabited by what could only be explained as a group of vampires, Julia's nerves began to feel a bit frayed.

Shadows leapt and frolicked upon the walls from the three candles, casting frightening imagery into Julia's overactive mind. All too quickly, she began to wish that she were not alone. She would have even preferred Jason's malevolent presence to none at all. The inside of this mansion was all too similar to a gigantic, wooden crypt.

In the short span of minutes, Julia had grabbed her jacket from the floor, and was out the door, into the cloudy evening. She would explain to Jonathan later, she thought, although the reasons why she had decided to leave would seem bit odd, even to her.

Following the dirt path, which led back down the gradual slope to her own home, Julia's fears began to melt away. Not even aware of it when she had stopped hugging her arms protectively, Julia's eyes, ears, and overall senses began to melt into the onslaught of the night. Filled with the awe and beauty of it, she wondered why she had never wanted to be alone in the night before.

The sounds were almost melodious. Crickets chirped, the wind blew through he shadowed leaves and grasses with a gentleness, that reminded her instantly, of Jonathan.

At the thought of him, her thoughts shifted, yet again. Where was he? Julia frowned, wondering why he had gone away and left her behind. Why couldn't I come?

Julia looked down at the dirt path, her eyes straining to adjust to the dim light. She could see tire marks there, in the road, a sure sign that Jonathan, and the other, had passed this way. But why had they gone back down the mountain without her?

When Julia arrived at the driveway, which led to her own house, she had come to a conclusion. She would not rest until she had found them. There must be a reason for all the secrecy, she decided, and that reason would be the one to prove whether or not these men were really vampires.

Julia closed her eyes, let her mind drift. She centered deep inside herself, to a part of her that she had been completely unaware of. Julia sent out her feelings in waves, careful not to call for Jonathan directly.

And then, she felt something. It was not quite Jonathan, but something related, and greater and altogether bigger, a thing that existed as a whole. She carried part of it inside her, and like two separate magnets, she let it pull her.

She began to run through the streets and backyards, upsetting gardens and sleeping dogs, paying no attention to anything, and not even realizing how fast her legs were carrying her. Julia focused upon nothing but the pull, the feeling of the whole, and as she got closer, the feeling increased.

Suddenly, as if she had actually run into the house, the feeling exploded within Julia and her legs stopped dead. As she blinked up at the huge, white apartment complex, Julia's concentration broke, and the overall feeling vanished.

Aware at once that she was lost, Julia looked around herself, at the cars parked in the over-large driveway, and at the all too familiar Harley-Davidsons parked next to the cars.

Walking around to the back of the house, Julia began to be filled with a new feeling, this one a sense of apprehension and dread. What were they doing here, and how in the world did I find them, she wondered, coming now to a door. The door, which led into the apartment, was slightly ajar.

Swallowing the fear, which had come up into her throat like bile, Julia grasped the door in shaking hands, and slipped inside.

Immediately, the smell of blood assaulted her. It came from everywhere and nowhere, all at once, yet nothing she could see would lead her to believe anything was amiss.

Julia's stomach tightened involuntarily, from hunger or terror, she could not place. She had no idea what she was going to find here, in this

63

darkened house. However obvious it was that someone had broken into this apartment, Julia did not know if it happened to be the men she was looking for. For all she knew, she had just become another burglar.

But the smell of blood could not be ignored. The more Julia dwelt on it, the more fear left her. Hunger was building within her, a hunger she instantly recalled from the other night, the night she had almost hurt Gayle.

Curiosity and hunger drove Julia from her spot at the door, and closing it behind her, she followed the smell through the downstairs rooms, to the front entryway, and up the stairs to the second floor.

It was here that the noise became audible. It was a soft sound, reminding her of infants, and babysitting. Pain jarring through her insides now, her thoughts were cut off, and she was momentarily blinded, her breath hissing out between her teeth. The blood smell had become stronger, hitting her in a wave, which had almost knocked her off the stairway.

Julia doubled over there, landing with a thud, painfully, against the sharp wood of the steps. Soon, however, the pain subsided, and she used the railing to pull herself to her feet, gasping for breath.

A low, deep growl stopped her cold.

Julia froze, looked up to the top of the steps, expecting to see some sort of rabid animal. What she saw almost caused her to scream, but all she could manage was a small, tiny yelp.

Jason stood at the top of the stairs, glaring down at her, with eyes like red fire. Streetlight from an open second floor window poured in upon him, glinting off two sharp little wicked fangs, in the upper corners of his scowling mouth. Blood coated his face and chin, and his hands pressed upon the railing, and the walls, were slick with it.

Julia's stomach lurched again, and she groaned, raising her hand to her mouth with dawning horror, as she realized exactly what was going on here. They were vampires, they were. And she was becoming one, too.

Julia watched, panic rising and overriding the hunger, as Jason began to descend down the stairs towards her.

"No," she whispered in denial, stumbling backwards, trying to get down the stairs without turning her back on him.

"You disobeyed my orders, little girl." Jason growled, coming down another step. His head cocked to one side as he laughed, horrible noise seeming to come straight from the grave. "What did you think you would find?"

Julia glanced backward, wondering why exactly she had come. "Jonathan," she whined, almost completely immobilized by pain and panic.

She could feel blackness coming on, and wondered if she was about to pass out.

"Not yet." Julia heard a whisper in her ear, and looked back to see Jason standing just next to her, over her, his terrible face leering into hers. He reached out for her, and she lurched back, preferring to fall, rather than let him touch her. She screamed, only to be cut off short by Jason, as one hand grabbed her shirt to stop her fall, and the other came down over her mouth.

Without another word, and faster than she could account for, Julia found herself standing with Jason, in the doorway of a room. "Watch," he growled out, commanding her to do what she knew she would regret, and she struggled against him, and the hands that held her.

But Julia could not help looking.

On the bed, in the center of the room, was Jonathan, his face nuzzling an older woman's exposed neck. It was obvious that she was far past struggling; she lay prone, beneath him. Devin was in a corner of the room, pressing down upon what appeared to have been an elaborate bureau; a pair of bare feet were poking out from beneath him. Andrew sat up against the wall, a small child, dead in his arms. He stared at Julia with the same red eyes, absently licking and wiping the blood from his mouth.

And right at Julia's feet lay a dead girl about her age; her neck torn to ribbons as well as her clothing, and the blood was everywhere. The smell was so thick; she could taste it through Jason's restraining hands.

Julia's stomach seemed to be on fire with hunger, pain jagged and huge, pressing in upon her ribs. She broke out into a cold sweat, shaking so hard, she was sure she would not have been able to stand there, unsupported. The blood was fascinating and appalling all at once, so warm that she wanted to touch it, to taste it. Her throat was so dry, and she was so cold.

"Let me go, let me go, I need to leave, help me…" she sobbed, hysteria spreading through her. Julia was torn between wanting to run, and wanting to go to Jonathan and beg him to share with her what he held there, in his arms, what he was sucking from that woman.

Julia could think of nothing but the blood and rage filling her suddenly, wondering why they could have it and not her, why she had to stand here, when she was starving. Muscles aching, her body tense and hard, her stomach demanded satisfaction. Her heart beat faster and faster; her temples began to pound, and her sight sharpened and focused, however, now filled with a distinct red haze she could not blink away.

Julia's struggles increased, her jaw ached, her tongue dry and rough against the roof of her mouth. Far in the distance, she could hear Jason begin to laugh, and now, instead of struggling weakly, she fought against him, really fought, trying to make him let her go. She needed the blood; the thirst was consuming her whole.

Pain ached and jabbed in her upper mouth, forcing some kind of obstructions down and stabbing into her lower lips, and she used these things to bite Jason's hands, and he freed her.

Julia fell to the ground. The girl on the floor was somehow uninteresting now, dead and empty, and Julia crawled over her, struggling through the aching hunger in her gut, trying to reach Jonathan, Jonathan, he'd help her, he said he loved her, he'd give her what she needed. She needed...

"Julia, what are you doing here?"

She looked up from the floor to see Jonathan standing over her, beside the bed. Not a trace of blood marked his face, only what appeared to be concern. His words pierced her madness for a moment, and the hunger subsided. He knelt down beside her, but much like a disoriented animal, she could not speak.

"What has he done to you?" Jonathan whispered, slipping his arms around her.

Something settled upon the bed. Blood wafted again through the air. Julia gritted her teeth in pain, as her stomach burned in agony.

"She came on her own," said a voice from the door.

Julia looked to the source of the voice, and saw Jason standing there still, grinning horribly around the fangs.

The fangs.

Julia calmed to the point of reason in Jonathan's protective arms, reached up with her tongue to her teeth, and there, sure enough, were the fangs, sharp, and ready for her to obey the driving need inside her. Drained of all strength, terrified for her very mortality, Julia saw the darkness coming once again, and embraced it, passing out in the middle of a nightmare.

Jonathan brought her home that night, but Julia was not aware of it. She clung to the cold darkness of oblivion as if it were a shield, and did not even attempt to resurface.

On impulse, Jonathan lifted Julia onto his shoulder, and used her open window as an entrance to her home. Sincerely worried for her, Jonathan undressed Julia to her bra and panties, murmuring soft words of concern, and threats to Jason's welfare.

After he tucked Julia's unconscious body into bed, Jonathan left the same way he had come to it. Because of the emotions raging within him, he had not taken precautions that he normally would have. He had been rather loud about the whole thing, unknowingly waking Gayle, who had watched, and listened, through a crack in the bathroom door.

10

When Gayle awoke the following morning, she stood a long time in the darkness of Julia's room, wondering what to do. Having been awakened by her sister's agonized moans, Gayle was the one who had caused the darkness, closing the window, and the shades, in order to give Julia some peace.

And now, Julia slept in silence.

Gayle watched Julia sleep, watched her sister's body move lightly with every breath she took. This was proof enough to Gayle that Julia was not yet a vampire. Julia did not sleep the coma-like sleep of the undead. Julia still breathed, after all.

Nonetheless, Gayle decided that something had to be done. She could tell that Julia's overall condition was getting worse. And, the things that Jonathan had muttered last night, when he had brought Julia home, could only lead her to one conclusion. They really were vampires. Jonathan was one. Julia would be one. What if she was next?

Gayle went into her own room, changed her clothes, walked downstairs, and called the twins.

They were excited about everything, and were more than willing to help Gayle. Much to her dismay, even Eyleen's spirits seemed to life with the prospect of what Ellen called, "A real adventure."

Ellen reminded Gayle that to return Julia to her normal self, they'd have to do one of two things. Either kill the vampire that had supplied her with the blood, or get some blood to test in order to find an alternative cure.

Gayle sadly told Ellen that she had no idea who had given Julia the blood, and that she also didn't know how to get vampire blood to test one. "After all," she practically whined into the phone, "it's not like I can just ask Jonathan to give me some of his blood."

"Gayle, you don't need to ask." Ellen said, gruffly. "Is he the only one Julia's been hanging around with? 'Cause if he is, we can just kill him."

"Ellen!" Eyleen exclaimed from the background.

Gayle swallowed down a lump, which had risen, in her throat. "I don't know."

"Well, then, here's what we'll do. The next time Julia goes off with this guy, you follow them…"

"Why me?" Gayle interrupted. Ellen continued on, ignoring the comment.

"See where they go because, where there's one vampire, there's usually more. They tend to be in packs, like wolves. When you get back, you can report back to us on how many there are, and maybe you'll even know who gave your sister the blood! Gayle, you have to go, it's Julia's only hope, you know."

Gayle considered the possibilities in her mind. What will happen to me if I do go? What will happen to Julia if I don't? In the end, Gayle agreed to be the spy.

It was after dinner that night, when the phone rang. Gayle, who had been watching television in the family room, lowered the volume with a remote, and answered the phone.

"Hello?" she said into the receiver, half expecting it to be Ellen or Eyleen. She was surprised to hear a man's voice answer.

"Ah, yes, Mrs. Jeanne Anderson, please."

Without bothering to ask the man to hold on, or to cover the talking end of the phone, Gayle yelled out, "Mom, phone!"

Gayle's mother entered the room, drying her hands with a towel. "Who is it, Gayle?"

"I don't know," Gayle answered, taking the towel from her Mom, and moving into the kitchen to finish the dishes. She was halfway done, when Jeanne burst into the room, ecstatic.

"Gayle! Gayle! I got my job back! I can't believe it! And with a promotion besides! They were sorry they laid me off, just like I said they would be. This means we can move back to Connecticut before school starts! We can leave in just two nights from now, isn't that terrific?" She ran over to Gayle, and gave her daughter a huge hug.

"That's great, Mom." Gayle said, but in her mind, she was saying, oh, no. Julia, Jonathan. With everything being as it was, how would Julia react? If Jonathan knew about all this, would he try to kidnap Julia?

Gayle sucked in her breath quickly, struggled out of Jeanne's grasp, and tossed the towel to her. "I'll tell Julia." she said, and ran to the stairs, biting on her lower lip, worried about how Julia would react to this news. Gayle bounded up the stairs, two at a time.

Gayle reached Julia's door in a huff, and raised her hand in midair to knock, but didn't. She heard the unexpected noises of someone moving within. Gayle lowered her hand and tried the knob. It turned.

Gayle opened the door wide and stepped inside. The only apparent light came from a dim orange bulb attached to a nightlight. The window was open, no moon tonight.

"Shut the door." Julia said, coming from the closet. Her voice had taken on a deeper, tighter quality, a sort of determined flatness.

Gayle shut the door as Julia asked, and blinked a few times in silence, in order to adjust to the lack of real light. When her eyes focused, Gayle could make out a suitcase lying on Julia's bed, filled over with clothes, cosmetics, hairbrushes and accessories, sunglasses, Walkman and tapes, towels, soap, and a toothbrush. Lying next to it, was her key ring.

"Julia, Mom..." began Gayle, but Julia cut her off.

"Yes, I know, I listened." Julia emerged from the closet holding her leather jacket, leather boots, and sneakers. She tossed the sneakers into the suitcase, and bent down to pull on the boots. Julia had already changed her clothes, and was now wearing a small black skirt and tank top.

"Where are you going, Julia?" Gayle asked, already knowing, and dreading, what the answer would be.

"Nowhere."

"Ha! I know where you're going. You're going to Jonathan's house, aren't you! He *is* a vampire, I knew it!"

Julia chose to ignore her sister, silently standing back up, and pulling on her leather jacket.

"I'm gonna tell Mom!" Gayle shouted, darting for the door.

"No!" Julia grabbed Gayle by the arm and pulled, perhaps subconsciously trying to pull it off.

Gayle howled in pain and fright, "Let go! You're hurting me!"

Julia let go immediately. "Sorry, I didn't mean to." Oddly enough, Julia felt as if she were on the verge of tears. She held Gayle's shoulders gently, and spoke softly, "Gayle, listen to me. I can't go back to Connecticut now; too many things have gone wrong here. I can't go to school now; I can't stand the daylight. I can't even go to the bathroom anymore. You can't begin to know what's happening to me, these temptations for blood. I can't change this until I find out for myself how it happened. I have to confront them alone, Gayle. Do you understand? Don't tell *anybody* where I'm going now. Not Mom, and especially not Ellen and Eyleen, and don't follow me, okay? Please, Gayle, just this once, promise?"

Gayle nodded, crossing her fingers behind her back.

"How you gonna get past Mom?" Gayle asked, watching Julia zip up the suitcase and jacket, grab for her keys.

"Don't worry about it. Cover for me Gayle, goodbye." Julia said softly, rushed. She looked at Gayle for a long moment, and then turned, walked to the window, and dove through it.

Terrified for her sister, Gayle ran to the window, only to see Julia land safely, all the way over, by the garage!

Heart beating wildly in her throat, Gayle bounded back down the stairs, yelling out to her mother that she and Julia were going out to the Park for the night. Grabbing a flashlight on her way out the kitchen's back door, Gayle all but flew around the back of her house, to where she had stashed her bicycle.

Gayle jumped on the bike, peeking around the corner of the house, just in time to watch Julia leave. Peddling furiously, flashlight clutched tightly in her left hand, Gayle followed Julia until her motorcycle's taillights were gone from sight. And then, braving the darkness, Gayle switched on the flashlight, and continued in the direction that Julia had gone, following the old dirt road.

As Julia pulled into the driveway of the old mansion, she prepared herself emotionally for what she knew must be done. She didn't really want to be here at all, knowing just who, or what, these men were. But as much as she wanted to be with her mother and sister, the truth remained that she couldn't. At least, not until she straightened this whole mess out.

Julia parked her small motorcycle next to the four larger ones, cut the engine, put out the kickstand and stood, pulling the suitcase off the back of the bike, silently. She stood for a moment, staring up at the old Victorian mansion, and at the flicker of candlelight, which seeped through the boarded-up windows.

"What am I doing?" she whispered, clutching the suitcase to her chest like a shield. She was, after all, really just a kid, and more frightened now than she had ever been before.

Summoning up what seemed to be the last ounce of courage within her, Julia trudged up the stairs, and to the big, old front doors. Without thinking to knock first, she pulled one of them open and stepped inside. The door slammed shut behind her, almost catching her in the back. She jumped, startled at the sudden noise, for the room was as quiet as the grave, ironically appropriate.

As Julia stepped into the light from the shadows, she looked up, only to see them watching her. Jason sat in an odd-looking chair, silently smoking a cigarette. Devin and Andrew stood near the fireplace, seeming to have been caught in the middle of a conversation. Jonathan sat alone on the small sofa.

Julia suddenly needed to speak, overcome with the urge to explain just why she had come. Anyone with half a brain would have stayed far away from these people, knowing what she knew, and it was completely obvious that the feeling was mutual.

"I...I had to leave," Julia protested meekly, surprised at her own voice. It was uncontrollably shaky. She moved further into the room, hands clutching the bag so tightly, she thought it might rip. "My Mom, she said that we're leaving Vermont in two days. We're going back home, to Connecticut. But I can't go."

Julia stared at the floor, knowing that the tears had finally come. Ashamed of herself, of what she had gotten into so voluntarily, she mumbled, "I can't leave. I don't know what's happening to me. I have no place to go."

Julia wiped the tears away violently, looked up at Jonathan with pleading eyes. She wanted to ask him if she could stay, but somehow knew that it was not his choice. Swallowing her fear and her pride, she took a deep breath, and turned to look at Jason. "Could I stay here? Please?"

A slow smile crept up upon Jason's lips. "Of course." he said, and motioned Devin to take her suitcase.

Devin took it from her hands, walked across the sitting room, and opened a door in the opposite wall, placing her suitcase just inside.

Julia watched him as he did this, knowing that the room was now to be hers. She swallowed down the panic with a hard gulp of air. Her fate was now sealed. She looked back at Jonathan, wanting to rush to him, to throw her arms around him and beg him to protect her from herself, from Jason, and even from him. But she couldn't do it, could not even say a word. Terrified of everything, she stared down at the floor.

Not even a minute had passed, when Julia was suddenly aware that they were leaving. Not her, not Jonathan, but the others led by Jason, they left the room, out into the night, to do things that she didn't even want to know about.

After the noise of their departing Harleys had faded into the distance, Julia heard Jonathan sigh, heard the creak of old springs, as he leaned back into the sofa. And then, suddenly, out of nowhere, she heard his voice in her mind.

Julia, come to me.

Her head jerked up, startled. She searched his face, slowly walked to where he sat. He looked concerned, curious. There was no threat there, she was sure of it, and so she sat down beside him. His hand, oddly warm, came to rest upon her leg, exposed by the skirt she wore, causing her pulse to jump profoundly.

Why did you really come back, Julia? You could have killed Jason in the daytime as he slept, and then left, free of us all.

Julia's tears painfully leapt back to the edges of her eyes. She cried out, "It was because of you, all right? More than anything else, it was because of you. I can't leave you, I love you! I just can't go!" Her voice finally broke into sobs, her control gone. She reached out to him, fell against him, crying into his shoulder as his arms embraced her, pulling her to him.

"Julia, Julia," he whispered, stroking her hair, "I know it hurts, I know. You don't trust me completely, but I love you, and you must believe that there was no other way. I wish there was some way to show you; I really do care for you."

"I know you do." she mumbled. "But how can I deal with this? What's going to happen to me after you're gone? Nothing lasts forever."

Jonathan gently pulled away from her, knowing exactly what she was referring to - her parent's divorce. "Julia, I won't leave you. I've searched for you for one hundred years, and I will never let you go."

Julia stared at him, for his words frightened her, just a little too much. Her tears flowed silently, she could not cry any longer. The truth was that she did not trust him, and how could she? But the love was definitely there, in the expression of his face, in the depths of his dark eyes.

Jonathan raised his hands to her shoulders, pulling the jacket Julia wore away from her body. She let it fall down her arms, and to the ground. The night air felt cool to her skin. She watched as he reached up to the back of his neck, devoid of the shirt beneath the jacket, fidgeting with the chain he wore. Finally, he held it open in front of her, the silver glimmering in the firelight.

"This was given to me a long, long time ago, Julia. No one has ever worn it but me, for I wouldn't let anyone touch it. It's part of my last link with my human life. I have a few other things kept from then, but not many, for Jason made me give them all up. All the memories, gone. But this," he said, placing the chain around her neck, fastening it in the back, "this is now yours. I am yours, and you are mine, and now we will never be apart. I will always be with you."

Jonathan's hands came to rest upon Julia's shoulders, raising a heat there that spread, quickly, throughout her body. Pulling back from his eyes, she looked down at the chain, touched the glittering silver, and the polished turquoise stones.

'This is the most beautiful gift anyone has ever given to me." she said.

"It doesn't compare to you Julia, my love." Jonathan rested his head against hers, pulling further into his arms. A few strained moments passed, until he groaned low in his throat.

"What's wrong?" Julia said softly, raising her arms to hold Jonathan against her.

Jonathan chuckled. "That skirt. You shouldn't have worn it tonight."

"Why?" she asked, her voice light, breathy. She looked up at him, only to see that his eyes were gazing down at her, taking in her legs.

"It's too short. I want too many things when I see you in it, things I shouldn't want from you yet." he said, and raised his eyes to meet hers.

The electricity in their dark depths caught Julia off guard. She sucked in her breath, as the short distance between them seemed to crackle. His hand came up to her neck, spreading waves of warmth and pleasure. Julia felt the heat of him close in around her, as he pulled her close, the sudden soft touch of his lips on hers, as they were now killing. Softly at first, as she ran her hands through his hair, pulling him ever closer.

Julia heard Jonathan let out a short, low sound, as if he were feeling pleasure and pain all at once, as if he were remembering something that he didn't want to remember, but still loved the moment with her.

Their kisses grew deeper, more passionate, as he leaned back against the armrest of the sofa, pulling her with him, so that she fell slightly on top of him.

Julia sighed against his lips, as she felt his hands run down her back, over her hips, and down across the back of her skirt. Their bodies intertwined, their mouths locked together in a passionate embrace, Julia grew brave, began to explore Jonathan's stomach and chest beneath the leather jacket he always wore. Her fingers slid over his soft, warm skin, and she was left wondering just why she had always been so afraid of this before.

Before she let things get too carried away, however, Julia pulled back, searching Jonathan's face for any kind of betraying emotion. But, there was none. The only thing found there, was exactly what he had told her of. Love.

Julia sighed, stretched out upon the sofa, her head resting on the portion of Jonathan's chest that was exposed, listening to his heart pumping softly with stolen blood. Her fingers tangled in his long hair; she wanted nothing more than to remain like this as long as possible. Lost in his embrace, his arms holding her tight and close, she felt as if she were free from everything.

"Jonathan," she whispered his name.

"Yes?"

"If only this could last forever." she murmured, becoming drowsy for some reason, which she couldn't place.

"It will my love, it will." he said.

Julia soon fell asleep. When she awoke, sometime later, she was alone. Upon opening her eyes, she tired to figure out where she was. She stared at the deteriorating wooden ceiling, listened to the crackling of the fire, and the ticking of the clock, and realized she was still in the mansion, lying on the sofa, with a few blankets gently draped across her body.

Julia sat up and rubbed her face, yawning. "Jonathan?" she called, but there was no answer. "Anybody?" Where were they? Not here, obviously.

Julia sighed as she got to her feet, gazing around the empty sitting room. The place carried the faint, combined smells of pizza, leather, cigarettes, mold, and the wood that lay, ignited in the fireplace, gave off a burnt aroma. Although there were no real decorations and nothing on the walls, the place was pretty cozy, for a vampire lair.

On one end of the large sitting room, there was what appeared to have been a stairway, although the stairs were now a mass of broken boards and carpet, which lay on the ground in a heap. Julia had to crane her neck to try and see up into the ceiling, where the entrance to the second floor was. There was nothing visible there but darkness, and so she began to inspect the rest of the first floor.

There were many doors scattered within the walls of the sitting room. Three of these were bedrooms, as Julia discovered, but the others were all locked up, tight. One door led down into a dark stairway, which she had to assume, was the basement.

Julia's room, the one in which Devin had placed her suitcase, was by far the most beautiful bedroom on the first floor. She was surprised to see that the room had its own fireplace, which somehow had already been lit.

It was a rather large room, occupied mostly by a big canopied feather bed, the kind that had been made in the eighteen hundreds. It was draped in mauve-colored blankets, and upon those, had been placed her leather jacket. The canopy was mauve as well, with white netting extending down from the top, gathered at the posts with strips of ribbon.

There was a window beside the bed, but she noticed that it had been boarded up. The curtains that framed the window matched the bedcovers.

There was a desk with a quill pen, ink and paper, and a crystal vase containing red roses. The desk was a dark cherry color of wood, resembling the woodwork of the bed. A large bureau of similar color stood in the corner. There was a large walk in closet set into the wall, and a black, Baby Grand piano stood in the final corner of the room.

"Wow," Julia whispered, taking it all in, rubbing Jonathan's chain lightly between her fingers. She wondered how they had acquired all these things, and why they all seemed to be kept in this room, alone. Why was the rest of this mansion in shambles?

Eventually, Julia let the questions rest, since she was obviously not going to get the answers she sought after, tonight. She began to unpack her suitcase, placing items with care into the drawers and closet.

After all was done, Julia placed her robe on a hook, near a wall-candle by the bed, exchanged her clothes for a red nightgown, and brushed out her hair.

She tried to read for a while, from a book she had brought from home, trying hard to ignore the creepy loneliness of the giant, old house. Soon, her eyes grew tired, and she put the book down on the floor, untied the net curtains, and sank back into the softness of the mattress, and the covers.

Julia closed her eyes, giving in to the mesmerizing sounds of the fire crackling, and the giant grandfather clock ticking rhythmically. By the chimes sounded out twice, Julia Anderson was fast asleep.

Gayle had ducked quickly into the bushes, when the man known only to her as Jonathan, had come out of the mansion. Frightened of him, panicking, she had forgotten her bicycle, where it lay beneath one of the mansion's windows. Seeing this, she squeezed her eyes tight, hiding her head in her hands, expecting to die now. But before she had to beg for her life, Jonathan was roaring away, on that big, loud bike of his and Gayle was all alone.

Sighing her relief, realizing her good luck and not stopping to question it, she crept back up to her place at the window, peering in through the cracks in the boards. Julia, where was Julia?

Gayle's eyes searched over the room, moving back to the little couch. It was where *they* had been together. The girl's nose crinkled at the memory. Kissing, yuck! Gayle couldn't believe how utterly stupid Julia was behaving now. Who knows where that guy has been, after all?

A sigh of relief passed through her when she saw her sister on the couch, fast asleep, cuddled up under a mountain of blankets. At least Julia was safe, for now. "Don't worry, I'll save you," Gayle vowed, a nervous whisper under her breath.

Tearing herself away from the window, she picked up her bicycle from where it lay in the dirt, and peddled frantically home.

Arriving there much too late, and way out of breath, Gayle snuck into the house from the back door, getting up the stairway, and past her mother, on mouse's feet.

Entering Julia's darkened room, Gayle used the phone that night, in order to do the one thing Julia had begged her not to do. She called Ellen. In order to save her big sister, Gayle decided she had to betray her.

Feeling like the biggest jerk in the world, she told Ellen where Julia was staying, and pinpointed the exact location of the mansion.

"Tell us how many vampires there are." Ellen said.

"Four," Gayle replied, remembering all of them sitting there, chatting away with poor Julia in the house. "Five if you count my sister."

"I don't think you want to count her in yet, Gayle." Ellen said, with a malicious chuckle, which made Gayle instantly regret her words. She ignored the comment, and went on.

She described each of the men to Ellen, what they looked like, how they acted, how strong they seemed to be. When she began to describe the one called Andrew, there was a sharp intake of breath from the other end of the phone; Gayle unknowingly cringed.

"Stop." Ellen interrupted. "He'll be perfect for us."

"Perfect for what?" Gayle asked, after a good pause. She almost didn't want to know.

"Don't worry about it, Gayle. Anything in the name of science, right? Talk to you tomorrow."

And then, Gayle was left standing there, listening to the dial tone, as she found herself once again, disconnected. She almost redialed their number, to demand from that little weirdo that her big sister not be hurt, no matter what happened. But she seemed to calm slowly, and she sank down onto the bed. Silently, Gayle hung up the phone and curled into a ball, pulling Julia's covers around her small body for comfort.

"Please be all right." she said, pleading to someone who was too far away to hear. Sleep came fast for Gayle, exhausted as she was, both mentally and physically, and at least, she had no dreams.

11

Ellen and Eyleen, the two sisters who would be vampire hunter, awoke sometime after dawn the next morning, armed themselves for battle, and traveled to the mansion.

Once there, they almost turned back. Not because of thoughts of fright, or even any nervousness upon their part. It was because the look of the mansion in broad daylight was so pathetically benevolent, and so rundown, unlivable they thought they had the wrong place.

"Come on, Eyleen," Ellen said quietly, all her malicious intent gone, completely disarmed. "Let's go have a look."

"But Ellen, what if we really find…"

"The vampires?" Ellen said, laying down her bike in the dirt driveway. "Well, then, our trip won't be wasted, will it?"

Eyleen laid her bike down as well, fidgeted with her backpack, and began to follow her sister to the house. "But Ellen, it's such a rat trap. How could anyone live here?"

Ellen shrugged, didn't slow her pace at all. "Vampires aren't people, Eyleen. Remember, they don't need human comforts."

Eyleen ran to her sister, grabbed her arm, "But Ellen,"

Ellen turned on her sister in a flash. "But Ellen, but Ellen, would you shut up already Eyleen? God, we're here to do a job. Either stop whining about it, or go home."

"Fine." Eyleen said, letting go of Ellen, and watching as she moved to the doors of the mansion, and gave one of them a tug. Amazingly unlocked, it squealed as it opened.

"Coming?" Ellen called.

Heart pounding in her chest, Eyleen followed her, silently, through the mansion. It was pitch black inside, the only given light streaming into the room from the open doorway.

From her position at the door, Eyleen could see a couch, a bunch of chairs, and something glowing in the corner; it could only be embers from a fireplace.

"Turn." Ellen demanded roughly, forcing Eyleen around, and unzipping the backpack. Eyleen waited until she was re-zipped, and turned once again to the sitting room, now illuminated with Ellen's high-beam flashlight.

"Take this."

Eyleen reached out, and took two carved wooden stakes from her sister, along with a glass jelly jar, which they had swiped from their mother's cabinet earlier in the day.

"Let's go." Ellen led the way, flashlight in her left hand, stake in her right.

"What are we looking for?" Eyleen said, as they began a search of the room, pushing against each door in the walls, most of which they found rusted, dusty, and locked. As they reached the ruined stairway, Ellen shining the beam up into the second floor, Eyleen sighed, letting her agitation be heard again, rather loudly.

Ellen groaned, shining the bright beam on her sister's face, who turned away, grimacing.

"Why are you so dense? You know damn well what we're looking for, and if you don't shut up, I'll..." Ellen's tirade was cut short by a moan, that came neither from Eyleen, or from herself. It had come from a door that they had yet to open.

Suddenly, the act, which they had come here to do, seemed very real. Silenced, the girls crept up to the door, each holding a stake in their right hand, ready to pounce.

Ellen counted, whispering to three, and then they pushed against the door with all their might, pushing it wide open. The beam wavered for a moment, and then, settled upon the figure clad in red, lying in deep slumber, upon the bed.

Eyleen realized she had been holding her breath, and let it out in a deep whoosh. It was only Gayle's sister, Julia, lying upon that bed. Not any kind of nightmare demon that she'd have to drive a damn stake into. Or, was she?

Just as Eyleen was about to ask that very question, Ellen said, "She's not a vampire yet. Look, she's still breathing."

And yes, as Eyleen watched, Julia took a deep, heavy breath, signifying that she was indeed, still human.

Eyleen backed away from the door, watching as Ellen closed it. This is terrifying, she thought, walking behind Ellen, as she went to the door on the other side of the ruined staircase. This was the last door. Maybe it too would be locked, unused, and then they could both go home.

No such luck.

The door opened, and the beam reflected off...descending stairs.

Ellen chuckled. "Bingo."

Step by step, the girls descended the old, creaky stairway, down into the dank, dark basement.

"God, it smells." whispered Eyleen, as the mold and dust of ages crept into her nose. Ellen didn't even acknowledge her sister this time. Scanning the darkness of the bottom of the stairway, she had found a pathway in the dirt and dust, one that was worn down, by at least a half a foot. Grabbing her sister by the front of her shirt, she pulled her off the stairs, and stared along the path.

The path wove in and out of some very old furnishings, boxes made of actual wood, swords, suits of armor covered in rust, and piles of things which they could only hope were clothing. Not to mention the rats, which scurried away from the light, were as large as small dogs, or the giant spider-webs complete with giant spiders.

And then, in the corner of the basement, which was the most damp, coolest, and farthest away from the stairs, the girls found what they were looking for.

"My God," Eyleen mouthed, crossing herself profusely.

Ellen's beam shone down upon the floor, an area trampled hard, and flat, by obvious years of usage. Upon this flattened floor lay four man sized coffins. Two were black, one dark red, and the other light blue.

Slowly, Ellen approached the closest one, a black coffin with ornate silver handles.

"Ellen," Eyleen whispered, edging closer. Ellen shushed her with a wave of her hand.

"Help me," she said.

Eyleen swallowed, resting the stake and the jar on the ground beside her, took one edge of the coffin, and together, they opened the lid.

It made no sound, not even a breath of air. As the lid opened wide as it would go, more of what was inside became illuminated by Ellen's flashlight.

For a moment, neither girl could move.

Inside the coffin lay the one called Jonathan, stretched out lengthwise, upon his back, resting amongst the black satin of the inside. His long, dark hair created a soft halo of sorts, gently resting upon the pillows, and fanning across the exposed flesh of his chest. The silver earring glittered in the intruding light, his face slack, his lips closed. His eyes did not move with the telltale signs of REM sleep. As a matter of fact, Eyleen took note; nothing on Jonathan was moving. There was no breath, no heart beat. His chest lay flat, like that of a corpse.

His hands were folded across his belly, clutching a wicked looking ivory handled dagger. Before Ellen could stop her, Eyleen reached out to touch the hands that held the dagger, curious to see what they felt like.

On contact, she drew back. They were as cold as death itself. Of course, she thought, swallowing down panic and nausea, he's undead.

Eyleen looked up to see Ellen standing, scowling down at her. "Stupid." she whispered.

Eyleen shrugged, rising to her feet, as Ellen closed the distance to the next coffin, the one that was light blue. Together, they opened this one as well, and as the flashlight shown in, Eyleen's heart sank. They had found their target.

There, amongst pillows of satin the purest color of white lay the boy vampire, Andrew. He looked so peaceful, so harmless, so unlike the other vampires. He looked like someone's older brother.

For a second the light left Eyleen, and she glanced up from her spot on the ground, to see Ellen returning to Jonathan's coffin, in order to pick up the forgotten stakes and glass jar. As she picked them up, she glanced nervously at Jon, and Eyleen had to wonder why her sister didn't simply close the coffin lid. Before she had the chance to ask, however, Ellen was back, this time handing the flashlight to Eyleen.

Eyleen pointed the light down into the coffin, at the body of the sleeping Andrew, wanting to apologize, or say a prayer or something. But then, the stake came down out of nowhere, hurtling into his heart with all the force Ellen could muster, piercing flesh, and muscle, and bone, as a bright fount of blood instantly came up, splashed the girls, and they screamed in unison.

Andrew opened his eyes, instantly bright red, and let out a shriek of his own. The stake hadn't fully penetrated, only about halfway through the heart. His mouth gaping, fangs glistening in the light, his arms swung crazily, reaching for the girls, who lurched backwards into the dirt.

"Quick! Get the hammer!" Ellen shouted, over the incessant howling from the struggling Andrew, who was slipping in his own blood, trying madly to wrench the stake out of his heart.

"I'm trying, I'm trying!" Eyleen shouted back, ripping the backpack off, fumbling around until she found the hammer.

Just as her fingers closed upon the cool metal, there came another shriek from the coffin. It was Ellen this time. The vampire had grabbed her by one arm, and was hauling her closer.

Something instinctual kicked in inside of Eyleen, something more primal than fear. Her twin was in danger. Her blood, her body. Standing steady now on both legs, Eyleen brought the hammer up, and swung it down with all her might, against the young, distorted face, and the reaching, gaping fangs.

There was another splash of blood, a muffled cry, and then, he lay back, twitching against the inside of the coffin. His face ruined, pulpy and cracked, Eyleen wrenched the hammer free of his skull, and dropped down on the blood-stained ground, next to her sister.

Without another word, Ellen snatched the gory hammer away from her, aimed it at the stake, and hammered it home. There was a thud, as the wood of the stake broke through Andrew's body, and landed against the coffin. His body arched up as he let out a deep, rasping moan, and then, all was still. Ellen grabbed up the jelly jar, filled it with the blood, still issuing nonstop from the boy, capped it tight, and said, "Let's get the hell out of here, Eyleen. It's been far too real for me."

Eyleen stared at Andrew, remembering how peaceful he had looked. "Yeah," she said, as Ellen pulled her to her feet, shoving the backpack once more into her sister's arms. "Way too real for me."

They followed the path quickly, and were out of the basement, up the stairs, in no time. Both were a horrible mess, each in shock, covered in dirt and blood. And that was why neither of them noticed Julia standing in the doorway of her room, watching them, too astonished to move, as the girls all but fell over each other, in their hurry to leave the mansion.

Gasping to each other about what they had to do next, they ran out of the house, closing the door with a bang, and peddled away.

Julia had been awakened by what she could only reasonably explain as 'a noise'. It was something that she had felt mentally rather than physically, but whatever it had been, it had woken her instantly and just in time to see the two girls stumble out of the mansion.

And now, as she stood there in the darkness that was not really all that dark, due to her developing vampiric night-vision, she began to realize that something was terribly wrong. Obviously, there was not supposed to be anyone in here during the day; that went without saying. But there was a lack of something, too, some oddity in the air, which hung like a curtain she couldn't place.

Suddenly, she became aware of a scent on the air, something distinct, and not altogether unfamiliar. It came from the doorway, she thought, but as she walked there, pulling her robe on over the nightgown as she went, she realized that it was not at the door where the scent began. It came from an open doorway, which she knew led to only one destination; the basement.

The meaning of all this became clear to Julia, the whole reason why those girls had come here, the feeling in the air, the scent. Panicking, Julia all but ran down the stairs into the darkness of the basement, finding her way along the path with her bare feet, easily.

She assumed what would lie at the end of the path, and find them she did, resting in coffins. Everything appeared serene, however, two of the coffin's lids were ajar, and the smell issuing from one of them was so rich, so dreadfully enticing and nauseating at the same time, Julia knew it could only be one thing. Vampire blood, and a lot of it.

Julia approached the first coffin, peering down into it, straining with her half-vampire eyes. It was Jonathan lying there, peaceful, calm. He wasn't hurt at all.

Relief flooded through her, just knowing that the one she loved was all right. But knowing what she must do, she summoned up her courage, and approached the second coffin.

As she looked down, she gasped, for there was no mistaking what it was that she saw. Andrew, or what was left of him, lay in a deep, dark pool of blood, his face mashed and mutilated, a stake protruding only about an inch and a half, from the cavity of his ruined ribcage. A hammer lay on the ground, coated with blood, dirt, and gore.

For a horrible moment, the sight of so much blood was almost a turn-on for Julia, the hunger sparking to life, deep within her gut. But then, something seemed to switch gears, realizing that it was indeed vampire blood, and it was one of what was now her own, which had died. More than that, she had known this boy, however short the time, and he had not deserved to die like this.

"Oh, Andrew," she whispered, wringing her hands for a moment, shifting her weight from one foot to another, and then louder, moaned, "Andrew."

Finally, Julia darted back to Jonathan's coffin, hands fluttering over his sleeping body, wanting to grab him, and shake him, but fearing the knife he held. In the end, she shook him anyway.

"Jonathan, wake up," she sobbed, frightened, disoriented, and having not a clue what to do. As she shook him, she watched the knife jerk backwards, clenched deep within his right hand. "Jonathan, please," she screamed out now, "it's me, wake up!"

Julia darted out of the way, as the knife came down in an arc, slicing only air. In an instant, his eyes opened, red as fire, and Julia crouched back, ready to flee.

A slow, deep growl rose from the coffin, Jonathan's body raising slowly from the depths, like some old-fashioned horror movie.

Julia backed away, decided to try once again, before running away from what seemed to be becoming a fatal case of mistaken identity. "Jonathan, will you listen to me? Its Julia, Andrew's been killed!" she yelled, tears running into her mouth, over her chin.

That did it. All at once, not only did Jonathan rise, but the other two did as well, Jason and Devin, coming out along with Jonathan, their eyes as red as his, as they gathered silently, at first, around Andrew.

Julia backed away from them at that moment, moving along the path to hide in the shadows, behind some boxes standing there.

Suddenly, their voices interrupted the silence, shattering the still, moldy air, with anger, and grief.

"Who would do this?" That was Jonathan, all caring, and all sadness for a dead brother.

"I don't care who did it, I want them dead!" said Devin this time, complete, instant conviction, and judgement.

"Julia would do this. And I let that wench into my home." Jason, it had to be. He was so ready to kill her Julia shuddered.

"No," Jonathan growled. "She wouldn't, what reason would she have? Wouldn't she kill me if she had to? Or what about you, Jason, for that matter."

"Now is not the time to try my patience with your petty arguments, Jonathan." Jason's voice again, tighter, hardly restrained. Julia sensed violence coming. "Andrew's dead."

"If Julia did it, I'll rip her in half." Devin now, already definitely enveloped within the physical vampiric changes.

"No," Jonathan demanded, almost on the verge again, himself. "Don't even think of it, Devin."

There was a roar, a crash, followed by fighting sounds. Julia decided that this was her cue to leave. She whipped around to go, ran straight into a suit of rusted armor, and brought it crashing to the ground.

The noise seemed to fill the old basement, bouncing off the very wall, and then, all was silence. Julia lay there, still as she could, hoping they hadn't heard her. No such luck. She heard their feet scuffing through the dirt, and in an instant, she had been hauled to her feet and off the ground, lifted into the air, by none other than Devin.

He laughed at her, as she tried to glare at him through her tears.

"A child killed by a child." He said through the fangs, grinning at her now. "Ironic."

"The only thing that's ironic, and sad," she said, trying desperately to sound tough and not to panic again, "is how crazy you sound, not even wanting to know the truth about how Andrew died, and I'm the only one who knows."

"Put her down, Devin." Jason said, calmly, rationally, placing his hand rather firmly on Devin's shoulder. "Now." Anger in that last word. Some control was being lost here, and Jason didn't like it.

Devin released her instantly, pulled back by Jason, like a dog on a leash.

Julia didn't even have time to look for Jonathan, who she knew must be closing the coffin's lid on that horror of a mess, at that very moment. Now, Jason stood over her.

"Julia, right now, I'm not going to listen to anything but the truth." he said, pulling the overcoat around his body, his hands in the pocket in order to perhaps look less menacing. His eyes flashed, even in the darkness. "You realize this?" he cocked his head to one side.

Julia nodded, looking away from him, brushing her robe off, wrapping it more tightly around herself. Why did he intimidate her so? His very presence made her shiver.

Jason's hands came up under her chin, forcing her to look up at him. "Who did this?"

Those girls, she thought, the one who had left in such a rush. Memories came rushing back, things Gayle had told unto her not that long ago, and suddenly, she realized that she knew who the intruders were.

"Julia, it is not good to make me wait." Jason all but hissed, fingers clenching just under her jaw. A small chuckle came from Devin, and Jonathan was suddenly at her side, ready to defend her.

"Jason," he began, but was cut off just as quickly, as Jason turned to look at him.

"Stop it," Julia said, swatting his hand off her face. She ignored the look in his eyes, and went on. "Ellen and Eyleen Pursivic did it. I saw them come up, out of the basement." She wrung her fingers together, her heart pounding furiously in her chest. Jason's eyes iced over, hard, emotionless, and cold. Julia stared at the ground, the rest of her statement coming forth in a rush. "If I had known, I would have stopped them. You have to believe me. I like Andrew. I would never have hurt him, I didn't do this." Julia realized that she was practically whining now, and tried to stop, to no success. "My sister told me they were Vampire Hunters, but I didn't believe it, after all, who would…"

Julia's words were cut off as she suddenly was pushed against the wall, falling before she could stop herself, or catch her breath, and realized just before her head slammed against the wall, she had said far too much.

A white explosion of light burst into her vision, as she crumpled into a ball on the dirty floor, and from far away it seemed, Devin was again ranting and raving.

"Your sister? Your sister? You are as much to blame for this then. She killed Andrew? So did you. You're dead, little girl, dead!"

Julia's night vision focused again, pain throbbing through her brain. Suddenly, she realized that Jonathan was standing before her, blocking Devin, holding him back as he shouted, eyes blood red, and tears like blood trailing down his face.

Jonathan, I am going to die here, she thought, rather calmly, still a bit in shock from slamming against the stone wall.

She watched, dazed, from so far away, it seemed, as Devin threw a punch at Jonathan, who returned it, and now, they were once again rolling on the ground, trying to claw, and bite.

Julia closed her eyes, falling into slumber, wishing she could do something, but knowing she was just too weak, too hungry, and too damn human to protect her little sister.

"Enough!" Jason's voice boomed through the basement, forcing Julia to open her eyes and drag herself to her feet, and halting the fight between Jonathan and Devin, instantly.

"Enough," he repeated, calmly.

Julia looked up at him, rubbing her head. To her surprise, Jason was watching her carefully, anticipating...something, which she could not explain. He came closer, peering down into her eyes. Julia backed up tightly against the wall, but couldn't seem to get away. She felt a tickling in her mind, some kind of door opening, letting memories out. From nowhere, she saw once again, the twins run out of the basement door, covered over in blood, and gore. And then, her vision focused upon Jason, once more.

"Devin, get Julia the wine."

"No."

"*Now!*" Jason roared, causing Julia to wince.

Out of the corner of here eyes, she watched Devin leave Jonathan's side, and disappear into the depths of the basement.

"You are telling the truth. And your sister was not part of this. Good girl, Julia, you told me the truth." At this, Jason left her, walking once again to where the coffins lay.

Devin returned then, forcing the bottle into her hands with an ugly glare, and stalked away, behind Jason. Jonathan stood by her as she drank now from the bottle, feeling instantly stronger, and refreshed, as the liquid poured down her throat.

"Julia." he whispered her name softly, hands brushing against her hair, "I'm sorry."

Julia pulled the bottle away from her lips, handed it over to him, and rubbed against him, holding him tight. His arms lifted to embrace her, as he gently placed his lips against her hair.

"Andrew is gone," Jason's voice echoed in the darkness, "and we will have revenge for those who destroyed him, but Julia and her sister shall remain as they are. They were not a part of this. That is my final word." With a breath of hidden air, and two light thuds, Julia knew that she and Jonathan were standing alone, in the basement.

"Julia, I have to return to sleep. I can't stay awake much longer."

"I want to stay with you," she pleaded, burying her face against his chest.

"No, Julia, I am not like you. I can't find sleep in a bed, I must stay here. And the sleep chooses me, not the other way around."

She looked up at him, grasping desperately to their love. "Tonight then?"

"Yes," he said, kissing her softly, "tonight."

She pulled away then, up the stairs and back into the sitting room, trying once again to brush off the fact, that her death was so close at hand.

12

Julia awoke the following evening to a pleasant warmth stroking the length of her neck.

She sighed, yawned, rolled onto her back. For a moment she thought it might be a dream, but then she remembered where she was, smelling the scent of burning wood on the air, the crackling of a fire filling her ears.

And then, the light, almost too gentle touch of a man's hands caressing her face, her lips, and her hair.

Julia stretched, opened her eyes to see Jonathan sitting over her in the firelight, his jacket lost to him somewhere, long, dark hair cascading over his shoulders. "Hi." she said.

"Hmmm." he replied, pulling the sheets and covers down, away from her. "How did you sleep?"

"As well as you might expect." she replied, sitting up against the headboard, pulling her knees against her chest. "Your, um, friends?"

"What about them." It was more of a statement than a question.

"Nothing, Jonathan. Unless, you count of course, that they all hate me." She made a dismissive gesture with her hands, than ran them through her disheveled hair.

Jonathan made a low sound of displeasure, removed her hands from her hair, and kissed them. "They don't hate you, Julia, it's just..." he trailed off, gazing into her face, looking blank.

"Just that they hate me," she finished for him, staring at the ceiling.

"But I don't."

"I know, Jonathan." Julia snuggled up against him. "I didn't mean to say that you do too, but just them. And Jason makes me feel weird. I don't like it."

Jonathan kissed her neck, her shoulder. He slipped one of the sleeves of her nightgown away from her, kissed the skin he exposed. Julia shivered, sucking in her breath, as his lips trailed downwards.

"It is because he turned you, Julia. You're feeling that bond, and you don't like him, so you don't like the feeling it creates inside you. You don't want him in there, inside your mind." Jonathan kissed her forehead. "Believe me," he said, gazing into her eyes, "I don't want him in there, either."

Julia stared at him. How can he love me so much, she wondered, rubbing her hands over his shoulders and back, wordlessly. How can I love him? Don't think about it too much, that's how.

She closed her eyes as he kissed her softly, pressing every part of her body against him, as they kissed. He lowered her to the bed, drawing her ever closer. She embraced him tighter, slinging an arm and a leg over him, as his hands roamed shamelessly over her body. The nightgown she wore suddenly felt so restricting; she longed to shed it, and was about to suggest they might do so, when a voice from the sitting room intruded upon their passionate moment.

"Julia, Jonathan, come out here! I have something to show you."

It was none other than Jason.

With a groan, Jonathan pulled away, hiding his head against her shoulder.

"I guess you had better change." he said.

Julia held onto him, not wanting to let go. "You can't protect me from him, can you." she whispered.

Jonathan ignored her question. He slid off the bed, through the curtains, and grabbed his jacket from where it lay on the desk. "I love you, Julia." he said, turning to look at her, as he reached the door. He paused for a moment with his hand on the door, as if he were going to say something else, but then he simply opened it and walked out, shutting it tightly behind him.

Sighing, Julia rose from the bed, pulling off the nightgown, as she walked across the room. Carelessly, she dumped it on the floor, opened the bureau, and pulled out a white lace chemise, blue V-neck sweater, and blue jeans. After she had dressed, laced up her sneakers, and brushed out her hair, she reached down to her neck, touching the chain that Jonathan had given to her. She knew that he loved her, and she loved him, but was that enough? She also knew, beyond any shadow of a doubt, that Jason had a hold on her. Somehow, she belonged to Jason, and not to Jonathan. She had been suspecting this for some time now, but only recently did it seem to be the truth.

"Julia!"

She sighed audibly, opened the door to the sitting room.

"What did you…" she began, but stood still in the middle of the room, as an overwhelming presence, like the scent of rotten fruit, overwhelmed her senses.

There, near to the front doors, by Jason's side, stood a young boy, younger even, than her. And something was not right with him. His buzz-cut, bleach blond hair was matted with dirt and blood, his light blue jeans seemed more holes than material, barely covering skinny legs, and the tee-shirt clung to his chest like a second skin. His sneakers were caked in mud, and at first, Julia rationalized that he was simply a little runaway.

But then, something clicked inside her mind. He was a vampire, but yet, not. It seemed as if he were something else, entirely. And then, she remembered. From the research she had done for her books, she remembered. He was a ghoul, or something almost identical to it. This boy had no idea where he was, or what had become of him. It was obvious from the way he scratched, and scratched at the palm of his hand until it bled, the way he stared at Jason, as if he were the only person in the room, to the slight bit of drool, running from the corner of his mouth. It had been too soon for this boy. The whole alchemical process of becoming a vampire had been rushed this very evening, from the bloodletting to the first kill, and it made Julia shiver with dread. And all this had happened to the boy because of Andrew's demise; Julia was sure of it.

Julia looked around the room, at the shocked grimace on Jonathan's face, to Devin, scowling, to Jason, watching her so intensely. Suddenly, he smiled.

Julia did not like that smile at all. It reminded her of the movies, the ones where a vampire would be so charming, so seductive, and lure the girl to die. She froze, not even breathing, as he said, hardly a whisper in that deep voice, "Julia, this is Dustin."

The boy turned to look at her even took a shaky step towards her. His eyes were those of a crazed animal light brown-gold, glazed and wild. He turned back to Jason, as if to ask what to do with this new person in his awareness, but then his eyes focused on the ground and he clenched his head in his hands, and moaned. He fell to his knees, in obvious pain.

"Stop it," Jason hissed at him, and the boy's moans ceased, instantly.

Julia almost laughed, almost, for the odd total control that Jason had over everything here, was unbelievable. *Everything here, except for me.*

"No, Julia. You are mine as well. Dustin is only a part of your lesson tonight," Jason's voice in her ear. She looked up he was gone. The place he had stood beside Dustin was empty. She jumped back a bit, as she realized that he now stood directly beside her, and she hadn't seen him move. *How? Oh, I know, he moved too fast for me, simple vampire trick, don't let him fool you,* she thought.

Julia looked up at him, innocently as she could, trying hard not to be scared. But there he was beside her, close enough to kiss...way too close for safety. Anger flashed within those eyes. *What had she done to make him so angry with her?*

"Don't you want to meet him, Julia?"

"No," she said, feeling suddenly quite small. She began to move away from him, but his hand came down on her arm, and stopped her dead. It was cold and stone hard.

Now she was frightened, and could not help but show it. "Let me go," she whispered. The look in his eyes told her that he had no intention of doing so, and was about to do something awful. A small chuckle came from Devin.

Julia pulled away again, but now his hand on her arm clasped tighter, like a vice, hauling her closer to him. She could feel him like that wall from the basement against her, totally hard, unyielding. A small sound escaped her lips, as acute pain shot up to her shoulder, and down to her fingertips.

"What do you want?" she said, sounding frantic now. "I didn't do anything, why are you doing this?"

"You need to learn the way of things here. You are a guest in my house. You exist here because of me. You are young, and have no respect." The smile vanished. "I must teach you."

The pain slightly increased. Julia gasped, and something inside overtook her, a strength flowing from within that she never knew she possessed. Instinct to fight or flee became instinct to fight. The pain in her arm heated the vampire blood inside her, and she kicked at him with all her might.

Now Jason growled at her, and she suddenly found herself kneeling on the floor, her arm twisted up behind her back, threatening to come free of the socket, and a scream ripped free from her lungs.

Jonathan then shouted along with her, his voice raising above the pain, "Stop it, Jason, she didn't do anything to you, leave her alone!"

For an awful second, the pain increased, her arm making an awful, tearing sound. Julia thought, My God, this is it, but she remembered how to save herself, and in the midst of it all, she shouted every prayer she had ever heard of, putting all the pain into words, and instantly, it stopped.

Julia was dropped to the floor like a stone, where she slid quickly backwards, putting some distance between them, cradling her hurt arm, and sobbing.

Looking at them, she realized it had worked like some sort of spell. They seemed in anguish, doubled over, everyone, their faces drawn in pain, all but the Ghoul-Boy, Dustin, and herself. Like a nightmare, Jason was the first to recover. "How *dare you!*" he hissed, and growling, lunged forward. Julia covered her face with her good arm, prepared for an attack, which never came.

"No!" Jonathan yelled out, followed by a string of harsh, French-sounding words. Julia looked up at them from where she crouched, watching in amazement as Jonathan pushed Jason a few steps backward, his voice rising in that strange language. He was fighting for her life now, and Julia knew it.

Julia ignored the tears trickling down her face, and pulled herself to her feet. As she watched, Jason backhanded Jonathan across the face with an awful smack, causing his head to jerk to one side, his hand rising to his jaw. Jason shouted at him in the same old language, and this time, Jonathan did not respond.

Devin added something, from where he stood, in a low tone, but Jason cut him off. Jonathan said something else now, pointing to Julia, but his arm slowly fell back to his side, as Jason shook his head no, and yelled out something else. And now, he hit Jonathan again.

Jonathan glared at him silently for a tense few moments, but turned, and walked away, past Julia without even looking at her, and into the furthest dark shadows of the sitting room. He sat in a corner, crossing his arms over his knees. As his head lowered, Julia met his eyes for a split second. His eyes were glowing red.

Jason grabbed Julia by the arm again, hauling her across the room, to where Dustin still knelt on the floor, as oblivious to everything as he had been, twenty minutes ago.

"Ow," she protested, but followed along, as not to upset him again. She swiped at her tears with one hand, as Jason lifted the other to touch Dustin's face. Julia jerked back on contact. It was awful touching him. The sheer wrong of him seeped into her flesh, directly from his.

"Dustin has something to give you, little wench." Jason's voice, seductive as a lover, in her ear, in her mind, as he breath fanned over her neck like a flame. It raised chills along her spine involuntarily; she shivered.

As Julia watched, the boy pulled from his back pocket, an old whiskey flask. He held it up, out to her, like a sacrificial offering.

"I don't drink," she murmured, flinching slightly as his right arm came up around her waist, holding her close.

"Oh, you will drink this, I assure you, Julia." Jason chuckled as Dustin opened the flask for her, once again holding it out.

"I..." The smell wafted up to her senses, with all the ferocity of a hurricane. Blood was contained within that flask. Not the wine-blood that Jason had given to her, and not the sticky smell of vampire blood. It was something rich, full of power, and sweet as life itself. Her stomach knotted up, hungry, demanding to be fed yet again. She found herself wrenching the flask from the boy's outstretched hands. She held it close to her lips, breathing in the scent, letting it curl around the hunger in her gut.

"Baby's blood." Julia whispered. She knew suddenly, what it was that had made Dustin this way. She hated him, hated Jason, but she was so hungry now, that she knew she was going to drink it. And she didn't care.

"Yes, Julia." He whispered. "The innocents." Jason laughed slightly at her lack of control. "The sweetest of the sweet. Now drink it."

And she raised it to her lips, and drank it down. The hunger inside her rose to meet the blood, and cooled, dissipating, as she consumed all of it into her body. Only, when it was gone, and she had dropped the flask where it clattered on the floor, she found herself standing there alone, feeling not quite as hungry, but perhaps even less satisfied than before. She turned and glared at Jason, who now stood a few feet back from her, grinning maniacally.

"Why are you doing this?" she gasped.

"To show you, Julia. You are only putting off the inevitable. The emptiness you feel will only continue on, with the hunger, until you kill. And you will kill, and join us very soon, I believe, or so your Jonathan tells me."

Julia looked down at the floor, overcome by shame. That baby who's blood she had drunk was dead, she knew it. How could this be Julia? She was not a killer. She was just a girl, after all. Wasn't she?

"Good evening to you both." Jason said, and with that, he, along with Devin and Dustin trailing behind, left the mansion.

Julia walked back into her room, collapsing onto the bed with a thud, finally alone, and let the sobs wrack her body. Soon, she heard the door to her room open, and Jonathan entered. He said nothing, as he sat on the edge of her bed, resting a hand lightly against her back, as she cried, and cried.

"It will be all right," he said softly, trying to reassure her.

Julia sat up swiftly, knocking his hand away. "No, it won't. How can you tell me this? How can anything ever be all right again? Do you know what it is you're doing to me? I wake up, and it's all a dream, just a dream, and then suddenly, it's real! How do you know what it's like? To be pushed by impulses you know are wrong, and to fear that one day you'll give in? And I know it's going to happen soon enough, and so do you!" Julia hiccuped for breath, swiping at her tears, watching Jonathan stare annoyingly at the floor. "How do you know what it's like to love someone like you, and to know that it can't be real, not really, when all you do is kill, and hate, and kill, and I...I left my family for you! What are you!" Julia sobbed, hysteria taking over. "What have you done to me!" He sat like a stone there, on the edge of the bed, and with a frustrated groan, she began to punch at him, over and over, slapping at him until he did look at her, and her tight.

"I can't, I can't," she sobbed, as his arms restrained her struggling body, holding her close.

"I know, I know Julia."

Julia sobbed, calming now, little by little, as his fingers stroked back her hair, and he kissed away her tears. "Julia, he hates me as well."

"No, Jonathan, don't talk about him." she whimpered. "Jason wants to kill me."

A small sarcastic laugh shook Jonathan's body. "If only you knew. I am the reason he did this to you tonight, my love. He did it to get to me."

Julia looked at him now, amazed to see the red of tears rolling down his face.

"Jonathan?" Julia sniffed, reaching out to touch those tears. He stopped her, still gazing off somewhere, to a place filled with pain, that only he could see. In a hushed, hurried voice, Jonathan told her that it hadn't always been this way. He told her that while he had been alive, there was a woman whom he had loved, and she had betrayed him, as well as many others, until there was nothing, no one, to keep him alive.

"When I tried to kill myself, Jason came for me. He had loved me like a father then; he saved me from death. But then somehow, everything changed. It was just as quick, Julia, and I felt I was dying again. One hundred years have passed by. I have been alive through it all. I have seen things no one should ever have to see. I wanted to die again, Julia, and then, I saw you."

He looked down at her, kissing her lips gently, pulled her against him tightly. "I have no father, but I have you, my love. Julia, I swear I will protect you, and love you, forever."

"Stop, Jonathan, I hate to see you in pain. It's awful." Julia held him tight.

"So you see, he does these things just to get to me. He knows it will hurt me to see you betray yourself. He flaunts it at me."

But why, Julia thought, but did not ask. "Jonathan, come lay next to me." She pulled him down to the bed beside her.

Jonathan took her n his arms, pulling her against himself, trying to make her safe with his actions, alone.

"I love you, Julia."

"I know, Jonathan." Julia whispered, a strange foreboding shadowing her words. "And I love you with all my heart."

13

The following morning, Gayle headed over the twins' house very early. She had gone spying before dawn, back to the vampires' mansion at 4:30 in the morning. She had actually gone to look in on Julia. She really missed her sister after all, and wanted to try somehow to convince her to come home. But what was Gayle to do? Go up to the door and knock? And so, she crept up to the window once more, and listened for any word of Julia.

She heard a lot more than that.

To her surprise, Julia and Jonathan were nowhere to be seen, and neither was the young one, the boy called Andrew. From Jason and Devin's conversation, Gayle quickly put together that Ellen and Eyleen had already been here, and had already had killed him.

No wonder why she hadn't heard from them at all, yesterday.

And something else had happened. There was a new boy sitting on the floor at Jason's feet, like some sort of pet. Gayle instantly knew that something was not right with him, but she couldn't figure out what. Soon, she didn't care.

As the sun began to rise over the mountains, she watched from her hiding place as Jason, Devin, and the boy stood, headed towards a door in the wall. She couldn't help but overhear the remainder of their conversation as they passed uncomfortably close to the window.

"Devin, I assure you, when the sun goes down, we will have revenge for Andrew."

Gayle gasped, held her breath until they were out of earshot. The twins were in trouble. They would have company tonight. And so, she had run as fast as she could in the early sunlight, down the mountain, past her home, and all the way to Ellen and Eyleen.

Once there, she pounded on the door, gasping for breath, until Ellen, who had already been up, answered it.

"What's up, Gayle?" she asked.

Gayle shook her head, trying to tell her the obvious, but so out of breath she could not speak, she simply brushed into the house, collapsing in the living room, onto the nearest couch.

Twenty minutes later, over cereal and orange juice, Gayle told both Ellen and Eyleen just what she had witnessed in the predawn hours, up at the mansion.

"We expected as much." Ellen muttered around her cereal. Eyleen said nothing, simply ate in silence.

"What are we going to do?" Gayle asked, slugging down the rest of her juice. Ellen smiled.

"I'm glad you asked." she said. "First, I've got to tell you, we've come up with a cure for your sister."

"You did?" Gayle asked, her voice full of new hope.

"Yes," Eyleen said softly, "but at a cost."

"No cost." Ellen corrected, all too cheerfully. "Only one vampire's life."

So Andrew *is* dead, Gayle thought, but then asked quickly, "What are you going to do to her?"

Ellen then explained that it was sheer logic that had found the cure, and not any amount of chemical testing. She had already known that Gayle's family were somewhat believers in the Christian Faith. This led her to believe that Julia must be a believer as well. And so, if Julia were still only half vampire, which she was, the thing to cure her would be, by Julia's power of conviction alone, almost the same as the thing that had started this whole thing.

"Huh?" Gayle asked, not following.

"She wants your sister to drink Holy Blood, Gayle. She thinks it will reverse the process. That Julia's faith alone will be enough to cure her. A mind over matter sort of thing." Eyleen said, finishing off her breakfast between words.

"Oh, I see." Gayle said, "But will it work?"

"I don't know." Ellen said. "But it probably will. I just haven't had a chance to test it, unless you two want to go up there to the mansion, and volunteer to become guinea pigs."

Gayle and Eyleen stared at Ellen. "Very funny." Gayle said, finally.

Ellen shrugged, wiping her mouth off with a tissue, and setting the bowl down on the floor.

"But Ellen, they're coming tonight. What's your plan for that?" Gayle asked.

"I'd like to know too, Ellen." Eyleen said skeptically.

Ellen ignored her sister's comment, and went on. "Well, we're going to need some traps. Maybe some nets doused in Holy Water. The vampires usually hate that stuff. We'll each need a crossbow, and dart guns with tranquilizers. We'll set up some ropes outside, in the trees, so we can get the drop on them."

"How can I help?" Gayle asked. "I want to get Julia home. I've been telling Mom that Julia's mad at her, that she's at a friend's house, but we're leaving tomorrow morning to go back to Connecticut. We've run out of time."

"Don't worry, Gayle." Eyleen said, patting her hand. "I'm sure that if Jonathan shows up here, Julia will be with him."

"That's right, Gayle. She'll want to try to protect you." Ellen said. "You just worry about trying to get her to take her cure. We'll take care of the reset. Just tell your mom that you and Julia will be staying with us tonight, and have her pick you guys up here tomorrow morning. Our folks actually left last night and won't be back for days, so it'll be cool."

"Okay," Gayle sighed, already getting nervous.

"Don't worry," Eyleen said again, and Gayle wondered if she was trying to convince herself of this. "Everything will be fine."

"Fine?" Ellen laughed. "Hell, it'll be fun." She threw her arms around her comrades, whispering the next words like some sort of demented secret. "Come on, girls. Let's go shopping."

14

Julia awoke a half-hour before sunset, for she could not sleep. There was something in the air tonight which bothered her. Not like this whole experience wasn't bad enough. But then, she looked down at Jonathan sleeping beside her on the bed in the darkness, flat on his back, not moving, not breathing. Even like this, she loved him. She could not deny it.

Julia snuggled back down into the covers, reaching her arm across his chest. They had spent the whole night in this room; simply talking until the sun rose, and sleep had claimed them both. Neither had wanted to go out, and Julia was positive that he had not fed, because of her. His skin was very cold to the touch.

In the morning, he had wanted to go back downstairs, to his coffin and his precious knife, but Julia had begged him to stay. They had simply closed the door, pulled the covers up over their heads, and giggling like kids, had fallen asleep in each other's arms. It had almost been normal.

But now, as Julia waited for him to come back from this little death he suffered every day, she couldn't help but feel the strange energy in the air. Something *was* going to happen, and it frightened her.

Finally, after much painful waiting on her part, the sun went down across Vermont, and Jonathan slowly awoke. He looked a bit disoriented for a moment, eyes searching the darkness for something Julia did not know of, but then they settled on her. A smile overtook him; he reached out to her, pulled her close for a kiss.

"Julia, what are you doing to me?" he questioned.

"What do you mean?" she whispered, curling her fingers through his hair.

"I have not slept in a bed for one hundred years, and now this little woman charms me into it, with nothing but a smile, and a kiss."

Julia laughed softly, holding him tightly as she listened to the footsteps in the sitting room, beyond her door.

"Jonathan, something's up." she whispered.

"Yes," he said, sounding disappointed. "I didn't know you felt it too."

"I don't want to," she said, kissing his neck, his cheek, and his lips. "Jon, whatever they're planning, let's stay here. I don't want to go. I'm frightened."

"Julia, I wish it was that simple. I really do. But it's not." He pulled back from her, gazing at her face in the darkened room. "We have all the time in the world to be alone together."

Julia nodded as he crept out of bed, pulling her with him. She wanted to believe him, but for some reason, it just didn't seem to be true. As he handed Julia her leather jacket, she became aware that he was studying her, watching her every move, as if to memorize this moment. Julia walked to him, pulled him close.

"I feel as if I will never see you again after tonight, Jonathan."

"No, my love, I will always be here." Jonathan kissed her head, her mouth, rubbed her back gently as tears filled her eyes. She could not deny the nervousness she felt; she wanted to beg him to stay here with her, but as he pulled her along with him, through the door of the sitting room, and out into the night where the others were waiting, she understood at once what was going on. The look in Jason's eyes could mean one thing only . . . death.

They were going to Ellen and Eyleen's house, walking down the road, and walking slowly, stalking their prey like a cat. Julia could only hold onto Jon's hand, going with them, because like him, she had no choice. She felt certain that Gayle would be there, and she had to protect her sister from Devin, no matter what the cost.

Soon enough, they were standing in front of the house, their hair lightly tossed by the breeze.

Julia watched it all from far away, not knowing what to expect or to do. She wanted to run away from it all, but loyal both to her sister and Jonathan, she stood still, waiting for whatever came next.

"Around back." Jason said, and led them through a stand of pine trees, into the back yard, where they stood in the darkness, until suddenly, the motion detector on the floodlights kicked in. The backyard was illuminated in harsh white light, and so were the five figures standing within it.

There was a moment of silence, it seemed, where no one breathed, not even the wind, and even the crickets were dead. And then a single word shattered the night.

"Now!"

From high above them in the trees, a nylon net fell, instantly ensnaring the Ghoul-Boy Dustin, who shrieked as if he were on fire.

Julia backed away from them a few paces, watching in amazement, as Jason reached down to grab at the net, winced in agony, and drew his hands back to reveal red, raw burn marks. What was on that net, she wondered, but had no time, really. Just as quickly as the net had fallen, there came a strange whistling noise, and suddenly, Dustin was silenced. An arrow protruded from the net, Julia saw now, and realized, along with the rest of them, that this had been a trap.

"Ahhhh!" Jason roared in frustration.

Julia glanced over to see his eyes shift to red once again, the fangs glittering in the false light. He gazed across the yard at another stand of trees, this one where the arrow had flown from. "I see you've been doing your homework!" he shouted.

Julia followed his gaze. Up in the tree knelt one of the twins, probably Ellen, from the war paint that adorned her face, and the fact that she had made the first kill of the evening.

"That's right!" the girl shouted back, loading another arrow into her crossbow. "Your boy Andrew helped us with that!"

"You're dead," Jason growled, stalking to the tree, dumping off his overcoat as he went.

"You first!" Ellen shouted, letting the arrow fly at Jason, who dodged it easily. Suddenly, he vanished from Julia's sight, appearing on the branch beside Ellen, and tossed her to the ground. She dropped like a rock, making not a noise as she fell. Jason jumped on her, not noticing what Julia did from across the yard. "Try this!" Ellen screamed, and pulled a hypodermic needle from inside her jacket, pushed it into Jason's neck, pressed the plunger. He made an awful groan, and fell to the ground beside her.

Julia didn't have time to watch anymore, as an arrow whistled down between herself and Jonathan. She jumped back a few more paces, looking up into the tree that the net had fallen from. There sat the other twin, taking shots at Jonathan with a crossbow of her own.

"No, don't hurt him!" she shouted, but too late. The girl was reloading her crossbow. Jonathan, however, had already jumped up into the tree beside her, snatched up the crossbow, and tossed it at Julia's feet.

Julia looked at the weapon, already loaded, waiting to strike.

"Don't even think about it." Devin said, this time growling at Julia like a rabid dog.

"Think about what?" she questioned, watching him carefully as he stalked up to her, covering the ground in a few paces.

"I know what you think about Jason, and I won't let you kill him." Devin snarled at her around the fangs, kicked the weapon away. It clattered against the tree, where Jonathan was undoubtedly choking Eyleen to death. "Julia, I know where your sister is."

Devin raised a hand to the house, pointed at the roof. She followed his raised arm, and yes, barely visible but for the top of her head, crouched Gayle, all decked out in army gear, also armed with a crossbow.

"Gayle!" Julia shouted, only to be silenced as Devin clamped a hand across her mouth and another around her neck.

"You make a move and she dies, got it?" he said, spit hitting her face.

Julia felt the heat and hunger rising once again. She bit into his hand, smiling as he jerked back. "You won't touch my sister."

"Bitch." he growled, raised the same hand she had bitten, and for one awful minute, she thought he was actually going to hit her again.

"Julia!" Gayle shouted from the roof, and Julia twisted in Devin's grasp, trying to signal to her sister to get back.

An evil grin crawled over Devin's mouth, showing off the fangs as he said, "Well, maybe I might just kill her to let you watch." And with an explosion of wind, he released her from his grasp.

Julia fell to the ground, coughing, as Eyleen jumped out of the tree and ran, with Jonathan close behind. Julia tried to grasp for him as he passed, but couldn't reach, and she fell over, onto the ground.

"Julia!" Gayle screamed, and Julia looked back to the roof, only to behold an awful sight. Devin, standing now upon the roof, had lifted Gayle high off her feet, and buried his face in the little girl's neck.

He was drinking from her!

Something snapped inside Julia at that moment. She was on her feet in an instant, not even realizing that the hunger was flaring through her body, her muscles tense, the aching in her jaw rising almost to pain. As she watched them, she rubbed her throat, running her tongue across the fangs that had suddenly grown down in her mouth.

Acting on impulse, she reached over to the base of the tree behind her, picked up the crossbow, and aimed it at Devin's arched back, just where the wind was blowing his golden hair away from the jacket he wore.

"Devin!" she shouted, her voice harsh, full of hate and pain, "I warned you!"

From somewhere in the yard, she could hear a voice cry out, "No!" but her mind was focused on Devin, who was killing her sister, and she could not rationalize. Pulling the trigger was easy. Just a simple click and the arrow flew straight into Devin's back.

Devin made no sound as the arrow dug into his body. He simply let Gayle go, turned, looked down into the yard, and fell. He landed against the soft ground with a thump.

As Julia walked forward, the crossbow at her side, she did not notice the fact that Eyleen had cut a rope and trapped Jonathan within a net, or that she too had tranquilizers and now Jonathan was completely immobilized. All she saw was Devin, lying prone on his back, the tip of the metal arrow protruding from his chest.

Julia knelt down beside him, watching Devin die. He stared at her, amazed, shocked, and coughing a few times, blood tricking from his lips. He didn't seem to realize who she was, or what in fact he was. He groaned a word, perhaps a name, something old and Irish sounding, and then, he fell still. The red seeped back from his open, staring eyes, leaving them green once more. The fangs were gone.

Julia left the crossbow at his side, standing, backing away, and breathing heavily as to calm herself. When she opened her eyes to look for Gayle, Julia appeared normal again.

"Gayle? You all right?" she shouted up towards the roof.

"Yes," a small voice replied, frightened, weak, but all right.

And then something took place, which Julia could neither rationalize nor explain.

Jason stumbled over from the other side of the yard, the drugs in his system already taking effect. He knelt beside Devin, cradling his head upon his lap. "Devin," he whispered. "Devin." Jason shook him a little, the arms and head of the dead vampire slightly rolling. "Devin!" Jason shouted. Sobs wracked his body as Julia watched, amazed. Jason, crying for this man whom was not a man, this thing that she had killed.

Jason looked up to the sky, red tears running down his face from red eyes, grimacing around wet fangs. He seemed lost for a moment, disoriented, not knowing what to do. And then, his eyes fastened on Julia. "You killed him." he whispered. "You killed my son!"

Julia took a step backwards as Jason stood up, the murder weapon held in his hand. "You killed Devin with this thing!" He removed the spare arrow that was strapped beneath the firing mechanism, tossed the crossbow across the yard.

"Do you have any idea what this will do to you?" he growled, holding the arrow in his hand as he slowly advanced on her. "I can make your death long and painful, you wench. You'll be lucky if I let you die as quick as him."

Julia looked around the yard, noticing Ellen and Eyleen running to help Gayle come off the roof, seeing for the first time Jonathan struggling inside the next.

"Jonathan," she moaned.

"*No!*" Jason shouted, almost in her ear.

Julia looked up to see Jason in front of her, waving the arrow in front of her face.

"Jonathan will not save you from me. He knows better. He can't do a damn thing. You are dead. You killed my Devin. He was my first born!" Jason shouted, slapping her across the face so hard, Julia fell to the ground, dizzy, trying to scramble to her feet. "Now you will die too."

105

"Jonathan!" Julia screamed, turning, climbing to her feet, running as fast as she could to where Jonathan lay, reaching out for her from inside the net. Suddenly, she was pushed from behind, and she fell just out of reach, as Jason came down on top of her.

Julia, squirming, turned over, screaming as he pinned her arms down under his knees, holding the arrow, metal point down, just inches from her right eye.

Jason laughed like a lunatic. "Now don't move. This might hurt." he said, arching the arrow up and over his head.

Julia screamed again, closed her eyes, but the final blow never came. She opened her eyes to see a tranquilizer dart quivering in Jason's arm, his eyes rolling up into his head. Julia pushed against him, and he fell off her, onto the ground. Pulling herself up, she looked to the house to see Gayle, standing on the ground, blood soaking her neck and shirt, a dart gun held in her hands.

Julia smiled at her sister, and then, turned back to Jonathan. She crept over to him, pulled him free of the net, knelt down beside him. "Oh, Jonathan," she whispered, watching as he tried to fight off the effects of the tranquilizer.

"Julia." he groaned his eyes cracking a bit open. "What an angel you are."

"Jon, I'm not an angel." she smiled, tears sliding down her face. She listened as the girls approached.

"They're going to take you away from me, and there's nothing I can do about it." Jonathan closed his eyes, sighed. "I wish I had listened to you." he whispered.

"Jon, no." Julia hugged him, trying to keep him awake, placing kisses all over his face. "I'll stay with you, I promise."

"Go with them." His voice was barely audible. "Not safe here now. I love you, will come back for you when it's safe."

"Jonathan, you promise me?" Julia sobbed, grasping his hand within her own.

"Yes. Keep my chain . . . part of me. Remember . . . love you."

"Jonathan I love you." Julia collapsed against him, sobbing, as the drugs took their toll.

"Don't you touch him!" she hissed at the girls as they came up beside her. She crouched beside him, ready to spring as she glared up at them, not really seeing them, but only a threat to the man she loved.

"Julia? It's Gayle, can you hear me?"

Julia looked up to the girl who spoke to her, now yes, seeing Gayle. She whispered her name, reached out a hand, and let the girl pull her to her feet.

"Come into the house with us, Julia. They can cure you."

Julia looked down at the body of her love, and then at the vampire who wanted to kill her, and the sister whom she had killed for. She went with them into the house, and drank down the Holy Blood they gave her from an old soda bottle.

The contents of the bottle burned her like acid, all the way down, and she tried not to throw it up. Gayle stayed by her side the whole time, clenching her hand, placing Julia on the couch to rest, as heaves and convulsions wracked her body. On the edge of consciousness, she heard Gayle on the phone with her mom, telling her where Julia's motorcycle was parked and that Julia had come in drunk, and could not go get it. She could tell Jeanne was not very happy, but her Mom agreed to retrieve the bike with the U-Haul.

As Gayle replaced the phone, Julia heard the twins go back outside, and rush in just as fast. The last thing she heard before darkness and sleep took over was what they told her sister.

"Jason and Jonathan are gone."

15

Julia watched through the Jeep's small plastic window, as the countryside gave way to highway once more. She glanced back at the U-Haul carrying her motorcycle, and ahead at the truck carrying all their furniture and other belongings. Sighing, she slid the sunglasses up over her eyes, looking at the backs of her sister's and mother's heads in the front seat. Julia had given up everything for them, and they didn't even realize it. Not really.

Julia thought back to the night before, to when she had awoken on the couch, somewhere towards the middle of the night. Gayle and Eyleen had been sleeping in blankets on the floor, Ellen sharpening a knife, resting on a chair in the corner.

As Julia stood and looked out the window, the young girl spoke to her. "They're gone."

Julia stared out the window, not answering. It was true of course. Even the bodies of Dustin and Devin had been disposed of.

"I mean really gone. They weren't at the mansion, when I went there to check."

"Yeah?" Julia asked, turning to look at her. "Maybe one day you'll be gone, too."

"Hmm." Ellen scoffed. "Maybe. Mom and Dad do want to leave Vermont. They say I'm running wild here, that I'm a bad influence on my sister. They want to go somewhere a little more developed."

"Well, I hope you like it." Julia went back to the couch, lying down, staring at the ceiling.

"I hope you thank us later for your new mortality." Ellen had said.

Julia watched the sky, as it turned from cloudless blue to gray. There had been warnings of storms this afternoon. But no storm could compare to the one raging inside her heart.

Jonathan. How could she ever hope to forget him? He might not be a part of her life now, but she still loved him, still felt linked to him. Julia brushed her fingertips over the chain she wore, watching out the window as the heavens opened up, and it began to pour. This now was her only tie to Jonathan, to the life he had promised her, no matter what that life would have been. He had loved her.

Julia looked again at her sister's head, at the girl who had saved her from death, from Jason. Gayle was so young to have that burden, and beyond everything else, Julia was proud of her.

Julia sighed. She would bide her time, and wait for Jonathan to come for her. And one day he would come. So she would write, and make a life for herself, whatever that life may be. Until the day he returned for her, and she would be held in his arms, once more.

PART TWO

The Reoccurrence (December, Nineteen Eighty Nine)

1

Julia Anderson had grown up.

She was nineteen years old, and quite an accomplished novelist. She had written several books that had ended up on the bestseller's list, gaining major popularity with other young readers across the United States, and Canada. She had completed High School back in Connecticut, and had obtained a two-year Associates Degree in Early Childhood Education.

Julia had become wealthy with the sales of her books, and was now living off royalties, along with her mother, and sister, in a classy section of the state.

Julia did not smoke, never did drugs, and only once had touched alcohol, upon graduation from Community College, which had, unfortunately, resulted in the loss of her virginity. She never touched the stuff again.

Her mother Jeanne had finally obtained a full-time position at a local grammar school, teaching music, and owned a BMW. Life seemed good, for the Andersons. Julia had no problems in her life now, but for one.

Jonathan.

It had now been three and a half years, since they came back to Connecticut from Vermont, and he had been on her thoughts ever since. He haunted her dreams. Sometimes, in the night, she could hear his voice, just too far away to understand what he was saying. She would awaken in the middle of the night and walk out onto her balcony, crying bitter tears for the love she had left behind.

Every day was pain for Julia, every night a lifetime of agony. It seemed that she wasn't really living her life, simply watching it happen. Ever since the Andersons had left Vermont, Julia had been this way, drawn into herself so deeply, she couldn't find her way out.

Julia never spoke much to anyone, never laughed, and never looked at the cloudless blue sky without scowling, never rejoiced the life her sister Gayle had given to her.

Many young men had become attracted to Julia, although all she ever did was ignore them. She had become beautiful, and even in her sorrow, everyone could see how she had changed, overnight it seemed, grown into a fine young woman.

Her blond hair fell now in thick natural waves, halfway down her back. She had grown a few inches taller; the curves of her body now complete and full. She always moved with grace. But deep within her blue-green eyes, you could see her sorrow.

Julia had kept her word to Jonathan, and never took off the chain he had given to her. She wore it always; a safety link to all that they had shared. It kept her company, made her feel loved, even when there was no love at all.

Julia had taken to other odd practices. She wore the color black constantly, to try to cover the hurt and emptiness she felt inside, but it simply didn't work. Nothing at all really worked. Friends couldn't help her, or relatives, or money. She wanted Jonathan. She ignored the world around her, knowing that her future lay in the past with him.

As for Gayle, at thirteen, she had cut her hair, curled it carefully. Her body was slowly growing more and more to resemble that of a young woman. Gayle was much taller now, coming right up to Julia's forehead when she stood straight.

Gayle was the bubbly one of the two sisters, the girl who always went to parties, hung out with her friends, had a new life, and loved it. She had not, however, talked to the twins in a while. Rumor had it that shortly after the incident in Vermont, Ellen had been committed to a psychiatric hospital somewhere. The rest of the family had moved to Canada, leaving the 'bad stuff' behind.

Gayle felt awful for her sister. Julia never talked to anyone but Christi, an old friend who came to visit every once in a while. Gayle was beginning to regret what had happened, that last night in Vermont. Part of her always wondered if Julia would have been better off with Jonathan, rather than without him. She almost felt responsible for what was happening to Julia. Being without Jonathan was slowly killing her, and Gayle knew it.

Maybe it was time for Julia to go back to Vermont. Because if she didn't, to Gayle, it was clear, Julia would die.

2

One evening, in the month of December that year, snow covered the ground. It was near to the Holidays by the Christian calendar, the season of 'perpetual hope'.

Julia Anderson was not in the Christmas spirit, for she was definitely running out of hope. In her eyes, there was no snow or ice on the ground, only in her heart. She did not feel the cold of the wind as it lapped at her face, or the stinging of snow flurries in her eyes, for she felt now as if Jon had somehow forgotten her.

Julia rode down the old New England roads on her Harley Davidson Sportster, an 800cc motorcycle, and the only one small enough for a woman of her stature to ride. Small, sleek and sexy, the black color of the motorcycle blended perfectly with the night, with her mood, with her.

Julia's friend, Christi, down for the weekend, rode behind her, clinging to her, on the back seat of the bike. Christi was the only one Julia had entrusted with her amazing story. And oddly enough, Christi had believed every word.

Julia concentrated on the feel of her Harley beneath her, the purring of the motor, like a wild cat, the wind blowing through her hair and her clothes, freezing her body. She thought of the wind, of flying, of Jonathan. God, she missed him.

Julia felt the familiar sting of tears rising into her eyes, shook her head to clear them, but she couldn't push him out of her mind. She slowed the bike to a stop, put the kickstand out, cut the motor and got off, collapsing on a street curb to cry.

Christi got off the bike, standing before Julia, shivering in the heavy woolen coat and gloves she wore. She stared at Julia, her wavy black hair in disarray, concern showing in the depths of her emerald eyes.

"Julia, look at me." she said.

Julia looked up, her cheeks streaked with silent tears, her body trembling.

"Julia, you can't keep this up. You look fine on the outside, but inside your mind, and your soul, you're dying! How do you know if he'll ever wake up? Or if he'll even remember you? Maybe he's been awake for years, and hasn't sent for you because he doesn't want you to come back."

"Christi," Julia sobbed, "don't you see? I can't stand these things you tell me, because they might be true. I've been dreaming about him every night, for the past two years. I think he doesn't remember me." She lowered her head to her hands, sobbing silent tears.

"Oh, Julia. Come on." Christi sat by Julia on the curb, putting her arm around her friend. "Let's not think about this tonight, okay? I hear that there's going to be some really great shows on those movie channels tonight. Naked guys, Julia."

Julia managed a small giggle for her friend's optimism. "Potato chips and beer too?" she asked, wiping her tears away.

"Yes," Christi grinned. "Lots and lots. Come on; let's go back. It'll be fun."

"All right," Julia said, standing, dusting her bottom off, starting the motorcycle back up. "Let's go."

Later that night, after many movies and beers, Julia and Christi sat up talking, into the early predawn hours. Sitting on pillows next to Julia's fireplace, they giggled, telling scary stories to each other, which were in all actuality, quite perverted.

They fell silent after a while, Christi dozing off, Julia staring into the dying embers of the fireplace. The fire crackling was the only sound through the house, that along with Christi's deep, even breathing as she slept.

And then, as Julia began to drift, she heard a voice in the night, reaching out to her across miles and miles.

Come back to me, my love, whoever, wherever you are.

Julia jumped up, instantly wide-awake. "Jonathan!"

3

Two weeks had passed since the night Julia had heard Jonathan's voice, beckoning her back to Vermont. It took that long to purchase a van, explain things to her mother, and to persuade Christi to accompany her on this journey.

Today she packed a light suitcase, nothing big, just a simple pack, which would hold a few changes of clothing, accessories, and a hairbrush. After all, this was a journey she might never come back from.

"But Julia, have you thought this through?" Gayle protested, tugging at her sister's arm.

"Yes, Gayle. I am going to see Jonathan." She shrugged Gayle off, and left her standing there, in the middle of the room. "Stop it, I have to pack."

Gayle stared at her sister, trying to reason with her, to no avail. "Julia, look. I know that the time away from him has been hard for you, but you can't just waltz in there like this. You don't know, Jason might be waiting!"

"But Jonathan's waiting," Julia replied.

"Who will go with you, how will you get there?"

"Christi's coming over. She's going with me, and that's why I bought the van, Gayle. We've been through this all before. I took out the middle and back seats so I could put the bike in there, a cooler, and our suitcases."

Gayle sighed. She thought of the time so long ago, when Julia had run away to be with Jonathan. And she thought of how miserable Julia had been, ever since she had come home. "All right Julia, go. I won't even try to stop you. I know you need to see him. I know you love him."

Julia smiled at her sister. "Thanks." She looked around her room, picked up her suitcase, jacket and purse, had Gayle carry the cooler, and left the room behind.

Downstairs, Julia wished her mother well, and said goodbye. Then, Julia headed out the door, met by Christi at the van. They exchanged greetings, piled their stuff in, and got into the van. Julia started it up, rolled down the window, and looked down at her sister.

"I'll miss you Gayle," she said. "But I have to go to him."

"No you don't!" Gayle said; she was so close to tears, and trying really hard not to let Julia see. "You don't have to go to him, you could stay here with mom and me, get your life together and forget him!"

"You know I can't do that." Julia said, reaching out and grasping her sister's hand. "I love him."

"I know Julia, I know." Gayle said, wiping her tears on her sleeve. "But I hope *you* know what you're getting into this time."

Julia smiled. "So do I little sister," she said. "Well, goodbye." With that, Julia rolled up the window, put the van in gear and drove away, leaving Gayle, her mother and her new life behind, back to Vermont, and Jonathan.

4

Eight hours later, Julia pulled into the driveway of what had been her old house in Vermont, and cut the engine. The old house looked radiant, in the diminishing winter sunlight. There was a new family living here, of course. Julia folded her arms over the steering wheel, and sighed. How could she have thought that things would have been exactly as before? Nothing remains the same.

Well. Of course not. This time, Julia would stay with Jonathan forever, no matter what the cost.

Julia pulled out of the driveway and down the remainder of the road to where the "dead-end" sign stood. There, she pulled the van onto the dirt road, and headed up the mountain. Luckily for her, it had not snowed up here; the path was in fairly good condition.

About halfway to the mansion, as Julia judged, she pulled the van to the side of the road. She wasn't really worried about anyone stealing anything, for she knew no one would come up the mountain at night. Years earlier, her mother had told her that people were prone to hear sounds up there at night, accompanied by an eerie presence that had made them quite uncomfortable. Hmmm. Could that have been vampires on the prowl?

Julia unbuckled her seatbelt, reached over to Christi who sat in the front passenger seat, deep asleep. "Wake up, Christi. We're here."

"Where are we? At the mansion?" Christi said, her voice full of sleepiness.

"No, but close. Get up. We have to get there soon. The sun is setting." Julia replied.

Christi yawned, rubbing her eyes. "What's the rush Julia? They'll still be here later tonight, won't they?"

"I don't know. And if we're still here when they leave, I don't want Jason to be the first to find us. Come on. Get your jacket on, and get ready to go."

Christi pulled her winter coat over blue jeans, and a heavy blue sweater; Julia grabbed her black leather jacket from the floor, pulling it on and zipping it up, over her tank top and jeans.

They ate leftover pizza and soda from the cooler for dinner, neither one saying a word, anticipating the night to come.

Not very far away from where Julia and Christi, the last rays of sunlight bathed the old Victorian Mansion in red.

Deep within, the Vampire Jonathan tossed in his sleep, suffering from the nightmares he was always subjected to just before dark. In all his time as a vampire, he had never stopped dreaming. The nightmares he had suffered as a human child had never left him. But the nightmares he suffered now were far worse than the ones he had become used to. They were not of death, violence, disease, or any other human fears. They were not of being burnt by the sun, or of his immortal soul being thrown to hell for all the sins he had committed.

They were of broken love.

These nightmares were of a presence, which he had cherished for only a short while, a lover that had been taken away from him, far too soon.

Too soon had this one and only love been pulled back into the light, to a place he could not follow. And try as he might, he could not bring about her name, or her features, or who she had been. It was the drugs that had done that, his dreaming mind rationalized. It must have been. Jason had told him so.

It did not matter. He knew only a love so strong, that he had wanted to spend forever with her, and now, he was left with a longing that he could not suppress.

Broken love.

In dreams, he saw a woman screaming his name over and over. He could not see her face, or even her body, he only knew that it was his love screaming. Children pulled her away. Children, they had caused this pain for him, and for her, this awful suffering. He tried to reach out to destroy them, but couldn't. He was paralyzed, couldn't move.

His love sobbed as they pulled her away, sobbed as he saw her in another place, far away from here. He called for her, as he had been for years now, calling with his mind . . . come back to me . . . but he knew that the summons was more powerful in the night, and he stopped.

He tried to reach out to her, but he could not. She was just too far. Suddenly, he could not breathe, could not even take in the air to scream, and suddenly, as if she had whispered her presence into his mind, her name came to him.

A great rush of air filled his body, and suddenly, he shouted for her, "Julia!"

Jonathan woke; the sound closed in around him, the sound of her name filling his ears and mind. His hands were clenched tight onto the dagger he slept with for his own protection. Breathing heavily, he placed the dagger on the floor of the coffin, his hand brushing against the satin lining, as he reached up to rub his face. To his surprise, his face was damp with sweat. It dampened his hair, probably staining the pillow red.

Jonathan did not sweat often. Not when he was hot or cold, for he didn't feel temperature as humans do. He didn't need to sweat to cleanse his body's pores, for any dirt he acquired could simply be wiped away. No, like all others of his kind, Jonathan only sweat after consuming a gloat of blood, or during times of extreme danger. His dream had come to him as danger. Not for him, but for Julia.

For the woman who wore his chain.

Suddenly claustrophobic, Jonathan pushed the lid of the coffin back, climbed out, and rose to his feet, only to see Jason standing there beside him, watching him.

"Dreaming again, Jonathan." Jason said, stuffing his hands into his pockets. "If that girl returns here, I will kill her."

Jonathan said nothing as Jason walked away from him, out of the basement and into the upstairs rooms. What he remembered of the night this girl left was somewhat limited. The tranquilizers he had been given had affected his brain because he had not fed that night, or the previous night. Jason had chastised him for it a million times over. A vampire that does not feed is a weak vampire. Yes, Jonathan knew all that, already.

But Jason had told him the rest. After his lover had left him, Jason had grabbed Jonathan, and fled the area, up to one of Vermont's many rocky caves, where he had also succumbed to sleep. Sometime later, they had both awoken, hungry and angry, though Jonathan could not remember why.

Eventually, they had returned to the mansion, and there, the dreams had begun. He had called for this girl several times, but even though he was not sure if she had heard him, he was sure she was mortal.

He knew Jason hated this girl. He knew she had killed Devin. But Jonathan loved her. Could not live without her. And even though there was danger for her here, he swore he would protect her. And for some reason, tonight he was convinced that she was coming here, back to Vermont, to danger.

Julia closed the van door and went to help Christi. They had untied Julia's motorcycle, and were now trying to pull it out of the van without dropping it to the ground, or breaking anything (including their bones), in the process.

They finally got the Harley on the ground, as the sun hung on the horizon.

Julia locked up the van, and climbed onto the motorcycle, with Christi behind her. She started up the motor, and then, once again, she started up the mountain.

"Julia, what will we do once we get there?" Christi yelled to her.

"Hopefully, I'll find Jonathan, and after that, who knows what will happen?" Julia yelled back.

"Julia, I hate to admit this, but I'm scared!" Christi shouted, the wind half whipping her words away.

Julia nervously chuckled. "So am I!" she shouted. The girls said nothing more, until they reached their destination.

Julia pulled up the long dirt driveway that led to the mansion. She got off the bike and cut the motor, after Christi had gotten off.

Julia took in a long deep breath, and let it out again. She felt Christi do the same.

Night had come on the way up the hillside, and the darkness was all around them, except for the silver light of the moon, which draped around the old mansion, like a picture out of a ghost story. Except the mansion didn't look old anymore.

Ivy clung to the walls still, the way it had before, but the upstairs rooms had been finished, and so had the attic. There was even a small widow's walk on top. The chimneys had been re-done; the house appeared newly painted, with authentic colors of the Victorian time period.

The mansion was beautiful, but it loomed towards the girls, forbidden and terrifying, all the same.

"Come on." Julia whispered to Christi. Julia walked the bike halfway up the driveway, and then, pushed it off to the side, into the bushes and hedges that framed it. When Julia assumed it was safely hidden, she put the kickstand out, and turned to Christi.

"You stay here, right here. Don't move, don't make a noise. If something happens to me, don't even stir until the morning comes, got it? These guys are vampires, Christi. They could rip you to shreds. Will you stay put?"

Christi nodded her emerald eyes wide with nervousness. She watched Julia dart out of the bushes, and called her name.

"What?" Julia whispered.

"Be careful, Julia." Christi murmured.

Julia smiled. "I will." she said, and then she was gone, leaving Christi alone with nothing but the bike for company.

Julia silently walked around the edge of the driveway. There were only two motorcycles in the usual parking space. Julia knew the big black

Harley Davidson was Jonathan's. There was also a new bike parked there, a gray one. Julia didn't stop to examine it, but she did notice that Jason's motorcycle wasn't there. She didn't remember exactly what his bike looked like, only that it was also black, and a bit smaller than Jonathan's.

Julia crept around to the back of the house, where the forest began to close in on the mansion. There was nothing back there, but for a pit full of charred wood, with giant logs lying on the ground surrounding it.

She stared up at the house for a minute, gazing at the boarded up windows of the bedrooms. Back here, the windows were boarded from the outside; in the front they had been boarded from the inside.

Julia shrugged, and went up close to the house. If her memory served her correctly, there was a very small window that led out of the basement. Her hands touched the side of the building, brushing the wood. It wasn't long before she found what she had been looking for.

Julia set to work, pulling at the boards with her bare hands, trying not to make a noise. When she finally had the boards off, she knelt down, and took out her lighter, holding it in front of the window. A glass pane reflected the light. Julia sighed, another problem.

Lucky for her, the wood that had been holding the glass in place had rotted. It took only a few minutes to pull the glass free.

The opening was a tight squeeze, even for a girl Julia's size, but soon, she fell down onto the basement floor on her hands and knees, in the heavy dust that remained.

Julia choked down a cough and got up, rubbing her hands on her pants to rid them of the dust. She blinked her eyes and tried to adjust to the total black darkness of the basement, but it did no good. She went into her pocket, and once again pulled out the lighter.

A glimmer of light suddenly flared in the darkness, and Julia could see several shapes of things that were stacked down here. Julia lowered the lighter, and now could visualize the single, straight path that the boys had tracked through the dust.

Julia followed the trail in the dust to the hidden corner, and found the coffins.

Two, Andrew's and Devin's, had been pushed to the side, with sheets covering them. Jason's and Jonathan's remained in the same places she had seen them, that long ago day in August.

Julia moved closer to gleaming black one with the silver borders, the one she knew to be Jonathan's. As she knelt down beside it, she felt tears rise in her eyes. She turned off the lighter and held it in one hand, as she stretched her arms across the coffin, and placed a kiss on the lid.

"Oh, beloved, how it would be if I could just see you again." Julia said, placing her head on the coffin, embracing it. She didn't hear the silent figure dart up on her from behind.

"You!" a deep voice bellowed, "Who are you, what are you doing there!"

Julia gasped and jumped up, trying to run toward the window, not knowing who the man was, and not caring, intent on getting away, praying it wasn't Jason.

The figure caught Julia, spinning her around, and backing her up against the wall. She tried to scream, but his hand was on her mouth, his other hand holding her arms down. Julia couldn't see a thing in the basement, she couldn't even see the man before her; everything was black. She tried to get her hands free so she could use the lighter, but that he wouldn't allow.

"Somehow you found out about us, this place. You must die." he said.

Julia thrashed her head wildly, tears welling in her eyes. She thought, I don't want to die not when I'm so close, I have to see him, just have to, just once.

"Who do you want to see?" the voice questioned, taking his hand off her mouth, and placing it by her head.

"Jonathan," Julia whimpered, "I have to see Jonathan."

"Why do you have to see Jonathan? Who are you?"

"I have to see him because I love him," Julia whispered into the darkness, "I love him, and I traveled thousands of miles to see him. I'm Julia."

The man sounded as if he was going to say something, but his breath caught in his throat. Julia felt his hand touch her neck, but she didn't move; she was afraid to. Then, she felt him lift Jonathan's chain slightly, the back of his fingers resting on her neck.

"Why are you wearing my chain?" the voice said, still deep, but not so angry.

"Your chain?" Julia asked, feeling a rush of excitement hit her.

"Julia? Are you the Julia that I dreamed of?" he said, releasing her.

Julia switched on the lighter, and brought it between them. It was Jonathan, all right. He looked dazed, as if he couldn't decide what to do. Julia, astonished, whispered his name through her tears. She put the lighter in her pocket again, and leaned forward to him, crying against his shoulder. He didn't do anything to hold her, or comfort her. Julia drew back as if she had been struck.

"What is it?" she sobbed, "What's wrong?"

"I…I'm sorry, Julia. I can't remember anything about you."

"What?" Julia whispered, and then, "*What?* You loved me forever, for an eternal night, and you can't remember?"

"I'm sorry, Julia," he said.

"No!" she cried, and crumpled to the floor, sobbing.

Jonathan stood over her, watching her with his night-vision. The girl was crying harder now, than when he had first come upon her. He tried to think of what to do. Soon, he had an idea. He picked up Julia, who offered no resistance, climbed the stairs, and entered into the sitting room, where his own vampire child, Timothy, was waiting for him.

Timothy saw him carrying her, and walked quickly to Jonathan, asking him what exactly was going on.

"If this is really Julia, I'll find out tonight." Jonathan replied, glancing over at his first son.

Timothy had been seventeen at the time of his changing, a month ago. He had longish dark brown hair, which fell in curls, into his dark blue eyes. He was smaller then everyone else in the coven, probably about five foot four inches, two inches taller than Julia now was. Jonathan had found Timothy barely alive at the scene of an accident, where he had been thrown thirty feet from his motorcycle. Jonathan had cared for the boy instantly, and made him an immortal, out of sympathy.

"If they return, let me know, Timothy. I must take care of her."

Timothy nodded and watched, as Jonathan brought Julia into her old room.

Jonathan closed the door behind him. He walked to her bed, and placed her gently on it. Then, he lit a single candle on her bureau, and turned back to face her. She looked up at him through wide, tear-shot eyes, as he came down onto the bed next to her.

Jonathan ran a hand through his hair, and thought about what to say to her. She had stopped crying all together and was staring at him, her gaze not wavering, expecting...what could she be expecting? Does she really know me? These were his thoughts, as he tried to choose the words carefully.

"I have to find out if you are who you say you are. I have dreamed, and dreamed of a girl, Julia, and I didn't even know her name until tonight. I could not see what she looked like in my dream, I did not know. I knew she wore my chain, as do you, but that is not proof enough. I could read your thoughts, but you could have gained this information about her, elsewhere. There are things someone like that could not know; feelings, secret thoughts, desires. These things I cannot read in thoughts. Only . . . "

Jonathan's voice wavered. How could he tell her? How could he make her understand?

"Do it." Julia whispered.

"What?" he said, moving closer to her side.

Julia sat up now, her mind only on what she wanted him to do. She wanted him to love her, more then anything in the world. "Do it, Jonathan. You must take my blood. It will show you the way, show you who I am. I love you, and this is my final sacrifice." With that, she removed her leather jacket, and let it fall to the floor. She exposed her tender arms, neck, shoulders, and stomach to the cold winter air, and to him.

"Do it." she said, and lay back down, onto the pillow.

Jonathan watched her lay down, the way her hair spilled around her like a halo in the dim candle light, the way her chest rose and fell with every heartbeat. He touched her cheek gently with his hand, and sighed.

Jonathan climbed up on top of her, feeling her legs adjust to his, her hot little hands slide up under his jacket along the flesh of his back. He looked into her eyes again, which were now filled with emotion.

"Do it." she whispered once more, as she looked into his beautiful dark eyes.

"Don't watch." he told her, and closed her eyes with his fingertips.

Julia felt one of his arms slide under the back of her neck, tilting her head a little, and his other arm move beneath her back; he pulled her slightly upwards. She felt him kiss her neck once, right on the vein, and she felt a chill run through her. Julia would finally know what it felt like, after all the years of only guessing to write it down in her books. Now she would be the vampire's victim, for real.

Julia sucked in her breath, as she felt him tense up under her hands. All his muscles had responded at the same time, and now his body was in a deadlock, completely ridged, and hard. She felt, and heard, his breath coming in irregular bursts.

"Just lie still beneath me." he said, his voice strangely contorted and harsh, "It will hurt you for a moment, but then you won't feel anything."

"Yes . . . " Julia sighed. Her body tensed, as she felt his jagged breath against her throat, every cell in her brain was screaming at her to run, but she did not move. As his lips touched her skin again in a form of a kiss, her body shook with revulsion. She felt his lips parting, his mouth so close to her raised neck, she could just barely feel it; she made a small sound of fright.

It seemed to hang that way for a long instant, him just next to her neck, when he let out a low growl, one that sounded like an angry animal. Then his fangs tore into her neck, and she moaned with the pain of it. It felt as if someone had dug two very sharp, and small, daggers into her neck.

Her brain told her to try to get away from him, but she didn't. Julia pushed herself upwards, her right hand leaving his back to push against his head, his fangs going deeper into her neck. She moaned again with the pain, but did not let go of him. She wanted this.

She felt Jonathan push down on her hard, sinking her into the mattress of the bed, and she wrapped her legs around him, her right hand pushing his fangs even deeper, so that she felt his mouth whole onto her skin, the fangs deep inside her, tearing, hurting terribly.

But Julia wanted this, and at this very instant, she knew that she had always wanted it, always to be the victim, to be loving every minute of the terrible pain, as if her whole life was for just this minute with Jonathan. Julia's thoughts were of this, as she sank into unconsciousness from the loss of her blood. Her hands and legs eventually fell away from him as he drank.

Jonathan had felt Julia pushing against him, drawing him into her even when it was hurting her, and he had wanted to go deeper and they had been like animals, together.

Together.

That was the perfect word for what they were now. Jonathan still existed as the beast on Julia, still greedily drinking her blood, even now when she had passed out. But he had wanted to be connected to her since the first time he had ever seen her, and with her blood pouring into him, he now knew it was Julia.

"Julia," he whispered into her bloodied skin, knowing it was his lover. As he drank her blood, her life, he began to read deeply, into the memories of her mind.

Jonathan felt her longing for him over the years they had been apart, he felt how she had been weeping for him, on that terrible night, when she had been snatched away from him. He saw them together on the couch the night when she had come to him, afraid to go home to Connecticut. He saw her memories of the time her father had left, and felt how angry she had been. He saw her in the seventh grade with her first boyfriend, the kid from down the street, and felt her first kiss. He saw Julia as a nine-year-old on a picnic with her family for a reunion. He saw her as a five-year-old child, sitting on a swing with her father pushing her, and he saw her as a three-year-old baby in a sandbox, flinging sand into the air, laughing, and laughing. Then, there was blackness.

Jonathan lifted up from her neck, and pressed his head against her heart. Just a small fluttering of a pulse remained. He looked up at her face.

His eyesight focused and cleared, the red haze fading away. Julia appeared deathly pale, her lips bluish. She was dying. Jonathan had seen the death look on his victims before. He had drunk too much, far too much. He knew that she would die.

"No," he whispered, looking down at her. "No!" he yelled. Julia was finally here, finally with him, he couldn't let her die, he couldn't!

Jonathan climbed off her, and gathered her into his arms. Julia's head was thrown back, she wasn't moving, wasn't breathing. From the wound in her neck, a little blood still trickled; two small puncture marks with a ring of red around them, from his mouth.

"Julia." he whispered. What was it she had said? Her final sacrifice? No, it couldn't be her final sacrifice! She was too young, too beautiful to die! There was only one way for her to live, he knew. To give her his blood, make her like him, like Timothy, like the others.

Jonathan shrugged his jacket off, first one arm holding her and then the next. He paused for a moment, debating what should be done, but no, "Julia, this is *my* sacrifice."

He reached back to his neck, and slashed it with his fingernails, forcing the blood up to the surface. It ran down his chest; a drop fell into Julia's mouth as he held her close to him.

With a shudder, her breath slowly returned, however, her lips remained blue.

"Julia, Julia." he called, slightly shaking her.

Julia moaned.

"Drink, you must drink. You will die if you don't."

"No Jon, not again, please don't." she whispered, her eyes still tightly shut.

"Do it now, or you'll die!"

Julia didn't answer. She began to slip away again.

Jonathan lifted her body, and brought her head to the wound in his neck, pressing her there; the blood ran into her mouth.

Julia's body trembled as she began to breathe, and she swallowed down the blood that was filling her mouth. Julia tasted the blood after the first mouthful. It was burning on her tongue, and tasted of a million souls sighing at once; stinging in her mouth. At the second mouthful, Julia's eyes opened, but she shut them quickly and reached up, grabbing Jonathan's back with both arms, for the blood was running into her at a steady pace now. It was better then anything she had ever tasted in her life. It was hot salty paradise, which claimed her soul in that instant.

Julia latched onto Jonathan harder, feeling the blood rushing into her in tremendous burning mouthfuls, and she was sucking at it so hard, that it hit the back of her throat and clogged her nostrils. But she wanted it now, yes, wanted it, and she clutched him to her even harder then before, sucking on his neck with more and more strength, crushing him to her.

The blood was heaven on earth, burning, but filling her with more life then she ever had, filling all the empty places in her soul, and Jonathan was inside her finally, totally, and forever. But all this wasn't enough. Every gulp she took left her more thirsty and hungrier then the last, and she bit into his skin, trying desperately to bring more to the surface.

She knelt before him on the edge of the bed, pulling him to herself, as if she were trying to devour him.

Jonathan held her as she pulled harder and harder upon him, taking more and more blood, and he knew he was transforming her. Suddenly a sharp pain whiplashed up his spine, and blinded him. His head began to swim, as his veins cried out to him to stop. Julia was taking in too much, too fast. He tried to pull away, but she wouldn't let go.

"Let go!" he yelled, and shoved her off him.

Julia fell, with a thud, to the ground. For a second, she could only stare up at him, like an innocent child. Then, as she looked at him, her hand went up to the place on her neck where he had drunk from her, and found the wound gone. Her tongue darted over her lips, licking some of his blood into her mouth.

"The souls." she whispered, wiping the blood off her mouth with the back of her hand. Only then did she look away from Jonathan, and notice the blood stain adorning her hand. She seemed to break from the daze then, and realize just what it was that had happened, and what she had done.

Julia stared at her hand with her mouth open, on her face a look of perfect horror, and she moaned, "Oh no! Not again!"

5

"*No!*" Julia moaned turmoil began inside her, inside her stomach. She fought the feelings, fought them hard. She remembered too clearly, what had happened three and a half years ago, and that she never had wanted it again.

Julia lay there on the floor, her head thrown back, her hands on her stomach, as she felt the heat begin inside her. The blood invaded her stomach now, creating a hot, burning sensation in there.

"I have to fight it." she whispered, more to herself as reassurance, than to Jon as an objection.

As she tried not to succumb to the feelings, which wanted to push her into a deep sleep, she was vaguely aware of Jonathan sitting beside her, his hand over hers. Julia finally gave up the fight, as she felt heat spreading itself over her body. She relaxed, her hands slipping away from her body to the floor, and let the heat consume her.

Before Julia gave herself over to sleep, she felt the soft bed underneath her, and realized that Jonathan had placed her there. He climbed up on the bed, beside her, one arm thrown protectively around her, the other propping his head up. He watched Julia slip away, not worried this time, for her body had known vampire blood before. Perhaps this time, she would give in more quickly.

Christi hid in the bushes by Julia's Harley, when she heard a deafening roar. Three men on motorcycles had pulled into the driveway. She ducked low, peeking through the evergreen shrubs to see the men more clearly. One of them wore nothing but black, carrot-colored hair streaking down his shoulders; he must be Jason, the one Julia had told her about.

There were two others accompanying him. Christi heard Jason call one of them Steven, told him not to get off his bike, go get a pizza.

Steven wore shoulder length brown hair, took in the world around him with hazel eyes. He looked fairly tall and definitely High School age. His clothing consisted mainly of boots, worn-out looking blue jeans, a black tee shirt, and a blue jean jacket. He nodded to Jason, gunned the motor of his bike, and left.

Jason called to the other one, Sabastian, "Come into the mansion."

Sabastian wore a thick mane of longish thick blond hair. He looked perhaps eighteen years old, clothed himself in boots, tight black jeans, a black net-shirt, and light blue jean jacket, adorned with band logos and safety pins. On his hands was a pair of leather gloves, and around his neck was a chain with a silver medallion hanging off it.

Sabastian and Jason had stood their bikes next to the others, cutting the motors. In the light emanating from the mansion, Christi could make them out clearly. Sabastian stood beside Jason now, and she could see that he was definitely the shortest of the pair.

"Jason, where's Lizzi and Cory?" Sabastian asked.

"They'll return soon, I'm sure," said Jason.

As they stood there talking, Christi gazed at Sabastian, drinking in his beauty. She was becoming mesmerized with him, never once guessing that it was the nature of his beast to attract the opposite sex. He seemed to her beautiful, and she sighed, "Sabastian."

Instantly, Sabastian looked in the direction of where she was sitting, breaking off his conversation with Jason. "Who said that?" Sabastian said.

Christi's eyes widened, and she covered her mouth to keep from gasping. She suddenly remembered what Julia had told her; vampires felt the instant someone said their name. This made them feel vulnerable and insecure inside, like an animal when it knows it's being followed.

"Who said what?" Jason said, his face also turning in her direction.

"My name, someone said my name." Sabastian insisted.

Jason looked around, but couldn't find anything, and didn't care, from the looks of it. "There's no one here, Sabastian. I have things to do. Let's go inside."

"You go ahead. I wanna look around, make sure."

Jason shrugged, walked up the stairs to the mansion, opened the huge doors, and went inside.

Christi crouched down and hid her face in her hands. She knew that they were vampires, killers. She knew Julia had instructed her to stay put. Christi was afraid; she wanted to get out of this place. Calming slightly, she decided to find Julia, and leave.

Christi stood, peeked through the bushes. Seeing no one, she began to walk through the bushes, when a hand clamped down on her mouth, and an arm around her waist, from behind. Christi knew the person holding her was Sabastian. She struggled and kicked at him, but didn't get free, until she bit his hand hard.

Christi crashed through the bushes and weeds, trying to get away from him. Suddenly, the bushes gave way to a path, and she ran down it as fast as her legs could carry her. What Christi didn't realize was that Sabastian knew where the path led to, and he was already there, having flown the short distance. He was ready to catch her, as she came running down the path, into the field.

Christi only saw him out of the corner of her eye; Sabastian standing with his arms outstretched, waiting for her. She made no sound as she slammed into him, and shoved him down. He fell backwards, and she tried to jump over him, but her timing seemed all wrong. Sabastian caught her left ankle, and Christi went down face first onto the cold, frozen ground. She squirmed onto her back, just as his weight came down above her, and he forced her arms above her head, grinning down at her.

Christi's eyes were wide with terror. She couldn't scream, couldn't move. She was paralyzed with fright, but something completely out of place clicked in her mind, the minute his grin turned into a wild smile.

Sabastian was gorgeous! The way he smiled with his beautiful mouth, the puppy-dog brown of his eyes, blending perfectly with his blond hair. Christi was attracted to him, immediately.

"Well, well. What a pretty little lady I found." he said, obviously amused with the whole thing. "Why don't you tell me why you were spying on us? Before I kill you, that is."

Christi said nothing.

Sabastian laughed. "You're going to make this hard for me, ain't ya?" he said now pressing harder against her.

"Get the hell off me," she squirmed, trying to get away from him, trying to ignore her body's reaction to his.

Sabastian laughed again, and let go of one of her hands to push his bangs out of his face. Christi took advantage of this, and slapped him with her free hand across his face.

For a moment everything was silent. Sabastian looked stunned. Christi drew back to slap him again, but this time he caught her hand, and forced it back down.

"Oh, so the pretty little lady's a wildcat too, huh?" he said, drawing closer to her again.

Christi shut her eyes and held her breath, waiting for the pain of his teeth in her neck, but instead felt the pressure of his lips on hers.

She opened her eyes to see Sabastian laughing again. "What was that for? I thought . . . "

"You thought I was going to kill ya, right?" he said.

"Yes,"

"Now why would I do a darn thing like that, to someone as beautiful as you?" he asked, helping her up, "Besides, killing trespassers ain't my department, it's Jason's decision. What's your name, darlin'?"

"It's Christi. Let go of my hands, Sabastian, come on."

"Nope, can't do that. Not until Jason sees you." He rose and started walking, pulling her along behind him

"Not Jason! No!" Christi moaned, remembering all Julia had told her, digging her heels into the ground as protest, however futile it might be.

Sabastian pulled her to him in one swift motion held her close. "Yes." he said.

Julia awoke with a start, and sat up. She stared at the canopy of the bed for a moment, until her eyes drifted to a lit candle. And then, she remembered where she was, and what had happened.

Julia touched her neck where Jon had drunk from her, but found the wounds gone. She licked her lips again, and tasted the saltiness there. She looked at her hand, the one she had wiped her mouth with, and gazed at the dried blood there. She whimpered a little, as she scraped off the blood with her fingernails, until her hands were immaculate.

Julia felt Jonathan's hand come to rest against her shoulder, and she heard him say, "Are you alright?" His voice was deep, mesmerizing.

"Yes, I think so." Julia softly replied. She turned, and looked at him. He was laying with one hand holding his head up, the other on her bare shoulder. She gazed at how his long, dark hair fell around his shoulder, down across his chest.

Julia lay back down against the pillows. She looked into Jonathan's eyes, the eyes that had penetrated her every dream. She took in his mouth, the softness of his lips, the soft boyish dusting of a beard and mustache on his face. He was watching her with a look of amusement, as if he was waiting to see what she would do next. But Julia knew what she wanted to do; she wanted to kiss him. Julia blushed, and turned away from him. As soon as she felt his hand drop, she felt stupid. She couldn't figure out why she was acting this way, it was only Jonathan. But then she realized it probably was due to the fact she hadn't seen him, for so very long.

"How long until I feel...pain?" she asked.

"Tomorrow night." he said, pulling her to him, "I'm sorry, this is all my fault. I should have known who you were, I should have trusted you."

"Jonathan, it's not your fault. Don't be silly. I told you to do it," Julia's voice trailed off. Jonathan's forehead rested against hers; he was watching her lips.

Jonathan raised his hand and traced her collarbone, up her neck, until he gently pushed his fingers into her hair. "My Julia." he whispered.

Julia watched, fascinated, as he kissed her, once, softly. Julia felt her body ignite, but he pulled back, his hand on her shoulder again.

"Jonathan, I'm not a girl anymore! I love you, and I want you! Kiss me like you mean it, and do it now!" Julia protested. This surprised him, and for a moment he couldn't do anything.

Julia grabbed him by the back of his neck, and pulled him to her. She kissed him hard, with urgency, and he immediately responded, kissing her back with the same passion, and strength. Julia sunk down onto the bed, pulling him with her, her hands sliding over his body, her mouth hungrily devouring his. When they finally slowed down, Jonathan pulled up from her slightly, and looked down at her. He smiled a wicked grin, and said, "You grew up."

Suddenly, the door was thrown open, and Timothy rushed in. Jonathan sighed, and sat up on the bed, pulling Julia with him. "What, Timothy?" he asked a little impatiently.

"Sorry, Jon, but they're back. And they have a girl with them!" Just as suddenly as he had appeared, he was gone.

Julia gasped and covered her mouth. "Christi," she whispered. She came down off the bed, grabbed her jacket from the floor, and pulled it on. She then reached down and picked up Jonathan's, passing it to him. "We've got to help her."

Julia walked to the door, and opened it a tiny crack, shut it quickly. She spun, grabbed at Jonathan's arms. "Jonathan, Jason's out there. You know what he thinks about me. If I go out there, he'll kill me! What will I do?"

Jonathan smiled. "Julia, there's nothing to be afraid of, now. Don't worry about anything he might say to you. You are mine now," he said, stroking her hair, "my child. He can't hurt you without going through me, first. He can't; I won't let him. Come on now." he said, taking her hand. "Don't be afraid."

Julia nodded, tucked her hair behind her ear. Just as someone called out that the food had arrived, Julia and Jonathan walked across the room, and opened the door. She felt the icy rage in Jason's eyes, as he turned to observe her entrance into the sitting room, his eyes fixed upon Jonathan's chain. His words sent chills up her spine.

"Well, well, Julia Anderson. Welcome home."

6

As Julia stared at Jason, she began to notice the change in the atmosphere, how everyone gathered in the room now stared at her, silently. She felt extremely uncomfortable suddenly, desperate to back out of the room, to not face Jason. She ignored these feelings inside her, and took a deep breath.

"Jason," she said, her tone laced with sarcasm, "You haven't changed."

He hadn't, actually. He was dressed the same way, and sitting there, in his chair, he looked like a nightmare. As Julia spoke, Jason's eyes narrowed; she felt Jonathan squeeze her hand.

"You *are* playing with fire, Miss Anderson. You know Sabastian has your dearest friend, Christi. He's in an upstairs room with her right now. What he does with her is none of my business, unless," Jason trailed off, smiled at Julia.

Jason turned, and spoke to a young man, whom Julia did not recognize. "Steven," he said, "go into the cupboard there." He pointed at a cupboard, which stood just to the right of the old grandfather clock. Julia didn't remember it having been there before.

Steven opened the cupboard, and inside Julia could see china plates, a box of silverware, tea-cups, mugs, and crystal glasses. There was also a bottle of Vodka, along with dusty old wine bottle, which Julia was sure that Jason had wanted

"Steven, get me the old wine there, yes, that's it, and a glass. Good." Jason said when Steven brought the items over to him. "You know what's in here, don't you girl?"

Julia nodded, but was confused. Why didn't he sense Jonathan's blood within her? The answer came to her soon enough. It was too early. Her blood was mostly human now, only a small portion vampiric. As the hours passed, Jonathan's blood would transform her more, and more.

Julia took a deep breath, as she watched Jason pour the blood-wine into a glass. She watched him raise it to his lips, and sip it.

Jason stood and walked to Julia, standing in front of her, towering over her. He looked at Julia's hand interlocked with Jonathan's, and glared at him.

Julia felt Jon let go, and take a step back. She glared up at Jason, who was grinning at her like a wicked boy, about to pull off a terrific trick. As he stared down at her, his orange hair shadowed his face. Julia stood her ground, watching, waiting.

Suddenly, Jason's grin disappeared, and his face became hard.

"I despise you." he hissed at her. "You killed my Devin, my son, my first-born. I despise you for that. You are a young woman now; perhaps you can understand these things better. I would kill you now, but no. I would not give Jonathan that pain. What I give you now is not immortal life, but immortal death. A life forever to live with me, in eternal hell. And do you know why?" he asked, his voice raising, "Do you know why, Julia? So when you are fully like me, and create a child of your own, I will show you the pain of losing it! *Now, drink!*" Jason yelled, and shoved the glass into her hand.

Julia looked down at the crystal glass in her hand, stunned. He really didn't know! She smiled at him, and raised the glass, as if in a salute. She then turned it upside down, pouring all the liquid onto the floor. The glass fell free of her hand, and dropped to the floor, smashing at Jason's feet.

"It's too late." Julia softly. "And I will never be like you."

Jason looked for a moment as if he was about to explode, but all the anger drained out of his face after she had spoken. "What do you mean, 'it's too late'?" he asked.

"I belong to him!" Julia said triumphantly, drawing back Jonathan's hair to reveal three angry red marks, lying against his throat. With a flustered expression, Jason backed away from Julia, moving towards the stairway. He placed his hand upon the polished railing, and for a second looked as if he were concentrating heavily. Then, rage came into his face, and he turned to look up the stairs. "Kill her!" he shouted.

"No!" Julia screamed, and ran to the stairway. Four steps up, Jason grabbed onto her leg, and she reacted instinctively, kicked him in the face. She leapt to the top of the stairs. A long hallway proceeded it, and she didn't know what door Christi, and Sabastian, was behind. She opened three doors, and no Christi.

Suddenly Julia heard a scream, and then a crash. She headed towards that room.

Christi had been trapped in the room with Sabastian, for quite a while now. He didn't speak to her, but sat on the bed, watching. Christi remained in the corner, head down, and legs pulled up to her chest.

When they had first come into the mansion, the judgment with Jason had been bad enough. Jason seemed to know exactly who Julia was, and that she was there, accompanying Christi.

"Take her upstairs into your room." Jason had told Sabastian, "Wait for my instructions once you get there."

Sabastian had forced her up the stairs, down the hall, and into one of the rooms. When he had first locked the door and let go, Christi had darted about, trying desperately to find a way out, to no avail. The two big windows were boarded from the inside; the only other door was to a closet that held his coffin.

This was Sabastian's room, and he alone held the key to the door. He had told her that if she wanted it, she'd have to come and get it. Then Christi had sunk, terrified, to the ground. There was no way out of this room now, and she knew it.

Christi looked up slowly at Sabastian. He wasn't looking at her any longer, but had turned away from her, and was now studying the curves and patterns of the woodwork, along his bedpost.

As Christi looked at him, she felt attraction, not unlike that which had pulled on her outside, in the field. Only now, it seemed stronger, much stronger.

Christi's eyes traveled slowly up his form, her eyes settled on his lips. They were just a little too red for his pale complexion, but even so, they appealed to her greatly, and she found herself drawn to him more then before. She wanted nothing more, than to kiss him.

Christi slowly rose to her feet, and for a moment, simply stood there. Sabastian had a kerosene lamp lit in the room; it made it easy for her to watch him, and as she did so, his eyelids half shut.

Christi slowly and carefully walked to the edge of the bed, reached out and touched the bedspread with one of her hands. From here, she could see his eyes better. Yes, his eyes were half closed, and glazed over. He looked as if his mind were far away. Christi walked to the side of the bed, he still did nothing.

Christi swallowed hard. What am I doing? Put the moves on a vampire? That's crazy! She wrung her hands together. But she couldn't deny that she was drawn to him, irresistibly.

Christi crawled onto the bed, until she came to lie next to him. She felt extremely unsure of herself; he was un-dead, un-trusted. She couldn't even explain exactly why she was doing it, but Christi, like Julia, decided to trust in her feelings, no matter what would happen to her.

Christi relaxed against the pillows, and slowly raised her hand close to his head. Biting on her lower lip, she gently touched his hair. "Sabastian." she whispered.

Sabastian turned quickly, his eyes wide, in utter confusion. He was apparently flustered, and his pride was a little hurt. She was brave; he'd give her that. Christi's left hand was resting on his cheek. He just stared at her for a moment, into her emerald eyes. "I thought you were afraid," he said softly.

Christi nodded slowly. She couldn't move for a moment, and then she felt his right hand come up on her left. "You're different then the other chicks I kill. You're stronger, braver." Sabastian said, and flashed her a wicked grin.

Christi was startled by his smile, and lost her nerve. She started to back off the bed, but before she could, Sabastian caught her, brought her next to him.

"At least try not to see me so intimidating, darlin'. I will do what I'm told, but if it were up to me, I'd give ya a chance." he said.

"A chance to what?" Christi asked.

"A chance . . . " Sabastian repeated, and kissed her. It surprised her slightly, not that he in fact was kissing her, but that she was now kissing him back.

Sabastian felt warmth pass through him and it was gentle, like a summer breeze. There was something special about this girl. No one had to tell him. Christi was different, and he knew it.

Christi sank down on the bed, as he leaned over her. She opened her mouth to speak, but he placed a finger over her mouth to quiet her. He traced her lips with his fingertips, and she closed her eyes. Her head was spinning with desire, trust, distrust, and fear. She wondered if this had been the way for Julia, and Jonathan. But somehow, nothing else in the world seemed to matter any longer; she was falling for this being.

Christi's heart raced as she felt his hair brush her cheek, his lips brushing by hers just as softly.

"I'm evil, Christi. I might have to kill you, but I'm beginning to doubt that I should." Sabastian said, holding tightly onto her, bringing her closer, to rest against him. Christi began to feel more comfortable than frightened, but the fragile peace did not last long. A terrifying voice pierced the tranquility of the room. It was Jason.

"Kill her!"

"Don't. Sabastian, don't listen to him, please?" Christi whispered. She hoped against hope for a moment, that he would not harm her. But then she felt his body become ridged, and his breathing become heavy. As he turned towards her, she gasped. Sabastian's face was rimmed with sweat, his eyes were red, and his opened mouth revealed two sharp fang teeth.

Christi squirmed away from him, knocking over a coffee table, and a vase of flowers, as she went. It fell, with a crash, to the ground.

Christi leapt across the room, away from him, backed up against the wall. "No, stay back." she said. She watched as he crept up from the bed, coming towards her. He looked like an animal, ready to pounce.

"Christi!" a voice shouted from the door. It was Julia! The door shook and rattled, but Julia could not seem to gain entrance.

Suddenly, Sabastian had appeared before her, holding her arms down, pressing against her. "I'm sorry," he whispered harshly, "but I must do as he tells me, he made me."

"Sabastian, don't do this to me, please." Christi cried. She saw nothing but those red eyes, gazing at her neck. Christi heard nothing but the hammering outside, as Julia threw her body at the door. Sabastian's head was slowly lowering.

"Julia, help me!" Christi shrieked.

"Christi! Fight him!" Julia shouted. *Thud. Thud. Thud.*

Christi twisted her wrists free and tried to hit him, but he twisted her arms behind her back, painfully. Sabastian bent over her, and sank his teeth into her neck. She screamed, but the pain faded quickly as her lifeblood flooded, free. She didn't even feel it when Sabastian laid her down, and began to drink.

Julia, hearing the silence from the room, threw herself at the door once more. The door gave and the lock broke. Julia rushed in. There was Sabastian drinking Christi's blood; his body arched like one of the vampire bats she had seen in an encyclopedia, as it drank from a dish full of blood.

"No!" she yelled, and kicked Sabastian in the side, hard. He rolled off Christi and growled, leaving the girl in a puddle of blood, quickly spreading on the hardwood floor.

Julia's courage began to fade slightly as Sabastian stood, and started towards her. She had backed almost to the door, when she ran into something behind her. She turned to see Jonathan standing there, glaring at

Sabastian. Sabastian glared back. They just stood there, like two soldiers at attention, and Julia realized that now was her time to move.

Julia fell to her knees beside her friend, the pool of blood next to her still growing larger, the blood still leaking from the wounds. Julia pulled Christi's jacket off, tugged the sweatshirt upward to the wounds in an attempt to stop the bleeding.

"I can't stop it!" she yelled, "Christi's a bleeder, a hemophiliac! Jonathan?" Julia said as she turned back to see Sabastian sitting on the floor, normal, staring at Jonathan, who was holding his shoulders. Jonathan looked up as she called him. "Jonathan, you have to stop this bleeding, she'll die." she said.

Jonathan walked over to her, looked down at Christi. "Move her clothes away from the wound." he said, kneeling down next to Julia.

Julia did as he said, and watched as he made a small cut in the palm of his right hand, with the nails of his left. He than closed his bleeding hand over the wound in Christi's neck, and held it there. When he drew his hand up, she could see that the wound on Christi's neck had closed, with only bloodstains left to prove that she had been bitten.

Julia then watched, amazed, as the blood stopped flowing from Jonathan's hand, dried up, and crumbled off in flakes, leaving only a red mark. "Wow." she whispered.

Julia turned her attention back to Christi. The girl had gone unconscious. "I need to bring her downstairs." Julia looked up, and saw Jonathan standing, looking towards the doorway, very still.

Julia turned, beheld Jason there; beside him was Steven and Timothy. Jason seemed focused on Sabastian, who was sitting, hunched over, his face in his hands.

Jason glared at Jonathan, Christi, and then Sabastian once more. "Look at me, traitor." Sabastian didn't move. "Look at me!" Jason hissed. Sabastian did nothing.

Jason growled, and yanked Sabastian's head up by his hair. Sabastian didn't say a word, just winced. Jason pulled the medallion over Sabastian's head, and glared at him, until he looked away again.

Jason walked to Jonathan then, and placed the medallion in his hand. "He's no longer my concern. He wants to listen to you, that's fine. I hereby give him to you."

Jason walked out of the room, Steven behind him. Timothy looked questioningly at Jonathan for a moment. "Go." Jon said, and Timothy left.

"Jonathan, please bring her to my room downstairs, please?" Julia asked him.

Jonathan nodded, but first he put the medallion back around Sabastian's neck, accepting him, without the use of words, as his own. "Julia," he said, "you can put her in one of the rooms downstairs, the one that's next to yours." *There is a door in your closet that will enable you to enter.*

"Why not just use the actual door?" she asked, after he had lifted Christi in his arms, walked out of the room.

"I'll give you the key, for safety's sake," he said, nodding back to Sabastian.

"Oh." Julia replied. As they walked down the stairs, she could not help but overhear the sound of three motorcycles pulling away.

"Is it comfortable in that room?" Julia asked him, as he shifted Christi to get a better grip on her.

"Yes. There's a bed in there and everything, it just needs a little furnishing, that's all." he said.

Julia thought for a moment about Christi, and then her thoughts shifted to Sabastian. What if…could it be possible he felt something for Christi? "Jonathan, go ahead. I want to check on Sabastian."

"Alright." Jon said with a sigh, perhaps in a way stressed, with the burden of all the new responsibility, which had fallen on his shoulders, tonight.

Julia made herself smile as she reentered Sabastian's room, noticing that he had remained on the floor. "Sabastian." she called.

Sabastian raised his head, his eyes wide. He had not felt her approach this time, as a human. Now it seemed, he felt the mixture. She was becoming half-vampire. "Who are you?" he whispered.

"I'm Julia. Don't be frightened. Look, I've come to odds with Jason before. I was his child once, and he tried to kill me. Believe me, it's better this way. Jonathan's really special."

"You love him, don't ya?" he asked.

Julia smiled, "Yes. Do you love Christi?" She waited for his answer, but he didn't have one. He just sat there, staring at her.

Julia, he was thinking, Julia, Jonathan's Julia, the woman of his dreams. She's right, I don't have to be afraid anymore. Jonathan is better. Sabastian sighed.

Julia stretched out her arm to touch him, but he shrank back from her, although the light from the lamp showed no change in his facial expression.

"I'm sorry for what happened to you tonight, it was my fault." she said, "If you need someone to talk to, I'll be here."

Sabastian nodded, and Julia left him. She went downstairs, and told Jonathan that she had to bring back her van. He nodded, told her to go.

Julia glanced at the grandfather clock on her way out the door. It was midnight.

Julia pulled her Harley out from the bushes and into the driveway, and put out the kickstand. She decided not to use the bike for transportation; she'd rather walk.

Julia walked down the hillside with her hands in her pockets, thinking of all that had happened this night. She hadn't expected it to go this way, and now that it had, a little part of her was nagging that she shouldn't have come. She was sure that Jonathan wouldn't let her get out of being a true vampire, this time. And even more then that, there was the matter of Christi to attend to. What had happened between Christi and Sabastian, if anything at all, was Julia's fault. And now, she didn't even know if Christi had lost too much blood or not. Julia shook her head, and sighed. She'd just have to take things one step at a time.

Julia finally got to the van, and brought it back to the mansion. She parked it a little further down the driveway from the motorcycles. The first thing she removed was the cooler.

Julia brought the cooler into her room, set it down beside the closet. Then, being curious, she felt around for the trap door. Her fingers touched a small square shape, about four feet high, and three feet wide. There was no doorknob. She felt around the sides of the door, and found a small indenture above the top. Julia pressed on it.

The small door swung away from her, and she stepped through it, finding herself in yet another closet. Julia opened the closet, stepped into the room. It was basically like Julia's, except Jonathan was right. It did need furnishing.

There was a small pine-colored desk and chair, a cushioned gold chair, which Jonathan was sitting on, a plain bed with pine-colored bedposts and brown bed covers, which Christi was lying on, and a small pine-colored coffee table. On the coffee table was a porcelain washbasin, a towel and pitcher. Julia went to look inside the pitcher, which was filled water in it.

"Where did you get these?" Julia asked Jonathan.

He didn't answer.

Julia gazed across the room at the fireplace. It was lit, and made of bricks. Above the mantle was a painting. The painting took place at night of a group of deer in the moonlight. Julia now remembered that she had seen several of these paintings. A few were in the sitting room, some upstairs. The paintings were all dark. Flowers, trees, sky tones, never the sun.

"Who painted these?" she asked Jonathan, pointing to the painting.

"Jason painted them." Jonathan replied.

"Was he an artist when he was alive?"

"No, I don't think so. He was looking at an artist's book at the mall one night, and said, 'That's simple art. I could do better then that.' The next night he started painting."

"Oh." Julia said, and went back over to Christi's side. Her jacket rested on the foot of the bed, and although she remained asleep, her breathing was normal.

She'll be all right in a few days.

"Jonathan, would you help me unload the van?" she asked him.

"Yes." he said, and opened Christi's door. Together they pulled the suitcases from the van, placing Julia's in her room; Christi's in hers. They decided to leave the mattress and sheets behind.

Later that night, Jonathan and Julia sat together on the sofa in the sitting room. Jonathan told her then, that there were two other vampires staying with them, besides those whom she knew now.

"Who?" Julia asked.

"Well, I'll tell you, and then Sabastian and I must leave. I have to meet Jason and the others at the park by two, in order to meet Cory and Lizzi."

Julia looked up at the clock. It was 1:30. "Who are they?" she asked, now genuinely interested.

"Cory is Jason's brother, more or less. He's from Paris, as Jason was. Cory's vampiric father was also Jason's. Cory has been visiting off and on here for as long as I can remember. But he's very…"

"Very what?" Julia asked.

"Very moody." Jonathan said, nodding. "Sometimes he is generous, sometimes not. But Julia, there's something you should know about him. He is a remorseless killer. He has no qualms about taking any kind of life, human, immortal, or otherwise. He takes what he wants, and usually gets it without a fight. Be careful around him. Promise me."

"Oh, Jonathan, of course I'll be careful, I promise, girl scouts honor." she said, holding up her hand, giggling. Jonathan frowned, and she covered her mouth with her hand, trying not to laugh. "OK, you win. I won't even look twice at him. Are you happy?" she asked when she was in control of her laughter.

"Yes, I guess so." he said with a sigh.

"Well, who's this Lizzi?" Julia asked.

"Before Cory was made a vampire, he was twenty five years old, and his wife had just died, leaving his real daughter, Elizabette, an infant. Cory brought Elizabette to his sister, and left her to raise the child on her own. Cory was planning to skip town then, when a group of hijackers overran him, took his money, and beat him, leaving him for dead. Then Jason's father had seen him, felt sympathy for him, and the evil beauty that Cory held as a mortal enthralled him. He made Cory a vampire. Thirteen years later, Cory heard that his sister had died, leaving Lizzi all alone with no other living relatives, and no money. Lizzi had become a prostitute. Cory went to her, and revealed to her the secrets of his life. Lizzi knew, of course, that he was telling the truth about all that happened, for she had seen etchings of Cory when he had supposedly disappeared, and they looked exactly like he did when he went to her. Lizzi agreed to go with him, and Cory had his maker endow her with the blood. So now they are forever father and daughter in the mortal sense, brother and sister in the immortal sense."

Julia let out a deep breath when Jonathan finished his story. "Wow." she said.

There was a movement on the stairs, and Sabastian came down, rubbing his eyes. He looked as if he had been crying.

"Jonathan, we have to go now." he said, standing next to the door, waiting.

"Good night, Julia." he said, kissing her forehead. He then stood up, and walked out the doors, followed by Sabastian, who shut them.

Julia stood, and began to roam silently over the rooms, looking over the repairs that had been made. The mansion was decorated now, and painted. It had an elegant nineteenth century look to it.

At 3 AM, Julia walked to Christi's doors and locked it, using the key that Jonathan had given her. She then went into her own room, and slipped the key into one of her desk drawers. She walked over to the baby-grand piano, opened it, and played a soft little melody she remembered, from the short time in her life when she had taken lessons. She then started a fire in her fireplace, and unpacked her suitcases, choosing a white lace and silk negligee to wear to bed. Feeling a slight chill, Julia pulled her red flannel robe on over it. She blew out the candle on the wall next to her bed, and put her lighter under her pillow, where she could get at it, in order to light the candle.

As Julia snuggled into the blankets and watched the fire, all the memories and thoughts of the years before came rushing back. She smiled, and sighed, as she hugged the pillow close to her.

The last thing Julia said before she fell asleep was this: "Julia, what are you getting yourself into this time?"

8

Julia slept through the day, never waking once, until something quite unexpected happened in the early evening. She slept, experiencing a rather pleasant dream, when she saw a pair of eyes in the dream, staring at her, watching her. She began running, but she couldn't escape the eyes.

Julia woke out of breath and scared, and she stared at the wall, lying on her side. Her sight had improved, over the time she had slept, sliding into night-vision, so that she could see every line in the wall, and the canopy. But she couldn't shake the feeling that she was being watched.

Julia heard someone breathing in her room. She couldn't tell who the person was. The person's scent was not familiar, and she couldn't bring the person's name out of its mind with newfound, vampiric telepathy, but it was there, and it was immortal, and definitely male.

Julia's eyes widened, but she tried to control her breathing, to lead him to think she had gone back to sleep. Maybe then, he'd leave. But it did no good. Soon, Julia heard footsteps coming, closer to the bed.

Julia gasped, pulled the lighter from her pillow, backed against the wall, and clutched her blankets to her. She turned on the lighter, and the room danced with the small flame.

There, standing next to the edge of the bed, was a man who looked about the age of twenty-five. He had waist length rusty-brown hair, and his eyes were hazel, with a little blue running through them. He wore very tight black jeans, which were tighter then Jonathan's even, jeans that he probably would have to peel off like a second skin. He had a pair of boots on, Julia could tell by the sound he made, as he walked.

He wore an immaculately clean white tee shirt, half hidden by his leather jacket, a certain type of jacket that Julia had not seen before. The arms, half of the front, and half of the back, were covered in small square silver studs. He wore no earring.

The man was thin, but not really so thin as to appear anorexic. He looked as if he were a bit taller than Jason, and Jonathan. But there was an evil look in his eyes, worse than Jason in all his fury. It made Julia tremble slightly.

As she sat there, holding the lighter between them, the man watched her, the same as she was watching him. No, not the same, she realized after a moment. He was watching her like he was a predator, and she was the prey.

Julia moved to the head of the bed, and lit the candle on the wall. She then put the lighter back under the pillow, and pulled the blankets closer to her. She swallowed heavily as she looked at the man. He had turned slightly to face her, but his face was unreadable.

"Who are you?" she whispered, but he didn't answer her, just came nearer. "Who are you!" Julia demanded now, with forced anger in her voice.

The man looked at her with a smile now playing on his lips. "You should know, Julia. From what I heard, Jonathan told you all about me last night." he said.

"Cory?" she gasped.

He nodded. "That's me."

"How did you know my name? How did you get in here? Where's Jonathan?" she asked, knowing she must have sounded like a scared rabbit.

"It was easy to reach your name, my dear. Your mind-block is not even developed yet." He chuckled, "You're not even a vampire yet! But you still tried to reach my mind. Why?"

"Answer my questions!" Julia said, feeling her cheeks grow hot with embarrassment.

"Alright." he said with a short fake bow. "The door was unlocked, I just let myself in. As for Jonathan, he's not here. In fact, no one is here but you, and I, and the girl you call Christi."

"You're lying to me." Julia said softly. She began to feel frightened. Jonathan had been right about him. He must have possessed evil beauty as a mortal, because he looked absolutely terrifying now. His features were perfect, but dark, without a bit of remorse. Even his voice teemed with the characteristics.

"I'm lying?" he asked, that chuckling coming from deep inside his chest. "If I was lying to you, do you think that I'd be here right now? Don't you think that Jonathan would be here instead?"

Julia didn't have time to answer him. He had vanished suddenly, and then he was next to her, sitting on her bed, his hand resting on her neck, two fingers on Jonathan's chain.

"It's a shame you have to settle with him," he said.

Julia pulled away from him, backing against the wall again.

"You could have so much more, Julia." he said, stretching his arms open, indicating himself.

"Please leave my room," she said. She looked into his eyes for a moment, and then, she realized her mistake. She couldn't move. He had trapped her there, in his eyes. Inside, she was screaming at him to let her go, but if he heard, he paid no attention.

Julia watched in horror as he climbed up onto the bed, close to her. She couldn't do anything to stop him, not until he looked away or closed his eyes, and Julia was sure he wouldn't.

Cory pulled the blankets away from her now lifeless hands, and then spoke. "Julia, I know you can hear me, so listen good. What I do now you are to tell no one, not a single soul. If you do, someone will die here. Either you or Christi or Jonathan, and I'm sure you believe me. If you move or make a sound while I'm with you, if you call for help in any way, I'll break your arm or perhaps even your neck. You won't die, but it will hurt . . . pardon the expression . . . like hell." Cory glanced away for a moment, allowing Julia to break free of the spell.

Julia was trembling all over, her eyes filling with tears. What is he going to do, she thought, rape me?

"No, nothing like that. I just want...a kiss, one kiss. If you obey me, no harm will come to you." he said. "Do you understand?"

"Yes." Julia said, now crying freely, but Cory didn't seem to notice. Julia stayed limp as put one arm around her, the other on the back of her head, his eyes roaming over her body. Julia covered her face in her hands, but he pulled them down.

"Julia." he said sternly. She turned her head and looked at him, just as his mouth came down over hers. She struggled feebly, but he was smothering her, his lips crushing hers, his hot breath fanning over her neck as his mouth lingered there. She pleaded, begged for him to stop, but he paid no heed until he was ready to let her go, put Julia back into bed, tucking the blankets about her, and closing her eyes with his fingers.

"Go to sleep, Julia. Go to sleep, and do not cry about this any more." he said, and then bent down, and touched his thumb and forefinger to her temples. "I'm leaving now, and when you wake, you will not remember this incident, so I now say. You will obey." He turned and left, closing the door behind him.

Julia had heard everything he had said, and she had fallen asleep, but when she woke, nearly an hour later, Julia did remember everything that had happened. Jonathan's blood had begun the process of transforming her.

Julia woke, and took in a great deep breath of air. Instantly all the memories rushed back to her and she sat up, her eyes darting around the room. The candle had been half burned down.

Julia jumped out of the bed, and with a heavy heart, she lit the candle on the bureau, and the two on her desk, and then put the lighter in the desk drawer. Then, she slowly crossed the room, and opened the closet door. She entered Christi's room by the secret passage, and leaned against the door; only then did she allow herself to cry.

Julia collapsed to the floor, sobbing in disgust for what Cory had done to her. She knew it was almost nothing, but she couldn't get the taste of him out of her mouth. She cried for herself and Jonathan. She wanted to tell Jonathan to get rid of Cory, but she knew that Cory had been telling the truth. He could kill everyone here probably, except, possibly Jason.

Finally, Julia picked herself up off the floor, and walked to Christi's fireplace. She started a fire, and stood there watching the flames, feeling thoroughly helpless.

A sudden voice broke Julia's revere. It was Christi, moaning.

Julia came around the bed, to the side where the coffee table stood. She wet the towel, and poured fresh water into the bowl. Christi's hands were clenched onto the blankets, so hard that her knuckles were turning white. Julia touched Christi's forehead, just to find out her friend had a fever. Julia pulled back and looked down. Christi's face was dripping with sweat, running down into her curly, black hair. Christi's neck was scratched and scarred, as if she had been clawing herself, and her sweatshirt had ripped as a result.

Julia placed the cold, wet towel on Christi's head, but the girl thrashed violently, and the towel fell off. Her eyes opened, and she stared wildly at Julia.

"What are you doing? Trying to kill me?" Christi shouted. Julia looked at Christi open-mouthed. It was now obvious that Christi had a fever for too long; she had gone delirious.

"Christi, it's me, Julia." Julia said, sitting on the bed and picking up the cloth. Christi's eyes settled on Julia's face, and this time, she allowed Julia put the cloth on her head.

"Julia?" Christi whispered through parched lips. Christi relaxed on the bed, her hands now lying flat against the covers. "I'm glad you've come. I'm so thirsty. Julia, can I have a drink?"

"Um, I don't know." Julia looked on the coffee table, and behind the pitcher, she found a small, porcelain mug. Jonathan must have put it there, she thought.

Julia filled the cup with clean water, and gave it to Christi. Christi drank the water greedily, and then gave the cup back to Julia.

"Thank you Julia, I'm so," Christi's voice trailed off as she looked around the room. "Oh no," she moaned, "no! We're still here, aren't we?" Christi grabbed Julia's shoulders, forcing her to look at her. "We have to leave. Julia, we have to go before they get to us."

Julia looked away from Christi. She knew what her friend meant now, before we go the same path as them, or worse. Julia knew what Christi meant, all right. That was because Jonathan had already 'got to her'.

Christi suddenly seemed to realize this. "No, Julia, no! It's not right, not possible!" Christi lay down, sinking into the blankets again. Then suddenly she appeared to have changed her mind. "Maybe it is right." she said, her eyes shutting again, her fingers scratching at her neck. "Yes, maybe it is right, if you love someone that much, and I...I...maybe I love Sabastian." Christi kept murmuring these things as she faded into sleep again.

Julia stood, placed the damp towel onto the coffee table. She hadn't turned yet, when she felt an arm slip around her waist. Julia gasped and spun around. She let out a sigh when she saw it was Jonathan.

"What's wrong?" he asked her, wrapping his arms around her, pulling her close to him.

Julia studied his face for a moment, gently touching his cheek with her fingertips. Then she looked into his eyes. His eyes stared into her soul, trying to find the source of her problems.

Julia felt a slight tugging in her mind, and she pulled her eyes away from him with effort, pressing her head and hands to his chest. "Don't do that to me." she whispered, close to tears.

Jonathan stroked her messed-up hair, holding her.

"I'm sorry love. I won't do it anymore. But what is it? There's something that you don't want to tell me, don't want me to know. You're scared of something. What is it? Tell me."

"No, I can't, I can't!" Julia was crying now, Jonathan could feel her tears. "Don't ask me about it, I don't want to talk about it!"

"All right, Julia. I won't talk about it. But if you keep crying, you're going to wake Christi." he said gently.

Julia sniffled and looked down at Christi. "There's something wrong with her, Jonathan. It's as if Sabastian poisoned her, or something."

Jonathan walked away from Julia, and leaned down over Christi. A few moments later he looked back up at Julia. "He has." he said.

"What?"

"She won't die, and she won't be one of us either. Sabastian has a human lover now, and he knows it. He told me he wouldn't rest, until she is his. He says he wants me to make her one of us, or he will find a way to get her. Says he doesn't want a human lover. He doesn't want a girl who will give him all her blood without a fight, and who is confined to bed. He wants Christi to be immortal, and he claims he loves her."

"No, not Christi. She's going to live, and she's going home to Connecticut." Julia said. Just then, she heard a sudden knocking at Christi's locked door.

Christi sat up, crawled to the edge of the bed. She raised her hand. "Sabastian!" she cried. Then her head cocked to one side as if she was listening to something. She whispered under her breath, "You must open the door, you must give him the key. If you don't, he will come through your room into mine."

Julia got up on the bed and forced Christi down. "Jonathan, take him away from here, hurry!" she yelled. No sooner then Jonathan had gone through the closet, the knocking on the door ceased. Christi fell back into sleep.

When Julia was positive her friend was out of immediate danger, she returned to her room to change blue jeans, her U-Conn. sweatshirt, and a pair of black boots. She pulled on her leather jacket, and entered the sitting room.

Julia observed for a moment, those within the sitting room. Steven and Timothy were sitting on the stairs, quietly talking Cory and Lizzi on the sofa. Cory didn't even turn to look at Julia, as she walked into the room. As Julia crossed the room, she looked at Lizzi.

Lizzi did look like a thirteen-year-old girl. She had the same rusty colored hair as Cory, but her eyes were violet.

Then Julia saw something that made her jump.

Jason was standing near the door with a young man, who was at least six foot four inches tall. He looked about twenty years old. He had layered blond hair that fell to his shoulders, and green eyes. He wore a gray shirt, and held a black leather jacket, which resembled Jonathan's, with black baggy jeans, and a pair of black boots. There was a small sword earring in his left ear.

But the striking thing about this guy, as he now leaned against the wall, slouching over, and looked at Julia, was the overwhelming sense that she had known him before. With sudden clarity, she realized. He, in many ways, resembled the one whom she had killed, so many years before. Devin.

Julia sighed, zipped up her coat, and walked out the doors. As she shut them behind her, she thought that anything was possible, in this place.

Julia looked out at the driveway, and at the items it contained. There was her van, her Harley and the five others, a small, well used, green Chevette, and a sleek black Porsche with tinted windows, all covered high in about two feet of snow. Julia decided that the Chevette must belong to the new boy, and the Porsche to Cory and Lizzi. It was just a guess, but she was right.

Julia came down off the steps, and into the snow. Her legs were encased with the frigid cold of the snow, but the coldness passed in a second. The next moment, her legs were tingling with small flecks of warmth, as if her legs had fallen asleep. But they hadn't!

Julia stretched her legs out as she walked, and she found that she could still move them. She pushed through the snow to her small bike, and dusted the snow off; pausing to glare at the snow bank that had accumulated around her bike. Suddenly a hand clamped onto her shoulder.

Julia turned fast, and let out a sigh. It was only Jonathan again.

"Why do you keep sneaking up on me like that?" Julia demanded, "You're scaring me, and I don't like it." Julia said, and turned back to her bike.

"What's wrong with you tonight, Julia? You're so jumpy, and nervous." Jon said, sounding concerned. When Julia didn't answer him, he moved closer to her, and put his hands on her back. He felt her rest her hands on the bike, for balance, and he leaned against her a little, slipped his arms around her waist. He pressed his body against the back of hers, and buried his face in her hair. A second later, he lifted his head and mumbled into her ear, "Where are you going?"

Julia turned around and looked up at him, tears standing in her eyes. "I had to get away from here. Not for good, just until…the pain comes, just before that."

Jonathan looked down at her, wondering why she was so close to tears. She was buried in some internal pain, and he didn't know what it was. He pulled Julia close to him, and raised her head, caressing her chin.

Julia rested against his zipped-up jacket, her eyes gazing into Jonathan's in the moonlight, and she felt little shock waves pass through her body. His head drew nearer, and Julia raised her arms upwards, her hands going beneath his hair, to the soft skin on the back of his neck. She closed her eyes, and a moment later they were kissing. She pushed one hand up through his hair and the other down beneath his jacket, onto his back.

Julia felt his lips gently moving on hers, widening in a soft open-mouth kiss. She followed his soft, passionate lead, not trying to deepen it, or ruin the moment. She knew this was what he wanted, a moment that was neither sexual, nor childish, simply loving. His hands remained where they were one on her cheek, one on her back. Then she felt his lips close, and she did the same. It seemed he wanted to speak, and so she kept her eyes shut, and listened, but not a word did she hear.

Talk to me Jonathan, I want to hear.

As if she had pressed some mechanical switch in her head, she heard his voice, whispering softly in her brain.

"Julia, Julia my love, you are strong this time, so very strong. It is the final sacrifice, the final bond between you and I."

What do you mean? Why are you saying these things to me?

Jonathan pulled away from her, abruptly. Julia looked at him questioningly, her hands dropped to her sides. He gazed at her for a long moment; his hands shoved into his jeans pockets. Then he said very softly, "You penetrated."

"What do you mean?" she asked again, this time more interested than before.

Jonathan smiled as he looked at her. "You came into my thoughts on your own, without me pulling you there, without my shield being broken. You were feeling the same as I. By channeling that feeling into my blood inside you, and from there into yours, you were able to enter my mind." He paused for a moment, and then spoke again, a bit more serious look on his face. "That, my love, has never happened to me before. I know that it had happened at times, between Jason and Devin, but never between Jason and I, nor any of his other children. It has not happened between Timothy and I."

"What does that mean? Did I do something wrong?" she asked, scared for a moment.

"No." Jon whispered, shaking his dark mass of hair. "It just means that you and I have a very strong link, and that you will be a very strong vampire."

"Is that what you meant by me being strong?" she said.

"Yes." he replied, sadness in his eyes.

Julia saw the change in his eyes and said very sincerely, "I will never leave you,"

For a moment, he said nothing, but leaned close to her. Finally, in a seductive whisper he said, "Come with me. I know a place you can wait for the changes."

Jonathan pulled Julia away from the driveway, down the very path that Christi had run, through a field, and toward a hemlock forest. There was no sound, but for the steady crunching of the newly fallen snow, beneath their feet. The moon was high overhead, full now, and bright.

Julia's hand held Jonathan's firmly as they trudged on, it being more difficult for her to walk in the deep snow, than for Jon. Then she noticed something unusual.

Their shadows were on the snow all right, a black reflection against white. But no vapors rose from their mouths, no steam, and no condensation.

When she asked Jonathan why this was, he said, "Because your blood regulates the changes in your environment. It lowers your skin temperature without changing your blood temperature. Do you feel cold at all?" and when Julia said no, he said it proved his point.

Once they were inside the hemlock forest, Julia came to realize, just how dense it was. The trees towered over their heads, and she judged that some of them might be a hundred years old. The trees had collected all the snow at the top, and so there wasn't much on the ground inside the forest. The ground was a carpet of pine needles.

Jonathan stopped beside one tree, and let go of Julia's hand, and looked up at one of the low branches. He jumped slightly, grasped the branch, and making a sharp, quick tug, broke it.

Julia quickly moved out of the way, as the giant branch fell, the end still hanging on a bit, by the tough bark. She looked in amazement at the branch. It was about eight feet in length, and as thick as Jonathan's thigh. Jonathan came up to her, took her hand again, and brought her beneath it. It made a sort of windbreaker, from the persistent winter wind.

Jonathan cleared out a spot of pine needles, and laid some dry sticks and twigs there. He went into one of his pockets, and pulled out a book of matches. He had a small fire going, in no time. Then he looked up at Julia, who was gazing at him steadily, and smiled. "Come here," he said.

Julia smiled in return, and gratefully went to him, resting on her side against him, and waited.

A little while later, a soft rustling of pine needles came into earshot. Soon after that, a fawn came from beyond the trees, close to the fire, gazing timidly at Jonathan, and Julia.

"Look." breathed Jonathan. He went into his jacket pocket again, pulled out a piece of dried bread. With his eyes fixed on the fawn's, he stretched out his arm, the offering in his hand. The fawn looked unsure for a moment, but it came to him, eating the bread from his hand.

Jonathan stroked the fawn's fur as it nuzzled his hair, licking his face with a long, wet, pink tongue. Jonathan chuckled, a low rumbling from deep within. He then took Julia's hand, and placed it on the fawn. They were both rubbing the animal's back now, and the fawn let them do it, not at all afraid.

Jonathan said softly to the fawn, "Go now."

With one last lick against Jonathan's face, the fawn turned, and ran away. Jon looked at Julia, who was staring at him, wide-eyed.

"How did you do that?" she asked, anxious to know the answer.

"I concentrated on its mind, exerted a bit of my will. There are a lot of things you can do, when you're like me." He gazed down at Julia, into her eyes. "Julia, this time, I want you to stay with me forever. There is no way out for you this time. No going back to the light," he said with a snarl, "no leaving me again, ever. Tonight you will make your first kill, become truly one of us. I need you beside me, and this is the only way."

Julia watched him look away from her again, the slight breeze blowing his dark hair away from his face. She leaned her head against him and began to cry.

Jonathan turned towards her, cupped her chin in his hand. "Don't cry Julia," he said, "it will be your rebirth."

"But Jonathan, I'm afraid!" she said, looking back up with wide teary eyes. "I'm so afraid."

"Don't be. I'll always be here for you. Don't worry, I'll be here through each step, no matter how painful they might be for me, or for you." he said, hugging her to him.

Soon, the pain inside Julia's stomach began, and she whispered, "It's here."

Julia felt Jonathan pull her closer to him, and then, she could no longer feel anything beyond her body. All she felt was pain. Burning pain, which began in her stomach, and moved into her heart. From there, the pain threaded through each of her veins, spreading throughout her body. The pain climbed into her brain, and she could no longer see; a blinding whiteness replaced her vision. A pounding began in her ears, which gradually increased to a roar. Her heart beat faster, faster, seeming like it would burst from her chest. The pain inside her stomach became excruciating, and her lungs wouldn't allow her to breathe.

Julia's blood interacted with Jonathan's, for the second time. Although, this time it was far more intense. Jonathan's blood cells were fusing with Julia's, giving her vampiric cells, making her a vampire. When her heart had slowed, and her breathing had returned to normal, the blood cells, now mostly Julia's, with traces of Jonathan's, lay in wait for more blood. They were hungry.

Julia opened her eyes, and gazed up at Jonathan, who had been holding her all along. She spoke then, the truth, what the new vampiric blood cells demanded.

"Make me whole, Jonathan. I am hungry."

9

As Jonathan took Julia back to the mansion, he told her briefly of the one called Rikki, the one who so resembled Devin. Jason had discovered Rikki, after he had given Sabastian to Jonathan. Tonight Rikki's blood would become vampiric, just as Julia's would.

Jonathan explained to Julia that victims were already in the house, having been there since Jon and Jason had picked them up, off the road, while Julia had been sleeping. These victims were trapped inside the basement.

Julia felt very confused about what was happening to her. She did not want to become this thing, this creature. But she had to, didn't she? After all, she loved Jonathan, and had traveled miles just to be here. If she had any second thoughts about what she was to do tonight, she was positive that Jonathan would make her do it anyway. Once Julia had her first kill, the spell would be irreversible; it would be too late. She would never set eyes on the sun again.

Julia wanted to scream, to cry, something, but she knew it wouldn't help, probably just make matters worse. She lowered her head, and trudged on after Jonathan in the deep snow. The tingling sensation had left her legs with the second step, and now the snow felt warm against her.

She didn't talk to Jonathan, he didn't talk to her. Julia opened her mind; perhaps he might be listening, and began pouring out her misery in thoughts, and memories. Sure enough, the tugging in her mind began, and she didn't care.

"Julia!" Jon said, in a shocked voice, and turned around so fast, that Julia didn't see it, and she bumped right into him.

Jonathan grasped her upper arms, forcing her to look at him. "If I did not do this, you would not be alive right now! You and Christi would both be in a shallow, unmarked grave, in this clearing right now!" he yelled, shaking her a little. "That is what Jason wanted. Do you understand?"

Julia was shocked at how angry he had become. However, as soon as he felt her become frightened, Jonathan's face softened, and he dropped his hands from her arms.

"I apologize for yelling." he began, looking at her face, "I just want you to understand, I couldn't let you die. Not when I had the power to save you. To make you live forever."

"I know." Julia whispered.

Jonathan stepped closer to her. "I love you. I will not let anything harm you. I know of the hell you endured, being separated from me. We will be together forever now."

"I love you, Jonathan." Julia said.

When they reached the mansion, another tragic surprise waited for them.

Julia stared at the couple on the couch, filled with an odd sense of familiarity. It seemed she was looking at herself and Jonathan all over again, three and a half years ago, except, it wasn't them. Christi and Sabastian sat together. In Christi's hands was a crystal glass, stained red but empty, which she twirled absently, in her fingers.

Again Julia wanted to scream, to shout, but she did no such thing. She walked to Sabastian, took a deep breath, and sighed. Then she looked at Christi, who refused to meet her gaze. "Take good care of her, Sabastian," Julia said; he nodded.

Julia turned her attention to the room, noticing that all former inhabitants were gone, but for the two on the sofa, Jonathan, herself, Jason and Rikki.

"Is she ready?" Jason asked, and Jonathan told him, she was.

"Come with us, then."

Rikki followed him, and Jonathan took Julia's hand, led her down the stairs into the basement. Although Julia had been here only last night, it seemed like years ago to her.

Once into the darkened depths of the basement, Rikki and Julia stood against the wall, facing Jonathan and Jason, and the victims, a boy and girl of early teen years. The teenagers didn't move or scream, their attention seemed completely focused on Jonathan, and Jason. Soon, their eyelids appeared heavy, and though they still stood, they appeared to be sleeping.

Jason made a long cut on the girl's dirty young face, a line of red running from her eyelid down to her chin. Jonathan did the same with the boy. Then the blood masters stood back, keeping the youths in a hypnotic sleep, waiting to see what Julia and Rikki would do first.

Julia could see in the darkness, for her night-vision had enhanced. She could see the blood running down the youths' faces. Her sense of smell was also stronger, something she hadn't noticed yet. Now, she couldn't help but notice. The smell of human blood filled the room, and her nostrils. The smell was sweet, and amazingly tempting. She could feel her body twitching in anticipation.

Julia pulled her eyes off the young boy for a moment, glanced over at Rikki; he was changing before her eyes. When all his vampire features were apparent, he stood there for one moment, as if he were unsure of himself. But then, he left the wall, and plunged at the young girl, pulling her off her feet, and ripping at her skin, in the clumsiness of his first time.

The young girl opened her eyes and screamed, but the scream didn't last long. She was dying.

The scent of mortal blood was all around Julia now. It was enticing, and she suddenly felt the changes wash over her, in a wave of starvation. The sweat on her forehead, the red over her eyes, her temples throbbing, her jaw aching, her stomach gnawing at her. She ran her tongue over her canine teeth a few times, encouraging them to grow long. Soon they became long and sharp, fang teeth for killing. And yes, she remembered it all, from before.

Julia stared at the young boy, with the sounds of Rikki, sucking on his kill, ringing in her ears. She was beyond all thought process now, and was functioning only on instinct, with the influence of Jonathan whispering inside her head to kill, and what it would be like, how it would taste.

Julia was not consciously aware of him influencing her in this way. She only knew she was growing more and more aroused, and she began to walk to the boy. Finally, she stood before him, staring up at him. She wasn't even aware, when Jon gave the telepathic control to Julia, and began filling her with provocative thoughts of killing, of blood, of life.

The boy's eyes opened as he looked at Julia, still in a dreamlike state; the look in his eyes made her run her tongue over the fangs again. She pulled the boy's name from his mind, Rusty. He was fourteen years old, hardly more than a child. His face was smeared in mud, and his hair was blond but dirty, a little runaway.

"Rusty," Julia growled, now so far in her hunger, she had forgotten her own code of morals as well. "Rusty, take off your shirt."

Rusty's glazed eyes looked at her, probably only seeing her because she wanted him to, for there was really not enough light in the basement for a human to see anything. Rusty nodded, and pulled off his grungy sweater, revealing his young, thin chest to her.

Julia pressed her hands to his skin, feeling the blood pumping underneath. She kissed Rusty's stomach, feeling a small quiver of excitement go through him. Up and up she kissed him, standing on tiptoes, teasing her hunger with the taste of his young human skin. When her lips caressed his neck, his hands raised to hold her there, Rusty's own lips against the back of her head.

Julia pressed her mouth to the place in his neck where the blood flowed close to the surface, along the jugular vein. She felt the boy tip his head back, encouraging her, his body trembling in sexual passion.

She laid her fangs flat on the surface of his neck, not piercing, but against it, and opened her mouth. She touched her tongue to his dirty neck, and felt the blood running beneath the surface, so close, so close. Her hands slid down his back, pulling him even closer.

Then Julia looked up at Rusty, at his face drawn with human emotion, his eyes shut, and a tiny voice screamed at Julia, breaking Jonathan's hold on her, forcing its way through her hunger.

It was the voice of her conscience.

Julia let go of Rusty, leaving him standing in the middle of the room, bewildered.

"No! I can't kill him!" she yelled, backing away with great effort.

"Julia, do it!" Jonathan yelled from behind her, offering no help.

"*Do it, now!*" roared Jason.

She turned and looked at them, Jon and Jason standing together, both glaring at her, *both of them angry with her.* She looked at Rikki, who was finishing his kill, and the sounds of him sucking pushed her again to the brink.

Sucking, Sucking, *Sucking.*

She turned and faced Rusty again, gazing through the red haze, which veiled her eyes.

Jonathan, help me. Julia silently pleaded, feeling compelled to the boy so strongly, she was rocking as she tried to stay where she was.

No answer came from Jonathan, not one word. She felt a more powerful stroking of thoughts being passed into her brain, and she heard Jason's voice, stronger than ever before. More seductive than anyone she had ever known. His will, being forced on her. His voice purring like a lover's, intriguing, and she became willing to succumb to him.

Julia, take him. He is young, soft, warm. His blood is fresh and free of disease. He won't try to stop you from taking him. He wants you; I could feel the passion building within him. Look at him Julia, see the blood inside him. Love the boy, Julia. Take him.

Then Julia moaned softly, looking at Rusty as Jason wanted her to. She saw all the veins, the red blood pumping his heart, his young moist heart. The beating of the heart filled her ears. It was a liquid sound, filled with blood.

Jason had come up beside her, now whispered in her ear. "Take him, Julia. Place your lips on his neck, and take the blood from him. Do it now. When you are finished, your lover will be waiting for you." he said, and then stepped back, leaving her to struggle alone. Julia knew, deep within, that he had meant Jonathan, but at that moment, she could have sworn that Jason meant himself.

With one final struggle of her own will, she cried out desperately for help, but none came. The combined pressure of Jason's and Jonathan's wills against her was too much for her to stand up to. Julia clutched the sides of her head and groaned aloud, trying to rage against them, and feeling the pain inside her as they pushed back, and won.

You are condemning me, both of you, to hell.

Julia could not resist them. The thoughts of blood filled her, and pushed her beyond the edge. She ran to the boy, pulled him down to his knees before her.

Julia yanked Rusty's head back by his hair, gazed into his surprised eyes. Then, without a second thought, she clamped her mouth onto his neck, sinking her fangs deep inside him.

At once, Jonathan and Jason withdrew their wills, leaving Julia to kill the boy herself. Jason brought Rikki upstairs, for he had passed out on the girl's body, and Jonathan stood, watching Julia with tears in his eyes. Even though he had preserved Julia, part of her would die tonight, her human morality along with the boy Rusty.

Julia felt their wills leave her, and found herself with Rusty under her fangs, only her animal instincts telling her what to do. The boy had gasped in shock as she drove into him, and Julia had been cautious about what she was doing. But then the vampire in her took over; she had tasted the blood.

The first mouthful of human blood spurted up and into her, flowing onto her tongue, and down her throat. The animal was unleashed now, and it took over. Julia pulled the boy harder to her, pressing against him as she drank.

Never in her life had she tasted anything like this. It was life, pure and simple. But unlike Jonathan's blood, which had brought her back from the dead, it was truly alive. The blood was alive with cells, and it danced into her, traveling down the length of her body, and gently stroking the hard hungry knot in her stomach, as it loosened more and more.

Julia's taste for the sweet, sweet blood increased with every hot mouthful, and she lowered the boy to the ground, and lay on top of him, loving every minute of this glorious feast. She opened her mind to the dying boy's, and she did not see any words or pictures, only felt the immense pleasure he was feeling at this moment, a feeling that he had never experienced in his short fanatic life with the girl, who was already dead.

Soon, Rusty's heart beat slower, and slower, and Julia had to suck on his neck more, and more to pull the blood out. Then as she felt the heart slowing even more, she pulled up from Rusty, and stared down at him. Her hunger ceased, and the vampire features left her.

Julia stared at the dying boy, her face smeared and dripping with blood. Her mind was in a state of shock, but her body was so warm suddenly. So strangely warm and caressing.

With a small whimper, she pressed her hand to Rusty's chest and felt his pulse flutter for the last time, his breath escape his body. Then, he was still.

Rusty was dead.

Julia had killed him.

Julia fell face first onto Rusty's still chest, trying to cry, but she found no way to cry for his death. Still, she was miserable, and she whispered softly to him, stroking his greasy, dirty hair. "Forgive me, Rusty." Still murmuring things to the dead boy, she passed out from exertion and the fullness of the kill in her veins.

Jonathan walked slowly to Julia, now whole and completely immortal, and let the blood tears run down his face. She would be at least a little different from now on, he knew. A bit more defiant, a bit more mature. Even her body would fill out more, and bring itself to the extreme beauty that Julia could possess. Even thought she had been beautiful before, she would now look to everyone around her, a goddess.

Jonathan picked Julia up off of the dead boy, and cradled her in his arms. He looked down at her face, and kissed the blood off of her, until there was none. Then, he brought her upstairs into her bedroom, and laid her down on the bed. He lit a fire in the fireplace, and extinguished the candles in her room.

Jonathan wiped the tears off of his face with the back of his hand, and unzipped his leather jacket. He approached Julia, who was sleeping now, breathing in and out with deep, even breaths. He unzipped her jacket and pulled it off her, letting it drop to the ground. Jonathan stared at Julia a long time, without blinking. She *was* changing. Julia's complexion grew somewhat paler than before, and her lips became red. Her dark eyebrows became a little darker, banishing the blond hairs in them. Her longish, wavy blond hair began to glisten softly.

Her fingernails grew a bit, just long enough to be able to cut something. The paint on her nails chipped off, and left them clean and pale. All the blemishes and birthmarks on her face, neck and body disappeared, leaving her without any marks, except her earring holes. Her breasts began to swell a tiny bit, growing slightly, to preserve her womanhood for all eternity. Julia's stomach flattened, and her thighs became a little rounder, and firmer.

Jonathan let out a long, deep breath when the changes had been completed, leaving Julia as he thought they would. She was now a goddess.

He climbed up onto the bed and lay beside her, next to the wall, with one arm around her. He hoped that her personality wouldn't change, for he loved Julia the way she was. Above all else, he didn't want anything to hurt her. Surprisingly, he felt overwhelmingly tired, as if he had just gone through the whole ordeal, not her. Within five minutes, Jonathan was asleep.

Some time later, Julia awoke. As she opened her eyes, she knew she was immortal.

She sat up swiftly, not using her hands or her muscles, and blinked a few times, looking down at Jonathan. She watched him for a moment, listening to him breathing. She watched him take each breath. Suddenly, she realized that she heard every sound his body made, as he dreamed. Her hearing had been perfected.

Julia turned away from him, and stared at the fire. A warning flickered in her head not to get too close, that the fire could kill her. But as she stared at it, she realized she was seeing all the colors in the fire now, blues, the whites, the oranges, reds, yellows. She could see the smoke particles rising up from it, and the heat waves.

Julia closed her eyes for a moment, and pressed her hands to her face. She felt as if she was going to cry. She was changed.

Julia shook her head, slid off the bed without making a sound. She landed on her feet gracefully, like a cat. She picked up her jacket, and without waking Jonathan, she pulled it on and left the bedroom, shutting the door behind her. She walked out into the sitting room, and looked around. There was nobody in the room, but she had a strange feeling that the others were upstairs.

Julia walked outside, and shut the doors behind her. It took no effort at all to close them now, whereas before, they had been heavy. She looked out at the newly shoveled driveway, and noticed that the black Porsche was gone, but she wasn't concerned with that. The thing that bothered her the most, was that Sabastian's motorcycle was gone, and so was her van, which Christi had a key to. Christi was gone, along with Sabastian. Julia realized that she probably would never see her friend again. She hugged herself tightly, wandered out into the drive. She looked up at the house, gazed at the candles flickering in the windows. Then, she looked up at the sky.

She wondered if she could take to the air, now that she was changed. Julia closed her eyes and made a silent wish, and then holding her breath, looked upward once again. Go up, she thought, and jumped towards the sky.

A huge wind grasped her body, knocking the breath out of her lungs, and she was propelled away from the mansion, to the stars.

Julia laughed aloud, as the wind blew back her open jacket, stung her cheeks and hands. She was in control now, as she soared over the treetops, reaching down to pluck the topmost branches. She dipped low into the valley, skimmed the surface of the river with her hands. She went farther, higher up, and soon, she found herself looking down at Getaway Park.

Julia landed swiftly there, on her toes, so fast that nobody in the park would suspect that she had just materialized there.

As she walked around the park, she was once again aware of her heightened senses. Inside all the lights she could see rainbows of colors, and hear higher and lower pitches of sounds. She could smell all the foods. But one scent stood out from all the rest.

The humans.

They smelled of hair spray, too much make up, sweat and blood. She could see the vapors rising from their mouths, as they breathed and talked to each other. The humans didn't arouse her now, like she had been by them, in the beginning of the night, because she remained full and warm from the kill. Even so, she was amazed at how she could pass so easily among them, and even more so how at how many young, mortal men, were staring at her with desire behind their eyes.

A while later, Julia went to the carousel. She remembered clearly, that long-ago August night when Jonathan had come to her. As she took her seat, waiting for the carousel to start moving, she felt a presence coming towards her. It was immortal, not human; she could tell by the walk it made, that it did not mean her any harm.

Julia glanced back over her shoulder, and saw Rikki approaching her. He came to her, and stood by the horse she was on, gazed at her intently. At that moment, the ride began to move.

Julia looked down at Rikki. Even though she was far up on the horse, he still came to her shoulder. For a few moments, all he did was stare at Julia, with those green eyes of his that reminded her so much of Devin.

"What's your name?" he asked.

"Julia." she replied.

He smiled at her, and then ran his tongue over his lips, as if he were trying to think of what to say next. "Listen, Julia," he said, "since we were made the same night, do you want to hang out with me? I won't do anything stupid."

"I hope not," she said quickly, receiving yet another smile from him.

"Yeah, well, you can see me as a big brother, or as a friend, all right?"

"Sure." she said. When the ride was over, she grasped his shoulders and jumped down. She held his hand, and they went off together, walking amongst the people in a comfortable silence.

"Jon's looking for you. I think he's mad that you left." Rikki said, after a while.

"I just got sidetracked. He'll understand." Julia said with a shrug. She didn't notice the worried look on Rikki's face.

Later, Rikki bought a cotton candy, and they shared it. The sugar of the candy melted in Julia's mouth and felt good in her stomach along with the blood. "What a pair we make!" Julia exclaimed through the mouthfuls of her candy, watching as a group of teen-aged girls passed by, giggling and gazing at Rikki. They were followed by a group of boys their age that glared at Rikki, but as soon as they saw Julia, blushed and turned away.

"Yes," he said to her, "a pair of blond-haired devils."

He laughed Julia with him, grateful for the break in the pressure of the evening. Even though Rikki looked a lot like Devin, he was nothing like him. Spending time with him was good, Julia decided.

After the park closed at two in the morning, Julia and Rikki walked together, through the town, in the valley. They visited all-night restaurants, and the Town Park, sliding on the frozen surface of the pond. The snowfall had been less in the valley, but even so, the Town Park's pond had been shoveled clean.

Some time later, while they were sitting on the park bench, gazing at the moon, Rikki suddenly spoke up. "Julia, I think it's getting close to dawn. You see the position the moon's in? We should get going."

"Yes, you're right." Julia replied. She took hold of his hand, and they took to the air together, into the night.

As they approached the mansion, Julia and Rikki felt anger vibrating up towards them. The anger seemed to be riding up airwaves themselves. Julia let her mind follow the anger, follow it all the way to the source.

It was Jonathan.

She knew that he sensed her in his mind, and he threw her out by mind-screaming her name with such velocity, she almost fell from the sky. But Rikki's hand on hers was tight and he pulled her back up.

"We're in deep shit." he muttered.

When they landed in the driveway, the first thing they saw was Jonathan glaring at them from the steps. He came to them in a blur of light and wind.

Jonathan grabbed Julia's arm, pulled her behind him. "I'll take care of you later!" he yelled. Then he turned to Rikki, his face twisted with rage. "You!" he hissed.

Jonathan lashed out with his right arm, his fist contacting with the side of Rikki's head. There was a loud cracking noise, blood came from Rikki's head, and he fell to the ground.

Julia ran between Jonathan and Rikki, pushing against Jonathan. "Jon, leave him alone! Stop it!" she yelled.

He snarled at Julia, and shoved her out of the way. She fell back onto her side, felt a sharp pain in her hipbone. Her eyes filled with tears, but she picked herself up again. Rikki had been so kind to her; she had to stop Jonathan.

Julia watched as Jonathan bent over Rikki, smashing his fists into Rikki's ribs and stomach. Rikki was attempting to fight back, but his attempts were feeble. The wound in his head gushed blood.

Julia ran behind Jonathan, and grabbed his arms, pulling him backward. "Stop it right now! You're hurting him!" Julia screamed. Jonathan shrugged her off without any difficulty, and pushed her hard, sending her back about six feet.

Julia stifled a whimper and got up again, running towards them again. Julia halted suddenly, when she saw Rikki gain enough strength to push Jonathan away from him, his face shifting to that of the vampire. Rikki got as far up as his knees, and Jonathan twisted Rikki's arm backwards, behind his back. Rikki twisted drove his fangs into Jonathan's free hand. Jonathan yowled; his fangs grew as he did. When he opened his eyes, they were blood red. "I'm going to *kill you*!" he shouted.

Julia couldn't move. She was scared by what she was seeing. Jonathan had never been like this before. He had changed, and she was petrified, and not one part of her body would respond. She couldn't even scream for help.

Jonathan twisted Rikki's arm again, so hard, that the bones almost broke. Rikki cried out with pain as Jonathan knelt on top of his legs. With Jon's free hand, the one that was trickling blood, he tilted Rikki's head back, and held him in this lock while Rikki struggled helplessly.

Julia suddenly could move, could breathe. She linked her mind with Rikki's, and she could feel the pain that he was feeling. She heard him whisper very softly and in pain, to help him, to get Jason. Then Jonathan's torturing cut off the link.

Julia clasped her hands to the sides of her head and screamed, falling to her knees with the sound of it. She screamed at the top of her preternatural lungs, the sound carrying out over the mountains. Then, out of breath and dizzy, she fell forward onto her hands, and could only watch what fate would await Rikki, for there was nothing more she could do. Julia watched in horror, so close, and yet so out of reach, Jonathan prepared to kill Rikki.

Jonathan lunged forward, his fangs grazing Rikki's neck, bringing some blood to the surface. Rikki let out a heart-breaking wail, but at the fatal moment, Jonathan was flung backwards by some unseen force, which Julia knew must be Jason. Rikki dropped, face-first, onto the ground.

Julia crawled forward, ignoring the pain in her side, and dragged Rikki back with her, away from Jason and Jonathan who were engaged in lethal battle. Jonathan was picked up and thrown into the air, a good twenty feet into a pine tree, which stood near the mansion's driveway. He hit with such a powerful blow against the tree; it would have shattered a normal man's spine. Even a vampire fledgling as old as Julia and Rikki would have suffered damage. But any vampire past one hundred years would not sustain much damage. Their bones were strong. The huge pine tree shook shaking heavy snow to the ground, as Jonathan fell.

Julia sat on the cold, damp, snowy driveway, with Rikki lying on her lap, unconscious. The wound in his head was still bleeding, and his arm was at an unnatural angle. Julia took off her jacket, and glancing at Jon and Jason fighting, ripped her sweatshirt in half down the front. She quickly shrugged it off, and pulled the jacket back on, zipping it up to the bottom of her neck. Julia wrapped her damaged sweater around Rikki's head, cutting off the blood flow. She wiped away the blood from a cut near his mouth, and kissed his forehead. Then, with tears streaking her face, she hugged him in her arms, and turned to look at Jonathan and Jason.

Jonathan gave a pretty good fight, but Julia could plainly see that he was no match for Jason. Julia didn't try to stop Jason, the way she had when Jonathan was fighting Rikki, because she was still very afraid of him.

Julia's heart leapt up into her throat when finally, Jason ended the fight by trapping Jonathan in the same position that Jon had trapped Rikki in. Jonathan struggled against Jason, but he couldn't free himself.

"There!" Jason yelled, now fully in vampire form. "Let's see how you like it!" Jason pulled Jonathan's head back by the long, beautiful hair, and set himself to lunge.

"Jason, no!" Julia cried, and he turned to her, and snarled. Julia heard Rikki moan, and she glanced down at him, stroking his hurt chest. She looked up at Jason, her eyes filling with fresh tears, her lips quivering. "Please, Jason." she whispered.

Jason looked at Jonathan, whose face was normal again, but in a barely controlled mask of fury. Then he turned back to Julia, gasping, the vampire characteristics draining from his deadly, handsome young face.

"All right," he said, his voice hurried, his chest heaving. "For Rikki, and you. But now you owe me one, girl. Don't expect another favor from me, ever!" Jason turned back to Jonathan, and with a look of disgust, threw him down to the ground.

"Don't you *ever* touch another of my children! Remember this; I made you, Jonathan, and I can destroy you." He walked to Julia, and plucked Rikki from her lap, as if she weighed less than a feather.

For a moment, he looked as if he were going to walk into the mansion, but he turned back to Julia, with a soft expression on his face she had never seen before. "Thank you." he whispered. Jason turned away quickly, and strode away into the house, the doors closing behind him.

Julia sat for a split-second, standing up when she heard Jonathan coming towards her. She ran to the mansion doors, holding the top of her jacket shut. By the time her hand rested on the door, Jonathan was holding her arm tightly. She could feel his bottled anger, boiling just below the surface.

"Let me go!" she yelled, trying to pull away from him.

"Shut up, get in." he growled at her.

Julia didn't move to open the door, so he opened it himself, dragged her inside. He pulled her across the sitting room, shoved her into her bedroom.

Once he and Julia were inside, he pulled a key from his pocket, and locked the door. Then he slipped the key into his pocket, and turned to face her.

Julia stepped back when he looked at her. There was a look of hatred in his eyes she had never seen before. The light of the fireplace showed this expression, clearly.

Jonathan took a few steps forward to Julia, and she, being frightened, moved away. She jumped up onto her bed, into the same corner Cory had backed her into.

Jonathan snarled at her, and turned away, looking into the fire. He yelled something, in French, Julia couldn't understand. Jonathan faced her again, stripped off his leather jacket, whipping it down to the wooden floor with a loud smack. Julia held the front of her jacket tighter, shrunk back further. He was furious.

"How dare you go off on your first night without me! With that other fledgling besides! He doesn't know half as much as you do about our kind. What was he going to do? Protect you?" Jonathan gave a short scornful laugh. "With his thoughts about you, the only person he'd be protecting you from is himself." Anger clouded Jonathan's handsome face as he glared at Julia. "He wants you, you know. He wants to do things to you that you wouldn't be able to imagine without reading a porno book. He just doesn't have the courage to defy Jason or myself that much. That cowardly bastard!" Jonathan pounded his fist into his other hand. "I've heard his thoughts! He deserved to die for even thinking of touching you! I've claimed you, *you're mine*!" Jonathan yelled, leaning over the bed, hands resting on the edge, dark hair falling over his shoulders in waves.

Now Julia understood. Jonathan was jealous. The thought made her want to laugh, but she immediately wondered what would happen if he found out how Cory had treated her. What kind of fit of rage would Jonathan be in then? He was too sensitive, too overprotective.

"Jonathan, I don't believe that." Julia said in a small voice. Jonathan raised his hands to his head, and turned away from her again. Julia rose, slid to the edge of the bed.

"Even if it is true, who cares?" she asked, her voice a little louder now. "Can any man, mortal or otherwise, help but not think those thoughts when he sees a beautiful woman?" She looked at him with concern. His hands were fists at his sides, shaking his head in frustration. "Jonathan, it's true! Look at me. Jon, I am beautiful now. I might have been before, but I am more so now. I have changed. I could see it in the eyes of the mortal boys in the park. As for Rikki, we only stuck together for safety reasons. We are friends."

Jonathan shook his head in denial, not willing, nor wanting to accept what Julia had told him.

"No!" he yelled, so loud, Julia's hands flew to her ears. "It is true, damn it! You aren't going anywhere with him, ever again!" he yelled, turning away from her yet again.

Julia was shocked. She couldn't believe that Jonathan was telling her what to do what to think who to be friends with. It wasn't fair. She wasn't going to let him do this to her, now or ever.

Julia jumped off the bed and ran over to Jonathan, grabbing his shoulder, and pulling him around to face her. "What can you do to stop me from seeing him? What will you do? You can't hurt me!" she yelled, realizing that the pain had gone from her side. "You won't kill me!" She glared up at him, into his dark eyes.

Jonathan's eyes narrowed, and he growled again from deep in his throat. Too fast for Julia to follow, he picked her up, dumped her onto the bed. He then flung himself on top of her, forcing her hands down to her sides with his arms.

"Get off me, now!" she yelled, trying to get her hands free.

"I told you to shut up," he said gruffly, and then he clamped his mouth over hers, silencing her. He forced his way into Julia's mouth, penetrating, and giving her hard, searing kisses.

Julia struggled against him, finally getting her hands free, trying to push him off her with tears trickling out of her eyes. Not Jonathan, he couldn't do this. Julia pushed against him, but he was just too strong for her. It didn't matter how hard she kicked or fought; his body wasn't going to move unless he wanted it to.

"No!" Julia screamed. "Don't do this to me, stop it!" Her tears now ran freely down her face, audibly sobbing.

Miraculously, Jonathan got off her, and off the bed, bending to pick up his jacket from the floor. He pulled on his jacket, and ran his fingers though his hair. He seemed oblivious to Julia's sobbing. "Remember, you are mine. I can do anything I want with you." He turned as if to go.

Julia watched as he neared the door, unbelieving of what had just happened. She sat up on the bed. "Jonathan!" she screamed through her sobs. She watched as Jonathan stopped moving and stood still, as if the pain in her voice had brought him back to reality.

"Jonathan, why are you doing this to me? Why? Don't you even love me anymore?" she cried, the tinted tears still flowing down her cheeks. "Why are you treating me this way? I let myself come back to you, I let myself become what I am for you!"

Julia watched Jon turn to her, his hands in his jean pockets. He didn't look angry anymore. He looked sad, in pain, as if he was listening to her now, and absorbing all of what Julia was feeling.

"I love you, Jonathan. Why are you threatening me this way?" she whimpered.

Jonathan took his hands out of his pockets, and walked over to Julia's bed. She moved away from him, still crying, clutching at the top of her jacket.

"Julia, I . . . " he trailed off. He didn't know what to say to her. He realized that he had done something terrible to Julia, something that could possibly jeopardize their relationship forever. He had lost control, again.

"Julia, I'm sorry." he said in a soft voice.

"How can I believe that?" she whispered, her tears finally slowing. "Is this how it's going to be between us every time someone looks at me the wrong way?"

Jonathan bit back an angry retort. "No," he muttered not looking directly at her. "I just don't want anything wrong to happen to you."

Julia gave him a dark look. "Well, you almost…"

"I know what I almost did, and what I was trying to do," he said, cutting her off. "That was the only thing I knew to do to stop you. I am very worried about you. I want to be the only person to love you. I don't want anyone to seduce you away from me." He looked up at her.

"Jeez, Jon, don't you know that no one can do that? I came back, didn't I?" Jonathan nodded rather sheepishly. Julia smiled at him. He took her hand, but then her face grew serious.

"Jonathan, I can take care of myself. Now more than ever, because of what you made me. I can take care of Rikki too, even if he is a bit more powerful than me because Jason is his father." Julia stared into Jonathan's eyes, looking for some sort of understanding. But she didn't see any. All she saw was blank, no emotion. "Don't you trust me?" she asked.

Jonathan reached his hand over, brushed a lock of hair back from Julia's face. His hand lingered there for a moment, and then it came to rest on her shoulder.

"Then, what is it that made you so angry?" she asked.

Jonathan gave her a sad smile, and pulled away again, moving away from the bedside.

"Is it just because of what Rikki thought?" Julia said gently, and watched as the muscles of his back tensed beneath the leather jacket.

"I wish it was that simple, Julia. I really do. But there are things about my world that you don't know about yet." he said, still turned away from her.

"Jonathan, come back here." Julia said in a strong voice, one that she knew would make Jonathan smile. She saw that she was right; he turned and walked back to her, standing in front of her, looking down at her on the bed.

"Jon, it's not just your world, anymore. I'm with you now. I'm here for you now. You aren't alone anymore. If you'll just tell me." Julia looked up at him, and grasped his right hand in her left again. "Tell me why you were angry."

Jonathan dropped down on his knees before her, his legs hitting the floor lightly, without any noise. He looked at her beautiful goddess-like face, and realized one thing about Julia had never changed. No matter how much she had matured, or how the vampiric blood had changed her, she still had those haunting blue-green eyes that were so knowing, so loving. With her eyes alone, Julia could bring out the strangest emotions in him.

"Julia, have you ever heard of The Wild Ones?" he asked her.

Julia looked puzzled for a moment, as if she was trying to remember something that she didn't really know anything about. "No." she finally said, quietly.

"Wild Ones are vampires who kill others of their kind, because they like the taste of the blood. They are insane, destroyers. They are El Diablo, the nightcrawlers. A menace." Jonathan frowned, seeming to be in heavy thought. "There's a law, a rule that we all have. Jason told me of it once, a long, long time ago.

"Vampires aren't allowed to kill others of their kind, but for two conditions. One is that we may kill our own fledglings. Two is that if we fight with another vampire, and they willfully fight back, trying to draw blood, we can kill them. Wild Ones do not pay attention to that law. They kill any others without exception. They kill any others who are weaker than them."

"Wild Ones . . . all they do is kill others?" Julia asked.

"No, they kill humans too. We all have to kill humans to stay strong, Julia. Vampire blood does not fill us. It immediately becomes part of us, unlike human blood that sits in your stomach for a while. We can feed on animals, too. But if we stay on that too long, we become weak, our powers diminish."

"Jonathan, why did you tell me this, about Wild Ones?" Julia said, raising her free hand to stroke Jonathan's arm.

"Well, because that is the other reason why I was angry, the other reason I was worried about you. I have felt young Wild Ones around here at one time or another, and they travel in packs to ensure power. I have always sent out a warning of how old my maker was, and what he'd do to them if anything happened to me. They have always left me alone. But that won't work for you, Julia. I'm young compared to most vampires. If they ever found you alone, or with Rikki, they'd kill only you, and leave him. He belongs to Jason. The only way they'd kill Rikki is if they were old enough to kill Jason too. But, Julia, they'd kill you. I would die trying to stop them. Our deaths," he said, making an awful face of anger, "would not be avenged. It would be considered my fight to protect my child, and Jason would not help."

Julia stared at him, at his grim expression. She gulped down nausea and fear. "What would they do to me if they caught me? How would they kill me?"

Jonathan shook his head. "I . . . can't tell you, I don't want to think of it."

Julia gripped Jonathan's hand between her own. "Jonathan, will Christi and Sabastian be hurt? Traveling on their own like that?"

"No, I'm sure they'll be fine. Jason made them, like he made me. He's powerful, Julia, he'd know if any of his children were in trouble in an instant.

172

I don't possess all the power he has. Power comes with time." Jonathan looked down, his eyes on Julia's knees.

Julia looked at him, and she realized, suddenly, how tired he seemed to be, how sad. But then, she remembered something. "Jonathan, didn't you say that we had a special link? That I could get into your thoughts when no one else can?"

"Yes."

"I can always call for you. And you'll always hear me, so don't worry." she said, trying to reassure him, but then he mumbled something that sounded like: "It's harder when the blood's more potent." And, "If someone more powerful is inside."

Julia looked down at his bowed head, and kissed the top of it, breathing in his scent. She had smelled it long ago, the scent of leather and woods. But now, distinctly among those scents, she smelled something male and vampiric. Jonathan's own personal scent, "I love you." she whispered.

Jonathan looked up at her, his dark eyes widening. "Even after what I did to you?" he asked her.

Julia smiled, and watched as his head hung down again. She let him put his hands around her waist, and press his head against her lap. "It doesn't matter anymore. I forgive you," she said, as she stroked his hair.

"There's something else." Jonathan said, pulling back and sitting up on the bed beside her.

Oh no, she thought, here it comes.

"Cory. He has something on you, doesn't he?" Jonathan said.

Julia's eyes welled up with tears; she turned away from him.

"That is what you do whenever he looks at you, whenever I mention him, or what has been bothering you. Julia!" Jonathan gasped her name.

Julia turned back to him quickly, tears falling. She watched as another dark cloud passed over Jonathan's face.

"Has he hurt you?" Jonathan hissed.

Julia reached out to him, and pressed her head against him, trying not to cry again. "No, Jonathan, no! You promised that you wouldn't make me talk about it, you promised! I don't want to talk about him! Just hold me!"

Jonathan wrapped his arms around Julia, trying to repress the anger he felt. If Cory hurt her, if he dared touch her, he'd . . . he'd . . . Jonathan let the anger go with a sigh. He didn't know what he'd do.

"I love you." Jonathan said softly. Julia pulled up, and wiped her tears away with the back of her hand. Dreadful to see a goddess cry, he thought.

"Do you?" Julia asked.

"Of course I do." Jonathan said. "This is our time, Julia. The night is ours to share forever."

"Forever?"

"Together forever." he said.

Julia leaned close to Jonathan slowly, letting him feel the softness of her body against him. She placed one hand beneath the jacket on his chest, her fingers blindly trailing up and down on his skin. She leaned forward, kissing him softly, and when she pulled back, he was smiling. She smiled too, looking mischievously at him. Julia looked into his dark eyes again, and touched her other hand to his forehead, smoothing his hair back. When he smiled again, the smile was one of amusement.

All right, Julia thought, you want to be amused, I'll amuse you. Her face grew serious as she began to lower her right hand, the one that was on his chest. She lifted her palm, just tracing him with her fingers, and her new nails. Down the muscles of his chest, around his nipple, down the hard flatness of his stomach, past his navel, and down to the front belt loop of his jeans. She tugged slightly on the loop, and watched as he took in a sharp breath. Julia giggled, and looked up at his face. His lips were parted, his amused smile gone. His face was flushed, his eyes sparking with desire.

"Why . . . why did you do that?" he asked between heavy breaths.

"Because, silly, you wanted to be amused." Julia said with another giggle, wrapped both arms around his neck. She watched as he gave her a lopsided grin, settled his mouth on hers. They shared a long kiss, and then he mumbled against her mouth, "Lay down."

Julia lay back down on the bed, letting him settle his long, hard body down against hers. There was nothing menacing in the way they kissed now, only love, and desire fired it. His hand trailed down against the length of her body as they kissed her ribs, her hip, her thigh, and her legs that pressed tightly against him. "How do you like it?" he asked her, pulling up to look down at her face, long hair draping downward.

Julia smiled warmly. "I like it a lot," she purred, "I like it just fine."

Jonathan smiled back at her, buried his face in her hair. It smelled like roses, and leather.

After a while, Julia spoke. "Jonathan, I'm real tired. I think that if you stay any longer," she yawned, "I'll fall asleep under you."

Jonathan let his powers collect sent them out towards the east. "Yes, you're right. The sun's still a way off, but it's coming. I'll leave you now."

Jonathan got up to leave. Julia came with to the door as he unlocked it. "Good night." she said as he turned to kiss her one last time, and then, he was gone.

Julia changed into her yellow gown this night, crawled into the bed. Just before she slipped into the covers, she pulled the ties off the curtains. As soon as she hit the pillow, Julia fell asleep.

10

When Julia awoke, she felt a strong, menacing presence in her room. She didn't have to cry out. She knew it was Cory.

Julia turned over, backed up against the wall. Her eyes took in the surroundings. The fire had burnt out, but a sliver of light was coming in from below her bedroom door. In that light, and in the sight of her night-vision, she could see Cory standing near the edge of her bed. A look of amusement played on his face.

"Get away from me Cory." Julia warned. She was frightened by him being here, but not as much as last night. No, now she was more angry than afraid.

She stared at him relentlessly, but an unexpected pain shot up from her stomach, into her ribs. She was hungry, and worried that Cory would notice it.

"Julia," Cory said, uncrossing his arms, "did anyone ever tell you that you look like an angel when you sleep?"

"Yes, my mother." Julia hissed.

Cory gave a short laugh and sat on the edge of the bed. "You don't have a mother anymore, darling. You have a father, and a lover, all rolled into one." He made a face. "How disgusting."

Julia glared at him. "Maybe to you, but not to me. Leave."

"No." he said softly, an evil look crossing his features. "I think," he said, parting the net curtains and reaching out for her, "that it's time you stopped giving me orders."

Julia forced herself not to slap his hand away; it came to rest on her shoulder. His fingers stroked the fabric of her yellow gown. She watched, repulsed, as he moved across the bed, closer to her.

The anger passed out of Cory's face and another look that Julia didn't fully recognize came in. It was sourness, desire, and hunger. A type of hunger only a predator could have. "I told you, Julia. I told you that you could do better than him. Come with me. Live in the darkness with me. I will show you the true nature of the beast." Cory stroked her neck; his eyes were fused on the spot where the blood flowed through the veins. Now his fingers stilled, and he tipped her head slightly backward.

Julia felt her skin rise with goose bumps, a chill of terror going through her. She tried to move her head, but she couldn't; his hand held her steady. She pushed at him with her hands, but his other hand caught hers, and he pressed them down against the bed.

"What are you doing?" Julia gasped. "Don't you know what I am?"

Cory laughed against her neck. "Yes, I know what you are, a very alert, but vulnerable fledgling vampire. Now here's a question for you, Julia. Do you know what I'm capable of doing to you?"

Icy fear swept over Julia, and she struggled against him. Thoughts were spinning in her head of what Jon had told her about him, and what he could do. She felt his lips touch her throat, her hunter's senses screaming at her to get away, that the hunter had now become the hunted.

No! Julia screamed silently at him, throwing all her power into that single word. Cory's hands went to hold his temples, and Julia shoved at him hard, knocking him off the bed, through the net curtains, and onto the floor. Julia darted off the bed and ran towards the door, trying desperately to get away from Cory, but something awful happened.

Julia was reached for the door, her hand outstretched, when suddenly, she couldn't move. It was as simple as that. Her legs wouldn't respond, her arms wouldn't move. Her hand was still in the same position; ready to open the door, but she couldn't move. She felt that it was a wonder she could still breathe.

Cory came up behind her, pulled her to him from behind, his hand pushing her arm down. His arms locked around her, and she thought even if she could move, she'd never escape his grip.

"That wasn't very nice, Julia. Hardly cordial at all." Cory bent and kissed her cheek, sensing the undercurrent of fear jetting through her bloodstream. He smiled.

Julia felt her eyes tearing, and could not stop it, could not push him away. His mind was not holding her there; his very will had locked around her like a rope of air. She could think and breathe, and even cry, but her body would not respond. How powerful was he, anyway?

"I am more powerful then Jason is, Julia. He would never be able to keep you this way," he said, seemingly answering her question. "He would have to use his mind to do it. But you already know that, don't you, Julia? I also think that you know what I'm capable of doing to you, and to those you love. Christi is gone now, but that doesn't mean she's safe."

Cory let go of his will; the invisible barrier left Julia. She immediately lunged forward, but was stopped short by Cory's arms around her. He pulled her tight against him, and she let out a sound of fright.

"Yes, Julia. Be afraid." he said in a deadly whisper, and then spun her around to face him. Again he pulled her tight against him, and she found herself face to face with him. "Be *very* afraid," he said. Cory's mouth descended on hers before she had a chance to recover, and now, his tongue was inside her mouth, rubbing on her canines.

Julia was horrified to discover her body responded to this treatment. The stomach pangs of hunger increased, the roots of her teeth tingling like crazy, and her head swimming. Her legs felt like they were melting, and she clutched at him for the strength to stand. Finally, he pulled back from her, forced her head to his chest.

"Come on, Julia. I can feel how hungry you are. Let the monster come out. Unleash it." he whispered, rubbing her back with one hand.

"No. "

Cory grabbed Julia by her arms. He grinned, held her in one hand. With the other, he pulled his shirt and jacket away from his neck. "Drink, Julia. Drink from me, and become mine."

Julia gazed at his neck, her eyes taking in the fine blue veins that ran just beneath the surface. That ran with blood. Julia saw her hand reaching out for him, voluntarily this time. She was so, so hungry. Her own veins were dry and parched, but he had fed tonight, she could feel it. There was plenty enough for her to drink without even hurting him. And then they could leave together. On this last thought, Julia realized that he had been putting these thoughts into her head, into her mind, which was not functioning properly because of bloodlust.

Julia clamped her mouth shut, grinding her teeth together, forcing her canines, which had just begun to lengthen, to stay their normal size. When she felt the hunger subsiding, she trusted herself to look at him again.

"No, Cory. No." she said angrily and firmly.

Cory laughed, let her go. She had almost given in that time. Almost, but not quite. He settled his jacket back into place, passed by Julia to go to the door. He looked back at her, and with a taunting smile, he said, "You were reaching out for me, Julia."

Julia clenched her hands into fists, glared at him. "Get out." she growled.

Cory laughed again with vicious cruelty. "You will be mine, Julia. You will." Then he turned, and walked out the door, shutting it tightly behind him. Julia fell, trembling to the floor.

Jonathan was just coming up out of the basement, when he sensed Julia in trouble. At the doorway of the stairs, he opened the door a crack, and watched, unbelievingly, as Cory strode confidently out of Julia's room, and walked to Lizzi, who sat on the sofa.

"Is she joining us?" the girl vampire asked.

Cory reached down and took her hand in his, pulling her to her feet. "Soon, my darling, soon. Come now, Lizzi, don't you want to go to the park again?"

Lizzi nodded, followed after Cory out the door, and into the night.

Jonathan emerged from the shadows, just as the door slammed shut. The firelight reflected the anger in his face. So, I was right, Jonathan thought. Cory has been hurting Julia, after all. Jonathan stormed across the sitting room, and threw open Julia's door.

Julia stood near the fireplace, brushing her hair. When the door to her bedroom had been thrown open, she assumed it was Cory, back to do her damage, this time. The brush clattered to the floor, and Julia crouched low to the ground, her mouth open, ready to scream. But it was then that she realized that it was Jonathan, not Cory, who had stormed into her room.

Julia ignored the angry expression on his face, and jumped up, running to him, throwing herself into his arms. "Jonathan!" she cried, tears flowing fresh. She felt him stumble back a few steps from the impact, as his tense muscles loosened in response to her crying.

Jonathan cast a look over his shoulder to see Jason and everyone else entering the sitting room. Frowning, he reached back, and closed the door. Julia was sobbing against him, not refraining from crying after what had happened tonight.

"Jonathan," she sobbed, "Jonathan, hold me!" She wrapped her arms tighter around him, pressing herself close.

Jonathan lowered himself to the ground, bringing Julia with him, realizing how vulnerable she seemed. Sobbing hysterically, not trying to stop, dressed in her soft gown, he could not help but feel anguish for her.

And then he felt rage. Rage against Cory, who was apparently ruining her new life. Jonathan felt the heat rise to his face, and he pulled Julia even closer to him, crushingly tight; if she were human it would have hurt her.

"I'm going to kill him." Jonathan said in a low, calm tone.

For a minute, nothing but the sound of her sobbing filled the room. Then, it stopped.

Julia pulled away from Jonathan, but he didn't let go of her. She stared into his dark eyes, unbelieving of what he had said. How could he know? How could he? Then Julia understood. He didn't really know what Cory was doing to her, but he knew he was causing her pain, and that was enough for him.

"Jonathan, don't do that. You can't go after him. He'll . . . he'll kill you!" she said.

"He's hurt you. I know Cory is hurting you. I could rip him to shreds for that." he hissed.

"No, Jon, nothing's happening between us." Julia lied fiercely. She knew better than Jon did in this matter, or so she thought. She had to make Jonathan believe everything was fine, no matter what happened. "You're wrong," she said, her voice breaking on the last word.

"Am I?" Jonathan said in a reprimanding tone. Julia looked away from him. "What is he doing to you, Julia? Tell me."

"No, I, I can't. You'll be hurt, Christi will die, and all the others." Julia said, her eyes filling with tears. It was terrible not to tell Jonathan. But she loved him; she was protecting him now.

"I don't give a damn about the others!" Jonathan shouted, forcing her to look at him. "All I care about is you! And if you don't tell me what's wrong, I don't have any proof! I can't go after him!"

Julia raised her hand to cup Jonathan's cheek. "I know." she whispered, and seeing his exasperated look, added, "It's because I love you."

Jonathan let go of his anger with a giant sigh. He knew it was the truth, he'd end up getting killed, or worse. He decided that he'd just have to catch Cory in the act. He dug into his jean's pocket, and found the key to Julia's door. "Use this," he said, pressing it into her hand, "to keep you safe. Lock the door every morning before you go to sleep. Don't unlock it until I come for you at night." Jonathan paused, looking to the door. "It won't keep him out. Doors are easily broken. But it should let him know that I know something's up. He shouldn't be bothering you much after that."

Julia stared down at the key in her hand, and stood, placed it inside her desk drawer. Then she turned back to Jonathan, wiped the tears away from her face. She sat near him, and watched as he retrieved the brush from the floor. He stared at it a minute and then said, "Turn around."

Julia did as he asked her, and soon, she felt his hands in her hair, caressing it. She felt the brush in her hair, moving with long, gentle strokes.

Jonathan's hand, the one that wasn't brushing her hair, came to rest against the back of her neck, against the sensitive part of her skin. She felt the brush come away from her hair, and she closed her eyes. The brush fell down to the floor with a soft thud. Jonathan's hand moved from her neck, his fingers spreading, and pushing up into her hair, along the back of her head.

Julia sighed as she leaned her head back against his hand, feeling his other hand grasp her around the stomach. He turned her, with one hand still in her hair, the other around her middle.

Jonathan pulled her into his lap, so that she was lying across his legs. He removed his hand from her hair to cradle her head, and watched as her eyes opened a dazed expression on her face. She was so beautiful in the firelight, Jonathan wondered if this was all just a dream. But the weight of her against him told him that it was true, that she was really here, and he wasn't dreaming at all.

Julia raised her arm to Jonathan's neck, drawing him slowly down to her, so she could kiss him. She wanted him to kiss her, to love her, and he seemed to know it. Jonathan bent and kissed her softly, and Julia felt a rush of love go through her. She loved him, really did, and for the first time, she was glad that she could spend eternity with him. When she looked up at him again, he was smiling.

"I love you Julia." he whispered.

She was about to reply, when she felt the hunger pangs begin inside her again, stinging her veins anew. Julia moaned as it seized her, blowing full force, and then leaving her.

Jonathan lifted her to sit before him again, and watched her face, carefully. In a moment, he spoke. "You're hungry."

"Yes." Julia said with a frown.

"It's all right to be so, Julia. You'll learn how to control the hunger, to put it off until later." He looked at Julia again, his face concerned, and then he spoke again. "You're ravished." He shrugged off his jacket, pulled his hair away from his neck. "Drink from me a little."

Julia gasped. "It'll hurt you!" she exclaimed, pushing back into the dark corners of her mind, the thought that Cory had offered her the same thing, not too long ago.

Jonathan smiled. "It won't hurt me, Julia. Not this time. I'm willing to give you some, and you'll know when you've had enough. You won't try to drain me this time. At least I don't think so." He chuckled.

Julia hadn't heard the last sentence, not really. She had laid her head on Jonathan's shoulder, her lips against his neck. He smelled so good; it was making her drowsy. But her eyes remained open, watching the pale blue veins filled with strong, immortal blood. "Are you sure?" she murmured against his skin.

Jonathan felt the heat of desire rush through his body, as she whispered against him. "Yes, because we won't be leaving for a while, and I know how badly young ones need blood."

Julia closed her eyes, willed the hunger to come back to her. It hit her with the force of a tidal wave, breaking out a sweat all over her body. Her vision sharpened extremely, filled with red. She was gazing through red at his neck, at the veins in his neck at the blood, in the veins, in his neck.

Julia opened her mouth wide, feeling the tingling in her canines grow to a resounding ache, which spread over the entire upper jaw in her mouth. The fangs were extending, growing down, long and sharp. Her forehead was pounding, one thud after another, over and over, until she couldn't stand it any longer.

Without a sound, Julia tilted Jonathan's head back, stroked the soft skin of his neck for a moment with her left hand, her right under his back. Then her hand stilled on his shoulder, and she pulled him to her, her mouth gaping, the fangs ready to pierce his skin.

Jonathan held Julia as the transformation overcame her; he held her as her fingers grasped him, bringing amazing feelings to his body. It had been a long while, since another vampire had drawn blood from him, a very long time indeed. Not even Timothy had ever been able to do this, for Jon would not allow it. Almost never had the blood been taken by force, with the rare exception. But not for very many years had anyone taken blood from him while they were a vampire, and he himself was also. Come to think of it, it had been Jason then.

"How ironic." Jonathan whispered, smiling, as he felt Julia become ready to drive her fledgling teeth into him. Jonathan felt her breath against him, her lips as they softly pressed against him. An age-old cry rushed through him that meant danger, but with a questioning of pleasure. He winced slightly, as Julia bit into his neck.

Julia moaned when Jonathan's blood filled her mouth. It was too good, too sweet, too much like biting into a candy apple. But it was delicious. She gulped instinctively, and swallowed as the second spurt of blood hit the roof of her mouth. She swallowed again, and again. She vaguely wondered why she hadn't tasted this wonderfully sweet elixir from his before, but she remembered that she had been human then.

She felt the burning need subside a little, but his blood was not in her stomach. It went directly into her veins, making her stronger, connecting her to him. Julia felt so good at that moment, with the sweetness of Jon's life inside her, she almost didn't hear the nagging voice inside her mind. But in the end, she heard it. Don't make a habit of this, Julia. You don't want to go crazy, to become a Wild One, do you? Julia tried to ignore the question by whispering against his neck, "But it's so good!" and the internal voice replied, yes, but it's not filling you. It's like eating candy for dinner.

Julia sighed, for she knew that the sensible part of her brain was correct. She had to stop this, before she became addicted or worse. She didn't want to hurt Jonathan. But she could feel it; he was in such a state of absolute bliss, that he wasn't feeling a thing besides Julia inside him.

Julia withdrew from his neck, not even bothering to watch, as his wounds closed up. She sliced her index finger of her right hand, on her fangs, before they receded. And then, relaxed, panting, and dripping with sweat, the goddess Julia held her finger out to Jonathan.

When Jonathan felt her pull away, it was like wakening from a dream, one that he hadn't wanted to end. But then, hazily, he saw Julia's finger, dripping with blood, held out to him like a gift. He tried to refuse her, but he couldn't in his state. In the end, she got her way.

Julia smiled as Jonathan took her finger into his mouth, his glazed dark brown eyes closing. She felt him sucking on her finger ever so softly, his tongue running back and fourth across it. He moaned now, with barely restrained hunger; she wondered why he wasn't letting it out.

Jonathan jerked away as he felt the hunger build slightly. He was supposed to give to Julia, not take. But when he opened his eyes again, gasping for breath, and saw the hurt in her eyes, he understood. She had wanted to give something back.

Jonathan grabbed her in his arms swiftly, and pulled her down with him, until they were lying side by side on the hard wood floor. Julia didn't say anything. She couldn't find the words. She just stared into Jonathan's eyes, searching for an answer to the question she didn't even know how to ask. She felt the pressure of his hands on his arms as he pulled her closer to him, so close in fact, that their bodies seemed almost one.

Julia pressed her head against his strong chest, listening to his heartbeat, and the blood pumping through it. She squeezed her eyes shut, tried to understand her erratic emotions, but none of the answers made any sense to her.

Jonathan felt her confusion as he held her painfully close, looking beyond her, at the fire. Something very important had happened between them tonight, something very beautiful. He knew that she had felt it too, but she didn't know how to say it, or how to ask him what it was. Jonathan himself didn't even know. He decided to ask Jason later what had happened. For now, he'd just hold Julia in his arms. "I love you, Julia." he said.

"Mahhummmphhooo." came from Julia; her face still pressed against him, the words muffled by his tight grip on her.

Jonathan smiled. Despite all the odds and problems, he knew that they were going to make it to the end of the world together. He'd bet immortality on it.

11

When Jonathan eventually left the room, Julia changed her clothes. Stripping off her nightgown, she put on clean underwear, jeans, shirt, sneakers, and her leather jacket. She pulled her hair away from her face, and fastened it against the back of her neck with a silver hair clip.

As she made her bed, tied the curtains back in place, she thought about what Jonathan had said before he had left; that Jason wanted to talk to her about something important.

Something important, she thought to herself, what could that be? More threats?

But then she realized that if Jason had wanted to threaten her or hurt her in any way, Jonathan wouldn't have permitted her to speak with him. "Or least he would have tried." she reflected with a knowing smile.

When Julia realized there was nothing more she could do to procrastinate meeting with Jason, she went into her desk drawer, removed the key to her room. She also took out the key ring that held her motorcycle key, house key, and a few others. She put the key to her room on the chain, stuffed it into her pocket, and went to the door.

Julia opened the door and stepped out into the sitting room. No one looked up at her as she moved into the center of the room. They were all indulged in a pizza that sat, steaming, on a large coffee table. Everyone ate, with the exception of Jason.

Lizzi and Cory were nowhere in sight.

Jonathan sat on the sofa, which was no surprise to Julia. He often sat there, as if it actually was his. She was now sure he had acquired all the blankets, which draped over it.

Timothy sat on a plush armchair to the right of the sofa Rikki on a wooden chair, and Steven on a rocking chair, creating a complete circle. Jason sat on the far end of the room in his wicker chair, near the stairs to the basement, where the shadows fell across the room.

Julia looked at Jason for a moment, watching the way his face was turned, how the smoke from his cigarette rose into the air with every puff he took. She could smell the smoke, a harsh type of tobacco, probably chosen for that reason. She wondered what Jason could want from her this time, as she watched him blow the smoke out from his lungs, into the air. Then his face turned, and his flashing blue eyes fixed right on her.

Her face burning from embarrassment, Julia turned away quickly and approached Jonathan, who was eating the pizza with wild abandon. She looked at the others who were eating, and they all appeared to her the same way. It was as if they couldn't get enough of it, as if eating this pizza was a life and death matter.

Julia looked down at the coffee table, pulled to the middle of the circle of seats, and down at the steaming pizza. Actually, she corrected herself, at the three slices that were left. She closed her eyes and breathed in all the scents of the pizza the pepperoni, the mozzarella cheese, the sauce, the spices, the hamburger, and the crust.

Julia heard a slight, distinct laughter surround her. When she opened her eyes, she looked at them all. Their mouths were stuffed with food, and they were all smiling at her.

"Go ahead, take a piece." the one called Steven said.

"Yeah, you can't get anything out of it by lookin' at it." Timothy said.

Julia looked at Jonathan and asked timidly, "Can I digest it?" Julia winced as another round of laughter filled the room.

Jonathan swallowed, smiled warmly at her. "It isn't blood, Julia. It will pass right through you."

"What will happen then?" she asked.

"Nothing." Jonathan said.

"It just means that early tomorrow night you'll be hitting the bushes out back or a gas station," said Rikki.

Julia grinned nervously, picking up the greasy pizza in her fingers. She felt clumsy holding it, like a baby, learning all over again how to eat. She wasn't hungry for it, but wasn't disgusted with it either. It just didn't appeal to her. Suddenly, she felt someone brushing her mind with theirs.

"That will change." Jason's voice came, from the far side of the room.

Julia felt Jonathan's hand stroking her leg, sending flames of pleasure up her body. In less than a second, she felt really silly, standing here in the middle of the room, holding this stupid pizza in front of her face while Jonathan was doing…whatever he was doing.

"Julia, just eat it," he said.

Julia shrugged her shoulders, opened her mouth. She took a big bite of the pizza, using her normal teeth, just as she had eaten when human. But something was wrong. It tasted awful!

Julia dropped the remainder of the pizza back down onto the box, and clutched at her throat. She was gagging. Her body did not want this food, this human food. It tasted like she had just bitten into a cardboard box.

"Julia, don't worry, just eat it. You'll get over it in a minute." Rikki was saying.

186

"You have to become used to the treats of humanity all over again, love." Jonathan said.

Julia nodded and chewed at it relentlessly, her eyes tearing, her breath coming in gasps. But soon, little tastes of flavor began to drown out the box-taste in her mouth. By the time it was mashed up enough to swallow, it tasted like a pizza again. In fact, it tasted like the best pizza she had ever eaten!

Julia swallowed the mouthful, pushing it down into her stomach. Once it hit, Julia felt as if she were going to throw it up all over the sitting room. She leaned over; her hand on her mouth as heaves wracked her body. But soon, the feeling passed. She straightened, shook herself, and smiled at Jonathan.

"Finish the slice." he said.

Julia had two more pieces, and by the time she was done, she could eat like a human again, no problem. Even her taste buds had increased, to the point where everything in the pizza stood out individually. She now understood why the boys had eaten it; it tasted exquisite.

As Julia stood there, licking her fingers when the pizza was gone, she listened to the boys talk. Her other hand rested on Jonathan's shoulder, and she wondered if she were truly immortal. But then, she felt the powerful stroking in her mind again, the presence she knew to be Jason.

Come, Julia.

Julia turned to see Jason extinguish the cigarette in a coffee can, stand up, and walk out the doors, shutting them behind him. She looked down at Jonathan, but he seemed heavily engrossed in conversation with Steven, totally unaware of what was happening around him.

Julia walked slowly, zipping up her jacket as she went. She opened the doors, stepped out, and closed them behind her.

Julia gazed up at the sky; the night was clear, the moon still out. The temperature of the air had increased a bit since last night, and the snow had melted during the day, leaving only a few inches on the ground.

She looked out into the driveway, making sure that Cory had gone. Then, as she looked straight across from her, a little ways into the driveway, she saw Jason.

He stood there with his hands in his overcoat pockets, his head tilted up towards the moon. His back was turned against her, and his hair fell back, down over his shoulders. The light from the moon made the orange hair shimmer, and appear glossy.

Julia walked to Jason and stood behind him, about four feet away. She still did not trust him. Suddenly, he began to speak.

"Did you ever wonder what it would be like to go up there? To touch the moon?" he asked her, his gaze still on it. "I used to wonder that a long time ago, when I was alone at night far away." Jason's voice came to a stop, and he took a deep breath. "People did go to the moon though. In the 1960's, for the first time. What a shock that was to me. Jon took it better. I guess that's because I was alive a lot longer ago then he had been. He had been expecting it I guess, not I." He turned and looked down at Julia and smiled. "It is always a shock."

Julia fell back a few steps, without realizing it. Being near him reminded her of the time he had hurt her, when he had almost killed her. When he had almost broken her arm. Her hand went up to massage that arm, without her thinking of it.

Jason's eyes followed her hand motions, the smile vanishing, his eyes becoming hard. "Are you afraid of me?" he asked.

Julia didn't answer right away. She shoved her hands into her pockets defiantly and shook her head. "No."

Jason laughed shortly, his icy eyes meeting hers once again. "You are." he said. "But you don't need to be."

His voice had taken on a quality she had only heard once before, when he had thanked her for risking her life for Rikki's. "What did you want, Jason?" she asked, a little shakily.

Jason smiled again. "We've always been enemies, haven't we, Julia Anderson?" When she didn't answer, he continued. "Well, I didn't want it this way. Why would I want and ongoing war with someone who lived in my own house? When you killed my son," Jason said, and icy flash in his eyes, "I hated you. And I couldn't have given you that damn wine without you hating me, for what I made you become. I won't blame Jonathan for any of this. He wanted you, he loved you. He never loved me. I treated him wrong, I was stupid. I wanted to help him overcome the grief that was consuming him again, like a hellfire."

Julia's eyes clouded over at the thought of Jonathan in pain, and she lowered her head. She felt Jason's hand come to rest on her shoulder, gently, and her head jerked up to look at him.

"Shh. I'm not going to hurt you," he said. "When you saved Rikki, it was like you gave my son back to me. He loved me, Rikki loves me. You cared about Rikki enough to put your life on the line for him. You helped him.

"Julia, I know that I started this whole thing in the first place. I should have kept Jonathan away from you that night in the park. I tried, but his love won out. I'm so sorry, Julia. It was my own fault. I took your humanity away." Jason turned away from her, removing his hand from her shoulder.

Julia stood there a moment, shocked, realizing how close to tears Jason had really come. He was showing her a side of himself, rarely seen by anyone. She didn't want him to be upset with this. She approached him, reaching out for him. "Jason," she began.

"Don't, Julia." he said in that voice, which seemed so uncharacteristic of him.

Don't what, she wanted about to ask, when he turned back to her again, the moonlight setting off his perfect features.

"You won't ever know how important it was to me, saving Rikki in that way, your own way. It was an act of…nobility." he said, smiling, a far-off look in his eyes. "I have thought about this for a while now, and I have come to a conclusion. I no longer feel that hatred towards you, girl. I just don't hate you. In fact, I'm grateful."

Jason took a step closer to her, so close that their bodies were almost touching. But Julia felt no menace, no threat, no lust - just simple warmth that spoke friendship. Julia smiled.

"I know you don't like me very much right now, and frankly, I don't blame you. I've hurt you enough for you to hate me forever. I hope you'll forgive me for what I've done. We'll live forever, Julia; there's eternity for that matter. But," he said, his hand digging into his pocket, "I want to give this to you, as a token of my appreciation."

Jason pulled out something from his pocket, held it between them. Julia stepped back, saw what his pale hands held out to her, and gasped.

In his hands, Jason held a bracelet of pure gold; emeralds embedded into the links. It was delicately woven, but appeared to be sturdy enough to withstand years and years, being carefully tucked away. The stones glimmered with a sheer radiance, which took her breath away.

"Go on, take it." Jason whispered. "I have plenty where this came from. I won't miss it."

Julia raised her right hand to touch the bracelet, her mouth hanging wide open. "I can't take this!" she gasped. "It must be worth a fortune!"

Jason pressed the jewelry into her hand, before she could object again. "It's not important to me," he said.

Julia gazed up at him, at the serene look on his face. "How could it not be important? Where did it come from?"

Jason stared at her for a moment. Then he said quietly, "It came out of my mother's collection."

"Your mother's?" she asked, unbelievingly.

"Yes, you see, I was born into royalty a long, long time ago. Things were very different then, from the way they are today. I suffered many hardships, before coming here to America. The problems began before my mother even died."

"How did she die?" Julia asked, immediately regretting the question.

"By fire."

"Oh."Julia did not press the statement, did not ask anything more of Jason's mortal life. His face was laced with pain. "Jason, when did you become . . . " She was left searching for a way to end the sentence, clutching the bracelet in her hand.

Jason smiled knowingly. "A vampire?"

Julia nodded.

"I was reborn to this world in the summer of 1700, in the slums of Paris, France."

Julia's eyes widened, her mouth falling open again in shock. "You're old!" she exclaimed.

Jason chuckled, and said, "I suppose that you could say so. I am precisely two hundred and eighty-nine years old. That is a long time, a very long time. I made Devin in Paris, Jonathan and Andrew here in Vermont. I have also created several others who live in America." He stretched his arms out, indicating what he was saying. "I like America. The blood here is good, the people are defiant."

Julia frowned despite herself. She still wasn't used to the blood talk that seemed so trivial, to all the others.

Jason took her other hand, the one that was empty, and said, "Come, Julia. Your lover's waiting for you inside. But promise me this. Put the bracelet away, and do not tell the others about our coming together. I want them to know on their own time."

"Sure." Julia said with a smile. They entered the mansion together, and Julia ran quickly into her room, tucking Jason's gift into a drawer in her bureau. She hid it where no one would find it. For the first time since she met Jason, Julia did what he told her to do.

Later that night, Jonathan took Julia into the surrounding mountains, and together they located a pair of old hobos, who were so miserable in poverty and disease, that they wanted to die. Jonathan took the old woman, Julia the old man.

The blood was delicious, filling. It gave her strength and power, and awakened tremendous feelings inside of her. Wanton desires, and animal characteristics, blossomed in her spinning head.

After the victims were dead, Julia had sprawled out on the cave's floor that the vagrants had been sleeping on, and pulled off her jacket. Jonathan crawled over to her when he was finished, his jacket off, dripping with blood.

Julia, swimming in her new desires, had licked off all the blood from Jonathan's body, her tongue tracing patterns on his skin. He did the same to her, and it ended in a kaleidoscope of frantic kissing and bodies entwining. Violent touching, groping, pressing, like animals.

Julia climbed on top of him, ready to beg him to take her body, when he scrambled out from beneath her, leaving her breathless and unfulfilled. He stared at her, the way she was crouched against the ground, her hair falling out of the clip, her mouth open, but mute. Her eyes were narrowed and burning with hidden fire.

"That wasn't right," he said, breathless himself. "It wasn't right for us. We can't do things that way."

"Why?" she growled.

"Think about it, Julia. You're only reacting to the call of the blood inside you, the desires it brought you. We can't love each other that way. Not like animals."

Julia pulled herself to her feet, her breath and reason returning. Her eyes were filling with tears. "But that's what you made me, Jonathan. You made me an animal." She sobbed, putting her hands in her face.

Jonathan sighed, pulling her close to him. She was still changing inside her mind, still adapting to the new feelings inside her. "Julia, it will happen when the time is right. When what we're feeling is love, not hunger."

"I know, I know." she cried.

"Come on, Julia. Let's go home," he said. He stooped down, getting their jackets from the floor. He helped her put hers on, and then put on his.

They exited the cave and stood in the cold, snowy, darkness. Julia tugged at his arm, and Jonathan looked down at her.

Julia looked up at him with wide, scared eyes. "You don't hate me for what happened, do you, because if you did I couldn't live with it. I think I'd kill myself."

Jonathan gaped at her, silent, trying to process what she had said. His mouth moved, but he couldn't find the words. Finally, he whispered despairingly, "I love you!"

Julia opened her mouth to say something else, but the words were cut off. Jonathan was kissing her.

12

A week in Julia's life went by. It was a week of awakening to new feelings, struggles, blood lust, and love. The whole week was one continuous night to her, but it didn't matter, for she was with Jonathan, the one that she loved.

Julia hadn't seen Cory or Lizzi, since the night Jon had given her the key to her door. She felt their presence sometimes, watching, waiting, but for what she did not know. She finally gave up the vigil for them, and grasped onto Jonathan, the most stable thing in her New World.

Julia was truly homesick this night, the night before Christmas Eve. Her mind kept filling with visions of how things used to be spending time with her mother and sister, sitting near the family room fire, the giant tree in the corner, eating the roast turkey dinner.

Julia clutched onto Jonathan's arm, shifted in her seat on the stairs in the front of the mansion, and sighed. Her eyes wandered up to the stars. It was a beautiful clear night.

"I want to go home." Julia murmured under her breath, momentarily forgetting how excellent Jonathan's hearing was.

"What?" he demanded.

"I want to go home for the holidays, Jonathan, and I want you to come with me." She turned her head and looked at him. With his lips slightly parted, he looked as if someone had just asked him to swallow a beetle. He was utterly shocked.

Julia smiled. "I want you to come as my fiancé, so I have a good reason to never come home again." Julia laughed at his new, puzzled expression, and kissed his open mouth. "Yes, as my fiancé! It's the perfect setup, the perfect plan. I'll tell my mother that you're a Vampire Researcher from California, and I'll say that I've become one too. I'll tell her we're observing vampires' sleeping habits, and that will explain why we sleep all day, and board the windows. My mom will give me one of those great 'Ohhh's', and then she won't bother us about it. I know that Gayle will go along with it."

Jonathan didn't say anything, just shut his mouth.

"Come on, Jonathan, please?" she begged, giving his hand a little squeeze.

Jonathan contemplated it for a moment, and then said, "Well, I guess so. I mean, if you really want to." He looked down and mumbled, "It's a very big risk."

Julia ignored the last sentence and laughed, hugging him. "Oh, I really want to! Tonight we'll get the rings and some new clothes for you." Jon's eyebrows went up. "Yes, clothes, silly. My mother wants me to marry a respectable gentleman. One who has good morals. Not a wild man."

Jonathan grinned, and trailed his hand upward on her leg. "So, I'm a wild man, huh? What do you think you are, little girl, a canary?"

Julia frowned, put his hand back on his knee. "Cut that out," she said.

Jonathan shrugged, pretended to pout. Julia giggled again, at his expression. Jonathan pouted some more, and Julia burst into a hysterical fit of giggles. She began to lose her balance, and almost fell off the stairs, when Jonathan put his arms around her, pulled her to him quickly.

Julia grinned, and climbed onto his lap, one leg on either side of his body. "My hero." she purred.

Jonathan's hands moved on her body. He pulled the tucked-in ends of her flannel shirt out of her jeans, and placed one hand on the bare skin of her back, and his other hand, the one that was still on the outside, went downwards. "I think it's time I lived up to my reputation. Don't you?"

"Oh yes indeed, my darling vampire boy." she said, her fingers playing with the zipper on his jacket.

Julia kissed him then, her mouth opening against his, and they began a session of deep kissing. Jonathan kissed her cheek, her neck. His teeth nipped slightly at the place where he had drunk from her a week ago. Julia's hands cradled his head, her back arching. Jonathan unzipped her jacket a little way, and unbuttoned the first button on her flannel shirt. He placed kisses near her collarbone, and then she pulled away from him, giggling again.

Jonathan looked up at her, saw that her head was turned to one side. "What is it?" he asked. He turned, and saw someone walking back to the mansion from the driveway, a cocky grin on his face. It was Steven. Jonathan smiled and looked down. Talk about being caught with your pants down.

Julia sat beside him again. Steven walked up to them, smiling down at Jonathan. "Nice night, isn't it?" Steven asked.

"Just go inside," Jonathan mumbled, and Julia blushed. Steven chuckled to himself as he passed them by, slamming the front door shut behind him

Jonathan stood up, dusting his pants off. "Are you coming or not?" he asked her after a minute.

"Where?" she asked, the idea completely had gone from her mind.

"The mall?" Jonathan sighed, exasperated.

Julia got up and put her hand on his shoulder, finally serious. "You're right, we should get going. Could you get some money? I'll wait out here."

When Jonathan came back, stuffing a rather large roll of greenback bills into his pocket, Julia had uncovered the bikes, for a length of large canvas had been spread over them.

Julia looked up at Jonathan and smiled, holding her keys in her hand. "Do you want to bring anything from inside?" he asked her.

"No, I don't think so. I still have some clothes at home that I can use. What about you?"

Jonathan smiled, opened his jacket, and dug into one of the inside pockets. He pulled out a sheathed ivory handled dagger, and a wrapped up package, which Julia supposed, was his feather. "All I need are these, my chain you wear, and of course, you." Jonathan put his things back into his pocket, closed his jacket, and grasped Julia's hands in his.

"Jon, we should leave." she said, pulling back, but not before he took the keys from her hand. "What are you doing? Give me those back."

"No, not unless you promise to ride behind me on my bike. You haven't done that since you returned, and it would make me feel better."

"About what?"

"I don't know, keeping track of where you are." Julia was about to protest, but he placed a finger on her lips, silencing her. "Please?"

Julia knew he didn't have to ask her. As her vampire father, he could make her do anything, really. Anything he wished. His blood was more potent in her veins, her will belonged to him. But she knew that he would never exert that power over her, and so she kissed his finger. "Alright, love. I will."

Jonathan smiled, and gave her the keys back. Julia tucked them into her pocket, and ran her hand over the cool metal of her bike. She had a strange feeling that she wouldn't be seeing it, for a while.

When Jon pulled his giant motorcycle out from under the canvas, Julia stared at the cover a minute, and then at the place where Cory had parked his car. Maybe she'd be getting rid of him this way, once and for all.

"Come on, Julia!"

Julia was shaken from her thoughts, as Jonathan called to her. His bike was ready, and roaring. Julia ran to him, and climbed onto the back, wrapping her arms around him. It felt so good to be near him, the Harley under her. She felt so strong.

As they pulled away, down the driveway of the mansion, Julia felt different. She felt scared and tense, the air around her thin. She felt eyes watching her, and for a moment thought it was Cory. But when she turned her head back to the mansion, she saw Jason standing in the driveway, a look of peaceful understanding on his face. He wasn't smiling while he looked at her, but his face seemed calm. He held up his arm, and raised his hand in a farewell gesture.

Julia smiled at him, waved back. Then they pulled out onto the dirt road, and the mansion and its owners were gone.

Inside the Valley Mall, Julia and Jonathan went shopping. Well, Julia was shopping, Jonathan was griping. He said he didn't want to look like a pinkie-boy, whatever that was.

So far, Julia had him buy a pair of good blue jeans, a blue button down shirt, and expensive sweater, a pair of black sneakers, one gray suit and white cotton shirt, a gray tie, and a dark blue ski-jacket. He refused to buy any dress shoes.

"I never wore them in my life, I won't wear them now!" he had yelled out a bit too loudly, receiving stares from many people around them.

They went to the jewelers in the mall, and decided on getting a diamond-studded ring for Julia and a gold band for Jonathan. They decided that the rings would do for engagement as well as the wedding.

The dénouement of the night was Jonathan's haircut. He moaned and groaned upon entering. He complained several times that he had never liked it short, and about the use of mirrors.

"Well, if you'd just calm down, you could make them think you have a reflection. You told me that you could do that."

"Well, yes." Jonathan replied, fidgeting in his chair like a little boy. "I can't. I'm not old enough."

"I know that." Jon said, looking agitated. Their whispers in the waiting room were getting louder. He watched as the receptionist said "Nexxtttttt?" in her sweetest voice, and winced. "That's me."

"I know that." Julia repeated him in the same agitated tone. She let Jon smirk at her, and kiss her lightly.

"I love you."

Julia rolled her eyes. "Just do it." She gave him a shove, and he stood up, fingering his hair. He gave her a pitiful look. "Just go! And when you get out, you can change your clothes." Jonathan frowned at her, but headed towards his assigned room.

When he came out, Julia almost cried. His hair was gone. In its place was a well-brushed short-clipped mop of dark hair. He had bangs in front, but the back of his hair didn't even touch his jacket's collar. He was pouting. Clasped in his hand was the dangling part of his earring. In his ear was the remaining silver stud.

"Oh, Jon, I'm sorry. I didn't mean to have them do *that*!" Jonathan smiled at her as he paid the blushing young receptionist.

Jonathan came to Julia, taking half the bags from her hand, pulling her to her feet. He pulled her close to him and whispered in her ear, "I think you should know something. It'll all grow back by tomorrow night. As the dead do sleep, know what I mean?"

Julia walked in silence next to him, as they headed for a bathroom, where he would change his clothing. "So that part was true too," she said softly.

"What? Oh, from the books, you mean. The vampire sleeps, and by day, the hair that was cut so carefully the night before, grows to the length in which he had died. It is mentioned in several stories and movies. But what they say is true, at least about that." he said gruffly. "It is natural to us. I have done it before, just don't like it.

Jonathan smiled down at Julia, who had stopped walking, now staring at him, open-mouthed. "I didn't know you read those books. In fact, I thought you would reject vampire novels all together."

"No, not I. I've read my fair share of them. Come on."

"But I thought . . . "

"What, that I don't read?

"No, I've seen the study and all the books there. I just have never seen any on vampires."

"That's because Jason doesn't like them. Tell me, Julia, Have you ever gone into the third floor? No? Why, because it's locked? You know what you are. Now, a little lock shouldn't stop you. Remind me to take you up there when we go home. It's my own refuge, and study." Jonathan left Julia, and headed into the bathroom to change.

Julia sighed at the thought of those words, when we go home. It seemed like forever, to her.

After Jonathan had changed, they started out for Connecticut. Jonathan's other clothes were packed snugly onto the bike behind Julia, as they were sped away. She kept her head buried into Jon's back for the first twenty miles or so, holding her breath as they zoomed past cars, and cut them off. A tirade of horns blew at them, and Jonathan's wild laughter filled the air. What little of air there was.

When she finally picked up her head and glanced out at the surroundings, which mainly consisted of blurs, she heard a police siren start up. Jonathan laughed again, and pushed the bike faster. When the cop finally caught up with them, Jon just stared into the cop's eyes, and the cop pulled himself over to the curb.

"The only way to travel, Julia!" he screamed over to her.

Julia sighed, closed her eyes, and held onto him tightly. How much more of this would occur, before they finally got to the border of Connecticut?

At about 12:30 PM, they pulled into Julia's driveway. Jonathan stared at the house in awe as he cut the motor, and Julia climbed off.

"Julia, it . . . it looks like a future model of Jason's mansion. I don't mean future, I just mean now." He smiled, shook his head. "I sound like a babbling idiot."

Julia pulled the bags from the back of the bike, gave them to him as he stood up, still staring at the house. "I know, it was my first reaction too. We used to live across town, but I bought this, and we moved here. Do you like it?"

Julia barely heard his answer. She had run up onto the front porch, inserted her house key into the lock, and opened the door. She heard Jonathan yell to her, but she didn't understand what he was so worried about. It was her home. There couldn't be any danger here.

Julia stepped inside the doorway, and into the room. Then she almost dropped her keys. Air pressure, hard and hot came down on her. It didn't hurt, just *pressed*. She could see the room around her, and hear the faint breathing of the people above her, but something else was happening here. Julia's night vision, that was usually clear, took on a sickly shade of pale green. She started to panic, when she felt Jonathan grab her, and slam the door shut in front of her face.

Julia took a deep breath of pure night air, and leaned against him. Then she looked at the closed front door. The pressure was gone, here on the outside. So was the eerie greenness.

"What happened?" she managed after a moment.

"You weren't invited in, Julia. I thought you'd know better than that," he said, reprimanding.

"But nothing happened, Jonathan. I didn't explode, or melt, or anything!" she protested.

"You watch too many movies, Julia. You know the feeling you were experiencing? You just feel that, until a human sees you. Then, by some part of our nature I don't understand, you will be thrown back out the way you came in, by a great gust of air. Just like Devin was the night he visited your sister."

Julia stared at him. "You mean he was in my house? Oh, yes, I think I remember now her nightmare, the man with the blond hair. Damn! I'm glad he's dead! He was going to kill her, wasn't he?" Jonathan looked at her, silent. Julia shrugged. "I don't care, anyway, that's all past now. Are there other rules about houses?"

"Yes," Jon said, and then looked up. "Put your keys into your pocket, Julia. Your mother and sister are awake."

Julia did so. "Well?"

"We can enter any house that vampires inhabit, without an invitation. We can take any human into our homes, to live there. If a human, or human family, is on vacation from their home, and no one is living there, we can enter, but when they return the effect is the same as before. We just can't enter a home that humans sleep in without that pressure, and the inevitable reaction if they see us. A home that just humans and no vampires live in. That's all." As soon as Jonathan finished speaking, the door swung open.

Jeanne Anderson stood there; hair messed up and in a night robe. "Julia! Do you know what time it is? Where have you been?" Julia shrugged, as her mother looked up to see the tall, dark man next to her daughter. "Oh." she said quietly.

Jonathan gave Julia a nudge in the back. "Mom? Can we come in? I mean both of us? I think I should explain."

Jeanne nodded, her eyes narrowing. "Yes, come in. Both of you."

Julia stepped into the now well-lit room, and smiled when she felt no pressure holding her down. The room felt normal. She looked up at Jonathan; he was right about all that houses stuff.

"Well Julia? Aren't you going to tell me who he is?" Jeanne said, indicating Jon. From the corner of her eye, Julia saw Gayle coming down the stairway, her hand over her mouth.

"Yes, Mom, I'd like you to meet my fiancé." She giggled as she heard her mother take in a quick breath. "Mom, this is…" She was just about to introduce Jonathan, when a small scared voice from the stairway spoke up.

"Jonathan!" Gayle gasped.

"Yes, his name is Jonathan." Julia said, frowning at Gayle. Gayle stared at Julia, as Julia let the sounds of her mother and Jonathan talking, pass completely from her ears. All her power focused on Gayle.

Shut Up!

Gayle stiffened and barely stifled a scream. She ran back up the stairs, her eyes tearing, and Julia's mind-voice ringing in her brain. It couldn't be, it just couldn't! Gayle flung herself down on the bed, in her room, and cried.

Julia looked down from the now empty stairway, wondering if she had done the right thing. She decided to deal with her mother first, and later talk to Gayle. She looked over at Jon. He was putting on the charm real thick, and Jeanne was having a fit over him.

Julia smiled to herself. She had always known this would work. Mortals on the planet would fall in love with Jonathan if he let them, and her mother was no exception.

"Oh, Julia, he's wonderful! He's just perfect for you!" Jeanne was saying, her anger forgotten. She hugged Jonathan, and then Julia.

"Yes, Mrs. Anderson, I've wanted to meet you for a while now. Julia's said so many good things about you. You are a really kind woman."

Jeanne Anderson blushed, shaking her head, her own dark blond curls flying. "Oh no, I'm sure Julia told you about me, but she must have stretched the truth. And please, call me Jeanne." She looked down at their clasped hands. "But, where are your rings?"

"Um," said Jonathan, and looked to Julia for help.

"We were waiting until we got here to put them on. Mom, I hate to tell you this so soon, but we can only stay here a little while. We have to get back home."

"To California." Jon put in.

"Yes, so we need to be married soon, all right?"

"Oh, all right. Well, come and make yourself at home, get everything settled, and you two can put on your rings. I want to see this." Jeanne said. She gave a glance up the stairs. "Gayle?" she called, and when there was no reply, she said, "I guess she went back to sleep."

After Julia had brought all of Jonathan's things upstairs, and took off her coat, she went back downstairs and into the parlor where Jon sat with her mother, holding two small velvet boxes. For some reason she felt like a giddy schoolgirl. She didn't understand why. This was all just an act, wasn't it?

"Come here, Julia." Jon said when Julia stood at the bottom of the stairs, not moving. His eyes were sparkling, and her mother's were watering.

Julia walked up to him, and took the box that held his ring from his hand. Jonathan knelt down in front of her, and opened the box in which her ring was in. The diamonds glittered in the light, and when she looked at Jonathan, there was the purest smile of love she had ever seen. In the seconds that followed, he spoke to her inside her mind.

Julia, when I say these words, I mean them with all my heart. I love you, and I want to marry you. We will be together forever and we should do things right.

"Jonathan." Julia whispered, her eyes filling over with tears. He really meant it this time. It wasn't just an act. Julia wiped her eyes.

Jonathan slipped the ring onto her finger and said, "Julia Anderson, my love forever, will you marry me?"

Julia opened the box that held Jon's ring, and put it on his finger. She raised her hand to his, and stared at their rings together. She couldn't believe that all this was really happening, and she forgot that he had asked her a very important question.

"I love you, Jonathan. I love you." she collapsed into his arms, holding onto him, not planning to let go, ever. She was dimly aware of her mother crying nearby.

"Well Julia?" he said after a moment.

"Oh, of course I'll marry you!" she cried out.

After all the excitement had quieted down, Julia told her mother her version of where Jon had come from, and the California Vampire Researchers.

She felt a bit guilty about lying to her mother about everything. Especially when her mother insisted on having the wedding in Connecticut. Then she felt worse, telling her mother that they had to have a judge, instead of a priest like her mom would have wanted, and nothing holy what-so-ever around them. But with a little mind persuasion, the scheme worked.

Her mother agreed to everything, and promised to have it all set up. Julia and Jonathan were to get married the night after Christmas, in the parlor.

Then, Julia and Jonathan went up into Julia's room with boards and nails, and heavy, thick curtains. They boarded up her windows, and covered the glass doors that led to her balcony with the heavy curtains. When she was sure that no light would be able to penetrate, she went to Jonathan, and hugged him.

"Vampires. To be married." she sighed.

"Why is that so strange?" he questioned her.

Julia pulled back and started to arrange the sheets on the spare bed. Christi used to sleep on it, when she stayed over. "It's not strange, just different, that's all. And I never though my wedding would be like this."

Jonathan watched her as she worked. "It's something that has to be, love. You know that."

"Hmmm." said Julia, and after a moment, "I would never have thought that you really wanted to marry me."

"Julia," he whispered as he came up behind her and pulled her up against him, so that her back was against his chest. She stopped what she was doing, relaxed against him. "I love you. I have made you my daughter, my lover, and soon you will be my wife. My first wife, and my only wife."

Can't you see how much I need you?

Julia closed her eyes and let his dark rich voice fill her mind. She pushed back against him, and her head tilted to one side. She felt his lips, soft as satin, brush against her neck.

Take me Jonathan. Take all of me into yourself. With you I am whole.

Jonathan sighed. "I can't now," he said sadly, releasing her. "Not now that we're engaged. That's the way it was, so many years ago."

Julia turned around to face him, her hand reaching up to touch his face. "That was a long time ago."

Jonathan looked down at her, his eyes filling with sadness. "I know. I can't help but remember her. You make me remember..."

Julia did not let him finish his sentence. She kissed him gently but firmly; cutting off the anguished memories that hurt her, as much as they hurt him. She felt his arms go up to hold her, his hands against her body, his body shaking very slightly. At that moment, she knew old rules or no, if she asked him to make love to her again, he would not refuse her. But, so not to abuse him, she resolved not to ask again, tonight.

Julia pulled back from him, staring up into his dark eyes. "No more tears, my darling. I'm with you now." she said softly.

Julia turned to her bureau, and after a few moments of digging, found what she was looking for. A pair of soft cotton jogging shorts that had belonged to her father. One of the many items of clothing he had left behind. Her mother had wanted none of it in her room, at the old house, Vermont, or here, and so Julia had taken it all into her rooms, for safekeeping.

As if he'd ever really come back, she thought, anger seeping into her face.

Julia shook the angry feelings off, turned back to Jonathan, placed the shorts in his hand. "You can use these for bed, if you want. They will be more comfortable than jeans in my sheets. I'm sure you'll understand. They belonged to my father. I think that they'll fit you."

Jonathan raised an eyebrow at her. She smiled and walked back to her old bureau, searching for something to wear to bed. As she looked through it, she listened to the sounds of Jon changing behind her. Her face was burning hot, and she had to fight off the urge to turn around. When she pulled out a long satiny pink nightgown, Jon said, "You can turn around now." And she did.

And gasped.

And dropped the nightgown onto the floor.

Jonathan was standing in the middle of her room, dressed in her father's night shorts. They fit him, barely. It was a really tight fit.

The shape of the top of his thighs and everything else was so apparent, her cheeks burned even more. His legs were lean, hard, and more beautiful than she had imagined, covered in a dusting of dark hair. Once again, she gazed upon his smooth, hairless chest, and the muscles of his arms and shoulders.

And then, at the smirk on his face.

"Oh, my." she said. "The body of an angel, with a devil's soul."

"Why, thank you." he said. "I could have said the same thing about you, once."

"Only once?"

Jonathan smiled, looked down at the shorts. "I think these must have shrunk, right?"

Julia became aware that her mouth was hanging open, and she shut it. "Yes, I suppose so. But it's all right, they look perfect. I mean, great. I mean...they're fine." She shook her head, and rubbed her face. She felt so stupid! When she looked up at him, there was a wicked grin on his face.

"Really. No problem?" he asked.

Julia saw the chance, decided to go with it. Well, she said to herself, why not? She stepped up close to him, just a small hairline of space separating their bodies. "Just one," she whispered, "Your beautiful hair is gone." She reached up, ran her fingers through the short hair. Her other hand pressed down against his leg.

Jonathan's eyes half shut and he gave himself over to her, to what her hands were doing. She now massaged his neck, now his shoulders, now his chest, and his stomach. Her fingers stopped at the border of the shorts. "Julia," he said, in a strangled voice.

"What?" she said slowly, becoming light-headed and dizzy. The closeness of him to her in this way was taking its toll.

"Do you have any idea of what you are doing to me?"

Julia stepped back from him, looking at him. "Some." she said. She looked down at her nightgown on the floor. "I have to change, I'll be right back." she mumbled.

Julia grabbed up the nightgown, headed into the bathroom. She then shut the door and leaned against it, resting her head on the wood. For a minute she just stood there, lost in thought. Then she turned to the light switch and flicked it on.

Julia turned, looking over her bathroom, and stopped dead when she looked into the mirror. She was not there. The mirror showed the wall behind her, but not one trace of Julia was left. The sight of it so empty seemed to mock her and call her Killer, even though that was exactly what she was. She stifled a scream, as an angry shot of rage went though her. Her hand went into a fist, and seeming to have a life of its own, smashed the mirror.

Julia stood back, watched as small and big shards of the mirror fell into the sink, and onto the carpeted floor. She was stunned. She couldn't believe she did it, and her hand wasn't even cut.

Julia turned back from the remains of the mirror, and changed into her nightgown. She left her clothes in a pile on the floor, turned off the light in the bathroom, and taking a towel from the rack, went out. She carefully stepped around the broken mirror, as not to cut her now bare feet.

Inside her room again, Julia stuffed the towel under the closed bathroom door, and looked around her room. Jon was sitting on the edge of her bed, hands folded and staring into her fireplace. He had started a fire, turned off all the lights.

Julia walked softly over to him, and stretched out onto the bed behind him. She lay on her back, stared at the ceiling.

"You broke the mirror, didn't you?" he asked.

Julia sat up, edged herself next to him. "Yes. Why did I do that?"

Jonathan just shrugged, still staring into the fire. After a few moments he said in a low voice, "It's a natural reflex to us. You have to learn how to refuse it."

Julia yawned, looked over at her bedroom door. "Did you lock my door? Did you put something under it so the sunlight won't get in?" She watched as he nodded, his eyes still not meeting hers. "What is it Jonathan? What are you thinking of?"

Jonathan raised his folded hands to his lips, and rested his chin on them. Then he turned his head to look at her. "Something...I have been putting off telling you, but I must tell you now."

Julia was a little bothered by the look in his eyes. It reminded her of the look that doctors gave their patients, when they told them that they were going to die. "Is there something wrong with me?" she asked.

"No." he whispered. He straitened up, and put one arm around her, holding her close. "I don't want to tell you this, It's a hard thing to accept. But I have to, and I don't want to."

Julia could feel the sadness anxiety rushing through him, and she focused on it, channeled it. "You don't want to tell me because . . . you brought it to me yourself?" she questioned, looking up into his dark eyes.

"Stop." He put one hand across her forehead, motioning for her to stop with more than words. "I want to tell you myself."

"So tell me," she said as his hand lowered.

He took a deep breath, and looking directly at her, began. "You know now, that by becoming a vampire, all your senses are increased. Your body is perfected and made stronger, and it will become even stronger with the passing of time. But there is one thing that your body drops forever, has no use for, and cannot be stimulated into doing. Ever."

"And what," Julia paused, not sure she should even ask, "is that?"

"Julia, vampires cannot reproduce children the way humans do. You cannot conceive life inside you, I cannot fertilize. Vampires are sterile. All the feelings of sexual intercourse are increased, but nothing becomes of it. We can only reproduce through the passage of blood."

Julia stared at him in shock for a moment. Then, very softly, she began to cry. "You took my babies. You took them from me!" She began to cry harder, but when she tried to pull away from him, he didn't let go. He sank back onto the bed, pulled her with him.

"I'm sorry, Julia. I'm so sorry." he whispered.

"I've always wanted a child, someone who was a little piece of me. One I could hold and love and cherish." She sobbed against him. She looked up into his eyes; her face was streaked with tinted tears. "Oh Jonathan, why didn't you tell me?"

"It wouldn't have made a difference, Julia. I wanted you, and I loved you. But there is a way around it."

"There is?"

"Yes, adopt a child. Bring it up knowing our ways, and when it is old enough and strong enough, make it one of us." Julia nodded, lowered her head, and cried on the blankets. "It's alright to cry, my love. I'm here for you."

Jonathan held her as she cried, and finally, towards morning, Julia fell asleep.

Jonathan put her into bed, tucked the blankets around her, and kissed her forehead.

Then, with the call of sleep ringing in his ears, he went into his own bed, and lay down.

14

Julia woke first the next night, probably because Jonathan had been relocated, and was not yet used to sleeping without his coffin.

She started a fire, and checked to make sure that no one had been in the room the whole day. When she was positive that no one had intruded, and had observed that her mother and sister were not in the house, she approached Jonathan.

He was lying flat on his back, long hair carefully tucked under him. It really had grown back. The covers were pulled to his waist, and his leather jacket was on. But none of these things disturbed her more than the ivory handled dagger he clutched to his chest. Something in her told her to stay back until he was really awake, and if anything disturbed him, that dagger would be embedded into her body.

With a mental shiver, Julia went back to her drawers, selected black jeans and a black sweater, clean underwear and socks, and went into the bathroom to change. After she had changed, she pulled on her sneakers and placed her old clothes into the laundry. Her nightgown she put on a hook on the back of the door.

Then, she picked up carefully all the shards of mirror, and dumped them into the trash.

When she went back into her room, Jonathan was awake, standing, and sheathing the dagger.

"Hi." she said softly, and went over to make his bed.

Jonathan shrugged off his jacket after he put the dagger back into the pocket. "I slept late."

"I know," Julia said as she finished his bed, going on to her own. "I kind of wanted to wake you up, but I didn't want to risk coming in contact with that knife of yours."

Jonathan made a low sound in his throat and went over to the fire. "Are you hungry Julia?" he asked after a minute.

Julia finished the last tuck on her bed and stood beside Jonathan, running her hands through his hair. "Yes." she said. "What are we going to eat here? Most people around here are really rich, and have top of the line security systems. Being the holidays, they're likely to have security really beefed up around here."

"Yes, I know. We will have to catch animals."

Julia frowned. She didn't like the thought of that, drinking the blood of animals. Then another thought came to mind, of a completely different nature. "Jon, I have to cut your hair. My mom isn't here right now, but if she sees you like this, she'll freak."

"Yes, we should cut it. Do you have any scissors?"

Jonathan went to Julia's bed, sat down on the edge.

He watched as Julia went into her bureau again, pulled forth a pair of silver sheers. He loved the way she looked in black, how her hair seemed to glow gold, and her eyes darkened. "I love you." he said when she came back to him.

Julia laughed. "What was that for? So I won't cut your hair too short? Really, Jonathan."

Jonathan pulled her to him, made her sit on his lap. "Can't I tell you that I love you without being questioned for it?" He kissed her, and then released her.

Julia knelt on the bed behind him, and took hold of his hair. She winced as the first cut took half of it off. She gave it to Jon, and he tossed it into the fire. The hair flared, went up in a puff of smoke. When his haircut resembled the one that the beautician had given him the night before, she led Jonathan into her bathroom so he could change.

When he came out, he was wearing the blue jeans, black sneakers, cotton tee shirt, and the blue button down shirt, unbuttoned. He looked like a model from a magazine.

"You look great." Julia said after a minute. Jonathan came up to her and touched her hair, her lips, and his chain that rested against her neck. She smiled, and said, "Come on, I'm hungry. Come on." She began tugging his arm, and he went with her. Through her bedroom door, and down the stairs.

At the front door, Julia opened it, and they stood on the front porch together. She shut the door behind them, and watched as Jonathan seemed to gaze out into space. She knew he was calling for the animals.

Soon, two squirrels approached Jonathan. They climbed up his legs, and onto his arms. He held out his hands, and they sat on them. "Take one, Julia. Concentrate on the squirrel's mind and talk to it. Calm it."

Julia reached out for the little animal, mind and body, and soon it was in her hand, in her power. The scent of the animal was musty, wild, and some part of her new nature longed to be free just like it.

Staring into the squirrel's eyes, she felt the hunger take over, felt her top canines lengthen into fangs, and her eyes glaze over red. She lifted the animal to her face, and when she moved the little head back, it did not resist.

The first taste of animal blood gagged her, the second did not. It was so different than human blood. She did not feel any power, or taste the sweetness of life. She felt something more raw and primal, and there was urgency to it; blood pumping through a little heart trying to survive.

Julia drained the animal to death, and did not get sucked under. She was not part of the death.

Julia looked up from the animal and relaxed, her bloody face returning to human form. She threw the squirrel into the street with one powerful toss, and licked her mouth clean.

Julia turned to Jonathan, who was leaning against the door, watching her. Even in the darkness that was slightly illuminated by the streetlights, she could see his dark eyes glittering.

"Why didn't I die with the squirrel? If it was a human I drank to death, to the last heartbeat, I would have died."

Jonathan looked at her for a long moment. "You said it yourself. It wasn't human." He paused, and the look on his face made Julia think of a sleek, cunning predator. "Let me ask you something, Julia. How do you feel, now that you drank the animal blood?"

"What?" she asked softly.

Jonathan smiled a warm smile, breaking the tension in Julia that he had unknowingly created. He always acted a little predatory after feeding, Julia reminded herself.

"How did the animal blood make you feel? I want you to learn to recognize your feelings."

Julia sighed and smiled at him. "Well, it wasn't like a regular feeding. It didn't give me any power or thrill, and didn't make me feel evil. It made me feel . . . like an owl."

Jonathan smiled again. "An owl?"

Julia laughed. "Yes. But for good reasons. I felt like a hunter that could be hunted. But I didn't like the taste. It was strange."

Jonathan now had a wise grin on his face. "What else did, or shall I say, didn't it do?"

Julia got the meaning of what he meant. "It didn't make me want you. It didn't make me feel sexual."

Jonathan nodded, turned, and went into the house. "Good, good." he muttered. As he entered the parlor, he stopped moving. Julia shut the door and went to stand behind him.

"What is it?" she asked.

"You have a Christmas tree up!" he said, like a surprised little boy.

211

Julia went up to the tree, pulled a candy cane off it, unwrapped it, and sank onto the couch, sucking on it. "Yes, we do. My mom goes out every Christmas Eve morning and buys a live one. Then she puts it up here, and doesn't take it down for a while after Christmas. When it begins to shed, she puts it outside and hangs things for the birds on it."

While Julia was talking, Jonathan had walked over to the tree, gently touching the branches. Now he cupped one little light in his hands. The ornaments brushed his arms. "It's changed so much in one hundred and three years. I thought I'd never be able to get this close to one again."

Jonathan sat on the couch next to Julia, and pulled her into his arms. "I don't care what Jason says, the holidays are a special time, even for us. Don't you feel it Julia? The love that is here and all around us?" He looked into her eyes. "Do you know that this is the first real holiday season I've seen up close since the year I died?"

Julia smiled, hugged him. "I love you," she said.

She reached over to the small, parlor coffee table, and picked up the remote control for the television, that was placed in the entertainment center on the opposite side of the room, switched it on to MTV.

Julia put the controller back on the table, and snuggled close to Jonathan. He put his arm around her and smiled. "I wish things could always be so uncomplicated, so without problems. Don't you?" he asked her.

Something in his words made Julia feel strange again, and she buried her face against his shirt.

"Julia, what is it? What did I say wrong?"

Julia couldn't help her feelings. She began to think about Cory all of a sudden, and she hadn't for some time now. The force of her fear came on strong, and she began to cry. It was as if he were nearby and watching them, mocking them.

Jonathan pulled her over a little, so he could see her face.

"Don't." Julia said, trying to hide her tears.

"Julia, what is it?" he asked again. He then made a strange face, and turned around. The big bay window behind them showed him nothing. Just her mother and sister pulling into the driveway. "We'll talk about this later, your mother and sister are home."

Julia nodded, sniffing.

Jeanne and Gayle came into the house. Julia and Jonathan stood, and approached them. Gayle took one look at Julia, and ran up to her room. Her mother seemed not to notice.

"Julia! All the plans are set. I can't believe the luck we're having for this last minute wedding! I was out all day getting things ready. The cousins are all coming out, I got a judge and the catering service, flowers, and all of your friends are coming." Jeanne frowned. "Except for Christi. I talked to her mother. It seems she came home in your van almost two weeks ago. She was with a young man. They took all her things and moved. Strange, strange." She shook her head, walked into the kitchen. Julia and Jon looked at each other, followed her.

"So, that means that everything is set. You said you didn't want bride's maids, and for your sister to be the maid of honor. I bought her a dress today." She went into the fridge and pulled forth a bottle of champagne. Then she got three glasses and gave them each one, pouring in the sparkly liquid. "Jonathan, you'll need a best man. You can either choose one of Julia's friends or send for someone, if it's not too late, that is." She sipped from the glass as she put the bottle back.

Jonathan took a long swig of the drink and then smiled. "That won't be a problem. A good friend of mine is coming down."

"Oh?" Julia said.

Julia's mom looked from Julia to Jonathan. She cleared her throat. "Anyway, all that's left now are Julia's gown, Jonathan's tuxedo, and his best man's. I have a dress."

"I'd like to pick them out." Jonathan said, setting his empty glass on the counter.

"What?" Julia and Jeanne responded, their voices blending in unison.

Jonathan put his hands in his pockets. "I know that it's not something that the groom usually does, but Julia's got to pack, and tonight is the last night before the wedding. If you ladies don't disagree." He gave them a puppy dog look, accented by his eyes.

Julia finished her drink, put the glass beside Jonathan's. "Well, to tell you the truth Mom, I don't care. I do have a lot of packing to do."

Jeanne smiled. "Yes, and I have to get some extra chairs. I mean a lot. And tables. Then I have to move everything out of the parlor, except the tree. It's fine with me." She put down the glass, reached for her purse and coat on the kitchen table. "Got to go." She gave Julia a kiss, Jonathan a hug. "Bye kids."

Jonathan smiled at Julia and said, "Your mother is really wonderful."

"I know." Julia said, reaching up to put her hands around Jonathan's neck. "But so are you." She kissed him, and Jonathan laughed. "What?" Julia asked, pulling back.

"You're determined never to let me leave here, aren't you?" he said.

"Fine. Go. Just go." Julia said, pretending to be pouting.

Jonathan smiled. "I will. Bye." And with a blur and a rush of air, followed by the door slamming and the motorcycle starting, he was gone.

Julia decided to head upstairs. As she walked past Gayle's room, she felt an urge to talk to her. She opened the door and went in. Her sister sat at the vanity; makeup was everywhere. Gayle was brushing her hair, and though she didn't see her sister in the mirror, she knew Julia was in the room. She could feel herself being watched, but she chose to ignore it.

Julia chose to ignore the mirror. She knew if she looked at it, she would smash it. She cleared her throat. "Gayle." she said softly.

Gayle put the brush down. Her fingers reached for something underneath her shirt. The other hand rested on her lap. She stared at the nothing in the mirror, rather calmly.

"Gayle, I can't tell you that I'm sorry for this. I wanted to be with him, forever, and now I will be. But you must understand. I didn't do this for glory, or for eternal life. I did it because I love him." Julia paused Gayle said nothing.

"I'm sorry for what this is doing to you, because I know how hard you tried to protect me. But you weren't protecting me! I would have killed myself if I hadn't been able to see him again. And then he would have done the same. I need him to belong with me."

Julia walked to Gayle, placed her hand on her sister's shoulder. Gayle glanced at her sister's hand, but did not say a word. Julia could feel the tension and fear, inside Gayle.

"I also need you to care about me, Gayle. You've been my best friend through the problems with Dad, you've been my baby, my sister, and I'll see you grow to be a woman, a wife, a mother, and a grandmother. I could offer you this life, but you wouldn't want it."

"What are you saying, Julia?" Gayle said in monotone.

Julia choked down a sob. "I want you to trust me, to be my friend again. I don't have too many left." She bent down and kissed her sister on the cheek. Then, she made the mistake of looking into the mirror, no reflection. Only Gayle, sitting with her eyes shut.

Julia fought back the angry scream ready to come forth, and with a burst of preternatural power, left the room in a blur of light and wind. She ran to her own room, and collapsed onto the bed, silently crying.

Later, she began to pack everything that she would need to bring with her. She was going to take two suitcases, and then have the local post office send the boxes of all her other things to Vermont. She wasn't going to let her mother know where to contact her, and besides, she was sending her things directly to a post office, in Vermont.

By midnight she had finished packing, and she felt Jonathan return to the house, accompanied by another of their kind. Julia opened the door and ran downstairs, vaulting over the railing near the bottom. She hit the floor softly and gracefully, and opened the front door.

Jonathan stood in the yard, holding a few bags. And there, near his bike, stood Timothy. They came into the house, and Julia shut the door behind them. "The best man, I presume."

Timothy smiled at her. "Yeah, well, I had to come. A wedding? I've never been to one before. I hope that I don't screw anything up."

"I doubt you will." Jonathan said. "I'll be right back. I have to put these in Jeanne's room."

"Can't I see them?" Julia asked.

"Not until tomorrow." he said as he left.

Afterwards, they talked a while. When Jeanne came home, Julia took them into the little computer room upstairs. Julia discovered that Cory and Lizzi had left for California the same night that Julia and Jonathan left, but later. That made the strange feeling creep back into Julia's mind, but she pushed it away. She didn't want anything to ruin her wedding.

They put Timothy up in a guestroom, telling Jeanne that he was just another Researcher. He took his bag with him into the room, and bade goodnight to Julia and Jon. Then finally, after an exhausting night, they were all alone, locked up inside Julia's room.

Julia and Jon sat on the carpeted floor next to her bed, with a big flannel blanket wrapped around them. Julia clutched onto him, feeling so strange; perhaps she was going to cry. "Jonathan?"

"Hmmm?" he said.

"I'm happy that we're getting married tomorrow, but…"

"But, what?" he asked, after she didn't finish her sentence.

"I'm worried about Cory. I don't want him to come here, to find me. I never want to see him around me again." She felt Jonathan stiffen up. "I don't want him to ruin this for us."

Jonathan looked down at her. "If he ever goes near you again, tell me. I'll kill him. He's not going to ruin this for us. I'll protect you from him, until I die from the effort. I know Timothy would too. Julia, I swear to you, I promise you, he will not harm you." He kissed her forehead. "I love you," he said as he pulled her into his embrace.

Julia tried not to cry as she felt that mocking, evil presence again, somewhere close by. She held Jon tighter. "I love you too, Jonathan."

15

Julia awoke suddenly. In the place between sleep and awake, she had felt Cory's presence. It was stronger than before, menacing and dangerous. It had seemed as if he were standing over her, ready to rip her to pieces, if she married Jonathan. She had heard him laughing.

Julia shook it off, sat up. Her digital clock read 6:30 PM. There were only two hours until the wedding. Julia lay back down, and stretched. She began to think of how the wedding would go, how most of the family should already be in the house. As she let her powers collect; she could feel them downstairs. Living, breathing humans, full of blood, her past. Her future lay with Jonathan. As the thought passed through her mind, she felt him slide into bed beside her, down into the covers. "Julia?"

Julia turned her head to look at him, his face shadowed by the long, dark, mane of hair. She reached up and touched his face gently, and his lips brushed her hand. There was something sad in their motions, as if they both knew something wrong would take place tonight. Julia could feel it in the air. "Jonathan, I'm scared." she whispered.

Jonathan lay down into the pillows, and Julia realized that he wasn't wearing his jacket. He pulled her close to him and kissed her forehead. "I know. I feel it too," he said.

Julia stared into his dark eyes, sighed. She wanted this to be so perfect, so right. Their wedding was to be like a dream. Not something to be afraid of.

Julia, please, don't think about it. Just focus on me and he can't get into your mind. Trust me.

Julia smiled, nodded, and pulled his head to her, kissing him full on the lips. She ran her hands through his hair, down his back. She opened her lips against his, and he kissed her deeply.

Desire radiated through Julia, fueled by a sadness of a loss she had not suffered yet. She wanted him to love her tonight so she would not forget. Why was she thinking like this? She didn't know, but he seemed to sense it.

Jonathan's hand brushed down the front of her body, and pulled her leg over his. With a little strangled sound, he turned over, putting Julia beneath him.

"Jonathan," she whispered against his lips.

"Shhh, my little bride, I will not harm you." he murmured in a low, faraway tone.

Julia's head swam, as she felt his hands sliding over her legs, pushing her nightgown up so he could lay down on top of her, both legs between hers. His weight came down on her, crushing her to the mattress. His lips met hers in a passionate dark kiss.

As Julia's hands caressed his back, she tilted her head upwards. His lips traveled across her face, down her neck, and onto her shoulder, where the nightgown hung off just a bit. When his fingers went to the buttons on the front of her gown, she did not stop him. She gave herself over to the sensations of his lips on her skin, her mind flying. Her whole body ached for him now, and all the pressure of his body on hers wasn't enough.

Julia was aware of him lifting her, pulling her up to kneel over him on the bed. She became aware of the nightgown sliding down her arms, the front wide open, but she didn't care any longer. She wanted him. She let the gown fall away from her arms as she kissed him hungrily and deeply, pulling him hard to herself, feeling his skin against her chest. She rocked on his lap, feeling him growing hard under her. She pulled away from him, staring at his eyes. His mouth was open now, his eyes so dark they looked black.

"Julia." he whispered in what seemed like a plea.

"Kiss me, Jonathan. Kiss me." she whispered back, and pulled his head to her chest. When his lips touched her breast for the first time, she felt the whirlwind inside, devouring her. His mouth was on her, and his arms were around her, and that was all that mattered. She knew in that moment that she could only belong to him, and there would never be anyone else.

Julia let her head fall back, her back arching. He was sucking on her like a baby would to a mother, and her breath escaped her in a soft groan. "Jonathan…" his hands on her body, sliding upwards on her legs, the softness of his fingertips against the most delicate, aching lower parts of her, moving slowly against the sides, teasing, teasing. She opened to him now, as a flower opens to the morning dew, and as they slid inwards, she gasped.

"My one and only love…" his voice breathy, rough, as he tossed her back down against the covers, his lips against her mouth, his tongue driving deeper, deeper.

"I need you, Jonathan, *please*…" Her mind could not withhold any tangible thought, frightened as she was that something may occur tonight, the presence of Cory in the air, and the aching need within her body for him, not very unlike the unquenchable desire for blood…

Her hands drew back from the hold she had on him, and as she wrestled with her clothing, and he with his, she burned for his touch once more, his kiss. Don't leave me, she wanted to plead, please, don't ever go… But then he was there, and she cradled him within her arms, her legs, and finally, with a desperate gasp issuing from them both, she held him within her body and soul.

"Jonathan, I love you…"

After they had dressed, holding onto each other, lying peacefully in bed came a slight, hesitant knock at the door.

Julia approached the door, unlocked it and opened it, and there was Timothy, standing in the doorway with a knowing look on his face. Julia blushed and yanked him into the bedroom, closing the door behind them.

"Jon," Timothy began, "We should start getting ready. I've got the stuff in my room." Then he looked at Julia who was withdrawing the scissors from her drawer, in order to cut Jonathan's hair. "That is, if you two aren't busy."

Jonathan laughed under his breath, as Julia brought him to sit on the bed. Julia cut off a chunk of hair. "Start a fire, will you Timothy?"

"Oh, sure." he said, and in no time had a fire going. Julia handed him the chunks of hair, as he tossed them into the fire.

As soon as Jon's hair was cut, he left with Timothy. About a minute later, Julia's room filled with aunts, cousins, and Gayle. They were all dressed for the wedding, in beautiful gowns; Gayle holding Julia's bridal gown, the one Jonathan bought for her.

Julia took one look at the gown, and gasped. It was beautiful, looked as if it was made just for her. The top was made of white satin with bead patterns everywhere. Upon the waistline, three separate branches came off of the top, extending downwards in a point of beads and pearls, in the front, and along the sides. Draping down bottom of the gown, was a long skirt of filmy white taffeta. The back had a tall of the same material.

Julia picked up the gown from Gayle's arms, held it to her with tears standing in her eyes. She couldn't believe that this gown was really hers. "I'll go put this on." she whispered. She went to her bureau, picked out underwear and a long slip. Then she went into the bathroom to change.

When Julia had the gown on, she couldn't believe how well it fit her. It was just like a glove. The top was off the shoulders and went just a little low down the front. The sleeves were short, but they also tapered off to a point going down.

Julia brushed her hair, and went back into her room, letting her aunts fix all the accessories. They gave her soft, netted gloves, adorned with pearls, a pearl bracelet, earrings, and necklace. They gave her white, high healed shoes, and veil. Julia held still as they did her make up for her. Her hair fell in glossy waves down her shoulders and back. When her aunts were convinced that she looked beautiful, they began fussing with themselves.

Julia was stood there, watching, until one of her older aunts approached. "Julia, you look beautiful. Why don't you have a mirror in here? You should be able to see how beautiful you look." Then, her aunt pulled a compact from her purse, and opened it. Julia shrank back, trying to get away, but she couldn't move; there were too many people in her room. Julia's mouth fell open and just as she was about to scream Gayle snatched the mirror away.

"You can't do that, Aunt Harriet." Gayle said in a calm tone.

"And why not?" asked Harriet.

Gayle looked at Julia, and then at the closed mirror in her hand. "Because the lighting in this room is all wrong, and Julia's best perspective will not show up. Then, Julia will be depressed for the wedding. You wouldn't want that, would you?"

"No, I'm sorry." Harriet muttered, took the compact, and moved to the other side of the room.

"Thanks, Gayle." Julia said.

"Yeah, well, I couldn't stay mad at you forever. That's a real long time." She gave Julia a hug. "I'll miss you, big sis."

"I'll miss you, too."

After Gayle removed Julia's engagement ring from the room, to place by Jonathan's near the judge, Julia began to drift amongst her thoughts. She had realized, tonight she would discover, for the first time, what Jonathan's full name was. He would also learn of her middle name, Deianira. She smiled to herself; Deianira of mythology had been the wife of Hercules. It seemed ironic that she was now marrying someone as strong as him, and just as legendary.

Julia became aware of hunger, stirring within. She hadn't fed tonight, and she could smell the blood of the people in this room...intoxicating. Julia choked down the hunger, pushed it into the back of her mind, as Jonathan had taught her. She sat down on the edge of her bed, staring into the very flames that could kill her, should she approach too closely. She shut her eyes, and she could visualize Jonathan waiting for her. He had been waiting for her for a hundred years, and tonight he would have her forever.

Sometime later, one of her aunts shook her to reality, and Julia stood up, grasping the bouquet someone had placed into her hand.

"Come on, Julia!"

Julia smiled at them, and walked out the door. She stood at the top of the stairs, waited for the music to start, as all the women went down.

Julia and Gayle were left, alone together, at the top.

220

16

Julia descended the stairs, gracefully, after Gayle, her feet barely touching the ground, so light and happy that she was. She would be bound to Jon forever in marriage, and in blood, but a little part of her nagged that with this marriage, the final link in her human life would be finished. She'd never see family or friends again. Strangely, she didn't care. She wanted this, all of it. She loved Jonathan more than anything, and would give up all she had, in order to go with him.

As she stood at the bottom of the stairs, and Gayle crossed the room to stand beside Timothy, the surroundings suddenly faded, replaced by images from the late 1800's. This was the time when Jonathan had been alive, when he had been betrothed once before.

Julia saw a girl leave on a train, and that girl resembled herself. Jonathan stood on the station's platform, sadly waving goodbye.

The room shifted in color and form, and found Jonathan waiting for her, with a Reverend in the front of an old wooden church, everyone in olden clothing. Jonathan was also wearing these clothes, his hair long, and braided down the back. Julia knew this was an illusion; his hair was short. She had cut it herself! When she glanced down, she found her wedding dress changed to authentic olden dress. She smiled up at Jonathan, and slowly the images faded. She was back in the parlor, late 1989. Jonathan looked gorgeous in his tuxedo.

Julia let out a sigh and smiled again, walking across the room to Jonathan. When she stood beside him, she handed her bouquet to Gayle, reached out for Jonathan's hand. The music stopped, and the judge began to talk.

"We are all here to experience a very special time in Julia and Jonathan's lives. They are about to come together, to bond together, and to meld their lives with each other. Marriage is the greatest gift anyone can receive, a gift that lasts a lifetime. Honor your vows as you take them, and you will honor them the rest of your lives."

Gayle now came forward, and gave Julia Jonathan's ring; Timothy gave Julia's ring to Jonathan.

"These rings are a symbol of never ending love. It's a circle that goes on forever, never stopping, never coming to an end. Are you both ready for this commitment?" the judge asked.

"Yes."

"All right then. Julia, take his hand in yours, be ready to put the ring on his finger."

Julia held his hand, and smiled up at him. She could see the love shining in his eyes. And the judge began to speak again.

"Repeat after me. I, Julia Deianira Anderson,"

Julia took a breath, and repeated him; "I, Julia Deianira Anderson,"

"Take you, Jonathan Jared Deschene, to be my husband."

Julia smiled. What a beautiful name he had. "Take you, Jonathan Jared Deschene, to be my husband."

"Through richer or poorer, in sickness and in health, as long as we both shall live."

Julia repeated him.

"Place the ring on his finger, Julia."

Julia did so.

The judge smiled. "Now Jonathan, take her hand the same way, and repeat after me."

Jonathan took her hand and nodded.

"I, Jonathan Jared Deschene, take you, Julia Deianira Anderson, to be my wife."

Jonathan began to repeat him, and Julia listened to not the words, but to the tone of his voice. It was very deep, very serious. She didn't hear the rest of his vows after that, for she once again felt Cory pushing into her mind. He wanted to speak, but Julia pushed back. In the end, he only got three words in, *coming for you...*

Julia shivered, and focused again on Jonathan, who was now slipping the ring on her finger. The diamonds twinkled merrily as his darker hand embraced her pale one.

"By the powers invested in me by the state, I now pronounce you husband and wife." the judge said.

Julia and Jonathan stared up at him for a moment, unbelieving of what they had heard.

The judge smiled. "You may kiss the bride."

Jonathan smiled back. "Thanks, I will." he said, and they kissed.

A cheer rang out in the parlor confetti filled the air. Julia plucked her bouquet out of Gayle's hand, and threw it into the air. One of her girlfriends caught it and laughed happily, looking at her boyfriend.

Jonathan picked Julia up into his arms and went up the stairway, down the hallway. When they reached her room, he set her down and said, "Go get dressed, and take as many suitcases as you can hold downstairs. Have Gayle mail your boxes. We have to leave this place, as soon as possible." He kissed her quickly, and left her, in order to change.

Julia entered her room, removed the gown and jewelry, replacing the pearl necklace with Jonathan's chain once more. She pulled on a dark red sweater, jeans, sneakers, and draped her leather jacket onto her arm, lifted two large suitcases. The rest of her room had been stripped clean, and packed in boxes lying all over her room. All that remained was an empty closet, empty dressers, empty desks, and two beds, nothing on the walls, or the floor.

Julia set down the suitcases and looked around the room, the room of a house that she had bought. She walked to the curtained glass doors, and pulled down the curtains. Immediately, moonlight came in through the doors. She threw the curtain onto the floor, and then walked to all her boarded windows, ripping the wood down, careful not to cut herself on the pieces. Then, she picked up the suitcases and her jacket again, and walked out of her room and down the stairs. She set the suitcases down beside Jonathan's backpack.

Julia quietly approached Jonathan and Timothy. Jonathan had dressed in his boots, black jeans, and white shirt. Timothy wore blue jeans and a black shirt. Jonathan put his arm around her, gave her a glass of champagne. Julia's mother began to make a salute to Julia and Jonathan, and then, it happened.

A high pitched, piercing scream rang out from outside. The humans couldn't hear it, but the dogs in the neighborhood could. The first things that Julia heard were the dogs howling and barking, and then, like a rush of blinding pain, the scream entered her range of hearing along with Jonathan, and Timothy.

They dropped their glasses to the floor where they shattered, clutching desperately to the sides of their heads. Through the blinding pain, Julia watched her mother approach, perhaps to ask what was wrong, but she couldn't talk, couldn't even breathe. Couldn't even warn her mother to get away.

The pitch of the scream began to lower, as glasses throughout the room began to shatter. The humans could suddenly hear the sound, and one by one, all Julia's guests fell unconscious. Other voices now joined the first, and the huge bay window burst. The screaming stopped.

Julia stood with Jon and Timothy, and for a minute, there was no sound or motion but the flapping of the window's curtains, and the crackling of the parlor fire. The moonlight came in through the window, and coldness filled the room.

"Jonathan," Julia whispered in terror.

For a minute he seemed to smell the air. Then he pulled Julia and Timothy behind him. "Damn it." he said.

A wind picked up suddenly, blew the curtains wide, and Julia clung to Jonathan as, out of nowhere, it seemed, Cory appeared in the center of the room. He stretched his arm out to her. "Come to me, Julia." he said.

"No!" Julia screamed, clutching wildly at Jonathan.

Jonathan grabbed her and yelled, "Go with Timothy, get out of here!"

"No Jonathan, I won't leave you!" she yelled, Cory's mocking laughter burning into her senses.

"Go!" he yelled, shoving at Julia.

"Jon, they've surrounded us!" Timothy cried.

Jonathan looked around him, and everywhere, he saw snarling vampires; Cory's spawn. Timothy, Julia and Jon stood back to back. "You're going to have to fight me for her!" he screamed at Cory. Cory's face transformed as he laughed. "Don't you touch her, you bastard." he snarled, the words issuing forth as a growl around his lengthening fangs, his hand locked onto Julia's.

Julia stared at the surrounding ring, at the vampires there. A part of her nature was telling her to flee, for there were too many to fight, and if Jonathan left her side, she and Timothy would never survive.

Jonathan, don't leave us!

But if he had heard, he paid no heed.

Jonathan roared aloud in anger and frustration, his eyes blood red. He ripped himself free of Julia and Timothy, and lunged at Cory. Cory laughed, caught Jonathan, and flung him backwards, against the wall.

"Come back!" Julia screamed, grasping at Timothy. The others were closing in on them now. Without Jon to protect them, they were vulnerable.

"Timothy, what do we do?" she whispered, her back to his.

"Fight them." he growled, and she could sense the change in him.

Julia let the changes come forth fueled by the raging blood lust inside her. She snarled at them, as the circle grew tight.

When the first vampire slashed out at her, Julia slashed back, her fangs grazing the side of his face. She backed up a little to find Timothy enveloped in the midst of ten or more vampires. He was fighting them off, but was losing.

Julia backed to a wall, snarling and clawing. "Give up, little girl!" a black-haired female said.

"Never!" Julia roared, and reached out for her, trying to scratch out her eyes. The female threw her to the floor, and was suddenly drowning in waves of faces, clawing fingers, and biting fangs. She tried to fight them, but there were too many. When she couldn't fight anymore, they held her arms and legs down, and waited for Cory. They were calm now, their faces normal in illusion.

Julia gasped for air, feeling pain throughout her body. She couldn't feel her legs, she knew they must be broken. She moaned helplessly and took deep breaths, calming down. Her fangs shrank down, the red haze lifted. Julia couldn't even cry for help. Something hurt in her throat; something had been damaged in there.

Cory did return, and as Julia looked up at him in the moonlight, she could see long gashes in his face, neck and chest. Dried blood caked his hair.

"Your little boyfriend fought well, Julia, but you know what they say. Survival of the fittest." He proceeded to lick the blood off his fingers. Julia knew it was Jonathan's, she could smell it. She tried to move her head, but she couldn't, her back hurt too much. She closed her eyes and tried to focus on Jonathan, but she didn't sense anything. She glared up at Cory, now sitting beside her. Tears flowed from her eyes.

"Don't cry, Julia. You're going to be with me now," he said.

Then his fist came down on Julia's head, and all she saw was black.

Cory motioned the others back. Julia's forehead appeared dented from the blow, and blood came trickling down. She was a mess, mangled everywhere. So were the others, Timothy and Jonathan. All in all, it had been a good night. Now, all he had to do was get her out of the East Coast. He looked down at the ring on Julia's finger, pulled it off.

"Start back with her. I'll be with you soon." He said to the others, and soon, they were gone.

Cory stepped over the still unconscious humans, and Timothy, and into the kitchen where he had left Jonathan.

Jonathan was lying on the counter. His arms and legs were broken, and so was his neck. His face was at an odd angle, his eyes were shut, and Cory knew that he would be concentrating on healing himself. His shirt was ripped and torn, blood everywhere. Cory waited until he heard the unmistakable snapping of bones fusing, and watched as Jonathan's head turned back naturally. He heard Jon's intake of breath, and saw his dark eyes open.

Cory approached, placed the ring on the counter by his head. Jonathan stared up at him. "I'll kill you." he whispered.

Cory laughed. He brought his head close to Jonathan's. "I doubt it," he whispered. Cory stared at the bones poking through Jonathan's torn skin and the blood still trickling out. He made a long cut with his nail on Jonathan's cheek. "I seriously doubt you'll be doing much chasing around after me, for a while."

Then, to Jonathan's absolute horror, Cory lowered his head until his lips touched the wound, and he began to drink. Pain lashed through Jonathan's veins as he felt the pulling grow stronger; the pain of another vampire stealing his blood.

"Stop," he groaned, in agony.

Cory lifted his head and looked into Jon's eyes. A thin line of blood ran down his chin. There was a dazed, hungry look in his eyes. "Your blood is exquisite, fine. Perhaps Julia's will contain some of yours."

"You're Wild," Jonathan murmured, aware of what little blood left in him was now healing his broken bones.

Cory laughed again. He tilted his head back, hugged himself. "No, no my dear boy, not Wild. Haven't you guessed yet? I must be…insane. I'm going now. Give my regards to your father." With a gust of wind, he was gone.

Jonathan picked himself up later and stumbled out into the parlor, where a few of the humans were now stirring. Summoning up his power, he put them all under a deep sleep. From Julia's mother he removed a plain silver chain, slipped Julia's ring on it, and put it around his neck. Then, he revived Timothy, took the suitcases, and after implanting the idea of mailing Julia's boxes into Gayle's mind, left Connecticut for Vermont.

17

Julia came back to consciousness three days later, in a cool, dark room. She didn't know where she was, but soon, she felt the presence of Cory close by.

Julia sat up on the bed, ignoring the pain in her head and legs. It didn't hurt as much anymore, but she knew she hadn't really healed yet. She reached over to the side of the bed where she saw a lamp, and switched it on. Light flooded the room.

Julia blinked a few times, and looked around her. The room was most definitely within a hotel, and from the slight salt in the air, and the distant sound of waves against the shore, she could assume a beach was nearby.

Disoriented, Julia gazed down at her clothing. They were blood clotted, torn. She lay back down on the bed, stared up at the ceiling. She thought of Jonathan and the wedding, and how could she possibly get out of here? With one look down at her hand, she knew, without a doubt, Cory had taken her ring. Where it was, she had no clue. At least she had kept Jonathan's chain.

Julia had just closed her eyes again, when she sensed a vaguely familiar presence approach the door. Lizzi entered the room carrying a change of clothes, and a glass of blood. At the smell of the blood, Julia's stomach lurched. She hadn't fed for nights now, not since before the wedding.

Julia looked up from the glass of blood, to Lizzi. The girl vampire looked annoyed that she now had to play nursemaid to Julia.

"Are you going to take these from me, or not?" Lizzi demanded.

Julia nodded and reached for the clothes, putting them on the bed. Then she reached for the glass of blood and held it in her hand for a minute, staring at it. It was a little cool, but it was human, she knew that much. "Where did you get this?" Julia asked, surprised she could talk again.

"Kevin got it for you." Lizzi answered. She turned and left the room, locking the door behind her.

Julia drained the blood from the glass, a little revolted that it wasn't fresh, but a starving vampire would drink any blood. Julia changed her clothes, tossing the old ones across the room. She lay back down, feeling strangely tired from the exertion of changing, and getting up, and she switched off the light.

Julia clasped the chain in her fingers, holding on to it tight.

She tried to contact Jonathan within the regions of her mind, but some sort of block wouldn't let her through. She could only guess it was Cory.

The tiredness and pain in Julia's body began to overwhelm her, and soon she found she couldn't stay awake. Before she fell asleep, she promised herself, no matter what, she'd get back to Jonathan. If it took a million years, she'd find a way.

"Jason, please! We must go after her! We have to! Can't you see? I'm not strong enough to do it alone, I need your help!" Jonathan pleaded with Jason in the sitting room of the mansion in Vermont. He had been for several nights, now. It was intolerable, this silence. He felt as if Jason would not even attempt to help.

"Jonathan, I've told you over and over again, we'd have no chance against Cory and his coven. He's stronger than me, he was made before me." Jason rested his face in his hands. Every night it had been the same, Jonathan pleading, crying, until Jason had enough, and left him there, alone.

"Jason, please! Don't you understand? We were meant to be together. I'll die without her!"

It was true, Jason thought as he looked up, slowly, from his hands. Jonathan appeared tired, ragged, and pale. His beauty had gone, he was starving. He hadn't had any nourishment; all he did was weep. "Jonathan, I wish I could help you, but . . . "

"Please, Jason, please." Jonathan fell to his knees before Jason, pressing his tear-streaked face to Jason's legs.

Jason put his hand on Jonathan's head, shut his eyes, and thought deeply. "I can see how much you love Julia, and what she means to you. She is very special to all of us, Jon, and I can't bear to see you in pain." Jason murmured. "There is one way."

Jonathan looked up into Jason's eyes. There was pain in Jason's face now also, and Jon simply knew he was about to make a great sacrifice.

"I have to go back to Paris, France." Jason looked out the window for a moment, and then back at Jonathan. "I'll have to find my father, Alexander. I know what Cory did was a sin, and only his father can punish him for it. Alexander and I did not part on good terms; I do not know if he will reconcile with me, or help us. I will search for him. I'll take Rikki with me, and you can stay here with Timothy, and Steven."

Jonathan nodded, swiping the tears from his face.

"It will work in time, Jonathan. We will get her back." Jason said, as he looked down at Jonathan. "In the meantime, hunt. It will build your strength." He pushed away Jonathan's hair from his face. Jonathan had gone back to wearing his black jeans, his leather jacket.

"I don't know if I can, Jason. I'm weak, I don't know if I could wrestle a human down."

Jason stared into Jonathan's dark eyes, for a lingering moment. He remembered watching Jonathan those long years ago, and how tormented he had been by those nightly visits. He remembered when Jonathan's fiancé had left him, and that night in 1886 when Jonathan had planned to take his own life. He remembered Jonathan lying in a pool of his own blood, and wrenching the knife free when he was about to cut his throat. Jason had told him that he was going to love him, and to accept his destiny to live forever. He remembered sharing the dark blood with him, the change in Jonathan, the family they became. He remembered the rapture of Jonathan's blood inside him.

A startling thought went into Jason's mind. He wanted it again. One hundred and three years later, he wanted it. He wanted to share again, with this young man forever his son. He realized that Jonathan had been staring at him the whole time, and read into the look on his face, and understood.

Jason pulled his soft orange hair away from his neck, and came down onto the floor next to Jonathan. He put his hands on Jonathan's shoulders, pulled him close. "Drink from me, my son." he whispered, words that had stood too long unspoken.

"Yes, father." Jonathan replied just as softly, his voice full of emotion that he had really never felt for Jason.

Jason felt Jon's fangs enter his neck, but there was no pain for him, because he gave his blood willingly, and Jonathan was his son. The beginning of the exchange of blood sent Jason's head swimming, a relaxed, drugged feeling overtook him. Slowly, as if in a dream, he moved Jonathan's hair back, let the bloodlust take over, and sank his own fangs into Jonathan's neck.

Jonathan winced a little, but not much. He just hadn't been expecting it. He felt himself being opened, draining from the source, but being drained, also. The taste of Jason's blood in his mouth was so hot and salty, and so old. It seemed like there never was a hurt, never Julia, never Devin, never any pain. He was again the young man caught between two worlds, and wanting desperately to be loved. Except this time, he possessed that love. He felt it, in the link bonding them together at that moment, and he knew that Jason would never neglect him again.

Finally, Jason pulled back, blood trickling down his mouth, and from the two puncture wounds in his neck. Jonathan wanted to grab for him, tell him not to let go, never again let go, but he knew he couldn't. He wiped at his mouth, as Jason did the same. He felt his skin close. He wasn't a young confused fledgling anymore. He was an adult male vampire, able to have fledglings of his own.

"But you still need to be loved." Jason said, reading into Jonathan's mind. Jonathan realized his weakness and quickly blocked his thoughts and endless cloud of gray. Jason smiled, his glazed blue eyes clearing.

"You ought to be strong now. Go out, hunt. I'll make things right, my son. Trust in me." He embraced Jon, pulled him up to his feet.

"Thank you, Jason. I'll never forget this." Jonathan said.

Jason nodded stoically, and retired into the basement, to prepare for the journey. Jonathan did as he asked, went out to hunt.

Across the continent, Julia tossed in her sleep. She feared, more than anything else, that she'd give in to Cory. No, she belonged to Jonathan, nothing like that could happen, could it? Cory couldn't stop her from dreaming, after all, and she was with Jon, in her dreams. His chain around her neck was a spark in the darkness, and she would never take it off again. It was his endless circle of love, which was there for her, in the midnight of hopelessness that surrounded her. And deep in her veins he was there, too.

PART THREE

The Search (April, Nineteen Ninety)

1

Four months had come and gone. Time had passed slowly for the members of Jason's coven. Changes had taken place, within them all.

In Paris, France, Jason and Rikki searched nightly for Alexander, Jason's "Father". They had not found one bit of evidence that Alexander had even remained all this time, within Paris. Sometimes they would feel a slight presence watching them, a fleeting shadow, but as they scanned with their minds, the presence would be gone.

They fit in perfectly with the Paris youth. Jason and Rikki went to nightclubs, art shows, dances and museums. Jason took it all in without saying a word. He had lived here, after all, and had seen it before. Rikki, the younger one, had grown up as a runaway, an orphan. He had been alone in Vermont all his life, until Jason had found him. He felt giddy at these places. Paris gave his inherited blood a thrill, one that he succumbed to, easily.

Rikki ate the French food with as much abandon as he drank the champagne. The alcohol had little effect on him, but if he drank it in high doses; it left him feeling a little drunk, for a little while. He would consume as much as he could, watch the world grow hazy and dizzy, smile at Jason, and do it again.

The women in Paris were beautiful and charming, but Rikki could outdo them anytime. He'd make them love him until the dawn.

In the operas, sitting with Jason, he disguised himself as a rich young man, handsome and daring.

Rikki was having the time of his life.

Jason was happy for him, but something weighed heavily on his mind. There were no vampires! It seemed as if they all had suddenly vanished. When Jason had been created, Paris had been swarming with them. He knew, of course, after so many years few would remain, but he had not expected this abandonment, this desertion. Something was terribly wrong here. They must be out there, somewhere, watching, waiting.

One night, in the lobby of the hotel where they were staying, a stranger came into their midst. Jason felt him first; an old familiar, menacing presence that he had not felt in a long, long time.

He looked up slowly from the glass of wine, which rested on a glass table, near his legs. He sat on a plush sofa, waiting for Rikki to return from the girl he was talking to. Rikki came to him at that very moment, and stood by him. "What is it, Jason?" Rikki asked, sensing the power in the air.

233

Jason raised one hand for silence, stared out into the night again, through the huge glass doors more than thirty feet away. The stranger stepped out of the Paris night mist, and placed one pale hand on the doors. And smiled.

Jason knew him!

Rikki saw Jason's blue eyes widen with shock, but nothing more in his expression changed. Rikki softly told the girl to go away. Her feelings looked hurt, but Jason needed him now. At least maybe, this creature would be worried by his appearance, if not his age. Rikki's blond hair was teased a bit, eyeliner outlining his green eyes. He had on a black net shirt beneath his leather jacket, and a pair of black leather gloves with the fingers cut off. Leather pants, and a pair of combat boots finished the outfit. The girl had helped him with the outfit. They had been going out, a trip to the clubs of Monmartre, but plans had changed.

He looked down at Jason, who slowly raised the glass to his lips and down again, as the man entered the building. Jason wasn't wearing his regular clothes tonight, although his heavy black overcoat lay just beyond reach, on the sofa, next to him. His orange hair had been tied back in a ponytail, making the chains on his earring dangle freely, against his neck. He had shaved his face clean, although he knew that the hair would grow back tomorrow, as he slept. He wore black jeans, his boots, and a light blue silk shirt the same color as his eyes. His clothing made him look thin, less menacing. Rikki guessed that he had created plans of his own tonight. In any case, they were now canceled.

The stranger approached in slow elegant strides. There was something about him, which practically screamed danger. He was a very old and powerful vampire. Very confident too, a trait which could possibly bring about his undoing.

The man halted directly before Jason. His hair was short, strait, and midnight black. He wore a small goatee that was also black, very characteristically French, a black suede jacket with a black shirt underneath, and blue pants, which lent a contrast to the rest of his clothes. On his face was a dark and very expensive looking pair of sunglasses. Rikki wondered why he wore them, but in the next second, he wished he hadn't.

The man took off the glasses, and gazed at Jason. His eyes were a light, light shade of gray, the color of half-dead brain tissue. It reminded Rikki of corruption. If you looked at this man from just the right angle, you didn't even see the gray. Just pale, empty eyes.

Jason looked up at him, not moving. He remembered this man, and although he had been far too young in his vampire life to fight him, he knew that Alexander and he, Jean-Luc, were enemies. Alexander had sworn to kill Jean someday.

"Bonsoir, Jastón." Jean said sweetly. "Good to see you once again. We never thought you would, but the prodigal son has returned. What is it you, and your satanic-looking fledgling, have come here for?"

Jason stared at Jean, his eyes never leaving his face. He set the wine back down gently, and folded his hands on his lap. "Jastón is dead along with Devin. Do you really think I'd use that name after Devin was killed? He was the last of my life . . . here."

Jean smiled again. "You don't have a life here, now. What did the young one call you? Jason? Ingenious. What is your American real estate under? Ah, yes. Jason Maura. You always have a way." An evil light went into his eyes. "Just like your father."

"Have you seen Alex, Jean?" Jason asked, his face expressionless, hard.

"Well, that again brings up the question of why you are here. To make amends with your father? Or to rescue a granddaughter?" Jean asked, his pale fingers rolling the sunglasses back and forth. He leaned close to Jason, his lips inches away from his face. "Perhaps to show the young one, how fast a castle can burn down."

Jason's fist flew out of nowhere, connected squarely with Jean's chin. The older vampire stumbled back a few steps, his smile gone. Jason sat still on the couch, but his lips were pressed tight, and deep in his eyes, flecks of red began to surface. He was trying hard to keep control, and Rikki knew it. Rikki took a step towards Jean.

"Be careful, young one. I always finish my fights," he said as he regained composure. Jason's hand extended and pushed Rikki gently back.

"It's alright, Rikki." Jason said in soft even tones. He glanced around and saw a few of the people in the lobby watching them, rather intently. He focused back on Jean. "What do you know?" he asked.

Suddenly, Jean's smile was back. "I know you, Jastón de Maurtiere. I know why you've come here, and what you want." He placed his glasses back over his eyes. "You and your child are not wanted here. Leave Paris or die." In a motion too fast for them, or humans, to follow, Jean was gone.

Jason sat back with a giant sigh, reached for his wine. He drank it, touched his fingers to his head.

"Jason, what's going on?" Rikki asked, a tone of fright in his voice.

Jason stood up, grabbed his overcoat and reached up to put his arm around Rikki's shoulders. "Come upstairs." he beckoned. He released Rikki, and began to walk up the golden winding stairway.

Located on the second floor were their joint rooms, very large, with the one odd stipulation that windows had been boarded up. How Jason had pulled this request off, Rikki did not know, nor did he ask.

Rikki followed behind Jason into one of these rooms, and sat upon the bed, Jason took a seat for himself on a large, cushioned chair. He placed his overcoat on the arm.

Jason took a deep breath, and began to speak. "Alexander, my father, was born to human life in the year 1255. Of course, he is not my real father, as I am not really yours, but he created me.

"I was told that Alexander was born of a good family, in a little village, outside of Moscow, Russia. He became the Captain of the Guard in Moscow, for the Grand Prince Daniel, in 1275. This was during the year of Mongol rule over Russia, when princes had to pay fees to the Mongol Lords, just to stay alive. Alexander would have been a mere twenty years old. He served Daniel in this manner for fifteen years, without any major Mongol attacks, or invasions. Then, on a dark, cold, lonely night in 1290, when Alexander was thirty-five, he had been ordered to forward supplies to another wing of the army, which stood a few miles south of his home village.

"There was a Mongol attack. It came out of nowhere, killing the other nine men, and seizing the supplies. Alex had been fatally wounded, but he was still alive when the Mongols checked the dead. He had fought bravely, killed thirteen of the enemy, before he was cut down.

"Alex couldn't see, couldn't breathe. He was in total darkness. But then, he saw a pair of glowing red eyes through the darkness of death.

"'You fought well, like one of us. I want you to live, to live forever.' A harsh voice whispered this, seeming to issue from the eyes.

"Alex began to feel a tingling sensation in his neck. He wondered briefly what those eyes were doing, but didn't have the strength to raise his head. In the end, he didn't care. He began to quietly fade away into oblivion, when he was thrown back into his body. The darkness faded, and now he could feel again, and see again. Something warm and wet was in his mouth, throat, and body, making him live. It was blood, the Mongol's blood.

"The Mongol sat, near to him, his wrist slit over Alex's mouth. Alex looked up at him, and saw the red eyes, the fangs, and his own blood running from the Mongol's mouth as he laughed.

"The morning after, Alex left for Paris, knowing that he couldn't live in Russia any longer. He knew he was changing; everyone he knew should think him dead.

"The sun hurt him. It burned his skin, and was too bright for his eyes. So he learned to only come forth into the world of man at night, to drink blood to survive, to become a hunter. A lion amongst the lambs."

Jason closed his eyes, touched his head to his hands. "Where did you come in?" Rikki asked.

Jason looked up at Rikki and gave a slight grin. "I was born in 1677, here in France, to a noble family, and was brought up in a castle. But my life was not as you'd expect it. It was hard; my father was full of contempt for my mother, and brother, and myself. They all died in a castle fire." A look of anguish passed over Jason's face. Rikki now understood why Jason had struck out at Jean earlier, for his comment about a castle.

"I had saved my father's wealth, took my fortune here to Paris. I had a few good years, but then disaster struck again. I can't explain now, and please don't ask. It is far too painful being here.

"Afterwards I again took to wandering, and developed a friendship with this man, Alexander. He took me into his home, where I found at least thirty others living, and all were vampires. After a period of living there and seeing strange things, hearing strange noises, I thought I had gone mad. But then Alexander, who had been my friend the whole while, revealed himself to me. He made me what I am in the summer of 1700.

"Alex and I always argued, and the last time this happened, he banished me from Europe, supposedly for good. I took Devin with me, and fled to America. He looked like you, Rikki, and was my first-born. I created Devin when I was so young, I could have died. I created a few others in America, Jonathan, and Andrew, whom you never knew."

"So why does Jean-Luc want us dead if you never went up against him? Shouldn't it be Alexander's fight?" Rikki questioned him.

"Yes," Jason said, "but it's not how the old ones do things. Everything they do is based on tradition and rules. I only met one vampire older than Alex in my life, but he left Paris a long, long time ago. I don't have any idea where he is now."

Jason seemed to be in thought for a moment, and then smiled again at Rikki. "Did you know, Alexander told me, the very first vampire was supposed to be Cain? The son of Adam and Eve, who were the first Homo-sapiens-sapiens. Cain slew Able and drank his blood. He wandered around in darkness for the rest of his days."

Jason stood up and went to the window, pulled back the shades, and opened the huge glass doors that went out to a balcony. "Cain bore the stamp of evil upon his head, and wherever he went, people feared him, and felt his evil. So he learned to disguise himself, and his evil. All his children became like him, and his children's children, and so on."

Jason pulled the elastic out of his hair, and the night wind swept it across his face. "The children of Adam and Eve, and their children, became the humans you see today. The children of Cain became the vampires. It must have been easy to feed back then. They slaughtered the ape-people that had somehow missed the link to evolve. They made their children by transfusions of blood to the healthier humans. Some of these vampires are still around, although many have perished in the sun. Some even say Cain is still alive, but perhaps that amount of time is too long for any of us to withstand. Too many changes have taken place in the world. However, I'm not sure if I even believe this tale, myself."

Rikki watched Jason walk out onto the balcony, now seeming to be thinking to himself. Sometimes, it was as if Rikki didn't even exist. "Jason, I'm leaving now," he said as he stood up. Rikki received no answer. He looked out onto the balcony, and saw Jason leaning against the rail, his arms crossed, and his head down. He knew better then to approach Jason at such a time. He left without saying another word.

Jason was now so locked up into his memories, that he never paid attention to the slight tremor of pain that Jonathan was experiencing. He never felt it when Jonathan slowly slipped into insanity.

2

In Vermont at this time, Jonathan had become a ruthless killer, deep in terrible grief for his lost Julia. Steven followed his example, mutilating the bodies, killing just for sport. Old, young, it no longer mattered to them.

Jon would now kill a wife in the bed of her husband, after the children had invited him in. He'd break the husband's arms and legs so he'd have no choice, but to watch as he killed the wife. Then he'd kill the man, leaving Steven to feast on the other occupants of the home.

Steven loved the recklessness, and the wild abandon, of which they fed. He took pleasure in watching people read about the "wolf attacks" in the newspaper, and how frightened they were. He followed Jonathan blindly into everything. The mansion was again in shambles.

Timothy, the quiet one, the one who shouldn't have been a vampire, had become disillusioned with the situation. He tried, to no avail, to halt Jonathan from these rampages, but Jon just laughed at him with tears in his eyes, cursing him, telling him he should have died. Timothy was of no use to Jonathan now.

They began to fight nightly, as Steven watched. Sometimes these fights were verbal, sometimes physical. One night while Steven was out, Jonathan and Timothy had their last and fatal fight. Timothy attempted to end Jonathan's existence, which only made things worse.

Jonathan had struck out at Timothy, causing Timothy to collapse against a wooden chair, his hands outstretched. As the chair broke beneath his weight, Timothy shrieked in pain, pulling back quickly and gazing at his hands, which had become embedded with splinters, oozing with blood. Timothy fought back the tears, and rage took over. As he watched, Jonathan stood calmly in the middle of the room, facing the fireplace, and let his jacket drop to the floor. His back was to Timothy.

Timothy painfully reached into his pocket for his knife, flicked it open. He rushed toward Jonathan, and with an inhuman scream, sank the knife deep into Jonathan's back. He pulled down on the knife and gashed deep and long, before pulling it back out. Without a sound, Jonathan fell to the floor, on his back. Staring up at Timothy.

Timothy's face contorted then, and with another scream, issuing out from beneath the fangs, plunged his knife deep into Jonathan's chest.

Jonathan lay there, crying inside for he knew now; he had to destroy Timothy. He wished the pain of the knife slashing him would hurt more, but it didn't. It couldn't. He closed his eyes, and let Timothy mutilate him.

"I will stop you, I will." Timothy's voice harsh garbled, as he slashed at Jonathan's legs, arms, and body. "Go on and bleed to death,"

Jonathan eyes filled over with silent tears, as he felt Timothy's knife sink into his heart, the cold steel slid in and out, puncturing. He wasn't crying because of the pain, but because he had loved Timothy as a son, and now he had betrayed him.

Timothy bent onto his knees, bloody hands dropping the knife. He touched Jonathan's forehead, and seeing no response, his own blood red eyes leaked red tears, as he drew forward, and sank his fangs into Jonathan's neck.

When Jonathan fell the pulling pain of his blood being taken without being given, he was reminded again of Cory.

Which pushed him further into insanity.

With a roar, he raised his hands to Timothy's head, and broke his neck with one sharp snap. Jonathan opened his mouth wide, shut his eyes, as he held Timothy's weakly struggling body in a vise-like grip. When he opened his eyes again, they were red; his fangs had grown down from his top jaw. Without any further hesitation, he bit into Timothy's broken neck, and slowly drank him dry.

He could feel Timothy's blood rushing into him, felt the captured vampiric soul detach from the body, and try so desperately hard to hang on. He felt Timothy's presence inside him for just a moment, as the soul gave a final effort, and then was gone.

Jonathan stood, watched as his wounds healed. As he shut his eyes and felt the beast leave him, curling up somewhere in his veins, he felt a little sick, but very powerful.

Timothy lay dead on the floor, his body completely drained of blood, a phenomenon of translucent, smoked glass. Only his red eyes and dark hair still held color. His mouth remained open in a silent snarl for all eternity, the fangs still very apparent.

Jonathan opened his eyes, now dark with the fire hidden behind them. His smile was that of a half-crazed maniac. "Poor Timothy. I told you. You should have died long ago." He carried out the oddly colored body to wait for the dawn.

Jonathan sat beside Timothy on the front stairs, watched as the dead vampire's body slowly cracked and splintered, flaking off into fragments, as shattered glass might. By the time Steven returned to the mansion, it was near dawn, and there was nothing really left of Timothy but his clothes, along with fragments of his skin, his eyes, hair and teeth. By the end of the day, nothing would remain but for a bit of ash, and charred clothing.

Steven slowly walked up the drive, approaching with caution because of Jonathan's sobbing giggles.

"Look!" Jonathan cried out, tears in his eyes.

Steven looked, and almost fell over from the shock. In his short life as a vampire, he had never seen anything like this, and it frightened him a bit to know that Jonathan could probably do this to him, as well.

Steven gave a short, nervous laugh, put one hand on Jonathan's shoulder. "Man, you are one crazy son of a bitch."

Jonathan wiped his eyes, and stood up, suddenly composed again. "Come on, brother. The sun's coming to meet him," he said as he gestured to Timothy. "Let's go inside."

Steven let Jonathan put his arm around him, flinching a little at the touch. He had to learn. He needed to learn. Steven just kept assuring himself of this, as he went down with Jonathan into the coolness of the basement. He didn't particularly care for it down there, but it was for Jason that he remained with Jonathan. To help him.

Steven sighed as he covered himself in blankets, just beyond Jonathan's coffin. Too bad for Timothy, Steven was the one with Jonathan now. And Steven loved his ways. "Those who adapt will survive." he whispered, remembering something from a long ago Science class, in a school he hadn't cared for.

Then it was gone as the darkness pulled him under, into dreams. The sun rose over Vermont.

3

Far away in California, the next night, Julia lay as if dead, on the bed inside the small hotel room; Cory's "grand hotel."

She had fallen into a deep sleep, a coma for a vampire. She could not awaken now, even if she wanted to. Her body had shriveled around her. She did not move, did not breathe. No thoughts processed inside her mind.

The previous evening had been the last night of consciousness, for Julia. She had been barely aware of her state and the world around her, but now, she was rendered oblivious.

The small amounts of dead, cold mortal blood had sustained her for a while, but they had lost their use. The blood had to be alive, in order for the vampire to live. Julia had slowly starved to death.

Kevin, the vampire who retrieved the blood for her, was a tall, handsome young man, probably about eighteen at the time of his transformation. He was about five foot ten, with shoulder length brown hair and brown eyes. He always dressed in black. Julia had only seen him twice.

The first time, her health had been better. They had talked for hours until Cory had found them, together. And then, there had been hell to pay. He had attacked Kevin, and even slapped Julia, screaming something about Jonathan dying, and starving forever. Then he had smiled that awful grin, and left.

The second time she saw Kevin had been the last. Even now, in her sleep, she could remember the look in Kevin's eyes as he saw her, barely conscious, deathly hideous. Kevin had cried. Actually cried. The blood-tears streaked his face, as he passed his hand gently over her body. He knew she was slowly starving, and he cried, sympathetic for her pain.

Kevin had sat there for Julia's last moments of consciousness, holding her hand. Julia had fixed her eyes on he alone, as the darkness came and swallowed her up.

The last thing Julia remembered was Kevin's tearful, frightened face, and Jonathan's blood crying out to her not to give in.

Now, in another part of the hotel, Cory had finished off a victim. A young prostitute, whom he had lured into his room, now lay drained, destroyed and dead, tangled in the bloody sheets.

Cory sat on the side of the bed, licking the blood off his long, naked body like a cat. He pulled on his clothes slowly, smiling at the limp, bloody form on the bed.

243

Cory chuckled to himself, pulled a clean white shirt over his head. "Stupid bitch." he muttered. He picked up her purse and rummaged through it, found a brush, and began brushing out his long rusty hair, pulling through the knots and blood clotted tangles. He stroked harder and harder, until his hair was gleaming and shiny.

Cory opened up the window and shutters, and gazed out at the sliver of moon in the sky. "You'll never get her back, Jason. Jonathan may die, but what do I care? I am the true evil, the true vampire!" Cory's voice rose a few notches in volume. "Neither you, nor your children, or even Alexander can stop me. You with your petty little peaceful worlds, so pathetic really, always are existing in seclusion. We were meant to create havoc and destruction." he chuckled. "As I will destroy Julia, and make her mine. None of you can change me. I am evil! I am the night!" he shouted, and then, realized there was no one in the room, but the dead girl and she didn't care anymore. He smiled to himself as he left the room, the maid sign fixed onto the door.

Cory walked down the hall to Julia's locked room. The key stuck for a moment, and he checked it with a frown. The lock had rusted. It hadn't been turned for over a month. Cory reached out to the knob, turned it quick, and sharp. There was a crunching noise as the lock broke. He pushed against the door, as the soft illumination from the hallway fell into her darkened room.

Julia lay on the bed with the bedclothes pulled up around her. Her appearance was grotesque. Nothing remained of the girl; it seemed a shriveled old lady had been left in her place.

Cory walked to her, knelt down on the floor beside the bed. He kissed her wrinkled forehead. He glanced contemptuously at Jonathan's chain around her neck, but did nothing more.

Cory bent over her and whispered sweetly into her ear, "Come, my dear, come back into the world of darkness. I beckon you."

He then dug into his jeans for a pocketknife, winced as he slit his wrist. He tilted Julia's head back and opened her mouth, letting the dark, rich blood pour into her.

A tiny spark ignited inside Julia's darkness. A dozen sparks followed that first one. They began to swim in the black, crashing and colliding, and multiplying. The sparks set off a fire inside her veins.

Jonathan's blood screamed.

Jonathan lifted his head from the first victim of the night. He had been drinking from her in his own driveway, but something had disturbed his feeding. He had felt something. A dying presence deep within. A strong tie perhaps being severed.

Jonathan wiped the blood from his mouth and lay back, allowing the woman to get up and stumble away, crying hysterically. He barely heard her scream, when she fell into Steven's arms. Jonathan attempted now, to focus on the severed tie. The pain hit him hard and without warning. It shot through him, and it burned.

Julia's eyes suddenly shot open, she jerked upward, but Cory's other arm held her down. She managed a tight gurgled scream. The blood was burning her, consuming her like fire would, or the light of day. She felt Jonathan's blood dying within her, and she knew she was running out of time.

Julia screamed again, this time with her mind. A white-hot lance of pain, agony, and rage entered Cory's mind, but he did not let her go.

Jonathan had curled himself up into a ball on the ground, hugging his arms tight. He felt a part of himself being killed by Cory, and he knew he was losing her. The burning pain was leaving him, making him nothing more than an empty shell. When he could no longer feel Julia at all, Jonathan Jared Deschene, Killer and Predator cried like a lost child in the night.

Julia's hands raised to hold her stomach, a feeble attempt to hold Jonathan in. She whispered his name, and she felt the last of him leave her. She appeared young once again, and beautiful, but she was so very empty. Jonathan was gone. Cory's blood had killed Jonathan's, and took its place beside Julia's own vampiric blood.

Julia almost cried out when she realized that Cory would now have influence over her, and would be able to control her desires and emotions.

The blood stopped coming.

Julia rose slowly, wiping her mouth off in disgust. She tried hard not to burst into tears, as she tasted his blood in her mouth.

Cory climbed onto the bed beside her, not even glancing at the wound in his wrist, as it healed. As he stroked Julia's hand, she didn't pull away. Instead, she slowly turned to look at him, her blue-green eyes rimmed with threatening tears.

Julia turned away from the smirk on his face, looked down at the floor. The blood tears ran on their own from her eyes, onto the carpet below. "He's . . . gone." she whispered.

Cory yanked her around so fast, her neck cracked. "Ow," she whimpered. She had no choice but to look at him. His eyes were narrowed, dangerous. There was a slight snarl on his lips, as one of his hands crept up to her face, gripped her chin a bit tight.

"You, Julia, are now and forever, mine." His voice was but a hiss. Julia pulled out of his grasp, put her face in her hands, and cried.

4

Jason sat across the lobby on a plush, gold velvet sofa, talking with three expensive looking, Parisian call girls. There was a blond and two brunettes, reminding Rikki of the vampire brides in that old classic novel, *Dracula,* by Bram Stoker.

These three girls, decked out in fancy garments and jewelry, were only human. They had no idea one of them would die tonight. In a way, they were playing a ghastly game of Russian Roulette. Jason would only choose one; Rikki put his money on the blond, being that Jason had a taste for the eccentric.

Rikki turned, gazed out the big glass window. Tonight he had dressed in a green sweatshirt, black jeans, and sneakers. At home he never would have changed so often. It was what Jason had said that prevented him. Humans in Vermont were used to their look, and only saw what they wanted, anyway. Perhaps they might have ever changed back home, if their clothes got worn, or bloodstained. His excuse for Julia was, she simply could not let go of her human nature.

Back home. That's where Rikki wanted to be right now. It was a place he could run free without fear of Wild Ones, or enemies. He could leave anytime he wanted, to go anywhere. Now Jason told him to stay inside, to wait for the girls. When they had come, Rikki had gone back to the window. They were too easy, like stealing blood from a child.

Prostitutes were usually that way. They went to bed with you for your money. They were too willing to give their bodies up. That's why Jason liked call girls. They were, in his opinion, sly and seductive. Rikki assumed they just liked like their job, and it made him sick. He needed a victim that would give him the thrill of the hunt, the chase, and the kill.

The thought of it all made him shiver. He needed to go out soon. He had to. He looked back at Jason, anxiety on his face. Jason, dressed in black once again, was holding onto the blond girl, leading her up the stairs.

Rikki smiled to himself. He had been right. And now he could leave.

He wondered what Jason would do if he found out he had left. He remembered what he had done when other sons had disobeyed. Jason could be gentle one second, and ferocious the next. But he also had said he'd never harm Rikki, never hurt him, because he loved him.

Rikki didn't understand the love crap, he never had. But Jason had helped him, and became the father he never had. Why would he hurt him now? He needed the hunt; Jason must understand.

Rikki opened the glass door to the hotel, and pausing only a second, slipped out into the night.

He jumped the stairs in one graceful leap, and then looked back up at the hotel. A few people were looking at him funny, but Jason was nowhere in sight. Rikki smiled, walked out into the continuous traffic of people and cars.

He strolled past the vendors with sweet smelling foods, past the couples holding hands. Past the stores, and shops, and museums. He looked behind him only once, to see if anyone was following him, but there was no one, and then, feeling rather safe, putt one foot far out in front of the other, and sprang off into the sky. No human had even seen him; his actions had been too swift for a their eyes to follow. He soared over the buildings of Paris gazed down on the people below. The wind blew the hair out of his face and rushed through his sweatshirt, tingling against his skin.

He swooped down in the darkened alleys, looking for some poor misfortunate creature that just happened to be out tonight.

In one of these alleys, he observed a young girl leaning over the ground. A dim lamp had been set before her. Rikki had found his prey. Now the fun would begin.

He swooped down over her, touching one pale hand against her head as he went.

The girl gasped, spilling a purse full of marbles down to the paved ground. They echoed off the walls around her like the tinkling of little bells.

Rikki landed softly on one of the surrounding rooftops.

The girl had forgotten her marbles. She stood up and gazed around with large, frightened dark eyes. Her face was smeared with dirt, as were her clothes. The coat she wore was tattered to rags. Her dark hair was matted and greasy, and she looked about eleven years old. So very young to be homeless.

The girl stared up at the sky and yelled a string of French words, which Rikki could not possibly understand. She reached into her pocket, while he watched, and pulled out a small gun. She cocked the hammer and held it in front of her, making a slow circle check of the area. She spoke again, this time under her breath, and stood her ground. When she was sure that no one threatened her, she lowered her gun to her side, and stood very still, listening.

Finally, she knelt back on the ground, and placed the gun in front of her. She began picking up the marbles, placing them into the bag.

When she had almost finished, Rikki decided he was tired of watching her. He leaned over the corner of the building, and called out: "Little girl!"

The girl snatched up the gun and spun to the rooftop, which he had been sitting on. Before she had a chance to see him, he leapt up into the air, landed softly behind her. "Bonjour." he said the only French word he knew.

Faster than he had anticipated, the girl whipped the gun around, aimed it up at his face. She screamed something at him, probably the French equivalent of, "Stop, or I'll shoot!"

Rikki smiled down at her, drinking in her fear. He let the changes come over him, never taking his eyes off her. He watched her as the red haze entered his vision, and pulled back his lips further to reveal his fangs.

The girl screamed and dropped the gun, her hands clasping her cheeks. She realized her mistake, bent swiftly to retrieve it. Rikki moved faster, and stepped on the gun so she couldn't. When she reached for it anyway, he kicked it behind him. The girl pulled back her hand, and stood, slowly. He was so much taller than she was; he appeared to tower over her.

The girl turned and ran.

Rikki watched her run away, folded his arms across his chest, and laughed.

She turned her head when she heard him laugh, saw him standing there. She briefly wondered why he wasn't following, but then turned down another alleyway, and kept running. Soon, she couldn't run anymore.

The girl stopped running, placed her hands on her knees, and panted for breath. When she closed her eyes for a second, she felt the sudden wind brush over her back. She turned and looked back at the entry of the alley. No one came in.

The girl smiled her relief, and turned back around.

Rikki landed behind the girl just as she began to turn, and as she made the complete circle, he stepped up to hold her.

She fell right into his arms.

The girl stared up at him for a moment, her face white, drained of blood. She looked like she was about to scream. But then, she shuddered violently, and shut her mouth.

Her hands fell away from Rikki's powerful arms.

The girl leaned forward, pressed her face into his sweater. She was tired of running, tired of the games. If his cold body repelled her, she did not show it. She simply gave up.

Rikki pulled her to him, cradled her small body in his arms. He sat down on an old wooden chair that someone had left in the street. He had only seen a few people give in without a fight, and this girl was one of them. It wasn't as good as a real hunt, but it would do.

He brushed the girl's hair away from her neck, and kissed it. Then, humming a song that he didn't know the words to, he shut his red eyes and tried to calm her shuddering body.

When she had relaxed a little, he got excited. When her fingers brushed his neck, he wanted more to rip apart hers. "Brave and innocent, your death gives me life." he whispered.

Finally, he couldn't stand it anymore. When he opened his eyes again, he found her looking at him with anticipation, as if she really knew what was about to happen.

He opened his mouth slightly, bringing his fangs to his bottom lip hard enough to draw blood. He licked the blood off, and turned her head with his hand. "Give it to me, now." he growled.

He sank his fangs into her neck, and instantly, the blood shot into his mouth. The girl did not scream. She sighed. She had known death was coming.

Rikki clutched her harder to him, his eyes open, but only seeing red. His mind's eye began to see the girl's life, to feel her feelings. He shut off the mind link, for he did not want to know. He thought only of the blood.

That is why he did not see the time in her life, when she had been introduced to Jean-Luc. Nor did he hear Jean's voice explain to her, every detail of what would happen this night. He wasn't even aware of it when, with her last ounce of strength, she pulled forth a tiny vial of bright blue liquid, and poured it down her throat.

The girl did not cry out, as it burned though her stomach and intestines, and poured into her blood stream. She couldn't; she was already dead. The shock of the liquid disintegrating her throat had stopped her heart from beating.

Rikki first thought that there was something wrong with the blood. It caught in his mouth and threatened to pull his teeth out from the roots. He kept sucking anyway. The blood was wrong, and tasted bad and stale, but he simply couldn't stop feeding, once he had begun.

He was suddenly aware of a great booming sound, somewhere outside of himself. His own heart began following in the same rhythm. Faster at first, then slower, and slower the booming heart outside of his body cut off suddenly, and he was aware that the first heart had been hers, and now she was dead. But there was still the brackish blood in his mouth, still coming. The blood was hurting him, he knew, and he needed to stop it, but he couldn't.

Suddenly, he felt the presence of the girl inside him, a feeling he had never felt before. It was a human spirit, a soul, and she was tugging at his heart. He could somehow hear her now, as she screamed at him. She wanted him to go with her into the spirit world. She pulled at his heart harder, and harder, and harder.

Rikki screamed in pain knocked her body away from him. It fell to the ground with a wet crunch. Rikki collapsed away from the body. The girl was still screaming inside him, and wouldn't release him.

"I didn't kill you! It was too soon!" He screamed, convulsing, bluish red blood coming in a stream from his mouth, nose and ears. "I didn't drink you down to the last heartbeat. Get out of me, please, let me go." He whispered to her, over and over. Finally, the soul seemed to understand. She let go of his heart, and slowly left his body.

When Rikki felt her gone, the pain in his heart receded, but his veins and his stomach were burning and throbbing on their own. Rikki began to sob, and as he did, the vampiric features vanished from his face. He hurt so badly, that it seemed the pain would never end. He looked up at the dead girl, and saw her skin. Then he knew he hadn't killed her.

Her whole body was pale blue, and her open mouth looked as if it had been eaten away by acid. Rikki painfully brought his hands to his face, and saw that they now contained the same, eerie color. She had poisoned him.

Pain entered his head, his very brain, and took the vision from his eyes. The last thing he saw was Jean-Luc standing over him, laughing.

Then his world was nothing but darkness and hurt.

5

Jonathan looked out into the valley, the cool spring wind blowing through his thick, dark hair. He had climbed up this mountain, choosing not to fly, but rather to feel the earth under his fingers, and feet.

The mountain was tall and high, taller than Deer Mountain, where he made his home. The peak at the top, where he stood, was rocky and jagged, but he had no trouble keeping his balance.

He looked down at the valley, at the mall and the park, and across at the house where Julia had once lived. Jason's mansion was further up, near the top.

Jon used to come here often, in those long-ago summer nights, after he left Julia slumbering in her home. Wishing he could be with her forever, was something he always had done. He had longed for her, and waited for her. Now he was here again, longing and in anguish. But this time, he felt as if nothing right would ever happen for him again.

Jonathan briefly considered suicide. He would have to stand here, until the killing warmth of the sun came to embrace him. It would be brief and agonizing, flames riding his skin, and in no time his life would be over.

Something inside him would not let him die. He knew that instinct would take over, and he would seek shelter in the rocky outcroppings of this mountain.

Jonathan sighed long and loud. He knew now that Julia was not coming back. She had given into Cory, perhaps didn't care anymore. His fingers brushed her ring on the silver chain he wore around his neck. Again he considered suicide, and again denied the thought. His hand lowered from the ring. He wouldn't get rid of the ring. He felt that he had to remember her.

Jonathan looked down at the thing he held in his other hand. It was a scarf of Julia's. The thing she had worn in her hair, the first night they had met. His eyes clouded over with tears, and he looked up at the stars in the sky.

The wind whipped his hair back away from him, smashing the chains on his earring, against his neck. The jacket was pulling at his arms, threatening to come off. But he felt nothing. He thought he could not feel anything ever again.

He brought the scarf up to his lips, kissing it gently.

"She's gone. I'll never see her again." he whispered. He shuddered, the tears flowing from his eyes. A soft sob escaped his lips.

Jonathan raised his arms, the wind whipping the scarf around his arm like a flag. The tears, a river of pain running down his cheeks as he cried out her name. The sound of his deep, loud voice echoed off the mountains, into the valley below.

He opened his hand and dropped his arms to his sides, watching as the scarf fluttered down into the valley, riding on the wind.

Jonathan sat down on the edge of the peak, covering his face with his hands. He cried until he had no tears left to cry. The pain of losing Julia was far worse the second time. He had been so close, so very close.

After quite a while, he returned to the mansion, only to leave again with Steven. They rode their Harley Davidsons to the park.

Jonathan walked through the crowds, with Steven beside him. He kept his head down and shoved at anyone who approached him. Steven didn't say much; he knew when to keep his mouth shut.

That night, Jonathan bought two six packs of beer, one for Steven and one for himself. He drowned his sorrows in the alcohol, simultaneously drinking the whole pack.

In the aggressive glorious high that followed, together they did more damage to the park and the people in it than ever before.

And Jonathan destroyed the carousel.

6

Two days later in California, Julia was being led out. Out of the hotel that had been her prison for four months.

She wore tight black jeans, a black half-top, black leather boots, and a small white blouse.

Cory had made a point to tell her, they had come off a dead prostitute. Julia had tried not to listen, but his words were there anyway in her ears, in her mind, in her blood.

Julia felt dead, truly dead. Without Jonathan she felt like nothing, could not feel the world around her. But when Cory wanted her to know something, she knew it, she felt it. He forced his powers on her constantly. The small traces of his blood insured that in her.

She knew now where they were, because Cory willed it so. He was pulling her out of the hotel by her wrist, down into the small Californian beach village. They eventually came to rest on a bench, beside a busy street.

Julia looked around her and frowned; she felt his arm slide up onto her back. She could see all the little houses and shops which lined the street, and the teenagers that walked along there. Towards one direction, she could see the Pacific Ocean, with late night surfers riding on the waves. A car came by as she looked across the street, and the stupid driver had the high beams on.

The teenagers around Julia rubbed their eyes, swore at the driver. The driver gave them the finger. Julia's sensitive night-eyes were now tearing. The glare of the light had blinded her for a moment, but now, only a burning sensation was left.

Cory was saying something, but Julia had focused on the kids, and the car. She glanced at the longhaired, tanned boy who sat down on the other side of her. All he wore were a pair of shorts, and sneakers. He had a piece of leather rope around his neck, and an upside down cross hung from it. His blond hair looked great with the tan. And his blood smelled good too.

Julia realized how hungry she was, and how badly she needed blood. She had just begun to lean towards him, when Cory suddenly forced his will upon her. His words came to her in an angry rush.

"Why haven't you been listening to me? I said that you are beautiful."

"Shut up." Julia whispered.

"What?" Cory asked, "Did you actually say something to me?" Cory grabbed her hair and pulled it, forcing her to look at him. "You'd better look at me when you talk, or I might not know what you're saying."

He took her hands, releasing her hair. Julia snarled and pulled back. If the boy behind her noticed, he didn't seem to care.

Cory laughed. "You're precious, Julia, truly precious. I'm so lucky to have you." He put both arms around her and pulled her close.

Julia pushed at him. "You only have me because you took me. Let me go!" She grunted, her voice rising in volume.

The look of amusement vanished from Cory's face, and it was replaced with a look of anger. One of his hands raised from her back grabbed a hold at the base of her neck.

"Look my dear," he said, "I'm your master now. My blood is in you. You can't order me. I could kill you easily, real easily. But I won't. Not yet. No, I've been after you for a while, and now when I finally have you, I'll do anything I want with you. You don't have to like it, and I honestly don't care that you're married or that you still wear that chain. It means nothing to me. You can wear it forever, but it won't stop me from touching you."

As if on a cue, Cory dragged her forward, kissed her harshly on the lips. Julia as first resisted, but something in her blood began to drag her resistance down to nothing. It took her will away, and forced her to like how he was crushing her to him, how his lips were hard and bruising against hers, how his tongue darted over her lips, forcing them open.

Before he could take her over completely, he stopped his attack. Cory pulled back and smiled, and Julia stared at him, shocked. Her hands were still against his jacket, but they had clenched around the front.

Cory's will drained away, and Julia removed her hands, wiping her mouth in disgust. The tears once again came from her eyes.

"Julia, I told you I could do anything I wanted, anything." He grew silent again, watching the people pass by.

Julia stopped crying, realized the boy still sat where he had been before. He hadn't done anything to help her at all, and that was strange for a mortal. They were always usually trying to help somebody.

Julia looked over at him, and found herself staring into bright blue eyes. It was that instant his friends had come over to him, all four of them girls. One was obviously his girlfriend. The others cluttered around Cory who had taken off his jacket, and let go of Julia.

The boy's eyes were like Jason's, but not empty and dead. They were full of sun and sky, and summer days. He had a blond mustache and beard. The girl next to him was yelling at him over and over, but he did not look away from Julia.

The boy, Don, finally looked over at his girlfriend who was now crying, and told her to go home. The girl ran crying down the street.

Don looked back at Julia again and smiled. Then she realized that Don was no boy. He must be about twenty-five years old. And he was interested. In Julia.

The thought almost made her laugh. Then it almost made her cry. Because somehow she knew that she'd kill Don tonight. The thought of the blood made her hungry, and she decided that she would go with it.

Julia turned to look at Cory, who was now standing, looking down at the other girls, flirting obnoxiously.

"Never mind him," Don said, and placed his hand on her thigh. "I know that type. He just wants to use you."

Julia laughed. "Don't I know that."

"I'm Don Tranize. What's your name?"

Julia turned back to him, smiled. "Julia."

"Just Julia?"

"Yes." And in a response to his hand motion in her leg, she kissed him softly on the lips. Not only was he making her hungry, but he was doing crazy things to her emotions as well.

"Julia!" Cory yelled.

Julia stood up. "What?" she questioned, in a tone that stated how angry, hungry, and aggravated she had become.

Cory smiled. "They are having a party tonight. Since Don seems to have lost his date, do you want to go?"

"Why are you asking me?" she said. Cory frowned, told the girls they'd go.

One of them left, reluctantly, and soon came back with a pickup truck, and they all piled in.

In the truck, Julia lost the small white blouse, leaned all over Don, who seemed not to have the slightest fear about anything.

When they arrived at the house, Julia could not help but smell the fragrances issuing from inside. Marijuana, beer, sweat, blood and sex she tipped her head back and smiled. This time, she was not even aware of Cory manipulating her.

They got in without difficulty. The house belonged to a vampire with long black hair and golden eyes, named Darin.

Julia smiled and said hi to Darin, who apparently knew Cory.

Cory almost immediately vanished up the stairs with all three girls.

Julia and Don found four marijuana joints and then, holding hands, also climbed up the stairs.

In the bedroom, Julia smoked two, and Don smoked two. The pounding metal music faded from the air, and Julia's head became light and dizzy. The drugs were affecting her more than they should as a vampire, and she suspected it to be the fact that she had never used them in her life.

She crawled on the floor to Don, and fell on top of him, kissing him and giggling. She tore off his shorts with just an exertion of strength, but he didn't say anything. Just chuckled low in his throat.

Julia pulled off the boots, jeans and tank top, and lay down on the floor beside Don. He kissed her forehead, her lips. His lips traveled down to her chest to where the bra started.

Julia shivered. She felt the blood on his face through her skin. His hands touched her and caressed her, and she wound her fingers in his hair. For a minute she imagined he was Jonathan, but he was just a human, although different from most, in a way she could not place. His fingers were doing wonderful things to her body, and in a whirlwind of drug induced haze, she dreamed that she had fucked Don. It reminded her of a bad thing that happened a long, long time ago and she cried out, and she was scared.

But Don was there, and when she raised herself to put him inside her, she knew what was different, and why he wore the inverted cross.

He was a Satanist, and had been since he was fifteen. He was a priest of his own coven, and he knew what Julia was, he knew what Cory was, and Darin, the vampire and owner of the house, was a blood god to him.

As they pounded back and fourth, Don chanted something that made Julia's hunger come out. She forgot Cory, and Jonathan, and everything that ever mattered to her.

She tilted her head back and howled, her fangs lengthening. Her eyes were scorching red, and the sweat poured from her body.

Julia shoved Don onto his back, her wet hair hanging in ropes. He kept chanting, stirring something so deep in her vampire nature, no one would be able to reach her at that moment. And Don knew what he was doing.

He ran his hands over her body, pulled her head down onto his neck. Julia tore into his throat and sucked out the blood that was so good.

Then she felt the knife enter her wrist, and the pulling, sucking motion that began there. She felt the pain begin in her arm, and whiplash up and down her body. She felt knives inside her veins, cutting her, and hurting her. Her heart was collapsing, and the very blood that she was drinking, flowed right back out.

Julia's fangs receded, and the red in her eyes faded out. She realized that they were still dressed, and the sex had only been a part of Don's spell. But he had wanted her blood, and now she was creating one of her own. But she had been tricked, and it hurt like hell!

Julia screamed again, this time in agony. She fell down beside Don, and tried to push him away, but he was latched there, and he wouldn't let go. She could feel her veins collapsing, one by one. Her head hurt. Her very brain seemed to be on fire inside her skull. A vacuum, namely Don, was sucking out her life. Finally, he let go. Julia watched as he twisted and moaned through the first pains of transformation, ravaging his stomach. When Don collapsed into a sleep, Julia stood, looked at her hands. Her arms and body were like bone the collapsed veins like ropes.

Julia gasped, staggered to the closet. She found a heavy blue blanket, wrapped it around her, in an attempt to hide her ugliness. At about this time, Don awoke.

"Am I like you now, Julia?" he asked.

"No, not until you make your first kill." she whispered.

Don approached Julia, and placed his hands on her shoulders. "Why are you wearing that?"

Julia let the pain and the hunger and betrayal come out. She ripped off the blanket and screamed, "Look! Look what you did to me!

Don stepped back, lowered his head. "I'm sorry. I . . . I didn't know you were so young."

Julia didn't answer him. She pulled the blanket back around herself, headed for the door. "Wait." Don said.

Julia stopped with her hand on the doorknob.

"I was hoping you'd teach me."

Julia was quiet for a moment, and then said, "Have Darin teach you, Satanist. If you ever come near me again, I'll kill you."

Then Julia opened the door, and fell right into Cory's waiting arms.

7

Julia looked up at Cory through her blanket. He was smiling.

With a small, terrified moan, Julia realized that he knew what had happened, and probably had even planned it that way.

Julia tried to pull away from him, but he wouldn't let her go. He pulled her closer instead and whispered into her ear, "How are you Julia? Do you hurt? You know that you shouldn't create anyone until you are at least one hundred years old. Then it doesn't hurt like that."

"Let me go, you bastard. You knew what he was capable of." Julia hissed.

Cory began to pull Julia down the hallway. She felt the other vampire, Darin, come up behind her, and enter the room she had just left.

"You look awful, Julia, a real monster. It's interesting that your first child would be created that way. And that you'd abandon him."

"I hate him, and I hate you. Let me go!" She struggled against his crushing arms, but she was too tired, and hungry, and hurting to even budge him an inch. Every time she brushed against his body with her skin, it hurt.

When Cory shoved her into his room, Julia could not stop him. He locked the door, and then told her to look up.

On the bed sat two of the girls who had followed Cory in. They held out their arms to him, and he shrugged off his jacket and white shirt, dropping them on a chair near the door. He lay down on the bed, and the two girls, who had remained fully clothed, began kissing him, touching him.

As they bent over him, Julia saw the bite marks on their necks, blood trickling out. Every once in a while Cory would raise his head to kiss them there, and they loved it.

Julia turned away from him, disgusted. To see two human girls, turned into devil's whores, was too much for her to bear. Cory would destroy anyone for fun, she thought.

Then Julia saw the other girl. She was sitting on the floor, playing with a bit of string that had unraveled from her sweatshirt. Her black hair was messed up, and her eyes had an empty look to them. Julia knew instantly that Cory had taken her mind. For some strange reason, he didn't want her anymore.

Julia let the blanket fall to the ground, positive that no one in the room was leaving here alive, besides herself and Cory. She knelt down in front of the girl, who was now staring at Cory. Her face still looked blank, but now, behind the emptiness, glowed an evil killing fire.

Julia looked back at Cory. He was now lying on top of one girl, as he feasted on her. The other was still kissing his back. But as he drank from the first, his blood red eyes were on the third girl, who sat complacently beside Julia. Julia looked from Cory to the girl, and then back to Cory. She heard his words echo inside her mind.

That one is yours.

Julia heard a sound issue from the girl, like that of a wounded animal.

She looked over at the girl. The girl had stopped gazing at Cory, and was now clutching at her head. Suddenly, she looked up at Julia, and growled.

Julia stared at her. How could Cory have done this? How could he transform his evil, into this mortal girl? She didn't have the time to figure it out. The girl attacked her, ripping at her hurting skin with her nails. Julia threw her off, the girl striking the wall. She looked down at her skin. Only a little blood came out. The girl came at her again. Julia received a fist in the head. Julia angrily grabbed the girl's arm and broke it with a loud snap.

The girl shrieked, and dropped to the ground. Julia smelt the living blood coming down from the splintered bone, sticking out of her arm, and instantly her facial features shifted to that of the vampire. She was so very hungry, after all.

Julia crawled to the side of the girl, and lowered her head to the arm. She licked at the blood there, and then began to pull the skin away from the bone. The girl shrieked again, trying to push Julia away with her good hand.

Julia, annoyed, broke her hand.

The girl went on screaming.

Julia smacked the girl across the face, hard enough to break her jaw. The girl was quiet after that, her face a mask of pure agony, and terror.

"It hurts, doesn't it?" Julia growled through the fangs. "You stupid bitch. You won't try to take my blood now. You can't even move!"

Julia turned the girl's head, raked her fangs down from the cheek to the shoulder, sheering the flesh off. The girl shuddered, but didn't make a sound.

Julia licked the furrows in the skin; tasting the blood made her skin tingle. Somewhere in the recesses of the room, a dark voice chuckled.

Julia couldn't wait any longer. The hunger was pain inside her ribs, an animal craving to get out. Julia pierced the skin on the vein, and the blood came rushing out, filling her veins and cooling her hurting skin. It healed her brain, and her heart, and her stomach. She drank until the girl was at the brink of death.

Julia sat up and smiled at her arms, now full and beautiful again. She licked the blood off of herself, shut her eyes as the girl died. Julia relaxed, losing the fangs and the red in her eyes.

When Julia opened her eyes, she gasped at what she had done. She had never, ever, done this before. She had never destroyed a body, or enjoyed it as much. She had always killed swiftly, mercifully, never causing pain or suffering. Now, this poor girl had died in agony, and it was all Julia's doing.

Julia stood up and backed away, feeling sick and nauseous.

She was positive now, Cory was winning. He was destroying her.

Julia looked at the girl once more and then at her hands. The blood had restored her body, but she felt sick about what she had done.

Julia looked over at the bed, and then raised her hands to her mouth, feeling sicker by the minute.

On the bed lay both girls, but they looked like one. Their limbs were intertwined, but broken. One girl had her head half ripped off her shoulders, the blond hair caked in red. The other had no hand on one arm. It lay on the floor, the fingers ridged and torn. The girl with no hand also had no heart. Her chest was a mass of dried blood and arteries, the heart on the pillow, shriveled and dead.

Julia shut her eyes to the sight of them. If she could have prayed, she would have. She began to cry, softly.

Then something grabbed her arms.

Julia screamed and spun around.

Cory stood behind her, his face, and whole upper body, drenched in blood. His fangs glistened white in the soft light from the cciling, and his eyes were burning red. His hair was slung back over his shoulders, and surprisingly not touched by the blood.

Julia moved away from him, crying. She huddled down on the floor away from the bodies, and found a cloth lying on the floor. She wiped the blood off her arms that he had put there.

She watched as he licked all the blood off himself, and used a dress hanging in the closet to get it off his face.

"Why did you kill them both?" she cried.

He turned back to her, the fangs now gone from his face. An evil light danced in his hazel eyes.

"This is a nightmare." Julia said to herself. In a rush of wind, Cory was beside her.

He knelt down in front of her, touched her hair.

Julia ignored him.

"Look at me," he said, but Julia didn't listen. Cory shoved her down onto her back, and Julia stared up at him, frightened.

Cory folded his arms across his chest and smiled. "You have done a good job." He looked around the room. "Not quite so good as me, but good enough."

"No!" Julia cried out. "This wasn't good! It wasn't me killing that girl it was you. I have never caused pain in someone like that. It was you there, killing her." Julia sat up, wiping the tears from her face. "You are destroying everything I've ever believed in! Why did you take me from Jonathan? I loved him, he was my life!" Julia glared at him. "I hate you for what you've done to me!" she screamed, and pulled back hard, and let her hand fly to his face, but it never connected. He caught it in midair, and kissed it.

The minute his lips touched her, Julia felt all the strength drain out of her, as Cory's presence built up inside of her. She stared at him, and his power held her motionless.

Never taking his eyes off her, he held her hand flat, pulled it down the length of his body, down his chest and down to his knees.

Julia felt repulsed by what he was making her do, but she had no choice. His presence inside her took total possession of her every emotion and move.

He pulled Julia up to him, and held her in his arms. "Hmm," he said smiling, "shall I just make you my prisoner, or shall I make you like those girls there."

Julia tried to pull herself out of it, but it did no good. She felt pulsating warmth in her veins, making her want to hold him. Julia fought at the power, finally it went away.

Julia took a deep breath. Cory showered kisses on her neck. And then, his head bent, and he kissed her stomach where the half top stopped.

Julia pulled back against his arms, but he would not let her go. One arm held her close; the other came up below her chin. "You are so beautiful."

Julia ignored the remark. "Please, please Cory. Just let me go. I want to be with Jonathan."

Cory pulled away and stood an angry gleam in his eyes. "Don't you understand yet? I brought you here, because I love you. I love every inch of your glorious body. I want you all to myself. Ever since Jason told me who you were, I've wanted you, and loved you."

Julia stood, tucked her hair behind her ear. She wrapped her arms around herself and could do nothing but watch, as Cory' anger began to rage.

"Jonathan. That worthless brat! Ever since he was made he wanted and got everything that he could acquire. Do you know he had a mortal lover, before he was turned? Yes, Julia, he did. It was a girl your age. She had blond hair and blue eyes. Her name was Deirdra. Now, is it a coincidence that she so resembled you? Or maybe your loving Jonny-Boy wanted it that way."

"No." Julia said, pressing herself against the wall. Cory came forward, and touched his hand to her cheek.

"She was the very image of you. You two are so alike you could be twins. I can remember how Jon and his brother had fought over Deirdra, and as a result, she left them both. I remember how Jason had stopped Jon from killing himself, how Jonathan swore never to love again. But he couldn't have resisted you. Not you, Julia."

Julia pushed his hand away from her face, and Cory placed both hands on the wall, directly beside her head. "Julia," he whispered his voice like that of a cunning snake. "I know you say that Jonathan loves you. But when he looks at you, is he seeing you, or Deirdra?"

Julia shook her head hard, the tears threatening once again. "No, he loves me. Me! He'd never lie to me. He loves me, and he needs me. I need him!"

Cory dropped his hands to his sides, a look of extreme displeasure upon his face. "He doesn't care about you, Julia."

Julia tried to shove him out of her way, but he wouldn't budge. The tears came from her eyes, as she shoved at him harder, and harder. "You bastard! He loves me, he loves *me*! Let me go to him! Let me go home!"

"No. You're with me, now. You might as well forget about a brat who doesn't care about you." Cory bent slightly, licked the tears from her cheek. "Love me instead." he hissed.

Julia slapped his face, knocking his head a little to one side. All of her power was in that slap. He grinned slightly, and touched that place, where it was beginning to swell and pulsate red. "You will learn, Julia, who wants you more." He went to his shirt and jacket and pulled them on. "You will learn who has the power to make you want them."

"Stop it! Stop it!" she screamed, sobbing. Julia sank back onto the floor, buried her head in her arms. "Leave me alone." she cried.

Julia was not at all aware of how she returned to the hotel, that night. She only knew she was there in the morning, before she fell asleep. She knew the nightmare was to be continued.

8

Jason sat still, ridged, staring in shock at the card he held in his hand. Scrawled upon it, in deep black ink were the words, *"I have your blond rogue called Rikki. Surrender yourself to us, or he will die slowly, in anguish."*

It was signed *"Jean-Luc."*

Jason looked up at the mortal girl, who stood uneasily before him. She knew what he was, that was obvious. Jason crumpled the card in his fist, dropped it to the floor.

He glared at her for a moment and said, in French, "What do you know about this?" The girl's brown eyes widened. She hadn't anticipated his ability to speak the French language.

This girl seemed to be on the verge of womanhood. Jason thought she might be about fourteen years of age. Her hair was dark red, knotted, and torn. He thought it was a wonder that the concierge had let her into this luxurious hotel. Her wardrobe consisted of ragged jeans and boots, and a huge flannel coat. She was covered in dirt, and carried the stench of all human poor.

The girl shook her head, the dirty red hair moving fast. "No, no Monsieur, I know nothing. I just do what I am told." she said in the same romantic language, which felt strange and fascinating at the same time on Jason's tongue.

The girl had begun to back toward the door. Jason's cold eyes followed her. The girl lunged the last five feet or so to the door, but Jason, never moving, lashed out with his mind.

He commanded the girl's body to halt, and it did. He could feel the panic in her mind at his presence there, but he did not try to soothe her.

Come here. He whispered in French power, into her mind.

The girl turned and moved forward, her head tilted back just a bit. She was frightened and pulling hard at Jason's power. But his mind had control over her body, and it obeyed only him.

The girl sat on the bed. Jason lifted his will. Humans were easy to control, but not for long periods of time.

The girl stood, Jason pushed her down again, and sat next to her, holding her arm in his pale hand. "Do you speak English?" he asked her, and she said nothing. Jason stared at her wide brown eyes. "I want you to tell me things. Tell me how you ended up with Jean-Luc. Tell me," he snarled, "Why they want my son!" The girl shrank away, and Jason let her go. He laughed under his breath. He had forgotten how menacing he could be.

The girl stood, fished in her pocket. When her hand came forth from its depths, she held a loaded, cocked revolver. In a blur, Jason snatched it away, bent it with his strength.

He then stood up and whispered, "I'm sick of these games, ma chere."

The girl then took out a flask of blue liquid. She uncorked it, raised it to her lips.

Before the first drop fell, Jason snatched that too from her, and then shoved her to the ground. The girl started crying.

Jason averted his attention to the flask. He sniffed at the liquid. It had no smell. He brought the liquid to a corner of his room where a waist-high plant stood. Jason thought a moment, and then dumped the liquid into the plant, smashing the flask on the floor. He watched the plant.

Starting at the roots, the green plant turned the same shade of blue. The leafy branches withered, until the plant had crumpled down into nothing, soaked through with the eerie, pale coloration.

Jason stared a moment, too shocked to do much else. This had been poison, an instant death of sorts. The girl had been planning to kill herself, and take Jason with her if she could.

The idea of this enraged him, and he moved fast to the girl, smacking her hard across the face. The girl began to cry again. Jason shook her by her shoulders, screaming at her in French. "Did someone do this to Rikki? Is that how they got to him? Tell me, where do they have my son!"

The girl was sobbing, trying to cover her face and her ears, trying to get away. "I don't know, I don't know."

Jason grabbed her hands, forced her to look at him. "You'd better tell me everything you do know, or I promise you, you'll be as dead as that plant, very shortly."

After the girl had calmed down, and gotten away from Jason, she was able to talk to him, to tell him everything she knew. Even though she sat on the pillows on the bed, and he on the opposite end, Marie decided that she could trust Jason more than Jean-Luc. Her face hurt, and he was menacing, but not as terrifying as Jean.

Jason listened to her pour out her life to him, and couldn't help feeling sorry for her. He didn't know if it was the childhood of Marie, or the city of Paris itself, which did this to him.

As for the children who wandered the back streets and alley-ways of Paris, Jean took them in. He and his coven made good use of them, so Marie told Jason.

They took little drains of blood from the children, but kept them in food, clothing and shelter. The children were supposed to obey the vampires' every wish. They were even supposed to kill themselves, if a human attacked them, or a vampire that lived beyond the confines of the coven, attempted to drain their blood.

Jason frowned. He hated human slavery, and always had. He saw vampirism as a curse. Not something to gloat over. Jean did it. Even Alexander had done it, but never to the extent of children.

"Why does he wish for me to leave?" he asked.

Marie touched her red, swollen cheek and flinched. "I can only think of two reasons. Either to hurt Alexander freely, or to help your brother, whom he always speaks of."

"Do you know where I can find Alexander?"

"No, I do not. But I can take you to the place where they last fought."

Jason moved next to her. Marie stopped fiddling with her hair and sat motionless. Jason touched the red spot on her face. Marie didn't move. She wasn't going to let herself be afraid anymore. She decided if she had to die, someone as handsome as Jason wouldn't be a bad way to do it.

"Wouldn't I be putting your life in jeopardy?" he asked softly.

Marie laughed, her laughter like bells. Jason closed his eyes. He was reminded of certain women, Paris in the winter, tragedy, love, and death. He opened them, and Marie was smiling at him.

"My life was over a long time ago. This now, it is not living. We are controlled, teased, toyed with. They torment us, Jason. They drain us almost to the point of death. They prick their finger with a needle to let us suck on. Only a drop, maybe two then we're sick in bed for days. They don't care. All of us, we're half starved, crazed maniacs, begging for mercy." Marie looked down at the quilted bed sheet. "And blood." she whispered.

Jason held her chin with his hand. Marie's soft brown eyes stared at him, her tears like diamonds falling down her face. He saw the pain in her eyes, the hope she carried that she would be immortal someday. She reminded Jason of someone, a young female vampire he had once known. She also had been very young, tender. Jason, moved by memories, drew forward, and kissed the young girl's human mouth.

Marie, entranced by his beauty, returned the kiss.

It was a long kiss, full of pain and sadness on both sides. Jason finally pulled back first, shaking. Kissing human skin was a sweet temptation. You could just feel the little veins beneath the surface. Jason closed his eyes, willing the hunger away. When he looked up, Marie was staring at him.

"Marie, I can help you. I can give you the blood that you crave. But only if you want it. I will not force this upon you. If you wish to leave here alive and well, you must go now."

"I do not have a family. I have no one to take care of me, or love me. No place to go home to." She smiled a sad smile. "I would rather die than go back to Jean." The smile faded, and was replaced with a look of determination and hunger. "I will be yours," she said.

Jason stood on the balcony while Marie showered. His body shook with silent sobs, as he gazed out over the Paris that he once had loved. Now it did not know him. He was a shadow within a shadow. A pale figure dressed in black. If he tried hard enough, he could remember the way Paris had looked in the daytime. The way the light had struck the cathedral of Notre Dame.

He remembered a beloved woman he had transformed, and she had thrown herself into the sun, unable to understand her new nature. He had tried a long time not to remember her, or the events that lead to her death, but Paris was bringing it all back. Paris, and the girl, Marie.

Marie's calling voice brought Jason back from his thoughts. He dried his eyes, and entered the room. She reclined on the bed, clad in the red robe the hotel had provided for him. Her hair was brushed out and dried, and now hung softly in deep red waves, just a bit below her shoulders. Her body was clean, and she now smelled like soap and water.

Jason checked the door that led to Rikki's room. It was still locked. Then he walked to Marie. He sat down next to her and removed his shirt. He smiled a bit, because of the way she was staring at him. He reached over and took her hand in his. "Lay back." he said.

Marie obediently lay down onto the bed. When her hair fell away from her neck, Jason saw the many purple bruises that covered both sides of her throat. He frowned, but did not say anything to upset her.

Marie smiled up at him. She let her hands wander over his body, feeling the smooth warm skin. She knew from experience that when a vampire's skin was warm they had fed. She tried not to think of that, and concentrated on the future.

Jason took her hands away from him, lay down on top of her. Transformation was different between a male and a female, he thought. There was a sexual element there between two opposite sexes. When he created his boys, the experience had been different, an exchange of blood from father to son. At times, he didn't feel anything, when they drank his wine. But for him, to create a female, was a dark, sexual fantasy.

Jason kissed her again, and she accepted more willingly this time. The kisses grew frantic. Jason's hunger built as Marie's lust built. Their bodies began to move together.

Jason kissed Marie's face, her shoulders, and her arms. He began to feel more of her upper body pressing against his chest as the robe loosened.

Finally, he couldn't stand it any longer. The fangs grew down, and the red curtain fell. He turned her head, and buried his fangs into her neck.

Pushing through her bruises was difficult. He caught images of others that had been there; who had drank her blood. But her blood was so very sweet, and he lost himself in it. He was blind to the others.

Marie ran her hand through his orange hair, savoring the texture. She was calm as she faded into sleep. Then suddenly, she was awake again. A hot, burning elixir began to fill her body. She opened her eyes, as she was pulled away.

Marie gazed at Jason. His blue eyes were glossy, his lips trembling. His neck was gashed, and a thin stream of crimson was running down his pale chest. "You choose." he whispered. The emotion in his voice scared him. He lowered his hands from her body.

Marie smiled at Jason, her master and creator, and bent forward to drink in her new existence.

9

Richard Thomas Grant stared up at the ceiling.

His vision had returned.

It had come in bits and pieces, like and old-time television slowly being turned back on. At first everything was black. Black as midnight, or as a crow's wing. Then there were subtle gray shifts in the black, as if someone was adjusting the light. His eyes began to tingle, as if a fresh new vitality was slowly taking place, and the gray developed into shift of color and shape.

Now, he could see every crack in the ceiling, every line, every dent, as if there was a soft white glow radiating in the room. But somehow he knew there was no light. There was nothing.

He lay as if dead on the cold dirty ground, his arms pressing painfully into the little sands of grime that coated the place where he lay. They hurt him, these sands, and as he dwelt on it, acute pain shot through him. He became aware of the pain echoing throughout his body.

He tried to think of where he was, and how he got here, but when he tried to remember, there was only pain inside his mind. The visions that came to him were visions of a car crash long, long ago and of the mutilated bodies of his parents.

He couldn't move at all. All he could do was lay motionless, and stare at the drips of moisture falling off the ceiling and hitting him in the cheek. So loud those sounds were to his ears. Like a drum in the middle of his head.

Splash. Splash. Splash. Splash.

Like the gasoline dripping out of the mangled car's gas tank, right before it had exploded. A memory of his mother screaming at him to get away and his father was already dead. Richard was two years old. He ran away as the car exploded. He was always running.

"Mommy." he formed the word, but only a hiss of air escaped the blue, cold dryness of his lips.

Richard Thomas Grant was so very cold and alone. He had always been alone. From one foster parent to another. No one wanted any part of a satanic child at the age of six. They'd take him to church and he'd scream his blasphemy. No one had wanted him.

He had finally run away for good, at the age of ten. Working for food, selling his body, he had done everything to survive. Now, ten years later, he lived like a prince. His father...his father was a king. A name, give me a name, he thought over and over. The pain wracked his head. Waves of sharp coursing pain inside his head, stomach and heart. He went into convulsions on the floor there, the pain curling his fingers, his long nails scraping the gritty surface of the floor.

The pain collected in his stomach. Every part of the pain rushed down from his limbs, veins, everywhere. With it went the blue skin. Everything focused there inside him.

The pain made him sit up, doubling over to hold his stomach. Very suddenly, the pain shot up, and he vomited blood all over ground. It was violet, the blood. It was bad, brackish blood that had combined with the poison, and as soon as it was all out of his system, Rikki regained his memory, and the pain went away.

Rikki held his stomach still, his breath coming in gasps. He hadn't remembered his parents in years. He had never remembered the crash.

He shook his head to clear it. Now was not the time to think about these memories. He knew that now, if he dwelt on them, he would begin to remember more and more, because of the powers he had.

But not now, now he had to get out of here.

Rikki sat back against the cold, damp wall. His sweatshirt was no where in sight. As he looked down at himself, he saw his skin was once again was pale. But he was covered everywhere in angry red marks, the kind a butcher knife makes. His chest and arms had been slashed, and probably his back was too.

It seemed to him that someone had attempted to drain him of blood, in this manner, to make sure that he'd die, but that actually was what had kept him alive. It had taken some of the bad blood out of his system.

Rikki leaned back against the cellar wall. He was tired, and very hungry. The hunger pains were already starting, shooting hard and hot into his ribs.

He had no concept of time or days. He had no idea how long he had been down here. He ran a hand through his blond hair, and wondered if Jason had been looking for him. And if so, how long?

Rikki suddenly became angry as he looked around the room. There was no bed, no clothes, no furniture, nothing at all.

He had been dumped here to die.

Rikki jumped up and glared at the wall.

He punched his fist right through it, creating a semi-round hole, winced as the fledgling bones broke with the impact. He pulled his arm out, and cradled his hurt hand in his other one. As the bones mended, he looked into the hole in the wall. Behind the first, and only concrete wall, was a wall of stones lined with mortar.

Rikki moaned. There was no way out of this. This room had been designed to hold fledglings. It would take forever to break out, and all the noise would surely attract others.

Rikki looked at the doorway. He placed his hands on the door. It was made from a certain type of very strong steel, he could tell just by touching it.

He was trapped.

The hunger shot up inside his body. He pressed his head against the cool metal, but it only made him angrier.

He paced back and forth a few times, but it only made him crazy. He had to get out.

As a vampire, a creature with animal qualities, he just couldn't stay caged like this. It would literally make him insane.

He was starving, and claustrophobic.

Rikki began to pound on the walls and door. He screamed, and howled, and yelled. He sent his hunger out in waves of power. He wasn't even aware that his fangs had come down, and each time he gritted his teeth, they cut into his bottom gum. His own blood in his mouth was making him frantic.

His red eyes searched for warmth in the darkness. Anything, just let it be alive.

Rikki collapsed on the floor again, biting his finger and sucking on it. He needed blood. He was now sure he had been inside the room at least two days.

He was just about to throw himself at the steel door, when he heard the heartbeat, and smelled a human boy on the other side of the door.

As the footsteps drew nearer and nearer, Rikki approached the door, and crouched down.

You want to open the door. You must open the door. Open it! Rikki commanded in powers, which weren't really all that strong yet.

The footsteps came to the door, and stopped. Rikki could feel the kid's fear. He closed his red eyes and projected his mind to the outside of the door. With great effort, he shot his will into the boy. He pictured his hand inside the boy's his mind inside as well. And this time, when he commanded, the boy acted.

As soon as the door swung open, Rikki grabbed the kid, giving him no time to find the blue flask he must possess.

The boy was four inches smaller than Rikki, and he tried desperately to free his hands. But Rikki held him stationary with one hand, the other around the boy's neck.

With a short laugh of triumph, Rikki tore the kid's neck open. After the boy was dead on the floor, Rikki left the room behind and entered the basement. There was a basket full of clean laundry next to the door; probably the boy had brought it here. He took out a black shirt and slipped it on. It was a bit big, but it fit.

Rikki was able to get through the house undetected. He couldn't shake the feeling that he was being watched, that they had let him go so they could chase him, but Rikki didn't care.

He took off out the front door, and ran into the night.

10

Jonathan and Steven looked down at the two couples in the convertible, from their perch on the rocks. The car sat precariously on the edge of the road, dangerously close to the drop, off the mountain.

Jon and Steven had been wandering aimlessly, when they had discovered the teenagers. It had been a marvelous stroke of luck. Jonathan had lapsed into the quiet deathly hunter he had become, Steven's anxiety building by the minute, as he gazed down at the couples. The two in the backseat were making out like crazy; the two in the front were just sitting there, miles apart. They hadn't touched yet, and Steven figured they were probably locked into some sort of argument.

Jonathan looked over at Steven, an evil, empty look in his eyes. It sent chills up Steven's spine. "You want to kill them now?" Jon whispered, and then looked back at the people. "Oh, yes, I think we shall. There's nothing better than death. Than blood." Jon was quiet for a moment, and then said, "I'll kill the guy in the back. You get the guy in the front. Keep the girls alive." In a blur of motion, he was gone. The music of death filled the air, and when Steven glanced back down at the car, he observed Jon attacking the guy in the back seat, the girl screaming, the guy in the front beating on Jon's back, and the other girl jumping out of the car.

Steven jumped down into the car, and grabbed the other guy's neck. He lifted him off Jon tossed him onto the ground outside the car. The teenaged boy hit the ground with a loud slap. Steven leapt out of the car, followed him as he crouched down, whimpering, and to Steven's surprise, he was holding the girl that had been in front with him, as a hostage.

"Holding a hostage?" Steven growled. "It won't do you any good. I'm not going to hurt her."

The girl looked up at Steven and smiled. Her face looked real calm, real beautiful. She wasn't afraid of him at all. Not of the fangs or the red eyes, or the hunger sweat that had beaded up on his chin. She elbowed the guy in the ribs, shook him off. She stood up to Steven and looked at him with hazel eyes remarkably like his. She shook her hair free of the ponytail, and it fell in light brown natural waves around her shoulders. She seemed the perfect match for him.

"You want to kill him?" she asked. "Go ahead. He's a prick anyway. Doesn't give a shit about anyone or anything. Kill him." Steven grinned down at the boy on the ground.

He was pleading with Steven, and the girl, Melissa.

"Shut up, Erik. We all have to die you know," she said, pulling away from him.

Steven was so happy he could have kissed her. He pushed Erik down on his back, and sank his fangs into his neck.

Melissa watched, entranced by the deathly grace the vampire possessed. She knew it was a vampire. She had seen enough television to know that. She just never really guessed such things existed. Now, as it killed her ex-boyfriend, she realized she was attracted to this one.

Jonathan was almost done with the one the girl called Billy. The flaxen-blond girl had been screaming Billy's name over and over, but had grown eerily quiet. Whether she was quiet because of him or Steven, he didn't know. While Billy breathed his last, Jonathan leaned back against the car's blood stained upholstery, and relaxed. He cleaned all the blood off his face and hands, and then looked at what he had done.

Billy's neck was nothing more, but a gnarled raw piece of meat. Jonathan began to laugh then, a dark bubbling laugh, issuing forth from deep within. They were violent laughs, which caused his eyes to tear. With his strength, he picked up Billy, who was now dead, and tossed his body over the cliff.

Then, he focused his attention upon the girl. She was still in the car, still staring at him, rather blankly. Jon looked for Steven. He had just finished off Erik, and was talking to Melissa, his hands on her shoulders. "Steven, get in here, let's go!"

Steven got into the driver's seat, Melissa next to him, a smile on her face. Jon moved closer to the girl, as Steven pulled away from the bodies, and headed down the mountain.

The girl in the back seat remained quiet, regarded Jonathan with dark green eyes, and an open mouth. Jon touched her cheek. "I'm not going to kill you," he said.

The girl smiled. "I'm Lena. Who are you?" Her face grew a bit serious. Jonathan was aware that she might be just a bit drunk, but the thought didn't stay too long in his head. Thoughts didn't process correctly anymore.

"What are you?" Lena asked.

"I'm Jonathan. I'm a vampire. I kill. That's what I do."

The girl giggled, and smiled. "You're lying."

"No. No I'm not. I just killed Billy, remember Lena?"

The girl looked puzzled, trying to understand what he was saying. "You killed him?" She looked back over her shoulder at the place where the car had been, and was now speeding away from. "Billy?" she called.

Jonathan pulled her close to him. She squirmed against him for a few minutes, but then was still, staring into his eyes. She looked at Steven and Melissa in the front, and then back at Jonathan.

"You really are a vampire, aren't you?" she said.

Jonathan laughed. Perhaps Lena was drunk, but somehow things were beginning to clear, inside her head. He looked down at the split-leg skirt, and the tank top she wore.

"Yes, I am," he said. He pulled her closer to him, kissed her lips. Lena kissed him back.

Steven did not mistake the noise. "Jonathan, what about Julia?" he called.

Jonathan looked up at him, a fierce look on his face. "Just shut up and drive." he growled.

Steven shrugged, gunned the motor.

Jonathan glared at the back of Steven's head, feeling Lena's lips trail along his face, his neck. "You're a strange girl," he said.

Lena looked up at him. "Why?" she asked.

"I killed your darling Billy, Lena. I could kill you. I'm a hunter, a killer. I'm evil," he said, emphasizing the words with a shake.

Lena laughed, throwing her head back. "Sure, Mister Jonathan The Vampire. But you won't kill me."

Jonathan gazed at the soft tender skin of her neck, the low cut top of her shirt.

He looked into her eyes. "You're tormenting me, girl. Don't you know it's bad to torment a vampire?"

He traced her lips, her legs that now wrapped around his body. "Don't you care about Billy anymore?"

Lena giggled, high pitched, tantalizing. "Billy who?" she said, pulling Jonathan's jacket away from his body. He let it fall off. "Hmmm, nice." she murmured, taking in his beauty.

She placed kisses all over his chest, nibbled at his neck. Suddenly, one victim didn't seem enough for Jonathan anymore. He needed more blood. He pulled Lena hard to him, gripping her shoulders as he bruised her mouth with his.

"I need your body . . . your blood." he whispered.

Lena finally seemed to grow serious. "Yes, I understand." she stretched her head back again, giving him full view of her tanned neck. "Go ahead."

Jonathan controlled his hunger long enough to say, "Steven, take us home. These girls are going to be ours."

Steven, driving already back to the mansion, was almost there when Jonathan had spoken the words. He understood why Jonathan liked Lena so much, why he himself had been so drawn to Melissa so quickly. But he did not tell Jonathan. He saw no need to. He wanted to cheat on Julia, so he figured he deserved whatever Lena would put him through.

Lena was not sorry for Billy. She wasn't even drunk. Melissa had told Steven the truth about Lena. Lena was a practitioner of some sort of Voodoo, and had been trying to steal Billy's soul. That had been why Erik broke up with Melissa, saying those awful things. She had told Erik the truth, and Erik hated her for even being friends with someone like Lena. He knew that Lena was going to hurt Billy. But Billy wouldn't listen, and he had said it was all Melissa's fault.

Steven had hugged her, searching her thoughts, finding the truth. She had not lied to him. Melissa cried freely on Steven's shoulder now. "He wanted to kill me, Steven. He wanted to kill me just for spite. You are my savior. My savior."

When they returned to the mansion a few minutes later, Jonathan immediately pulled Lena out of the car, and inside. She was giggling, he was grinning.

Steven and Melissa followed them in, closed the doors behind them. Steven watched, angry, as Jonathan led Lena up the stairs, and probably, into one of the rooms. He was cheating on Julia, big time now, not just a kiss here, and there. He was going to transform Lena. He probably would make love to her. Steven respected Julia. She wasn't just some kind of pleasure seeker, after the power of immortality, she was wonderful and beautiful, and loved Jonathan more than anything.

Melissa rubbed his shoulders and back. "Don't worry about them," she said.

Steven looked at her and he forgot Jonathan, Lena, Julia, everything. She was beautiful and inviting, and he wanted more than blood, more than her body. He wanted her love. He wanted her beside him, forever.

He made love to her next to that roaring fireplace and he only made small cuts on her human skin with his fingernails to tempt himself, to tease himself. He knew he could not transform her himself.

He gave her the wine. Jason's wine.

By the end of the night, there were two new fledgling vampires in the mansion.

One was Jason's, one was Jonathan's. And both of them would have a rather short existence.

11

Julia sat motionless on the balcony off of Kevin's room. He sat beside her, on the edge of the railing, holding her hand in his. His cool fingers felt comforting to Julia. His friendship soothed her, in this time of pain.

Julia could not forget the night of the party. She remembered Don, and the pain she suffered. She remembered how badly she had mutilated that poor girl. She went hunting every night still, with Cory right there along with her. He wouldn't let her leave to go anywhere, without him.

Julia was a little grateful for his company. She didn't for one minute forget about that girl, and his presence served as a reminder of what not to do. She took her victims quietly, without pain or agony on their part. Cory would laugh. He'd laugh and laugh.

Julia felt as if someone had sucked away her entire life. Her whole code of morals had gone down the tubes, when Cory had brought her here. She would rather been a corpse in a coma now, than living this life.

It was pure hell.

Julia looked at Kevin and found him gazing at her with those kind, sad eyes. "I want to help you, Julia. You know I want to help you, more than anything. I've been trying to escape this place, for a long time. I came here when I was a fledgling. I was alone, and afraid, and Cory took me in. I realized what a mistake I had made in hours. That was fifty years ago. He won't ever let me leave. I know he would kill me if I tried."

Kevin gently touched Julia's cheek with his free hand. She didn't even move. She felt cold and indifferent inside to everything going on around her. "Julia, I have seen many, many girls come in here, like you. You aren't the first he has stolen, but I wonder, will you be the last? You resist him, unlike the others. You're a challenge to him. And he becomes more and more frustrated every night."

Julia looked over at him. "What are you saying?" she asked.

Kevin looked over his shoulder, up at the rest of the hotel. He closed his eyes, undoubtedly scanning for Cory. When he opened them, he seemed puzzled a moment, and his lips formed unspoken words.

Then he looked back at Julia. "Come on, let's walk." he said.

They jumped down from that fifth story balcony, landed soft and gracefully on the ground. Kevin took off his leather jacket and gave it over to Julia, who gratefully pulled it on.

Julia snuggled against the soft leather of the jacket and against Kevin's arm as they traveled down the street. It was the same every night cars, kids, parties, and more cars. The lights were blinding.

Kevin reached into a pocket, and withdrew a pair of dark sunglasses. "Use these. They'll help your eyes until we get to the beach."

"Thank you." Julia whispered, almost in tears. It had been so long since anyone at all had been good to her. It was hard to accept these things Kevin did for her, with grace.

When arrived at the beach, Julia and Kevin sat side by side on the sand, watching the surfers glide and soar through the gigantic, roaring waves.

Julia removed the glasses, and put them in a pocket of the leather coat.

"Kevin, what did you mean earlier, about Cory getting frustrated? What will he do to me?"

Kevin took a deep breath, hardly visible by the way his black tee shirt was being blown by the wind.

His eyes searched Julia's face, his lips pressed tight then relaxed, tight, then relaxed.

"Tell me," she said, patting his hand.

"My guess is," he sighed, "he'll either let you go or force himself on you."

Julia stared at him a moment. She knew there was no way Cory would ever let her go. Never. He'd go to the limit; he'd force her. I have to get out of here, she thought.

"Yes, you do." Kevin said after a moment. Julia immediately built up her mind block.

Kevin smiled. "You must keep that strong, if there's any hope of you leaving this place. I will try to help you Julia. I can take you half way, but after that, you'll be on your own."

"Thank you." she half-sobbed, falling into his arms. She cried against him, hugging him, her only friend in this terrible New World.

"We'll leave tomorrow night," he said.

This was about the time Cory began searching for Julia. He had felt Kevin trying to get into his mind earlier, and had just played with him a bit, not bothering to find out what he wanted. He had screwed up Kevin's perceptions a bit, which would generally serve to upset someone that age. But Kevin didn't care.

Now, after he had his meal of the night, he was curious why Kevin had attempted to contact him, when he normally resented Cory so much. It must have something to do with Julia, he thought to himself.

He walked down the corridor, in elegant, arrogant strides, stopping only in front of the huge marble-framed mirror. As he stared at the nothing in the mirror, he remembered Julia's reaction to it. She had stiffened in his arms, and growled low in her throat. And then, by some means, she had broken free and hurled herself at it. Cory had caught her, of course, but he almost hadn't. It had almost been a huge marble-framed mess.

Cory chuckled. Then he had showed her the mirror-trick. Julia had screamed and thrashed in his arms, because she knew she couldn't do it.

Cory smiled, leaned forward, and touched the mirror with his fingertip. With his mind's eye, he saw himself. He remembered how he looked in other vampires' and humans' thoughts.

And then slowly, very slowly, he pushed the thoughts out through his finger and onto the glass.

At first it was pale, a shadowy, ghostly phantom figure. As he pushed harder with his mind, the form began to flesh out. Colors came in, and his clothes. Then with one little exertion of power, to give the reflection life, he stepped back.

It moved as he moved. It frowned as he frowned. It finally faded back into nothingness, when he couldn't stand the strain anymore. It was a good trick, but a hard one.

The better trick was always to let the humans think they saw you in the mirror. That was simple. Just implant the memory.

Cory sighed, and turned away from the mirror. On to better things, he thought.

His good, if somewhat demented spirits did not last long, however. On that floor he did not find Julia. On Kevin's floor, he did not find Julia.

As he stood out on Kevin's balcony, he searched with his mind, and realized neither of them was there.

This infuriated him. Where were they? Where was Julia? Why wasn't she here, in this place, in his chains, where she ought to be!

Cory paced back and forth on the balcony, muttering to himself. He had thrown his jacket in a corner, and eventually sat down beside it. Julia meant nothing to him, really. But she was his possession, until he got what he wanted from her. She was his key to happiness, so to speak.

Total submission from that one would be good. But within the package would be the destruction of Jonathan, and apologies from Jason. If Julia wanted him, there would be no way she could have been kidnapped. It would also leave Alexander out of his life, which was where he wanted his father. Far, far away.

283

No little vagrant would keep him from all that glory, not even if he had become part of the family.

Cory mused to himself on Kevin's darkened balcony, as he waited for their return. His temper flared on and off, but mostly he thought of Julia. She was an interesting creature. She fought him, always. Never gave in to his powers, even when he forced his will on her. Julia was a temptress, even though she herself did not know this.

All this made Cory desire her. Her resistance, from the very start, made him want to conquer her. Her blood, he had not yet tasted, seemed to fire her wants and needs, and keep her just beyond his grasp. When he had her, and he would have her in the end, he would break her will, and she would become his mindless vampire slave, to do his will, always.

A sudden rustle, a movement in the dark, caught him in his thoughts. He looked up towards the railing of the balcony, and there, climbing over the side, were Julia and Kevin. She wore Kevin's jacket, and smiling, held his hand. Kevin spoke quiet reassuring words to her, about how they would leave someday, together.

They hugged then, Julia throwing her thin arms around Kevin's neck. Cory got to his feet, feeling the anger rise to his face, the heat spreading up his neck, and down into his arms. Quietly and stealthily, he approached them, never letting them know he was there.

When he stood quietly behind Kevin, he waited, and he saw the hair on Kevin's arms raise. He heard Julia gasp. They knew he was there, that they were being stalked, with nothing more than a predator's cunning.

Kevin spun around, pushing Julia off and away. But he shouldn't have turned. Cory's hand closed over Kevin's neck, cutting off his circulation, and his air. Kevin gasped, his fingers clawing at Cory's, his nails drawing blood there.

Cory ignored all this, and with his strength, lifted Kevin off his feet, into the air. He heard Julia's scream, but ignored it. His arm shook a little with the weight of Kevin bearing down on him, but he held him there. The muscles in his arm strained, but still he held him.

Kevin stopped struggling now, concentrating on holding himself in the right position, so the blood would not stop circulation to his brain. He didn't need the air, he needed the blood.

"Where have you been gone to so long, my young friend?" Cory said in deep measured tones. Kevin gave no reply. "Very well." Cory said, and let Kevin drop to the ground.

Kevin took in a deep gulp of air, massaged his hurt neck. He lay there and stared up at Cory, as Cory stared down at him. Kevin did not speak now.

Out of the corner of his eye, he could see Julia standing very close by, her face tear streaked, wringing her hands. But he couldn't help her. Cory was standing just above him, his chest rising and falling quickly, trying, for some reason, not to lose control.

Cory knelt down on the floor beside Kevin, pushed him flat to the ground. As Cory leaned over him, Kevin felt his breath against his cheek, his long hair brushing over his chest, his warm arm where it pinned him down. He heard the savage hiss in his ear.

"I could kill you for this Kevin. And I want to, yes, very much. But . . . I won't. No. I want you to suffer, and live to see the time when she will bend to me. To want only me. And the day when you yourself will become a sniveling little weakling, begging for our attentions. And I know you will want them."

Kevin clenched his teeth and shut his eyes, his body tremored from anger and guilt. He wanted to strike out, at the one who mocked him so clearly. But that was entirely impossible. Cory wanted him to do it, just so he could kill him. And he would not strike out at him.

"Keep away from Julia, my young friend. You will be very sorry if you do not obey me."

And just to prove what he said was indeed true Kevin felt the pinch of his teeth, very light against his neck, drawing only a little blood.

Kevin held himself still, and when Cory stood up, he smiled at him, that horrid, evil smile, and licked his rouged lips. His hazel eyes were dark, the seething madness only slightly hidden.

Cory turned to Julia, and all but ripped the jacket off her. He flung it down against Kevin's stomach. "See to it this never happens again." he said, reached out, and dragged Julia away by her wrist.

Julia was crying, and straining to stay with Kevin. She reached out for him, but he could not help her. He would die if he moved to get up, he knew that now.

"Help me, help me," she sobbed as Cory dragged her behind him, only stopping once to pick up his jacket. They went in through the doors, Julia crying, and calling out to Kevin. Then they were gone, and Kevin closed his eyes, shedding tears of his own.

"Let me go!" she screamed, as he dragged her through the room, and through the hallway. He ignored her totally, holding onto his jacket, dragging her as if she weighed nothing.

Others passed in the hallway, but did not stop, and did not look. Some glanced sideways at Julia out of the corner of their eyes. Some laughed. But no one stopped to help her.

285

Julia saw that they were going to the elevator, and she stopped struggling after Cory roughly shoved her inside.

Julia stared at him in a rage, as he pulled his jacket over the clean, white shirt. As soon as he bent his arms back to pull his hair out of the jacket, Julia exerted all the energy she could muster, and threw herself against the giant, well-lit control panel. Julia jammed her hand onto the number one, pushed it through the panel. With a sizzle of electricity that jolted her body, and slammed her onto the floor, the elevator began a rushing decent to the first floor, and the easily deceived humans.

"Bitch!" Cory screamed at her as the elevator dropped, faster and faster. Julia looked at him, amazed as her vision, the vision of a vampire, began to blur, her body thrown against the wall, as the elevator took momentum.

"Oh yeah, Julia, you had to pull something like this, didn't you?" He was screaming at her, at the same time, punching open the emergency exit at the top of the elevator. "Come on, bitch!" He grabbed her again, tried to pull her out of the opening in the top. She tried to hold on to the ceiling, but she couldn't. Cory plucked her off like a fly from a wall, and yanked her through the opening. He flew straight up, with Julia dangling from his arm.

"You just had to try something, didn't you girl." he kept saying over, and over. "I will never let you escape me, Julia. Never."

"Let me go you bastard! I'll see this place burned to the ground, you and everyone else dead!" Julia shouted at him.

He laughed and kept flying, up to the floor that was his. Once there, he wrenched open the door and flew inside, just as the elevator hit the ground floor, and a fireball burst high up the shaft.

Julia was let to lie on the ground. She caught visions from the floor below. Human terror, screams, the vampire overseers talking to them, telling them everything would be all right, all right, all right.

Cory was pulling at her again. "No!" she yelled.

She felt his arms under her body, the swift motion in which he slung her over his shoulders.

Julia bit her bottom lip, trying to hide the anguish and the tears threatening to come again. She pounded uselessly on his back. Her strength was nothing compared to his. Nothing at all. She pulled at his long rusty hair, but he just laughed again and again.

Julia let out a long, heartbreaking moan as he entered the room. She watched as he locked and dead-bolted his door.

"Are you ready Julia? Are you ready to take me on? That's what you want, isn't it?" Cory turned and dumped her down onto the bed. As soon as

Julia hit the lavishly furnished, soft bed, she jumped right back off again. "Let. Me. Out." she said evenly.

Cory laughed again. Julia put her hands over her ears. It was like a corpse laughing. So evil and grating. But what was he doing? There were no lights on, only a soft orange night-light showing through the bathroom door.

Cory was pulling off his jacket, his shirt, even his boots and socks. Then he sat down on a tall plush blood-red armchair, snuggling into it. "Take a look around, Julia. You aren't going anywhere."

Julia looked around herself, taking in his room. The bed was large and black. Black comforters, black pillows, black headboard. The walls were painted black also. There was a glass desk and a silver brass chair, a dining table and chairs, red roses on the table, a small refrigerator, and the bathroom.

A bureau stood next to one side, the same glass and silver as the desk. Julia gasped, for resting on it were several sculls, mostly female, few men, two vampire sculls with the fangs still in. There were jars of disgusting little things. A cat fetus, eyeballs, tongues, ears, rats, and jars and jars of hair.

Julia backed away from these things, feeling her stomach convulse. There was an open doorway extending from the room, she saw as she backed away, one that smelled awfully of death. A human wouldn't know it. It was like a fingerprint you couldn't wash away. Julia stepped inside the room, and found it plainer, duller. It seemed to be his second room. Julia could feel the women he slaughtered in this room, screaming for help. The room was littered in posters and clothes, but the bed sheets were immaculately clean, and the windows weren't boarded.

Julia returned, and closed the door.

"What's wrong Julia? You look awful." he whispered into the dimness of the room.

Julia leaned back against the closed door, her eyes shut, and trying not to scream, or to throw up.

"Come here, girl. Now that you've seen your ground, let's let the games begin."

Julia mouthed the word no, but even as she did it, she felt Cory pushing his will into her again. Julia shuddered, fighting it, fighting against it. When she fought, a pain of white rage shot into her head.

Julia cried out in pain, holding her head, falling to her knees. She stared at Cory, who remained calm and composed in his chair, the blue in his hazel eyes somehow showing up more clearly, perhaps because of the orange light.

"Stop, stop this now." she hissed in pain.

"You don't like that, do you, Julia? Come here to me, now."

The will came again, burning through the fog she had created, in order to protect her mind from his, burning down into her limbs, forcing her to get up.

Her legs began to move, and as she fought against it, the pain came again. Julia fell again, this time down at Cory's bare feet. He came down, and sat beside her, while the pain paralyzed her thoughts and actions.

"Get up. Now." he said, pushing into her again. Julia's own will was weakening, and this time, he got her up without much difficulty, without much pain.

She sat there, trembling, hurting, and staring at him. "How could you do this to me? How could you?" she cried out, raising her fist, punching him squarely in the jaw, with all the power she had left. His face went back and he smiled, gingerly touching the place she had struck him.

"Good. I was afraid you'd make this too boring." he said.

Julia screamed then, with all the rage, and pain, and anger that she had held in for days, and as she felt the fangs come down and her sight become red, she knew she had to fight Cory, even if it caused her death. She attacked him then, clawing at his snarling face, ripping at his throat with her fangs. The beast within had come to the surface without Cory's help, and now, she fought him.

Cory's teeth snapped inches away from her face, and every time he came close to striking true, she hit him, and kicked him. The attack had at first caught him off guard, but now he fought her, with the knowledge that no matter what occurred, he would win in the end.

Cory tossed Julia backward, and she landed gracefully on the bed, crouched, hissing and snarling at him. He stood now, wiping the blood away from his mouth. He ran his tongue over his fangs. "I knew you wouldn't let me down, Julia." he spoke in harsh throaty tones.

He leapt up onto the bed and she met him, her fangs sinking into his shoulder, just missing his neck at the proper time. Cory grabbed her head and held her away from him. "Oh, you like this, don't you, bitch. Yeah, I knew you would. You want me to get rough, don't you?" he growled.

Julia twisted out of his hands. "Shut up!" she screamed, the voice of a monster coming from her. She lunged at him again, striking right this time. It caught him off guard again, surprisingly, and he twisted as she held him against herself.

I'll take all the blood from your veins; you won't hurt me, anymore!

Her mind threatened him. But the blood was good, and just for a moment, she tasted the candy-richness of another vampire's blood. She felt that she was conquering the beast, which had hurt her. But she tasted in his blood the consuming, darkened evilness. And she realized that he was striking out at her, and it hurt.

Julia was torn off him in one great punch to her ribs. The blood was flowing out of her mouth and out of the ragged tears in his neck, and down onto the black comforter. Her blond hair fell down into her eyes as she felt herself become strong, and ready for whatever he could throw at her. But she wasn't really ready, not really.

"That's it! I'm done with playing games. You will be mine, now!"

Cory sent spasms of pain down into her body, and into her stomach, where the blood she had just taken from him resided, using her own defenses against her. He thrust his will deep inside her, raping her of all conscious thought, and will of her own.

Julia fell off the bed, slamming her head against the hard wood floor. Her head hurt tremendously, knocking the fight out of her. Her lips closed over the fangs, covering them.

Julia felt sticky. What was it? Oh, yes, Cory's blood. No! Her fangs receded, her eyesight cleared. Cory stood over her, torn, covered in blood. She smiled; dreamily thinking she had done it herself. The room was a mess; she'd have to clean it later. *What?* Her brain screamed, what are you thinking, Julia? You have to get up, he's coming, he's coming, he's . . .

But he was already there, lying beside her, his fingers tracing over the vein in her neck. Instinct was screaming at her to run, to flee him, but she couldn't move. Her power was gone. Cory's will had striped her bare.

She closed her eyes, shivering, feeling his hands slide down her body. He was undressing her, rendering her even more unprotected and defenseless. Soon she lay in nothing but her panties and half-top, cold, bloody, and weak. The floor was hard and cold. Every thing around her was cold, and merciless.

When she opened her eyes, he was there. "I hate you." she whispered softly, in pain.

Cory smiled a horrible grimace, around his fangs. "Yes, Julia. I know. Hate me if you like. But I love you. I will have you for myself. You can't resist me any longer."

His hands pushed hers away from her body, and pinned them behind her head, as he lay down on top of her. Julia began to cry as she felt his breath against her neck. She was helpless against him, she couldn't move if she tried. His blue-jean legs were rough against her skin, and holding her steady.

When he entered her neck, it hurt dreadfully, like rusty nails being forced through meat. She cried out softly, pitifully, and the tears ran down her cheeks. When he began to suck, to pull at the wound in her neck, she cried out loudly. It hurt terribly, worse then Don ever had. Her veins were on fire with undeniable pain. He was stealing the blood that flowed within her, that kept her alive.

Julia scratched at his hands with her nails, but feebly. She couldn't stop him. It was as if he were cutting her deep inside, over and over, sucking every part of her being out from those two holes. Pain radiated from her brain down her spinal cord, and from her heart into her whole body.

Then, suddenly, it was over. He got up, ripped off the blood-soaked comforter, and threw Julia down onto the bed, climbing on top of her once again.

"Your blood was exquisite, fine, just as I thought it would be. Wonderful. I have had your blood. Now I want the rest."

Julia's eyes widened, and she stopped crying, as she realized what he meant to do. Somewhere deep inside her, she regained the strength to fight him off. Maybe it was a quick thought of Jonathan, or maybe, just maybe, it was her strength coming through.

"No," she said, "*No!*" She shoved at Cory, pushed at him. Kicked him. He wrestled with her, rolling on the bed. Julia slapped at him, dug her nails deep into his chest and neck, but this time, nothing seemed to stop him. He was relentless.

Cory finally pinned Julia down, and he ripped at the top, breaking one of the shoulder straps. She screamed. She struggled and fought as she felt his legs coming down hard, parting her own. Julia screamed as loud as she possibly could, louder even, then the time she had screamed in Vermont all those months ago.

Julia realized, as the piercing cry slowly died away, that Cory had suddenly become very still. His body was rigid, and he was no longer attempting to move against her. Julia looked up at her would-be rapist, and saw him looking over to the right. He was taking slow, deep breaths, and the fangs and redness in his eyes had vanished.

Julia's eyes traced the path of his vision. The first thing she saw was the door, smashed to bits, and lying broken on the floor. Then, as she looked more near to the bed, she saw Kevin standing there. His own breathing was shallow and quick, his brown wavy hair falling into his eyes. He did not wear the jacket, and Julia could see the muscles standing out on his arms.

Kevin stood posed, a piece of the broken wooden door held in his right hand like a spear. There were splinters on the wood, and she could see the blood trickling down his arm. But his face showed no pain. Just rage.

"Get off her, Cory." he no more than hissed.

Julia saw Cory look at the rough wooden stake, at Kevin, and then at Julia. Slowly, he backed off of Julia, sitting gracefully on the edge of the bed. Julia squirmed free of him, shuddering, and ran to Kevin.

"What are you doing, young one? Do you know what it is to cross me?" Cory spoke softly.

"I know." Kevin said raggedly.

Julia glanced up at him, and then pulled on her jeans, and socks, and boots.

"I could call everyone else to me, before you could throw that, you know." Cory said, his eyes on the stake.

"Try me." Kevin said, a bit more controlled this time. Still looking at Cory, Kevin tossed something dark and big at Julia. She caught it, and saw it was a sweatshirt. She pulled it over her head.

Then she looked back at Cory. He wasn't moving, but was now staring into Kevin's eyes. Kevin didn't flinch, didn't even move at all.

"No, not this time Cory. I won't let you touch her. No." he said after a moment. And then added, "Get out of here, Julia. Go back to Vermont, to where you will be safe. Go now."

Julia looked at Cory, whose eyes were now narrowed in anger. If looks could kill, she thought. "Kevin, come with me," she said, tugging his other arm. "He'll kill you, if you don't come."

"No, Julia, I can't go. I have to keep him here. Just go. Go now!"

"But Kevin . . . "

"Go!" he shouted at her, pushing her away from him.

Julia looked at Cory again. A low, deep growl came from him, and his eyes burned redder than before. His lips had drawn back, and she could see those fangs, just now coming down from his top jaw.

Kevin's steady arm had begun, just a little, to shiver.

"Please go, Julia." he whispered.

Julia gazed tearfully at him for a moment, and then said, "I will never forget you." She ran to the far wall of the room and to the oak doors that she knew led to the balcony. She flung them open, and she heard Cory yelling after her, "I'll find you no matter where you go! You can't escape me!"

Julia ran off the balcony, and flew full speed into the night sky. She never looked back, but in her mind, she could sense that Kevin was dying awfully and slowly, in terrible pain. She heard Cory's awful laughter. He laughed at Kevin, he laughed at her.

Julia cried silent tears, but she did not stop.

She had to get home.

12

Jason stood still, holding Marie's soft, warm hand in his.

She had taken him here, to a place from his memories. A graveyard, an old, broken down Parisian graveyard. Standing here now, a ghost in the shadows, memories drifted to him on the cool spring wind.

It was here, where his human wife and son had been buried, and here where Alexander had found him. Here, he had carved himself a stake, and had wanted to kill himself. Here he had broken stone, and the bones in his fist as a fledgling. Here he and Devin had once conversed under the moonlight. And here, where he had taken . . . taken . . .

No, better not to think of that, he told himself. Not to think of his doomed one. His first daughter. No.

"Why have you brought me here?" he asked, after a moment of reflection. "Do you wish to cause me pain? There are no signs of a struggle between immortals in the recent past, in this place."

"I brought you here," she whispered, her hand clenching Jason's, her head pressing into the fabric of his overcoat, just below the shoulder. "I brought you here because a voice told me to do it. I . . . I could not resist. It was so strong."

Marie wrapped her other arm around him, as a shudder ripped through her body. He raised his hand to touch her head.

Just then, he thought he heard his name being whispered softly, very softly. It was a man's voice. It had a slight, distinct accent, and held the flavor of the aristocratic.

Jason's head jerked up, his night eyes searching in the shadows of the old graveyard. "Alexander?" he called, his voice ringing out alone and sounding very much like the frightened young mortal he had once been.

Jason gently pushed Marie's arm off his waist, but her other hand had no intention of letting go of his. It was her first night as a full vampire, and true to the fact that she was still a child, these little things seemed to really scare her.

He went deeper into the old graveyard, following a path his retreating mind did not want to remember. Marie came along quietly, just a little behind his footsteps.

Jason stopped, sensing the powerful presence in the air, and felling it truly, with all his senses, with his blood . . . and he knew it was Alexander. But where was he?

"Come to me, my beautiful one, bring the little one. Come to me . . ."

"Alex, why are you bringing me here?" he whispered after the voice had faded out. He could feel Marie's hand clenching his tighter, as he pulled her along the path. She could feel the power now, Jason was sure of it. And she didn't like it. What fledgling vampire would want to meet a seven hundred-year-old vampire on their first night out? What vampire would, come to think of it.

Jason saw his steps on the soft ground as steps into the past. He remembered carrying his baby's casket by himself, as the others carried his wife's. He remembered how they had died horribly, in agony, at the hands of Alexander's vampires. Alex had been there, naturally, and for some reason, had chosen only Jason to pull from the jaws of death, literally.

He recalled their last fight, Alexander's and his, when all the 'laws' he had broken on that fateful night had finally been found out. He knew shame that night, and guilt, and rejection. He was never to return.

And here Jason was now, finally, standing at the foot of his own grave, where his wife and child had been buried. On it, faded as the centuries had passed, were their names, years and places of their births, and deaths. On this elaborate crypt, inside which their skeletons still lay, Jason's name had also been carved, on top of everyone else. Yes, the name, the date of his birth and the place, but after that, nothing.

Everyone that Jason had known died thinking bandits had killed him, but it had never been known for certain. And so out of respect that he might come back, they had left it untouched, forever.

Jason smiled as he looked at this, and at the little keyhole that had become overrun with weeds, and vines. He still had the key, which fit this lock. It was kept in a secret box inside of his coffin, his true resting-place.

Jason was ousted from his thoughts by the sudden increase of power, and Marie's tiny gasp. Jason turned slowly, as Marie went behind him, still clutching at his hand, and feeling the way every hair on his body was standing on end. The remainder of the old blood running through his veins made his body tingle, knowing it was so close to its long ago source.

As Jason turned fully, he beheld the final past, the illusion of a middle-aged man, the dark father, the leader of Russian armies. As he looked slightly upward he thought these things, and he gazed upon his blood master, and creator, for the first time in many long years.

Alexander stood there, tall and proud, his full height of six foot two. His hair was a perfect blend of golden-brown that came down halfway and wavy, on his back. He had a thick, old-fashioned mustache of the same color, and his eyebrows were a bit darker. They framed the icy blueness of his eyes, which were so like Jason's own.

He wore soft suede boots laced high with strips of rawhide. His dress slacks were a faded black, so faded they appeared almost gray. His shirt was white silk, its top two buttons open to reveal the skin underneath, which was almost as pale as the shirt. The tails of the shirt were not tucked in; the wind flapped them against his body. He wore an expensive looking French leather jacket, and no jewelry, but for a small golden chain around his neck.

To Jason, he hadn't changed a bit. He still imposed the startling, handsome Russian/French nobleman mix, and although he had no French blood, he had lived here long enough to acquire the characteristics.

Now he crossed his arms, and waited for Jason to speak first.

Jason reached in back of himself and pushed away Marie by the arms, feeling the cotton sleeves of her dark blue shirt against his fingers. Yes, she is the cotton, Alex is the silk. He knew that Marie had stepped back against the stone wall of his crypt as he stepped up closer to Alex.

"Alexander." he whispered, addressing him finally after so long. "I apologize for the intrusion, but I had to come back here."

Alexander stared down at him, waiting.

"I . . . I need your help." Jason bowed his head, regretting that he had to swallow his pride.

"You have begun to learn, my son." Alexander said in a very, very old language. It sounded like a rusty gate creaking in the back of Jason's mind. It took a minute before he remembered.

Latin, the language spoken in the old coven.

Jason shook his head, saying without words that he could no longer speak this old language.

"Ah," Alex said, and then, began again, in French, "You have begun to learn, and to understand. You grow wiser as you grow older. I have seen this as I have seen my other children. I have watched you since the day you left here. I have seen that which abandonment had done to you, making you careless, thoughtless, and yes, even a bit mad.

"I know that it took an offspring of one of your own children to make you understand, to finally bring you to your senses. You have accepted your life in America, which should be the place you make your home for now, and until one day when you become the lone wolf. That would be the day you and I, perhaps, will live together again. I have allowed you to return from America, because you have finally become the generous, trusting creature you once were in life. And also, because there has been harm done unto the female that awakened you, by one of my own sons."

Anger passed over Alexander's face.

"This I will not allow. Courchenne, the one who has long ago taken to calling himself Cory, thinks treasonous thoughts against his own father, against the one who has created him!"

Alex pounded one fist into the other, the first animated movement made by him yet.

"He will not be allowed to put this plan into effect. He does not know that I have seen his thoughts within my own mind as he slept, and as he dreamed. That is how I watch over my children."

He smiled at Jason now, his pale face becoming less and less of the stiff white statue, and more like that of a thirty-five year old man. "That is how I know that you wish to be called Jason. How I know that you are still a very rich man, your once millions becoming billions, with each generation saying you are this cousin, or that son, making your life lawful, but a secret."

"And that is the way it should be." Jason whispered, realizing that he had done this thing out of instinct alone, never but now remembering that law, *'Make your life lawful and secret; this is the way it should be.'*

"The old rules are gone, my son." Alex said sadly. "The old coven has dispersed over the years, most have gone, or have perished. Only a few of my children have remained. There are always new children, and this you know. Some elders still come to seek council. There are also the young ones, coming to seek the great Alexander." He laughed slightly here, going on to say, "Do you know, once it was thought I may be Alexander the Great?"

Jason smiled. Here he was, and here he had always been. Alexander, his father, and his home. "Do you bear me ill will?" Jason said, after a moment of silence.

"No." Alex said quickly. "I do not. Your heart has changed. You are no longer what you were when we argued last."

Jason smiled, and watched as Alexander closed the gap between them, opening his heart and arms to Jason, as they embraced.

"My beautiful one returns." he said, and, releasing Jason, approached Marie, where she stood in the shadows. "Marie, do not be afraid of the powerful. Most do not destroy the weak."

She took in a sudden breath, as she realized he had taken her name from her thoughts, but smiled and was not, at least she hoped, afraid.

Jason felt as he walked with Marie and Alexander, exiting the graveyard, that in the end, things were going to be all right. But then, he felt cries of a terrified child enter his mind, with such stunning force, he almost collapsed. In a flash, he saw Rikki running, crying out.

When he looked up, he saw Marie and Alexander gazing at him with concern. "Where is he?" was all that Alexander asked.

Jason did not answer. He used his senses to locate Rikki, and then flew up into the night, with Marie and Alexander just behind him.

13

Rikki ran faster.

He was beginning to tire himself out at this preternatural speed, but he knew he could not stop. He knew that he was being chased.

He could feel them behind him, above him, all around him. He could feel their outstretched hands, their snarling, laughing faces. He could feel his own death coming.

He ran past mortals who saw him as a white blur without a face, a strong wind. His lungs hurt, his face hurt from being stung from the wind. His pride hurt for being chased like this. Here he was, the vampire, being hunted down by others of his kind. Just like a rat in a trap.

Rikki did not know where he was going, or how to get help. All he knew was to get away, to get away. The alleys of this part of Paris were like a never-ending maze, and he did not know how to get out. Sweat poured down his body, and he knew he'd have to stop soon, or he'd collapse.

Suddenly, he struck a wall. His face and hands hurt where he had hit. Rikki had not known this wall had been in place. It was made of brick and mortar, and should not have been there.

He could sense that the open street was on the other side.

He could tell that the wall had been built just a day ago.

Rikki moaned low in his throat, as he realized what had happened. They had planned this. They had planned to catch him here, against their wall, which they had built. They had known all along that this was the direction he would, in the end, choose to run.

Rikki's attention was drawn to the top of the wall, to the one who sat there, laughing at him. She mocked him in strange words, and Rikki covered his ears to block out the French sounds. His eyes darted frantically about, watching with horrid fascination as they stepped from the shadows, surrounding him, laughing at him.

"No!" he cried out, and reflexively, he flew straight upwards. A hand shot out in the darkness, cold and pale. It grabbed his arms, pinning them behind his back.

Rikki gazed fearfully at the face of the one that held him, and the cold, dead eyes. It was Jean-Luc.

He smiled at Rikki, awful to see one with no eyes smile. Then, he lifted his hand back and Rikki saw what he held. It was a stake, which came down in a sweeping arc, and buried itself in his thigh.

Rikki let out a piercing howl, and felt himself being dropped to the ground. The pain in his leg made him weak, and he could not stop himself from falling, down, down, to the cement.

He hit the ground with a resounding crack, knowing that his spinal cord had snapped. His mouth remained open in absolute pain, and although his hands grasped for the stake, he found he couldn't pull it out. He had no strength.

As he looked up at the figure of Jean-Luc, he felt the power of the wood enter his body. It was fire; it had to be fire! His entire leg was on fire, as if the sunlight was shining on his body. The fire had begun to spread up his torso, and his blood could not do what it needed to do, in order to heal his broken spine.

Rikki looked down at his leg, and found it a horrible mistake. Where the stake was sticking into his leg, a fountain of dark blood bubbled up and over him.

"You won't die yet, child. Not until the fire consumes your heart. Then you will know that all your blood has gone. It is a slow and agonizing process. Do you wish me to continue?" Jean said, his fingers stroking his chin.

"No." Rikki croaked, his fingers twitching around the stake, slipping in the blood.

"Very well." he said with a sigh. Then he looked around himself, at the dark-clothed figures gathered there. "My children are hungry. I think it's time they fed."

He stepped over Rikki's leg, caught some of the blood in his mouth, and reached down. With one mighty pull, he wrenched the stake free.

Rikki yelped and convulsed, splinters hanging back in his skin, and muscle. The pain was very great, but at the very least, his spine was now mending.

Rikki reached down and touched the ragged wound on his leg. The fountain of blood had stopped, now having slowed to a trickle.

As he slowly and painfully sat up, to cover his leg feebly with his hands, he could see them surrounding him, all around him. Jean had stepped back, smiling, letting them do what they wished.

Rikki looked up at all of them, dreading the fangs, dreading the death. "Get away from me! All of you! Are you all Wild Ones to chase and hunt down your own kind?" he screamed at them, ignoring the pain in his back and thigh. Most looked at him with sheer indifference; they did not understand his language.

"You are all sheep to do this, to obey him like this! Don't do it! Leave me alone!" Rikki tried to make them listen, but he knew by Jean's persistent laughter, they were relentless.

"You little fool!" Jean laughed, "They will not understand you! They are my children, and the enemies of Alexander. They obey me, for they do not understand the words 'Wild Ones'." He looked out over his group, a slight frown upon his face, "And I shall kill any that do not obey me."

He looked at Rikki once more now. "Farewell child. This has been a marvelous hunt."

Jean-Luc disappeared from sight and they fell in on Rikki, surrounding him in pain and blackness.

Rikki struggled briefly. There were too many to fight. Too many fangs, too many hungry mouths. He felt the cloth being torn from his body, the nails against his skin, the teeth pressing into him from all sides. And he shut his eyes.

He was a roasted pig, a meal, a feast. Rikki felt the pain flowing through him and out of each new hole they made in his body, but he would not let them get his neck. Rikki put his hands around his neck, oblivious to the beating fists, the growls, the chunks of bloody skin they ripped from him. He knew that if they got at his neck it would be over. He would die swiftly.

A piercing scream suddenly entered the feeding frenzy. A name was whispered among each Wild bloody mouth. *"Jean-Luc, Jean-Luc..."*

Rikki became aware, slowly, that they were leaving his body, that each of them were no longer hurting him. He curled up into a ball, and his bloody, naked body shook with sobs. If he had looked up then, he would have seen a sight, which would have given him the satisfaction of pure revenge.

Jean had been so much enjoying the killing, he never saw the shadow glide up on him from behind. He never saw his old enemy, and his new one, that had come to kill him. But he had seen the stake as Jason picked it up from where it lay, and drove it through his intestines with a snarl of fury. He had felt Alexander's hand as it ripped open his chest, and wrenched out his very heart. Jean-Luc had watched, dying, as Alexander sank his fangs into the heart, spurting the blood over Jason's laughing triumphant face.

And he had felt it when Alexander bent over him, drawing the blood from his throat. It was the pain, and perhaps the young fledgling girl-child watching in the shadows, that made him tell his pack of demons to retreat.

And then, he died.

Alexander stood then, when Jean had died, looked down at the red pulp he still clutched in his hand. It was the heart.

He dropped it on the ground then at once, licking his hands clean.

Jason smiled at him, his eyes, those icy blue eyes, reflected the same fury in his own. He watched as Jason went to Rikki, Marie following him.

Alexander looked at the Wild Ones, who with their evil bloody mouths, stared down at their fallen master. "He taught you wrong. All of you. Even those of you who have known me seemingly forever. I was never the devil in Paris. It was the thing lying dead here, at your feet. Find the right paths, and I will never hunt you down."

They dispersed then, some staring at Jean-Luc, some at Alexander. But all were grateful for their newfound freedom. It could be seen within their eyes.

Rikki came back to awareness slowly, flinched when he discovered arms around him. But then he saw Jason, his father, and he knew he was no longer in danger. There were tears in Jason's eyes. Real and true, now running down his face. But the face showed no emotion. It was all right, though. Everything would be fine, now that Jason was here.

Rikki accepted the overcoat Jason wrapped around his body. But he could not move, he hurt far too much. For the second time that night, he felt that he might die. He felt pain still, though his back was mended. The splinters in his muscles were like embers from a fire. The flesh on his body ached where it had been bitten, and although it longed to be healed, it could not. The blood was gone.

With the last of his strength he could muster, he leaned forward, trying desperately to get at Jason's neck. "I cannot help, Richard." Jason said, in that tone, in that voice he had only heard the night of his death to the human world, and the night that Julia had saved him from Jonathan.

"Jason . . . please . . . " he croaked out, and then finding himself unable to finish, *I don't want to die, Not from the wood, not from the blood loss. I want to live. Help me, Help me. Father!*

He closed his eyes and felt Jason's body shake, once, just once. "I cannot help the wood. I can stop the hunger, the pain in your skin, but not the wood . . . not the wood. It is deadly to us."

Rikki was going to protest, when he felt himself being lifted. Power in these arms, in this embrace. He was frightened, and his mind called for Jason.

"Relax, child."

A voice now, dark and rich, the voice of the past, the future, it was deep and melodious, and he knew in an instant, it was Alexander.

He opened his eyes a crack, and though it was blurry, he saw Jason holding a young female vampire close to him, his eyes staring wide, blank.

The female clutched desperately at Jason, for all she had seen had been terrible.

My sister, he thought, and a voice reassured him. He looked up at Alexander, and saw the magnificence. And then he saw the blood, red and deep as rubies, slowly falling down his flawless neck.

Rikki found the strength to lean up and catch the first ruby in his mouth.

And then he began to suck.

14

Julia awoke in a basement of a small house, just out of St. Louis, Missouri. At first she didn't remember how she had got there, or even why she was here.

But with a sudden clarity, she remembered.

Julia rose from the old, rotted sofa, which she had slept on during the day, and stretched. It was good that she had found this house, for the people who lived here had gone on a vacation.

She had been able to deduce this from the stack of mail that had been thrown on the table, and the lack of clothes in the closet. But now, night had fallen. And it was time for Julia to move once again. She did not wish to be caught by Cory, and she was sure he was already looking for her.

Julia walked a long while. As she entered the city, her mind was full of thoughts of Kevin's tragedy, and the night before. A little while later, she stopped by newsstand, reached for one of the papers. The date upon it read April 20.

Julia lowered her head and sighed. Almost five months. Had she really been separated from Jonathan that long? Julia closed her eyes and silent tears fell, dripping, from her eyes. They soaked into the paper, and made the ink letters run in a messy gray and pink stream. Julia threw the paper down and was about to walk away, crying, when she felt a human man come up behind her.

"Hey, gal. Wanna go fer a ride?" he asked. "Ya'll look friendless."

Julia turned to look at him, wiping off her tear-streaked face. She took note of the slight southern drawl, looked over his features. Built enough, nice tan, dark short hair, dark blue eyes. He wore cowboy boots and a hat, of course, and his whole wardrobe looked as if he had just stepped out of a country western video. Julia noticed, as she observed him now, that he had a goofy, drunken look on his face.

The man took Julia's hand, and immediately she gripped it, turning it over and rolling up his fringed coat sleeve. She began to stare at the blue veins underneath. The alcohol in his breath, and the blood inside him, made her stomach lurch. She remembered that she hadn't fed last night. In fact, blood had been taken from her by that asshole, Cory.

The more she thought about it, the hungrier she became.

"Take me somewhere nice." she said, her voice choked with sorrow and lust.

They got into his old, beat up truck, and pulled away. They drove through the streets, their destination at a high point that looked over the city and all the shining lights.

"Nice, ain't it?" he asked Julia, slipping one tanned arm around her, his fingers beginning a maniacal pattern down the inside of the sweatshirt.

Julia looked out at the lights, ignoring the fact that his big clumsy hand was now headed down her tank top, as well. She threw his arm away from her, tears welling up in her eyes again.

"What'sa matta, gal?" his voice slurred.

Julia touched his hand, linked with him only long enough to discover his name. Terrance.

"Please, Terrance, you touched my chain. I don't like that." she said, her hands instinctively clasping around the stones, tears spilling over her pale cheeks. Her lips began to tremble.

"I'll take it off for ya," he offered.

"No!" Julia screamed at him, leaning forward.

There was silence for a moment.

"Sorry, gal, won't do it 'gain." he said, sliding his hands around her waist under the sweatshirt, pulling her back. He made a little gagging sound, and then said; "You're cold."

Julia smiled through her tears. "Yeah," she said bitterly, "That's because I'm not human."

Terrance was now kissing her neck, shoulders, and pulling the sweatshirt off, over Julia's head. She let him. Julia reached back and knocked the hat off his head. "I know you ain't human, little darlin', you're a goddess." he said, happily, drunkenly.

Terrance pulled at the ripped tank top, and Julia looked down at her one bare shoulder, reminded yet again of him…Cory…and wondered if perhaps she would never escape the scars of this ordeal, even if she did find a way to return home. Julia's tears were flowing heavily now, and she struggled not to sob.

More and more of her body had become exposed, as Terrance pushed the other strap down.

Why am I doing this, she thought, why am I letting him do this to me? She knew in the next minute why. She touched his hands to stop them, and found the palms sweating.

Human sweat.

Julia licked the palm of his right hand and then sucked on each finger. She could feel the pulsing of his tiny veins, could taste the salty sweet skin, and by his pinky finger, he was ready to take her.

Julia's upper jaw had become an aching, throbbing thing, just like Terrance's manhood.

She held his hands tight as a shudder ripped though her, starting at her stomach and circulating at her canines.

With her eyes still tearing, she tilted her head back, opened her mouth. The throbbing in her canines slowly, achingly, lengthened them into fangs. The world had become a red pulsating place, the darker the red, more the heat, and the more the heat, the more the blood.

Terrance was one giant sack of blood.

Julia placed her other hand on his thigh, and absently sliced her nails through the jeans, deep into his skin, making five long furrows of blood.

Terrance flinched, but didn't pull away.

"Sorry." she said in a weird, strangled sound. Then she turned, and held his face in her hands. "Look at me!" she cried, her voice grating against the change in her anatomy. "I didn't want to hurt you, he made me like this, he changed me. Can't you see?"

Terrance just stared at her, too drunk to even understand what he was seeing.

Julia was hungry, starving. The smell of his blood intoxicated her. Terrance was practically bursting out of his pants. Just looking at Julia intoxicated him.

Terrance brought her head forward, and kissed her mouth, his tongue sliding in against the fangs. Julia struggled not to bite down, to rip his tongue out of his mouth, and suck up the blood. His hands got what they wanted, seeking and finding.

Julia climbed onto his lap and ripped his cotton shirt down the front, popping buttons. She rubbed her hands against his human skin, and withdrew her head from his.

She shut her eyes tight, and sank her fangs deep into his neck. There was a shudder, a slight moan, and Julia did not even have to look to see the wetness spreading on his pants.

The blood rushed into her; hot and wild laced with the alcohol. She held onto him as she drank, rocking back and forth.

There was something inside her screaming to rip his head free of his body, and catch the blood in her mouth, as it would gush up.

No, she thought to herself, not like Cory, no.

She let go of Terrance as she felt his movements slowing. "I'm not going to kill you," she said raggedly, gasping for breath, straining against her instincts and her needs. "Remember me, Terrance. My name is Julia."

She then kissed his head, and all but tore the door off the hinges to get out of the car. Outside, with the smell of blood locked up inside, Julia adjusted the tank top and pulled her sweatshirt back on. She licked her lips and nails clean of blood, and tried desperately to relax.

Julia ran all the down the hill, back into the city, and by the time she got there, the hunger had almost hidden again. The fangs had retreated, and only the most insignificant specks of red remained in her eyes.

Julia walked onward; hugging herself, when she by chance passed by an old wooden tavern that appeared polished, but worn. On a sign that had faded long ago, Julia could just make out the word, *NOSFERATU*.

Nosferatu? Vampire? She wondered. Julia tried to scan the place with her mind, but there was some sort of mental block on the place, which wouldn't let her mind penetrate.

Wiping the last traces of Terrance from her mind and her mouth, she bravely headed to the old wooden doors, and pulled them open.

Immediately they shut behind her, and she was enveloped in the atmosphere and structure of the place.

There were vampires everywhere; the power of so many gathered was unnerving. Some were sipping at glasses of blood with alcohol spiked into it. Others were drinking vodka, and pure grain alcohol. The ones who were drinking pure grain looked a little woozy from time to time, and so Julia bought a whole bottle of that.

Dim red and blue lights lighted the place. Old music was being played; Italian, French, Spanish, Russian, Celtic, and Classical. They were alternately played through well-concealed speakers.

Julia sat down at a corner table, looking around at the place. It was all very elegant, very old. There was a giant staircase leading upwards to rooms, which were visible from the first floor.

A vampire tavern. Julia's mind raced back, a thousand gears clicking at once. This had to be one. It was the only explanation for these many gathered here. She had heard of them, read about them in novels, but this was the first time she had actually ever seen one.

Julia had just taken her first swig of the pure grain stuff, when she was approached by a female vampire. Her scent was . . . familiar to Julia.

"Julia?" the girl called.

Julia looked up, startled, and gazed at someone who had once been her best friend.

It was Christi, the friend who had left her side.

"Sit down, Christi. Tell me, how are you? How is Sabastian?" Julia smiled weakly, took another swig off the bottle.

Christi sat, relayed her story to Julia. Sabastian and she had left Vermont in order to be together in safety, to be away from Jason. Julia told her Jason had changed, however, Christi didn't believe her. Julia shrugged.

Anyway, Christi said, they had left and hooked onto a group of vampire bikers, gone to Canada, Oregon, New York, and then here to St. Louis. They were planning to go to New Orleans soon.

"Why?" Julia asked.

"Why what?"

"Why are you going to New Orleans, with those bikers?"

Christi laughed. Julia took another swig.

"We aren't going anywhere with them, they left two days ago. We're going ourselves."

Julia asked if that was wise. Christi didn't care. Same old Christi, she thought.

Here, now, they had joined up with the group of vampires that ran this tavern. They called their group The Bleeding Hearts, to signify they were a suffering kind. Sabastian hung out with a lot of the younger ones, going here or there in the city. Christi usually did the same, but had stayed here tonight.

"Perhaps it was destiny that made me stay here. To see my old friend again." she reached over the table, patting Julia's hand. "I'm sorry I left you there, Julia."

"I'm sorry I brought you into this mess." Julia said with a sad, knowing smile. Christi's face mirrored her own.

"What's going on with you and Jonathan, Julia? Why are you so far out here?"

Julia leaned back in her chair, closing her eyes. Christi's fingers tightened around her own. She senses my trouble, Julia thought. "Do you trust me to show you?" she asked Christi.

"Yes." Christi whispered.

Julia opened her eyes, and stared into Christi's. She felt the block surrounding Christi's mind melt away, as Julia's did the same.

Julia's fingers clenched onto Christi's, and she pushed through all the images of what had happened since the time that Christi had left. Then, to Julia's wedding, her capture, and finally yesterday in California. Julia showed Christi one last image, the image of Terrance in the truck.

Then she let go of her hand, and pulled back, building up her shield once again. She was trembling because she had to relive everything. Christi was trembling because she had seen it.

"Oh, Julia. I had no idea." she sighed.

"Well, it's almost over now." she said, drinking again from the bottle. "I'm almost home. Christi, I feel so old."

"I understand, Julia. I really do. And I'm so sorry. Maybe some day I'll come back to Vermont."

"That would be good." Julia said, and then, tipping her head back, drank the rest of the bottle, gulping the whole thing down. When it was empty, it fell to the wooden ground, breaking into a thousand tiny, fragmented pieces. The world grew blurry around her, as the room began to swim. She could faintly hear Christi saying, "Goodbye, Julia. Good Luck. And please, be careful."

When Julia awoke later from her personal blackout, it was without a hangover or some stupor. It was with a start, as if someone had snapped their fingers. She realized that she was no longer in the outer room, but in some kind of lounge. There was a man sitting next to her, gazing at her in a strange way. He had curly short blonde hair, so blonde it was almost white. His eyes were a rich amber color. And his skin was very pale. He was wearing all black, black jeans, black shirt, and black jogging sweater with a hood in the back, unzipped all the way down the front.

Finally, he smiled at her, breaking the tension in Julia.

"Hi. I guess you can't hold your liquor, huh?"

"No, I guess not." Julia smiled at the man, sitting up and rubbing her face with her hand. "I couldn't do it when I was alive either. I'm not very good with that stuff."

"I see." he said.

Julia looked at him again, this time taking in all the little things, the things only a woman can see when she is sizing up a man. He looked good.

The man smiled, placing his palms down on the plush, blue velvet couch. "I do, do I?"

This startled Julia. She had her mental cloud up, all right. She had not wanted to be overheard. How had he done this? Julia began to shake. She started to get up to leave, but his smile vanished, and he said, "No, please. I'm sorry, don't go just yet."

Julia sat back down and sunk into the couch, feeling the velvet slide against her neck. It was a nice feeling. Although, for some reason, she felt uneasy around him.

"I saw you earlier talking to a girl, Christi?" he asked in a demanding, but polite way. She nodded. "Sabastian has joined with us. The Bleeding Hearts. You know of this, yes?"

"Yes," Julia said, "but where is Christi now? Did she leave?" The man nodded, and Julia frowned.

"She asked me to help you, and I agreed. I am Dominic. I was originally from England, and was twenty-four, once. I kind of like to keep things a bit personal to myself, so I probably won't tell you much more. I know all about you, Julia."

Dominic smiled again, and this time touched five pale fingers to Julia's neck. A sizzle, like lightning, flowed from his fingers into Julia, and it strangely attracted her to him. She pulled back, biting her lower lip, staring at him in suspicion.

"You shouldn't be afraid of me, Julia. I only want to help you. I once had a lover like you do, but it wasn't meant to be. She was strong. She left me." He sighed, brought his fingers up to run them through his hair. "But that's in the past, isn't it? Past is dead. Hey, you know Julia? We are a lot alike, you and I. Maybe if you hadn't gotten married, I could entice you to stay here?" his eyebrows raised at the question.

"Maybe," she replied, staring into those strange, unique eyes.

"How has your journey been?" he asked sincerely.

"It's been hard. Very hard." she sighed. "I've been seeing a lot of things that I thought I never would, or should. I have been meeting new people, like you. I suppose that if there was one good thing to come out of all this, it would be those who tried to help me."

"Yes, I agree with you." he said, his eyes wandering from her face. Someone had come in the door, and Julia glanced up. It was a woman.

The woman looked at Dominic, smiled, and went back out.

"Privacy here is a thing that comes not too often, Julia. You have to learn to deal with it." His hand waved in a formal gesture.

Julia smiled, looked down at his hand. She was surprised at the paleness of it. "How old are you? When were you made?" she asked, sounding like a kid in a fairy tale. When she looked up at him, he was smiling.

"Julia, come on, I told you not to ask me questions."

"All right, I won't." she said softly.

"Julia," he said now, leaning close to her, so close in fact, that his lips almost touched hers. She found it difficult to look into his eyes, and she lowered them. He clasped her hands in his. "Julia, I will help you to return to Vermont. It is a terrible thing that this Cory has done to you, and to your family. I will not let him harm you."

Julia stifled a sniffle, and was surprised when she felt Dominic's arms around her, shutting out the pain. There was that strange electricity again, but somehow not as strong this time. It was like a shield around her, protecting her.

311

"Why are you willing to help me?" she asked him, her face now against his shoulder.

"It's part of the reason I'm in this society, The Bleeding Hearts. I still care about people, humans and vampires alike. If something goes wrong, I think maybe I could make a difference." He let go of Julia and held her out at arm's length. "And when Christi told me you were in trouble, you were sleeping like a little angel. I had to help you. There was no way around it."

Julia smiled. "Thank you. But you should know, the last person who tried to help me got killed."

"Yes, I'm aware of that, but I also know this. Cory simply does not possess the power to kill me. Perhaps with a thousand followers and the sunlight, but not on his own."

"I'm grateful for this, Dominic."

"I know, child." he said, stroking her hair. "You're thinking, I'm not a child. Well, you are to me, babe. You don't have to try harder to get me out of your head like that." Julia stared at him, speechless. "Don't worry, I won't read your thoughts anymore. But you're too young to stop me."

He was joking now, she could tell. It was in the way he smiled, the way his shoulders shook with silent laughter. "Come on now, let me get you a place to stay for the daytime. It will be here soon, you know." He got up to leave, taking her hand in his.

"This won't be too much trouble for you, will it?" she asked as they exited the lounge and entered the main room, and started up the stairs there.

"No, no trouble at all. There's an extra room, up near mine. I'm a good friend of Pete's, the manager here. I'll just tell him that you're using it for a while. Okay?"

"Yes, thanks." she said.

They went up together into a long, old darkened hallway. Candles, which had been separated with great distances between them, served to produce the only light here.

Julia watched the shadows disappear, as a switch of some sort kicked in the back of her mind, and her night vision came on.

Dominic stopped between two doors. "Julia, listen now. My door is the one to the left. If you need any help with anything, let me know. Just knock or scream my name. This door here, the one to the right, is yours. I am going to lock you in tonight." He pulled out a set of keys, and unlocked the three bolts on the door.

Julia pulled it open, and entered the room. It was dark inside, but she could see everything in perfect detail. A switch was hit in the darkness, and a fluorescent light came on overhead. Julia squinted, adjusting herself to the light in the room.

"This is it." spoke a soft, gentlemanly voice behind her. The door shut with a thud.

Julia looked around the room. There was a peculiar looking bed in the corner; four posts as thick as two-by-fours extended upwards, at the top, met by a long, thin, wooden board. The board was nailed to the posts to create a top of sorts. There was a heavy, dark cloth extended down from the top, and all the way around the bed. "It's like a giant coffin." Julia said.

"Yes, that is how all the beds here are designed." Dominic said.

Julia pulled the curtains back, and looked up at the top board. It was painted black to match the curtains. But as she looked down at the covers, she had to chuckle. The covers were completely white. "Nice touch." she muttered.

Also in the room was an old wooden bureau, its paint chipped and cracked. The walls were painted a sky-blue color, and the floor was wooden. There was a small bathroom to the side, with just a toilet, and a sink with a cold-water faucet.

Julia came back out to Dominic, smiling. "There's blood stains on the bathroom floor. Did you know that?"

Dominic gave her a sheepish grin. "Well, I must admit to you. I sometimes keep guests in here."

"Ah-ha." Julia said, nodding.

They stood in a comfortable silence for a moment, and than he said, "Well, I should get going. I have to…ah . . . meet someone before the dawn. There are boards on the window, and there are bolts on the door. But you already know this. Well, what I mean to say, is that you can open them from the inside. Just turn the switches," he said, gesturing to them. "Do you have any questions?"

"Yes," Julia said, sitting on the edge of the bed. "Who runs this place during the day?"

"Don't you know? Pete's human cousin does. He knows about us, what we all do here. He runs the tavern during the day, and he also serves the people food. He puts up a giant chain on the staircase. There is a sign on it that reads, *'Manager Only. All violators shall be thrown out.'*

"So far, no one has been thrown out. We keep our doors locked during daytime. Pete and his cousin split the earnings of what we make here. The vampires can have low-priced drinks, since we don't drink much. They charge more for the rooms."

"I don't have any money!" Julia exclaimed, jumping to her feet.

"Don't worry about that, Julia. I'm paying for these rooms already, remember? Just have a good sleep. We'll talk again tomorrow evening. Good-night."

He almost left the room then. He was halfway out the door when Julia called out to him, "Dominic?"

"Yeah?"

"I've been through so much. Will Jonathan still want me, after what happened? What if Cory finds me?"

He went to her, sat down by her side. She was amazed at how gentle he was.

"Oh, Dominic, I'm so scared."

She lowered her head, wrapped her arms around herself. Dominic pulled her close again. Electricity. Didn't he feel it? If he did, he didn't say.

"Don't worry, little girl. You're safe here. Everything will be okay. If Cory comes here, he'll be sorry he did. You'll be fine."

"Are you sure?" she asked, looking up into his eyes.

"Yes," he whispered, "I'm positive. Nothing can touch you." No sooner had he faded into the gentleman; he lapsed back into the free spirited, boyish creature. He grinned at her, stood up, and ran his fingers through his curls.

"See? You'll be fine here. The place is cool. Goodnight, Julia."

He left her then, and as soon as the door shut, she heard the sounds of locks clicking into place.

Julia sat still for a moment, reflecting on the evening, and the generosity of this man. Then she pulled off her boots and socks and jeans, leaving them in a puddle on the floor. Last, she took off the sweater, threw it on top of the jeans.

She inhaled and exhaled deeply, as she looked down at the damaged tank top. She tied the two ends of the strap together, and rubbed her exposed belly. She was still hungry, but more exhausted than anything else.

Julia went into the bathroom again, and found a brush in a little closet that also held skin cream, blankets, and several towels.

Julia brushed her hair out as she strolled back into the room, closing the door on the small bathroom. When she was finished, she put the brush down on the bureau, yawned, and stretched.

Julia walked silently to the door, pressing her ear against it. The commotion downstairs had finally begun to thin out. She checked the locks on the door, and shut out the light.

With her eyes adjusted to the darkness of the room, Julia crept onto the bed, pulling the heavy curtains shut around her. She snuggled into the covers, and almost instantly, fell asleep.

15

Jonathan brutally pushed Lena down to the sofa.

She had attacked him again.

She wanted blood, received none.

Something inside of Jonathan had prevented him from letting her kill. It was something about her, something which had to do with the way she acted. The way she had looked at him after that first night when he had given her the blood. The way she made love. It was too fierce, too powerful. There would be a disaster, if she were permitted to become fully a vampire. And so Jonathan kept her imprisoned here.

Now, a week later, Lena was starving, going insane with bloodlust. She would try for anyone, anything. She had sprung at Melissa and Steven a few times. Even tried for the rats in the basement, and the birds in Jonathan's attic.

But he would not let her get at anything. He kept her in his watch, in his care. And several times, she had stolen just a taste, of Jonathan's blood.

He stood here now, turning back to the fireplace, his hands at his sides, helpless. His jacket was off; his hair was brushed down, soft. He felt extremely tired and sad, as if Lena's madness had taken away his own. He did not feel that overpowering anguish and insanity devouring his mind. No, he knew now that he had brought it on himself, all these problems. He knew that he had become like Cory. It made him feel sick inside.

Julia, he thought, when will I see you again? Ever? Take me away from my wretchedness. Then he thought of Lena, and what he had done. "Perhaps Julia has also quenched her needs." he whispered to himself.

There was a sting then, in his throat. Strong, desperate arms wrenched him backwards. The sting became pain, as Lena pushed her fangs deep into his neck and pulled, taking another mouthful of blood this time.

Jonathan gasped. She had caught him off balance. Pain jarred him as she took in another mouthful, and another.

Jonathan twisted, knocked her down onto the ground.

She screeched at him from where she had fallen, his blood dripping down from her mouth. Lena clawed at his legs, trying to get more of his blood into her mouth. She succeeded in pulling him onto the ground, and came at him again, growling and moaning. Her teeth sank into his arm, the part of his body nearest to her.

Jonathan slapped her this time, across her forehead, hard enough to break her off him. As she lay there on the floor, clutching her head, Jonathan climbed on top of her, letting his fangs come down. She scratched and hissed, and grabbed at his neck.

Jonathan finally held her arms above her head with one hand, and forced her head up by her chin with his other hand.

"No Lena, never shall you drink human blood." he watched as she squirmed at the word. "You will never again attack me, Steven or Melissa. Never shall you drink blood. You are only half vampire, and you will die as such. I will take my blood back!"

Jonathan sank his fangs into her, tearing back the flesh. She screamed and struggled, but out it flowed, half-human, half vampire, all into Jonathan.

"Jonathan...don't." she whispered, as she died. Jonathan pulled back then, and watched as the last breath escaped her lips with a sigh, her eyes rolled back into her head. He stood, chest heaving, as he stared at her. There lay a drained human. Human flesh, human bone. She was solid, not transparent. She was just a human. Never had been a vampire; never had been one of *them.*

Jonathan returned to the chair he had lain his jacket on and retrieved it, loving the feeling of cool leather sliding against his skin. He picked up Lena's body, and brought it with him out into the field, leaving the doors of the mansion opened.

The night was cool outside, and he loved it. As he dug deep into the earth with his own two hands, he loved it. As he watched the night creatures with his own preternatural sight, he loved it.

He dumped Lena into the hole he had dug, and covered her up, the dirt feeling good against his hands. Yes, it felt good once again to be one of the Dead. To do the things which Lena will never be able to do.

He dusted the dirt off of his hands on his jeans, and took a patch of dead, dry grass to the dirt that remained behind.

Returning to the mansion, he closed the front door, turned and looked over the place in Vermont, his home, his domain. He belonged here. Not as a raving, crazed lunatic, But as himself, Jonathan Jared Deschene. The only one, he was original. Only one thing was missing, he thought with a sigh, as he walked toward the bushes.

There, covered in canvass, was Julia's motorcycle. He pulled the covering off, and it fell like a curtain. There it was, still clean and smooth, beautiful like her, shimmering in the first quarter moonlight.

He ran his hand over the furnishings on the bike. Yes, he could feel her presence here, and here. Everywhere on the bike screamed Julia's name. It felt . . . as if . . . she was right there beside him! Jonathan spun, but all he saw was the mansion, and empty scenery.

Her presence, it seemed to be everywhere now. In his heart, in his mind. Breathing softly down his neck. Goosebumps rose on his skin. His hands rubbed his neck and chest. He shouldn't feel like this, shouldn't be so afraid.

Where was Jason?

Jonathan shook his head to clear the bad feelings from it, looked once more toward the field. He had killed another one. Another fledgling. When would these feelings of self-hatred stop?

Would Lena and Timothy come back to haunt him?

Jonathan breathed slowly and deeply, wishing Steven and Melissa hadn't gone for the night. Wishing Jason was home. Wishing, hoping, praying Julia would come back to him.

He covered the motorcycle back up. A soft breeze blew against him, blowing his jacket and hair back from his body. The chains on his earring rattled, the only sound to be heard.

Suddenly, he was angry. He stared at the white lump in the bushes. He was angry with himself, angry for being so scared, and desperate, and alone. He was hungry. He needed to hunt soon. No, hunt now.

Jonathan strode quickly to his Harley, slid on, and started the motor. It growled to life. The huge bike roared with the intensity and hunger that Jonathan himself felt.

Like a sleek, cunning predator, the bike descended down Deer Mountain to the unsuspecting civilians below.

Jonathan roared through the valley, past the park, past the mall, to the outskirts of town. He sent his hunger out in the waves of dreams, seeking . . . seeking . . . finding.

No sooner had Jonathan located the girl who wanted him, he was there, pulling the bike to a stop outside her window. Yes, he could feel her there, the girl was dreaming about him, the dark mysterious one she had seen at the park. He stared up at her window, looking past it, into the room, and there she lay.

There was a tree beside the window, bathed in shadows. Its branches reached up to her window, so thick and close; he could just see the girl climbing down to get away from her abusive father.

Perfect, he thought with a completely malevolent, sadistic grin.

Jon got off the bike and proceeded to the tree. One, two, three, four handholds, and he was there. Scratch, scratch at the window. He saw the girl wake up; her eyes take him in. Endlessly dark they were, so like his own. Her face was ageless, beautiful ebony hair like midnight. And the blood rushed to her face.

Yes, darling, I am here. I am hungry, ask me in.

"Oh." she said, not bothering to move from the bed. "Come in then."

Jonathan slid the locked window up with expertise, not making a noise as the lock broke, and the glass slid up. He crept close to her.

The girl stared at him. "Is this a dream? I dream about you all the time."

"No, it's not a dream." he said, slowly waking from one himself. "I'm sad, weak, angry. I am hungry." He slipped into bed beside her, his fingers closing around hers.

"You're cold." she whispered.

"Yes, I know. I need you to make me warm again. Your dreams will all come true."

A look of understanding passed into the girl's eyes. She had dreamed of death by him, and Jonathan knew it. Lucky he was to be seen by those who desired him.

The girl snuggled close to him, pressing herself against him. She shivered in the small nightgown.

Jonathan's fingers passed over her throat.

The girl sighed.

Jonathan was lost in a dream of blood and ecstasy.

When Jonathan finally returned home, sedated and full, it was close to morning. He was so full from the fresh kill and Lena's blood within him, that he was sweating blood. The sweat oozed slowly down his face, his chest, and his hands. In fact, the only parts of his body that were sweating, were those which came in direct contact with the air.

As he pulled into the driveway of the mansion, his senses became aware of something. It was a singular power, cloaked, but strong. For a second, he wished it were Julia. But when the presence sensed him, all shields were thrown down. Still outside, all that power scared him. Jonathan almost turned the bike back around. But Jason was here; Jonathan could feel that too. And slowly, he entered the mansion.

Inside, he stared as the doors shut behind him. Melissa and Steven were there, and she was clutching onto him, staring up at something, which Jonathan didn't want to see just yet.

Jason was there, with a redheaded girl standing at his side. She was talking to Jason, speaking broken English with a thick, heavy French accent.

Rikki sat heavily in an armchair, his head in his hands. He appeared sad, tired, dressed in jeans and a blue shirt.

Jason turned, saw Jonathan and smiled, walked to him, embraced him. He was saying now, how much he had missed Jonathan, yes, and he loved him.

Everything would be all right now. He's here. He's here. "Jason," Jonathan could not say any more. The tears came then, blood red with the excess still dripping from his body. Jason's smile vanished, his face hardened.

Jonathan turned to go, to run, but he was stopped. Jason turned him, held him. Jonathan was humiliated, but the pain and madness had now fled forever, and he knew it was because Jason was here. He was aware of everyone leaving the room, all going upstairs into the study. All except that power, that thing that scared him so.

Soon the tears stopped coming, the blood had stopped flowing. A hand, pale long fingers held a cloth out to him.

Jon looked up at the figure now, the man that stood before him. He seemed old and young at once. Jonathan stared at him as he wiped the blood off his face, hands and chest. There was no trace now, it was all gone.

"Jonathan, listen now. This is Alexander, my father. He has come for Cory. Julia will come back to us now, with his help."

Jonathan looked over at Jason as he spoke these words, and then, reassembling his dignity and pride, welcomed the ancient man who stood before him.

16

Cory approached the tavern with a smirk on his face.

Julia had left a trail for him, so obvious, that he had tracked her without any difficulty. First the basement. Oh, that had been real easy for her, with the people gone, no one living there. The whole place had contained her scent, along with the scent of fear. And then there was the man, Terrance. Still wandering around the night after the feeding, looking for his 'goddess'. Julia had been real stupid not to kill that lovesick pup. He was spouting her name everywhere. And when Cory had got to him, now that had been real fun. Sinking his teeth into those two little wounds, touching the five marks on his leg, he could feel Julia everywhere in Terrance. Then yum, yum, Terrance was all gone.

Julia's path through the city was an easy one. Her instincts had led her to this place without her realizing it. And she was still here.

Cory looked up at the old wooden building; the big glass window in front was heavily draped. Nice place, he thought, but not good enough to hide someone.

Cory grinned at the two friends he had brought with him.

Snake was Mexican, short dark hair, dark eyes, dark complexion, and mustache. He spoke with a Mexican accent. He had come to Cory as a wanderer. He was a great assessment to Cory; Snake was as ruthless as he was.

Jayme was a beautiful Southerner from Alabama; she had been created at the time of the Civil war. She was tall, strong and mean. Cory had once been attracted to her. Her hair was long, curly and auburn, her eyes soft green. She had a permanent pout on her sweet heart-shaped face.

They were the two best suited for this type of job. They had no relations to either Cory or Julia, and they were both with Cory because they wanted to be. They were cunning killers, perfect in Cory's eyes. Cory was proud of these two, happy to have them as friends. They were there when he needed assistance. When he expected trouble.

Now they stalked up the stairs and entered the tavern.

Dominic glanced up from a poker game when he heard the front doors slam shut, just as he had been doing all evening. He watched for the one called Cory, the one who Julia was afraid of.

So far, there had been no one to fit the description, however his one just had to be the Cory Julia spoke of. His hair was that strange rusted color; his hazel eyes reflected a bit of blue as they darted around the room. His jacket had those small square studs on it. He had arrived with two others. Yes, Julia had said he might indeed come with others.

Dominic laid down his cards, spoke softly to the other members of The Bleeding Hearts around him. "Keep them busy for me."

They nodded, and being as quiet and calm as possible, Dominic escaped up the unchained stairway. He looked down to see the guys he had been playing poker with rise, and intercept Cory. One sent him a quick telepathic message, *It's him.*

Dominic descended the hallway, digging for the keys to Julia's room. He hadn't seen her come out yet. He suspected Sabastian had brought her a meal, but they hadn't spoken yet, tonight.

He unlocked the door, and went in, locking it behind him. "Julia," he called softly, not wanting to disturb her, facing the door. For a moment, only soft sucking sounds could be heard from the bed, followed by antagonized breaths, and the shearing sounds of skin being ripped. The smell of the blood in the room increased.

Then he heard her growl, low and very feminine, in her throat.

Dominic turned around.

Julia lay on the bed, her arms stretched over the almost dead, disfigured male, clad in only her tank top and panties, blood covering her face and hands. Hunger and pain were etched together in her face. Obviously, she did not like what she had been doing to the man on the bed, who just now breathed his last. The skin on the guy was ribbons, his flesh a patchwork of bloody pulp.

"Oh, Dominic," she sighed; now realizing who stood within the room. The red in her eyes flickered, dimmed, went out. She looked down at the mess on the bed; all over the white blankets, and began to cry. "Oh, help me. Help me!"

Dominic erased all thoughts beginning to seep into his mind of how beautiful she was, and what it would be like to kiss away all that blood. He went to her, picked her up in his arms, pulled shut the curtains of the bed. Stepping over her clothing, he entered the bathroom.

He sat Julia gently down on the toilet, retrieved a towel from the closet. He wiped all the blood off her face and arms, and held her as she cried. He began to notice now, how every time he touched her, she flinched.

"Julia, listen to me. Please, don't be upset when I tell you this, now."

Julia sniffled, wiped her eyes, and looked up at Dominic. "What is it? I . . . I can handle it."

"Come on," he said, gently taking her hand, and leading her to her clothes. "Get dressed quickly. Cory's downstairs."

Julia's eyes widened, and a look of pure terror crept into her face. But she was true to her word. She did not cry out, but began to pull her clothes on, systematically. First the jeans, than the boots, than the sweater. Then she looked up at Dominic, taking him in with her night-vision. His strange amber eyes were staring at her.

"What is it?" she asked him.

"Nothing really. Just wondering to myself why I have this overwhelming urge to protect you, until the day I die." He shook his head, grasped her hand. She flinched again. Why? He didn't ask. "We better go. I don't know how long the boys downstairs can keep him. I'm going with you, Julia."

Julia nodded, took a deep breath, preparing herself for the worst.

They went out into the hall, Dominic locking the door again, this time, from the outside. They didn't notice the three figures at the dark end of the hall, lurking about in the shadows.

Cory watched as they came out of the room. It had been easy to talk his way past the others downstairs. It was Dominic he had to worry about. He was strong, powerful. But with his two, all their power together could quite possibly overwhelm that of Dominic's. And once he was out of the way, Julia would be no problem.

He smiled as he saw how jumpy Julia was, with his presence in the building. He felt his friends become fidgety. They wanted to attack now. "Wait." he told them. "Julia." he hissed, in a low, low tone.

Julia turned in Cory's direction. Her name had been spoken, this she was sure of. His presence was everywhere, she felt it. But when she looked down into the shadows, he stepped forth, followed by the two others.

Her hand clenched on Dominic's, her mouth dropped open.

Cory began to approach her, slowly, and smiled.

Julia screamed.

Dominic looked up, stunned, and pushed Julia out of the way, behind him.

Julia was in a state of shock. Cory was coming. Slowly, dreadfully and steadily. Julia couldn't breathe. He had her now; his eyes locked onto Julia's, his mind descending into Julia's like a hurricane.

Julia's last effort of freedom was to wrap her arms around Dominic. She felt his body harden, tense up, and then, from somewhere deep inside him, a roar came out, echoing into the hall. The electricity zapped her hands, made her shake. The power issuing out of him was tremendous.

Cory roared back, he and Snake changing instantly. The three of them came at Dominic, and Julia felt him falter, just for a second.

Suddenly, out of nowhere, all the members of The Bleeding Hearts surrounded Cory and his friends, cutting off Cory's mind link. "Hold on." Dominic whispered to her.

Dominic leapt over the staircase and flew straight for the huge, draped glass window.

Julia held tight, shut her eyes.

Dominic and Julia crashed through the window. It shattered behind them, and as they flew into the night, Julia could hear Cory screaming with rage.

They flew away from the tavern faster and faster, putting a great gap between them and Cory. When a good distance had been completed, Dominic let go of Julia.

He lapsed again into the Puck-like character, turning complete somersaults in the air. "Yahoo!" he yelled, laughing in his deep, throaty way. "See? I told you, no problem!"

Julia came to him smiling, the wind blowing the hair about her face, tingling against her skin. "Dominic," she said, and he put his arm around her.

A strange feeling overcame him then, as when he first met her, and when he saw her kill tonight. Though now, it was more pure, more intensified. She was beautiful. Her lips were so close he could almost taste it. She gazed up at him, puzzled, feeling some sort of attraction. The same strange thing that made him want to kiss her, to overpower her, made her want surrender to him.

She realized, without really knowing, all flight had stopped; they were slowly descending. She held onto him, her fingers pressed into the sweater and the cool pale skin of his hand, his amber eyes taking up her whole world.

He felt her small soft body in his arms, a little thing that was helpless without him, depending on him alone, for everything. One who was so young, so very young.

They touched down quietly in a forest, beside a pond. His fingers rested gently on her neck, where the pulse ran clear and sweet. His head descended slowly, and Julia shut her eyes.

They kissed.

The crackle of energy from Dominic seemed to wake Julia up. But now, she couldn't help what was happening. His power had descended over her; she was in a swoon. He kissed her again, and this time, there was no energy. It seemed as if the energy that had lingered around him for nights had just done its job. He was taking over.

Something whispered in Julia's mind, about the powerful taking over the young. The fledgling vampire's blood being a sweet temptation to the older ones.

"No," Julia whispered, "Dominic, stop it. You're going to hurt me."

Dominic pulled back, his eyes hazy, and a tinge of red showing through. His lips were slack, and Julia could just see a bit of fangs beginning to extend.

He pushed Julia away from him, disappeared into the trees.

Julia collapsed onto the bank of the pond, her body trembling from the power, which had made her limbs grow weak. Slowly, she was able to rise to a sitting position, and stare at the moonlit water. Where there should have been a reflection, there was none. She threw a rock at the nothing, breaking the perfect surface.

Julia later heard the soft footfall behind her, on the mossy ground. She knew it was Dominic. He carried with him the scent of many animals; rabbits, a squirrel, even a deer. It took all that to get rid of the hunger?

"Yes, you're right." he said, reading her thoughts. "I feel strange about what happened, Julia. That has never happened to me before. I have heard about it from others, but..."

Julia wrapped her arms around her chest as Dominic sat down. No electricity now, no power.

"I suppose all along I was trying to get you alone, to myself. It was instinct, I suppose, to kill the lesser power. I don't know everything about our ways. I don't know why I tried to seduce you into giving yourself over to me. If I had hurt you in any way a while ago, I know I would be sick with grief now. What I want to say is, I'm sorry."

Julia looked up at him. His face was smeared in pink; he had been crying. She hugged him. No more power surges. "Dominic, I understand. I know it's not your fault. You're still the same person you were. Now you just know what to do if it happens again, what to look for as a warning. I'm sorry too."

"I will not hurt you." he said, more of a promise to himself, than to Julia.

"I believe you." Julia said, getting to her feet. She reached down to grab Dominic's hand. "Now let's get me home."

17

Jason stood inside the decorative bedroom on the second floor with the girl, Marie, trying to convince her to stay put. Alexander had explained to Jason that he felt Cory coming, and if Cory was returning, so was Julia. He had warned Jason to put Marie somewhere safe, so she wouldn't be hurt. But Marie would not listen.

"Marie, this could get a little messy, what we're expecting tonight." he said softly as he watched her pace around the room.

"But why must I stay here, Jason, why?" she asked him in thick, accented English.

Jason approached her, placed his hand against her face. "It is because I care about you. Marie, it has been so very long since I've cared about anyone, do you understand this? You are the first in many years."

"That's not true!" she said, stomping away to the bed, throwing herself upon it, pouting. "You care about this Julia."

Jason appeared before her in a blur of wind, lit the lamp on her bureau. "I do not," he said, narrowing his eyes, and blowing out the tiny match's flame. He then sat down beside Marie, falling under her watchful eyes.

"You do! You wouldn't have done this if you hadn't, and don't tell me it's for your son!" She switched to French as her anxiety built. "Jonathan needs you, it's true enough, but Julia needs you too. You've done this for her because you like her. You respect her and you like her. Admit it Jason, admit it!"

"I admit nothing, ma chere. You know that." he spoke in French. The truth was he had begun to realize that he did care for Julia, and this realization agitated him. He got up to leave.

"Jason, stay with me!" she pleaded in English.

"I cannot. Stay here, Marie. You'll be safe, here." Jason turned, and walked towards the door. He ignored the pillow that flew at him and hit him in the back. As he closed the door, he heard her yell, "Jason! I won't be caged up like this!" Jason smiled and walked down the hallway, down the stairs.

In the sitting room, Jonathan and Rikki sat on the couch, together. Rikki seemed empty, vacant. His health was improving, though he still walked with a slight limp. He owed this to Alexander. However, he had become far more withdrawn, since his ordeal in Paris.

Jonathan however, was another story. Since the news of Cory's return by Alexander, he had been trying to reach Julia, to no avail. It tortured him that Julia was no longer a part of him, that she belonged to someone else, who possessed more dangerous emotions than he.

From the soft spoken voices Jason heard from beyond the mansion's doors, he could tell that Steven and the new girl, Melissa, lingered on the steps outside.

Jason went to the couch and looked down at Rikki. Their eyes met, and Rikki didn't have to be told that Jason wished to be alone with Jonathan. He rose, went outside with Steven and Melissa.

When the doors shut, Jason sat beside Jonathan on the sofa. He looked for a minute at Jonathan, the way his fingers just barely were touching his chin, the way his eyes wandered over the room, and finally came to rest on Jason.

"Do not worry, we will retrieve her." Jason promised.

"And if we don't?" Jonathan asked, his fingers falling away from his face, to rest alongside his other hand, on his lap. His face was pure anguish. "Do I stay this way forever? Half in and out of sanity? Killing my own children? You cannot imagine the feelings inside of me, the things I have thought of." Jonathan pushed his hair over his shoulder, grabbed onto Jason's steady, strong shoulders. "I will not go into a coma. There will be no more sleeps for me. I begin to want the sun. To feel it . . . on my face." His hands rose to his face, he pressed himself into the couch.

Jason watched his son, emotions of sadness and anger passing through him, at the same time. How dare he say this to me, he thought, and fought back the cold anger beginning to seep into his mind.

"Jonathan, you will not say such things to me again." he said in a cold, steely voice.

"I'm sorry." Jon mumbled from beneath his hands. "I don't want to be this way, Jason."

Jason took a deep breath, sat back on the sofa. "You'll pull through, you know. You did with Deirdra."

Jonathan's hands fell away from his face. For a long moment he said nothing. Then softly, he said, "Deirdra means nothing to me now. Besides, you were there for me."

"I know, Jonathan. But I am trying to tell you that when you care for someone, you can't just stop because they are a little different than you remember. Julia will always love you. No matter what happens between you both, she will always be there. I feel this inside of me, for certain. You must remember this; Julia loves you."

Jason turned back to Jonathan and found himself looking into a pair of endless, dark eyes. Jon was listening to him, really listening this time! On this subject, Jason decided to say one more thing. "Jon, don't turn her away, just because you know Cory's blood is inside her. You were the one who changed her, who turned her. Julia will always be bound to you, for that reason alone, if nothing more."

Jonathan sighed. "I know, but it's not that easy, Jason. I don't feel right knowing that he has won, that he can force her to do anything to me. To me! I don't feel her coming. I can't feel a thing." Jonathan looked down at his hands, as if they were the lame part of his body. "Perhaps I should have just kept Lena with me, and forgotten Julia." he mumbled.

"I know you don't mean that. I know you still have love for her. Open your mind!" Jason said, and then, his eyes shifted to the door. His children had sensed something, and were now afraid.

Jason stood up.

"What is it?" Jonathan asked, standing by Jason.

The doors opened, and Steven, Melissa, and Rikki backed into the room. Rikki's face was shocked, Melissa was trembling, and Steven was holding her close.

They retreated to where Jason and Jonathan stood, and gazed at the doorway.

There was a rustle of cloth, and a tall dark man, with curly flaxen blond hair, came into view.

He looked over the room, searching the place as if to make sure that there was no one to harm him. He stood in the doorway, waiting, perhaps, for something . . .

Jonathan heard Alexander come down the stairs, to stand beside them.

The man in black's eyes widened at Alexander, but not too much, Jonathan noted. This man wasn't afraid of Alexander, but out of courtesy, perhaps respect, gave Alexander a curt little nod. He looked over the rest of the room, at those standing there.

When he felt the man's eyes fall on him, Jonathan looked up, and there was a strange connection. He felt his name recognized, and at the same moment, he was allowed to know the man's name, *Dominic*.

Then, as he stood, eyes wide and staring, five smooth fingers reached out to clasp Dominic's hand. As if she were a demoness gliding in from the night, Julia appeared beside Dominic. Her eyes rested on Jonathan.

Jonathan gasped. He could not help it.

She looked...so like Cory.

Alexander sat up on the smooth leather couch he was lying on, reading a book by the light of a candle. He brushed the hair back from his face, and closed the book with a gentle finality.

He rubbed the muscles of his arms, and wondered what had disturbed him enough, to cause him to put down this book.

He closed his eyes, concentrated. It came to him in a flash.

A sense that Courchenne was coming. That he was near, very near.

Another sense that a closer presence had come into their midst. Female, small, Cory's blood running through her. This must be Julia.

And yet another sense. A strong presence. Just one hundred years younger than himself.

Alexander concentrated harder, followed the power to its source. Male, yes, and quickly approaching with the girl.

Alexander rose from the couch, pulling on his jacket. He blew out the candle and left the room, shutting the door with a thud, behind him. As he descended the stairs, he could feel in Jason unrest.

In the doorway stood a man, the source of the power. There was a quick exchange between this man, Dominic, and himself. The basic thing between older vampires when they met; I will not harm you, nor will I you.

Jonathan gasped, and Alexander's attention focused once more at the doorway.

A woman with blond hair had appeared. And this must be Julia, he thought.

Julia and Dominic approached the mansion on foot. They had chosen to walk up the mountain, so to prepare Julia for whatever kind of reaction the coven might have.

They stood now in the beginning of the driveway, bathed in the soft, dull lights emanating from the downstairs windows.

"He is here, my love is here. Look, there. That's where my motorcycle is." Julia said to Dominic, grasping his wrist, as if she was afraid to let go. Indeed, she must be. She looked at the figures on the steps, just now sensing they were there, going into the house, while leaving the doors open.

"I'm gonna miss you, Julia." Dominic said, giving Julia a sad little smile.

Julia smiled up at him, and gave him a kiss on the cheek. "I'll miss you too."

For a second, they just looked at each other, and then Dominic said, "Come on," and he disappeared from her sight.

Julia was engulfed by a sudden strong gust of wind, and when it died down, she looked up to see Dominic standing in the doorway of the house.

By the time Julia had come to his side, it seemed that everyone present had congregated in the sitting room, in order to see whom the stranger was. Julia slid in beside him, and looked up at Jonathan.

He gasped. Then, as he blinked, letting his hands hang down at his sides, he whispered her name.

"Julia."

Julia slipped past Dominic as he turned and closed the doors, shutting out the night.

"Jonathan." Julia sighed. She walked to him, as he stood there with a dazed look of amazement upon his face. "Jonathan, I've come back. I've come home!" Julia raised her arms to hold him as she stood before him, and was shocked as he took a swift step backwards, almost colliding with Steven.

"What's wrong?" she asked, feeling so close to tears it was undeniable. He was shocked, she could tell. "What is it? Why won't you come near me?"

"You're filled with him." Jonathan said in a low, monotone voice.

"No, no, it doesn't matter!" Julia cried out, the tears now spilling from her eyes. Julia reached out for him, he backed away. The others moved away from them. "Stop it!" Julia cried, trying desperately to reach him. He wouldn't let her. He kept mouthing the word 'no', his eyes seemed startled.

"Jonathan!" Julia pleaded, her body shaking from grief. In all her preparation for the consequences of what Cory had done, Julia never would have expected this. "Please, hold me," she sobbed, backing him almost to the fire. She stopped moving towards him, embraced herself, and sobbed. "You hate me now, is that it?"

Someone stepping in front of her, between herself and Jonathan, blurred Julia's vision. She looked up; it was Jason. He took hold of her shoulders. "Julia, he feels Cory inside you, and it intimidates him. Since Cory can control your emotions and feelings, Jonathan believes you are dangerous to him." Jason said, his once cold eyes now searching Julia's face, trying to make her understand.

"No." said a voice from near the staircase. Julia looked up to see a powerful man approach them. "She is dangerous to all of you, now. Cory will arrive soon. I've seen him, though he has not seen me. I've made sure of this. He can destroy all of you, with perhaps, the exception of Dominic. Julia is dangerous to you all."

"Who?" Julia asked Jason, without looking up at him.

It took a minute for him to answer her, perhaps because he was trying to locate Cory himself. He could not. Jason decided to answer Julia. "Alexander, my father."

Julia nodded.

Alexander turned back towards the group. "It is best that you all have the chance to confront Cory on your own, before I set out to destroy him. He will not suspect my being here, if you do this. Do you all agree?" Everyone gave their silent consent.

"Cory is one being, but he is not acting alone. I know that he accompanied by two others. I want for you all to be careful." He walked to Jason, placing a hand on his shoulder. "I will go upstairs now, and wait for the proper time to come down to you." With that said, he was gone.

18

Julia stared at Jonathan, wringing her hands.

He stood with his back to the fireplace, his eyes no longer on her. He seemed intent on studying an ant, which made its way across the floor.

Steven and Melissa had retired to the shadows, Jason spoke quietly with Dominic near the doors, and Rikki had retreated to sit on the stairway, to rest. They had left Julia and Jonathan alone to sort out their problems, hoping it would work.

Now Julia approached Jonathan slowly, as not to upset him again. "Jonathan, I . . . " she didn't know how to begin. He looked up at her when she stood but three feet away from him, the saddest expression on his face. She raised her hand to his chin, not touching him just yet. Please, don't move, she thought to herself. She was just a little aware of something seeping out of her mind, striking Jonathan.

He didn't move. His breathing quickened.

Julia noticed that Dominic and Jason had stopped conversing altogether. But for some reason, all her being was focused on Jonathan, praying he wouldn't move.

It suddenly occurred to her that he could not move, that her mind was holding him there. Cory's blood had given her some strength over Jonathan. Caught off guard, he was less powerful than she was.

Julia touched his lips now with her fingertips, love for him breaking the hold she had over him.

Free from Julia, Jonathan started away from her. "Oh, Julia." he moaned. "No." He broke free of her fingers, and bolted down the stairway that led to the basement. Jason rushed after him.

"Jonathan, I'm sorry!" Julia yelled. Julia walked slowly to the stairway. "I'm so sorry," she said quietly into the dark shadows.

Julia turned back to the room looking for Dominic, but he was gone. There was no trace of him in the room; he had completely vanished. "Where's Dominic?" she asked, her voice ringing through the silence of the mansion like a bell.

No one answered her. The fire crackled, the grandfather clock ticked. From deep in the shadows came the soft sounds of kissing.

Julia went to the door, opening it slowly. There seemed to be an eerie stillness outside, cold for spring. "Dominic?" she whispered. Did he leave? Why would he leave here like this?

Julia crept down the driveway and out into the road, trying to located the whereabouts of Dominic. She couldn't see him anywhere, couldn't tell where he was.

With a heavy heart, she began the walk back to the mansion, when seemingly out of nowhere, a hand clamped down hard over her mouth and another around her waist, lifting her off her feet. She immediately knew it was Cory.

Julia pulled at his hands and kicked at him, but it did no good. He wouldn't let go. "Ah ha, my Julia. Did you think I'd let you get away from me that easy? Huh?" His grip on her tightened, his fingernails digging into her cheek, drawing blood there. Julia screamed, muffled by his hand.

Julia heard laughter, and two others touched down in front of her. One woman, one man.

"These are my friends, bitch. Jayme and Snake. Together we're going to destroy this coven, and you're going to help us."

Julia struggled against him, as he pressed her tightly to him. She heard his voice rasping into her ear, chanting that she would be just like him. Like Cory, like Cory, like Cory.

His will descended over her, painfully as it had that night in California. This time, however, she could not resist. His anger, his coldness, his hunger, everything that made Cory what he was, seeped from the blood in her veins, taking over.

Then, mercifully, she saw black.

Julia ceased struggling, put her arms down at her sides. Cory set her down on the ground, kissed her neck. He laughed. Julia made no move to get away. Her eyes glowed red as his.

"Come now, my darling girl. You have a husband to kill."

Cory took her hand in his, leading her, along with the others, into the mansion. He threw open the doors, giving his friends the silent command to kill.

Steven and Melissa had recently come out of the shadows to the sofa. Now Steven jumped up, ready to defend Melissa to the last. He was too late. Jayme and Snake descended on them both, draining them quickly, without remorse.

Rikki lay still on the stairs.

Cory and Julia stood near to the sofa, hand in hand. He watched the feeding for a while, and when Steven and Melissa had been drained, now lying dead and translucent on the floor, he called for Jason.

"Hey, Jason! Come on out! I'm here!" He laughed Jayme and Snake laughing with him.

There was a soft breeze in the room, as Jason appeared in the downstairs doorway. He looked at Steven, dead, glass-like, and limp on the floor, with Melissa the same, next to him. He couldn't believe it. Steven had been a worthy son, had taken care of Jonathan for him. He had been warm, caring, had loved this girl Melissa. Now they were both destroyed, utterly.

He glared at Jayme and Snake, the cold blue ice within his eyes enough to cause them to back away from the bodies. He approached Steven slowly, bent down and touched the remnant of his face. Only the hazel eyes and brown hair were left. As Jason's fingers disturbed the skin, the whole body shattered, leaving a pile of dust and clothing where Steven had been.

Echoing laughter came from Cory across the room.

Jason straightened, clenching his fists, squeezing his eyes tightly shut. He let the overcoat fall off and onto the ground, between Melissa and what was left of Steven. His fists brushed the leather of his pants, so soft, reminding him again of Steven.

Jason looked down again at Steven's remains, his orange hair falling over his dark-clothed shoulders. When he glared at Cory his eyes were burning red, full of hate. "Bastard!" he hissed through the fangs.

"Julia, go see to Jonathan, hmmm?" Cory said when he observed Jason, transformed. Julia turned and slowly descended the stairs, as if walking in her sleep.

"You!" Jason roared, "are finished!" He ran at Cory, determined to destroy him, himself.

The impact of Jason flinging himself at Cory shook him, slightly. Cory fell to his knees, Jason slashing away at his face. Cory growled, and got to his feet, pushing Jason back a couple steps. Jason and Cory's arms locked like two vicious fighting beasts. They growled and roared both trying to sink their fangs into the other's neck.

Jason fought Cory well, and although Cory had a bit of extra power, Jason was enraged. Jason's fists struck out at Cory's stomach, making him gulp for air. Cory gave it right back.

On and on it went, the two powers colliding, struggling, and fighting back well-aimed fists to the temple, the pressure point in the head. Then something happened to turn the tide.

"Jason!" a frightened voice shouted from the stairway.

Jason turned his head slightly at the sound of the girl, Marie's voice, and at the same moment, Cory's fist cracked against his temple.

Lights exploded before Jason's eyes and he went down onto the floor, bleeding, dizzy, and dripping with sweat. His sight, for a moment, would not clear.

Marie rushed to Jason's side, trying to get him up, but he could not move. And then she beheld his attacker. This was the one Jean-Luc had always spoken of. The traitor, Courchenne. She knew without having to ask. He looked horrible standing there, his face streaked with blood. His harsh laugh was more an animal's, than anything resembling a man's.

He kicked Jason in the side, causing him to convulse in Marie's arms. "You're killing him!" she screamed in French. She jumped at Cory, her nails like claws, her fangs aiming for the jugular vein.

Cory caught her easily, ripped her neck open from ear to shoulder. Her skin came off, like a piece of meat, hanging down on her neck. She shrieked like a banshee.

Cory caught some of her blood in his mouth, tossed her like a rag doll onto the floor. In a swift motion, he grabbed the closest wooden chair and smashed it down onto the floor, breaking it into a handful of stakes.

He then grabbed one, and kicking Jason again so he wouldn't get up, sat down on Marie's stomach. She sank her nails deep into his legs, but Cory didn't even flinch. He brought the stake down and through her heart, satisfied at the sound of the stake grating against the hard, waxed wood floor. This done, he rose up.

Marie screeched and convulsed, trying to pull the stake out of her heart, but her fingers seemed not to work. From her mouth erupted a stream of blood.

Jason crawled to her. "Marie," he whispered, grabbing her hand. Her fingers closed around his, so very tight, for a moment, and he felt as if they might truly break off.

Her head thrashed once, twice, and a final third time. Then she let go of Jason's hand, relaxed on the floor. A look of peace came over her face; she let out a long, pained breath, and died.

Jason blinked back tears through the red haze in his eyes. "Just a lost child," he murmured. He slowly stood, breathing heavily. Cory mocked him; even now he mocked him.

"A little slut, you mean. She wasn't even worth the clothes you dressed her in!"

Jason spun around, glaring at this evil, wretched thing in the middle of his home, his mansion. He wondered why he had put up with Cory all these years.

"Come on Jason! Come on! Fight me you little fool, you little fucker! Take your best shot!"

Jason lunged at him.

Rikki leapt off the stairs when he saw Snake and Jayme coming at him. He did this in trying to get away, but instead, he became cornered between them, pressed against the wall.

They snarled at him, turning his blood cold.

Snake closed in for the kill, wrenching Rikki's chin upwards. At the fatal moment, Snake shrieked, foul spittle spraying over Rikki's neck and face.

Rikki stared as he fell down at his feet, a stake sticking out of his ribs.

Dominic stood there, dusting off his hands on his pants. He had come down from upstairs, where he had been talking with Alexander. "One down, two to go." he said referring to both Jayme and Cory. "But first," he said, turning his dazzling smile on confused Jayme, "how'd you like to meet up with Robert E. Lee?"

Julia crept down the stairs, slowly, stealthily.

Jonathan watched her from around the corner, but this she did not know.

Julia went directly to the coat of armor, which she had knocked down so long ago. Taking heavy, deep masculine breaths, she searched amongst the armor until she found what she was looking for.

It was an ax, old and rusted, laying in years' worth of dust. Julia gripped the ax in both hands, carrying it high like some twisted banner.

To Jonathan's coffin she went, stumbling slightly under the pressure of Cory's will. Once there, she opened the coffin, taking out what was inside. The feather, the dagger. Cory wanted them thrown on the fire. Yes, that was it. She placed them in the dust on the floor, and closed the coffin's lid.

Julia swung the ax high and back, and let it fall. She was thrown off balance by the impact of metal against fine polished wood, but did not falter in her actions. Again the ax fell, again, again, again, until the coffin was nothing but a rubble of wood and silk.

"Jonathan!" she cried out, her voice monstrous, and contorted, and strangely deep. "Come out and face me!"

Alexander paced in the darkness of the study. He knew that Cory had no idea he was present in this mansion, and that was the way it should be. But much blood was being shed downstairs, and he could feel that Jason was in agony for the losses.

Jason and Cory were waging a war of their own, while Dominic killed off the other intruders, with Rikki's help. He knew Dominic would do this much for him, even though it was not Dominic's battle. When Alexander knew that both his sons were exhausted, and were each now attempting to destroy each other, he started down the stairs.

At the bottom, Alexander observed the carnage. There was the poor young fledgling Marie, staked, along with the body of Cory's Mexican friend. There were three other dead vampires; one's body was completely gone except for the clothes, the wind from the open doorway having begun to blown the dusty remains about the room. The other two were drained, the first one almost to the point of her body collapsing, the other just recently dead, with both Dominic and Rikki sitting placidly beside it.

Alexander moved to the middle of the room, Dominic and Rikki's eyes following him now, instead of the fight.

Jason and Cory hadn't even heard him come down.

Alexander stared at them, Jason obviously now tiring, lying on the ground with his fist in Cory's mouth so he couldn't bite. Cory was twitching, clawing and kicking at the same time, trying to dislodge the fist from his mouth. Alexander frowned a little. This is what people did to mad dogs if attacked. Not to a mad vampire. A mad vampire needed to be silenced, killed. A fist in the mouth wouldn't stop him for long.

True to Alexander's thoughts, Cory jerked away from Jason's fist, vomiting a thin stream of blood on Jason's face. Jason gagged, reaching out to grab at Cory's neck.

Ah and here would be the end, Alexander thought.

Cory caught Jason's hand and wrestled his arm to the floor, grabbing the other arm also, and pinning them both on Jason's own stomach. Jason struggled and twisted as Cory sank his full weight down on him.

And then, grasping Jason's wrists so hard to keep them still in his one hand his knuckles turned white, he grabbed Jason's head and wrenched it to the side.

"Enough!" shouted Alexander.

Cory stared at Jason blankly for a moment, his hand loosened on Jason's wrists. Jason took advantage of this, and tossed Cory off him.

Cory rolled over and stood up, ignoring Jason's bloody and torn figure retreat to where Rikki stood, waiting.

Cory gasped for breath, his red eyes flashing as he took in Alexander. "So, I see you have come to help them instead of me. Once again, you have chosen Jason."

"Cory, it is not I who has chosen sides here, it was you. It always was you. You have made me despise you." Alex said, removing his jacket, beginning to unbutton the white silk shirt, so not to get Cory's blood on him.

Cory grinned at Alexander, watching him do this. His own clothes, jacket and shirt, had become a mess of bloody ribbons. "I suppose you mean to kill me now, Alexander. Over what?" he uttered a short scornful laugh. "A woman?"

"You stole her from here, Cory. That is not allowed." The silk shirt slid off his equally smooth skin, fluttered to the sofa where his jacket lay.

"It was only one little bitch. I wanted her. I have no regret for what I did. She had great promise. That brat, Jonathan, could do nothing for her."

"It is not only that, Cory." Alex said, looking calm and serene, compared to all the faces filled with hate in the room. "You and Jean-Luc were going to come for me by the use of those children. You betrayed my trust to my enemies. For these crimes, you must be reprimanded."

Cory scowled at him, using the fangs to their fullest potential. "Are you to be my judge Father? All you others a jury?"

"Look at these bodies here, Cory." Alexander said, using his arms to indicate the room around him. "These have died for your selfish needs, for your selfish longings. Ours is a limited race, you know. The young ones have foolish notions about us, about our ways. They fall into despair and meet destruction by the ever present, cumbersome vampire hunters. The older ones grow tired of living eternally, and eventually destroy themselves. We need to keep our race alive, just as do the humans, the werewolves, or any other type of creature.

"You are blind, Courchenne, so blind." he said, shaking his head. "So young to me, and still so ignorant. Perhaps when you are gone, and Elizabette lays claim to your businesses, she will right all the wrongs you have committed. Perhaps she will come to me for guidance."

"Lizzi will never come to you!" he growled, rage pulsating in his eyes. "I am sick of this talk!"

"How many more lives will you sacrifice for your sick-minded goals? Jason's? Rikki's? Jonathan's? Even mine? Your creator, your father, who pulled you back to life?" Alex asked, stepping closer to Cory.

"Yeah, you're right Alex. Right as you always were about everything. But I don't care. I shall not be extinguished! I'm relentless, and I will see that you are destroyed, once and for all."

Alexander began to laugh now, starting softly at first, and grew louder, and louder, until the room shook with the density of his deep laughter. He threw his head back, the small golden chain reflecting the light of the candles in the room and the fireplace. When he lowered his head, his power made an impressive sight.

From beneath the heavy mustache two sharp fangs showed through, moist and glistening. His laughter ceased now as he approached Cory.

"Courchenne, my forsaken child, I know it will not be I who is destroyed tonight."

Julia hissed and struggled. Jonathan had climbed above her, holding her down. His face held no anger, only sadness.

"You are not my Julia," he said, trying to pin her struggling arms down. Her nails grazed his cheek, drawing blood.

Jonathan growled, and struggled to push her hand down and away from his eyes. "You are . . . a creature that . . . Cory . . . has made . . . You are not . . . Julia!"

He succeeded in pushing her hand down, but in one swift motion, she threw her leg over him and was suddenly on top.

She roared into his face.

Alexander whipped out his arm, sending Cory backward into the half-opened door. It shut with a bang.

Jason watched from where he sat, silently laughing to himself. Cory didn't stand a chance. Sure, Alex had been bruised a few times, but nothing compared with Cory's wounds.

Cory now jumped up, slashing at Alex's chest with his fangs.

Alex threw him off again, down to the floor.

Alexander leapt upon Cory, like a great, giant beast pouncing on his prey. His fangs sank into the life-giving vein in Cory's neck. Cory cried out, smashed his fist against Alexander's face with all his might. Alex tore off him. But now the blood was gushing from Cory's neck.

Julia clawed and punched Jonathan, as they rolled through the dirt and rat droppings, which covered the ground. The dust kicked up and swirled around them like some sort of black tornado.

Jonathan held her hands in check.

He would not fight Julia, only restrain her.

Alexander stood and gazed down at Cory, who seemed to be bleeding all over. His face, neck, arms, chest and legs were covered in deep lacerations.

He had lost the fangs and the redness in his eyes; for once he was afraid.

Upon seeing Cory as a helpless figure propped up against the bloodstained wall, Jason, Rikki and Dominic had got to their feet, swiftly closing in on him.

Cory was afraid for one reason alone. With all the blood he had lost, he would never be able to hold them off. He was afraid they'd take his body and tear it into tiny little pieces, while he was still alive.

Alexander watched them advance in a detached sort of way. He knew they would do something dreadful to Cory if he let them, and looking down into his pleading hazel-blue eyes, he knew he could not let them do it.

"Wait." Alexander said, stretching his arm out before them all. "I will finish it." He knelt down on the floor beside Cory, and after a moment's pause, cradled him in his arms.

"You gave me life, Alexander. Now you will take it away? I'm your son, Alex, you created me, don't you remember, three hundred and twenty years ago?" Cory gasped, shuddering a little. He was really afraid now, afraid of death.

Alexander seemed to think on it a moment. Jason and the others were restless behind him. "Yes, Courchenne, I remember. I am truly sorry, but I must do this. It is either they or I, and I would rather it be me that must to do this thing. I must undo what I have done."

"No, please," Cory moaned, too weak now to even struggle.

Alexander didn't reply. He rose now, with Cory securely in his arms, and opened the door. The cool night air reentered the mansion, sweeping up a breeze in the room that blew the particles about, from the now collapsed bodies of Melissa and Jayme.

He went down onto the ground in the driveway and then, cradling Cory to his chest, began to drain him. The moment Alexander began to suck, Cory moved dreadfully in his arms, spasmodic wildly, but the struggle was only brief, and feeble.

His blood was running out.

Julia screamed and rolled off Jonathan, the pain breaking Cory's power over her.

He was dying now, she could feel it. It was a pulling in her veins, in her heart. It was an outside force strong and demonic, trying to pull her down with him to hell.

Julia mercifully fell unconscious from the force of the driving pain.

Jonathan crawled to where she lay, exhausted from their confrontation. He observed her quietly, and knew what was happening. Somehow, for a reason he did not know, and could not be explained, Cory was trying to take her with him. He shook Julia, but she wouldn't wake up. She was very still, very cold.

"Alexander! *Alexander!*" he cried, knowing that he would be able to help. He removed his jacket, laid it across her body. "Julia, don't go with him again. Please, love, don't leave me now."

In the driveway, Cory's body was losing its color. Drained now, almost to the point of death, he could not move any longer. His soul, half gone from his body already, made its connection with Julia.

As he shuddered once more, his pale body translucent as glass, he smiled up at Jason who stood, watching, above him.

"I have her," was all he said. And then, taking a deep, rasping breath, his immortal life was over.

Alexander pulled away from the glass figure of a man, laying it down on the hard ground. "We must be fast. Julia is in desperate trouble."

Jason turned with the sound of Jonathan, calling for help. And then, the little surviving group reentered the mansion.

Alexander, Rikki, Dominic and Jason ran down the stairs, into the dark midnight of the basement. They located Jonathan and Julia, and went to them.

Alexander knelt beside Jonathan in the thick heavy dust. He cut Julia's sweatshirt down the front, ripping it open to reveal her throat. Without using words, he expressed to the others that he had no choice, but to withdraw Cory's blood from her, before it killed her like poison.

He had to be careful that Julia was never without vampiric blood cells, the stuff that had already soaked into her brain, her heart, and her stomach. If the blood he removed pulled these cells along with them, Julia would die. There was also a chance that the transfusion would not work, and she would become a raving lunatic. This was something that would ensure her self-inflicted death by the sun. He could not stress enough, if Julia were for one minute deprived of vampire blood, she would die. No one would bring her back, ever.

Jonathan collapsed beside her heavily, folded his legs up beneath him. He closed his eyes, lowered his head. This was something that he could not bear to watch.

Jason approached him, a mess in bloody rags. He placed one hand on Jonathan's right shoulder, Rikki's hand on the left. Dominic sat steadily on the other side of Julia, not speaking, watching Alexander carefully.

Alex bent over Julia, and gently, as if he was her lover, pressed his teeth into her throat. He drank and drank, until the final danger, when the last drop of blood was about to come forth. Until she was a dangerous shade of extreme paleness.

Alexander pulled away from Julia, slicing his finger on his receding fangs. A drop of deep red blood issued forth and this he smeared upon the wound. This stopped the blood from coming. Then, very swiftly, he slashed his wrist, and pressed it to her cold lips, staring down at her unblinking eyes.

"Drink," he whispered, and then, sending a burst of power into her mind, *Come, Julia, my young ones need you here.*

Julia, at first, would not take the blood. It dribbled down her chin and into her hair, turning the blond crimson. Alex slashed his wrist again and pried her mouth open, working the fount of blood into her mouth. And then, as they watched, Julia's throat moved. Without even being aware of it, she had swallowed.

Jason gripped Jonathan's shoulder harder, and he looked up at Julia. Her throat moved again and again. Her eyes glazed over with a glassy film, and suddenly, she blinked.

The great dark haze that had imprisoned Julia was clearing away. She could see it now.

First she had been falling, she knew that much. A giant dark tunnel had surrounded her, lined to the brim with pain. She tried to call out, but she could not. Cory's laughter was all around her, binding her in chains.

Then, slowly, the laughter died away. The chains had been cut the tunnel was gone. However, Julia was not aware of where she was. It was foggy, dark and hazy here. She could not see, did not possess the night-vision she needed. There were things moving in the darkness around her, but she could not touch them. Her arms were heavy; she could not move them.

She felt something then, something warm and refreshing inside of her, and she realized with joy that she had a body again. She tried to move her eyes, her lips, something.

Water fell like raindrops in her eyes, and when she tried to clear them, it worked.

Julia could see them now, their outlines dark against the fog. The haze had begun to clear little by little. *I'm coming back!* Her thoughts to whomever was helping her, whomever was the shadow leaning over her.

Yes, Julia, you are. But you must drink now. You must drink to get better. Lift your hands to hold my wrist there, drink deeply the lifeblood.

This was the voice of Alexander, she knew. Julia tried desperately to reach out to him. The shadows were clearing up, and she found herself forcing Alexander's blood through her limbs, lifting her arms like two heavy logs, slinging them over his arm. She forced her lips to close around his wound, and she began to pull on it.

Alexander remained a long while, feeding Julia. Perhaps Cory's blood had been poison to her in his purified state, but now, as Alex's strong, ancient blood devoured Cory's blood, Julia was healing. Alexander's blood, a miracle to her, was healing, rich and pure. Finally, he pulled away.

Julia stared up at them, now having her full ability to see in the dark, to breathe, to allow her heart and brain to function. But her limbs were uncoordinated, her body not listening to her commands. "More." she whispered.

Jonathan leaned over Julia, slashing his wrist. She whispered his name softly, closed her mouth over the wound. She sucked at it hard, drawing Jonathan's life deep into herself. It strengthened the tie, which bound them together, and healed her even further.

When the pain was too great, Jonathan pulled away, his body aching.

Dominic came to her next, and his blood was indeed powerful and nourishing, strengthening places where the others could not, because he was from a different bloodline. Her nails grew a bit longer, her muscles a bit harder, and her reflexes a little quicker.

Julia let him go long before he was hurting, and reached for the next offered wrist.

This she had known before. This was Jason, charming, dark, mysterious, magnetic. As she looked into his blue eyes, for a moment she saw herself as sixteen again, drinking the wine on the sofa.

When he pulled away from her, she almost snatched him back, thought better of it.

Julia laid back, closed her eyes. The blood inside her from so many was healing her body well, and swiftly.

Julia opened her eyes and looked at them all, one by one. They all cared about her. Even Jason's creator, Alexander, had cared about her tonight. She had though he was here just to destroy Cory and make amends with Jason. But maybe she was wrong tonight. Maybe . . .

Julia sat up, smiling at them. Her family.

"How am I?" she asked them.

Jonathan looked stunned, Dominic and Alexander smiled at her, standing up and out of the way. Rikki looked on, quietly, detached. Jason answered her in barely a whisper. "Radiant."

Julia smiled. "Thanks, Jason. All of you." Then she looked at Jonathan. Without a sound, she fell into his arms. He embraced her tightly, remembering and loving the feel of her body against him.

"You are never leaving me again," he said in a deep, somber whisper.

"Never." Julia said, backing out of his embrace just far enough to kiss him.

"Never."

19

They filed up the stairs when Julia could find the strength to stand.

Jonathan had picked up his dagger and his feather, slipped them into his jacket, and was now holding onto Julia around the waist, determined not to let her go. Julia was pleased at this. She had been away too long it seemed, but she'd never have to worry about that again.

She talked with them and they welcomed her back. They were her family now, truly her family. Their blood now flowed, as a whole, through her veins. She had understood this when Alexander had said; "You're a child of the family now, Julia."

They reentered the battleground, the sitting room, and fell silent.

The place stunk with death. It was worse than the smell of human death. It was immortal death, and yes, it even scared Julia a little.

"Someone get rid of that shit." Dominic said, pointing to the clothes of Jayme and Snake.

"Yes, I suppose we should clean this." Jason said quietly.

Jason, Alexander and Rikki removed all the bodies, and the clothes, from the house and the driveway. They built a fire in the pit behind the house, burnt everything within it.

Julia, Jonathan and Dominic, meanwhile, swept the dust that the collapsed bodies had left behind, and brought it all outside, letting the wind catch it and blow it away. Then, Jonathan produced a mop and a few jugs of water and soap, and they wiped all traces of blood from the floor and walls.

Afterwards, they reassembled in the sitting room, tired, drained, and heavily grieved. The group assumed a quiet conversation until sunrise.

"Alexander, Dominic, stay here today. Take any room you wish. My home is yours." Jason offered.

After they agreed, Julia interrupted. "Please stay with us a while." and getting a surprised look from Jason added, "That is, if he wants you to. I mean, it would make me happy if you would."

"Sure, babe." Dominic said. And Alexander made a curt, little bow to Julia.

"You don't have to do that," she said, blushing.

"A good evening then, to everyone. I know I've had enough adventure, for one night." Jason said. He gave Jonathan a clap on the shoulder, and then, with a mischievous grin, whispered in Julia's ear. "I'm glad you're back. Things weren't the same without you." Then he was gone, down into the basement to sleep alone.

Julia couldn't help but smile at his retreating back.

Rikki and Alexander left too, murmuring good nights, and retiring upstairs.

Dominic came forward then to Julia, lagging back until everyone had gone. "I'm glad you're back with him, but I'm also not." Seemingly frustrated, he scratched at his blond-white curls. "I don't know what I'm talking about, I'm not good with words, so I'll just say good night."

He hugged Julia and said to her, "If you need me, I'll be here." He stepped back grinned at Jonathan. "Be good to her before you go to sleep now, you hear? Julia's special, she's important. I know she's going to be a true Immortal."

After Dominic left them, Julia stared at Jonathan. "What did he mean by that?"

Jonathan looked at her. "He meant that you're going to be around for quite a while."

"Oh," Julia said. She was a bit confused by that, but it didn't really matter. She was home.

Without warning, Jonathan turned to Julia, swept her off her feet into his arms.

"What are you doing?" she laughed.

"Well," he said as he stared across the room, "it seems to me that it is customary to carry the bride into the bed-chamber after they have been married. I've been married to you five months, and I haven't done that yet!"

Julia laughed delightedly and kissed him deeply, as he unlocked the door to her room, and set her down inside it. He turned, shut the door and locked it, lit the candle on her desk.

"Remember these?" Jonathan asked, holding up Julia's keys.

She smiled, took them from his hand, laid them on the desk.

"Look around, my love."

Julia turned, and a surprised little gasp escaped from her lips. Everything she had packed away, back home in December, had been unpacked and fixed neatly in the room. All her lamps, pictures, posters, make-up, everything had been set. In the open closet hung her clothes.

"Jonathan, I can't believe you did this! You kept this up all the time?"

He nodded sheepishly. "It was all for you Julia." Then, he removed his jacket, and dumped it carelessly on the floor.

Jonathan took Julia's hand and brought her to the bed, where the net curtains had been pulled back. He set her down and reached into his jean pocket.